Smoke and Mirrors

A Vampire Romance

By

ELISE NELSON

Smoke and Mirrors: A Vampire Romance

You can follow author Elise Nelson at
www.elisenelsonauthor.com

Cover design and formatting by Covers and Cupcakes LLC
www.coversandcupcakes.com

Published by Shattered Glass Press

Published in Canada

Printed in Canada and the United States of America

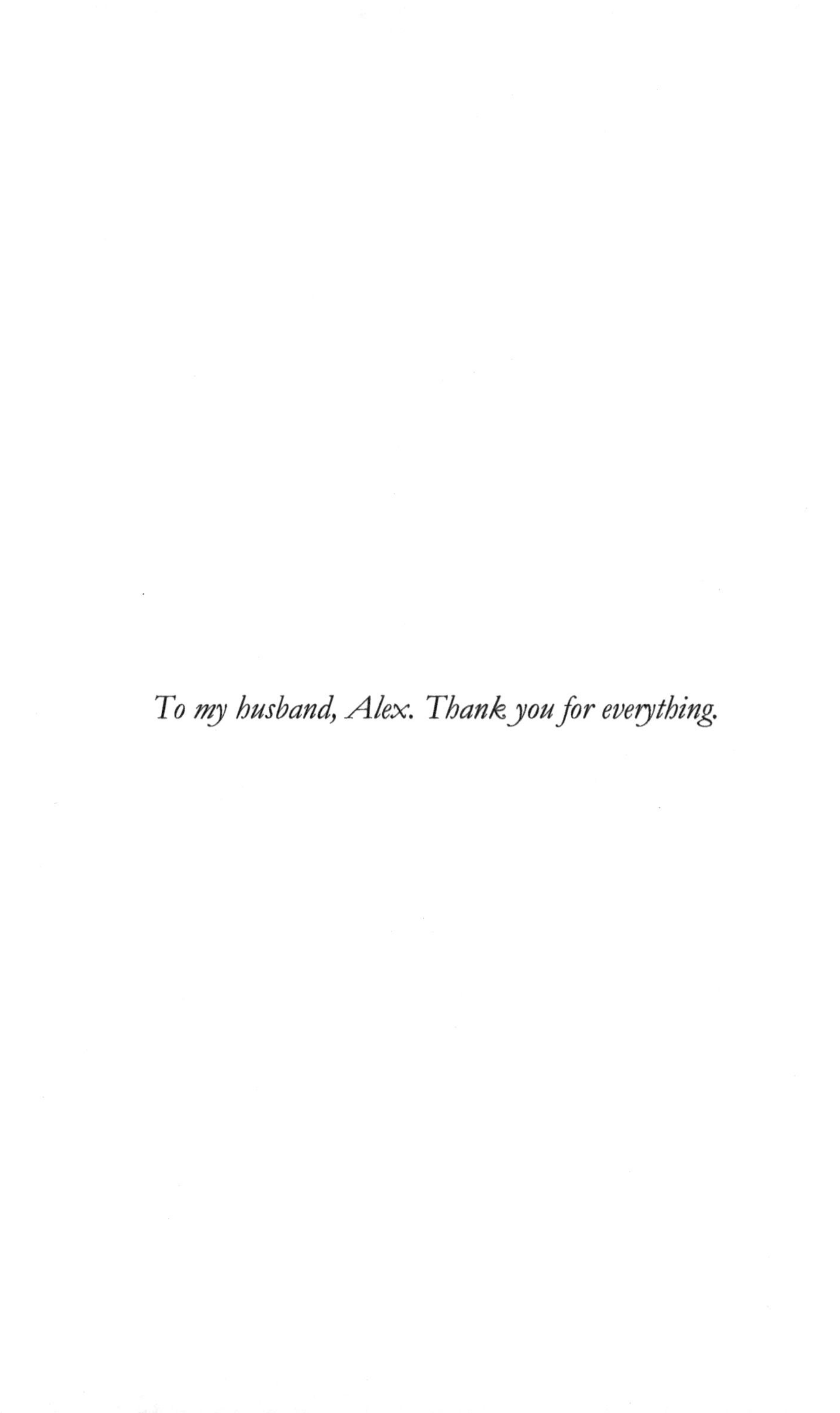

To my husband, Alex. Thank you for everything.

CHAPTER *One*

I could never forget that day. There was an eerie stillness in the air as we stood there, waiting. Chills dimpled deep into my skin, and I swore it was watching me. It was watching all of us. A thing too far away for us to see but close enough to feel the slimy chill of its gaping stare. Like the unnerving lick of a wild animal. Or being scratched in that spot of your back that you can't quite reach.

I could never forget how it all felt. The stale air clasping my skin, as if paralyzing me in place. The blind panic coursing through me. The sound of muffled breaths and stifled cries suffocating the air around us while we did our best not to make a sound.

None of us really knew what we were waiting for, and somehow that made it worse. Maybe we wouldn't have been so utterly petrified if we'd known what we were up against. But we didn't. We just stood there in the dark, the dewy mist of twilight teasing our tired eyes, and tried not to scream.

My aunt always told me to beware of the monsters in the closet. Of demons and shadows. Mythical beings she read stories about at bedtime. Creatures from the corners of our eyes and the echoes in our footsteps. She sang me eerie lullabies of cautionary tales, sinking in stories rich with disaster and fear so I would recognize any such creature if I ever saw one. When she'd speak these rehearsed sermons of the undead, her hands would tremble, and her eyes would go wide and far away—the shocking blue around her pupils turned into stagnant crystals ready to drop and shatter at any moment. It was as if she had left this world altogether and I had to wait for her to return.

I always wondered where these stories came from and why Maggie recited them to me every night before I went to bed. As a teenager, I thought she was simply out of touch with reality—that there was something about her that wasn't quite right. I heard it when she spoke and saw it in those wide crystal eyes. Her lyrics never made their way into my mind, at least not until I was much older. They just swirled inside the little head that she cradled and brushed before bedtime. I was a very protected child in a small home, in a small town, hidden deep within Western Europe.

When she died, I left the only place I'd ever known. I had no one else in Fairbrooke worth staying for.

So I moved to Brakerton Heights.

I placed my trunk on the bed and cringed at the dust that puffed out from the sheets. The room was a little dirty from lack of use but spacious. It was furnished with an adequate bed fitted on springs and a small nightstand covered in a film of dust, complete with a small oil lamp that somehow looked both brand new and very old. The only part of the room that held any kind of beauty was the oak vanity table pushed against the wall opposite the bed. The dusky wood was shiny and glazed, from the rim of the mirror to the feet on the floor, and gave off the fresh scent of a forest full of pine.

Still, part of me was hoping for more from a big city hotel. Well, "big city" might not have been the best way to describe a city with just over two thousand people, but I came from a town of around 300, give or take a few. So, I supposed I expected a hotel that looked a little more occupied. It was strange. I was the only guest at the only inn in town, and it was beautiful here. With fall just about underway, the cool mountain air was matched with rolling hills and crisp leaves falling from color-changing trees, soaking the air with fluttering bouquets of tangy orange, bright rubies, and rusty golds. Why was I the only guest here?

I sighed and let myself fall onto the mattress, coughing as more dust flew into the air. I wondered when the last time the room was used or cleaned. I couldn't complain either way. The innkeepers were kind enough to let me stay here at a fraction of the cost that any respectable inn would charge. They knew whatever job I'd be able to get would pay little to nothing, and they were gracious enough to work around that.

By the time I got settled in and changed into my best wool jacket and dress, the delicious smell of warmly baked bread and wafts of cinnamon rose like an autumn sunrise through the cracks in the floorboards. My stomach twisted in hunger. I wasn't used to eating so little, but ever since Maggie died, I had to split the costs of living and eating to make the meager sum I was allotted last. It was tough living in this world as a woman. I wasn't given the option to keep my aunt's home, despite the fact that I'd fixed it up so many times that I practically built it myself.

The whole thing was outrageous, and it was one of the reasons I hoped to work as a reporter for the newspaper *The Woman Speaks*. Their mission was to change the world's view of our sex and to run the country's first-ever all-female newspaper. I didn't have much experience writing, but I had a strong will and determination to help the cause. Hopefully that would be enough.

I opened and locked the door to my new room and walked down the stairs to greet the Clarkes. I had only met Mr. Clarke when he gave me the key earlier and offered me a small tour of the front lobby and dining area; his wife hadn't been home at the time.

When I rounded the corner, taking a sharp right into the dining area, I saw the woman with her small crown of white hair and long pleated skirt. She was slicing a thick loaf of cinnamon coffee cake, the knife releasing small puffs of steam from the top. I tried to keep my mouth from watering, but my eyes betrayed me. As soon as the woman saw me, she smiled and handed me the first spongy piece on a small plate.

I tried not to look too eager as I carefully snatched it from her. The scent overpowered me, and I realized I couldn't remember when I'd last eaten. Maybe last night? Yesterday morning?

"Thank you," I said and waited until she was cutting into the loaf again before shoving the first bite into my mouth.

"Of course," she said, cutting more slices, moving along the body of bread with perfect precision. "My name is Flora, by the way. You must be Caroline." She looked back up at me, her small eyes set against her plump cheeks like rising suns. I smiled, my cheeks full of bread so warm I wished I could fall asleep on it.

I swallowed. "Yes, I am. Thank you for having me. I appreciate all you and your husband are doing for me." I watched as she cut the last piece of the bread. She peeled the heel off and moved toward the trash can, and I practically gasped. "Are you going to throw that away?"

She looked at me with raised brows, then laughed. "Do you want it? I'm sorry. My husband and I don't like the heels of bread, and it's been so long since we've had guests, I must have forgotten that some people do like them." She laughed again and handed the piece over to me, giving me the other heel as well. I could hug her.

I ate one of them as she wrapped part of the loaf in a clean rag, leaving two pieces out and putting them on plates. "Why has no one stayed here in a while?" I asked, folding the other heel of bread into my handkerchief and tucking it into my bag. "This place is so beautiful."

The woman froze, her hands suspended above the plates of bread, like a clockwork doll that needed winding. I waited for her to say something or even open her mouth to say something, but she just stared blankly at the plates below. Just before I was about to ask again, the sound of the front door opening pierced the silence with a fierce *ding* before slamming shut.

"Mmm! I smell your famous cinnamon bread, my love," Tom Clarke's booming voice sounded through the lobby, growing louder as he strode toward us, coat and hat in hand. When he saw us, something on his face registered that there was an awkwardness floating in the air. I was too confused to know how to explain the situation. Did I ask something I shouldn't have?

I thought he'd address the suspicion, but he just smiled and said, "Good evening, Ms. Blake. How has your stay been so far?"

"It's been perfectly lovely, thank you. And your wife here graciously gave me three pieces of bread," I motioned toward Flora, who returned to her warm, mobile self.

He laughed heartily. "Is that so, dear?"

"Well, two were heels," she said with a laugh. He strolled over and took a piece from one of the plates and gave a deep, satisfied *Mmmm* as he took a bite. "Would you like some tea, Caroline?" the woman asked as she grabbed hold of a teapot from the counter behind the table.

I looked at the clock. 3:47. I needed to get to the newspaper office before five or they might close, and I'd have to wait until tomorrow to inquire about the job.

"Well, I have to get to the office before five—"

"Oh, stay for a cup of tea! It will only be for ten minutes or so," the man said, his mustache twitching as he brushed crumbs off his face with a napkin. I looked at the clock again but then remembered their generosity. The fear settled into my stomach that I wouldn't have anywhere else to go if I messed this living situation up. I might as well stay for a cup of tea.

"All right," I said, trying my best to smile, "Thank you."

"Atta girl!" Mr. Clarke said in his earth-rattling voice. Flora padded over with two teacups and poured the two of us tea that smelled like blueberries and peppermint.

"Won't you join us, Flora?" I asked.

"Oh, I will, dear. I just need to fetch another cup." She placed the teapot down and shuffled past the counter, disappearing into the adjoining kitchen.

Mr. Clarke took another slice of bread from beneath the rag and ripped a piece off to pop in his mouth. In the silence, I was vaguely self-conscious of the sound of my gulping. I tried my best to take a small sip before asking him the same question I'd asked his wife.

I placed the teacup on the table and looked over at him. "This town is so beautiful, Mr. Clarke. Why doesn't anyone visit?"

He took a deep breath and sighed. "Well, they used to." Flora shuffled back into the room.

"What happened?" I asked. The older woman flinched, and her husband's look turned solemn. He swallowed a piece of his bread and put the rest on his plate. I found myself regretting asking the question. I hoped Flora didn't think I was here to torment her for reasons unbeknownst to me. Another moment of silence passed by, with only the ticking clock marking each second as they seemed to grow further and further apart.

Just when I thought I'd be sitting in silence until my tea went cold, Mr. Clarke spoke up. "Well, when my father first opened this place, it was always booming with guests." He chuckled softly, his eyes bright and wistful as they trailed into the past. "I have a lot of great memories of greeting guest upon guest as they arrived through those doors. My mother checked people in and had me show the guests to their rooms."

I took another sip of my tea as he continued. "I loved being here. I loved the smell of candy that wafted through the lobby each time someone opened the door and came in from the cold. I loved hearing the laughter and chatter when droves of people would make themselves at home, especially on the nights of the annual festival—" He barely finished the word when his mouth clamped shut. Flora froze again, but this time she made a small involuntary squeaking sound. When I looked over to her, I saw deep lines forming cracked rifts above her brows, and her eyes, wide and somber, looked horrified.

The man sighed again before continuing, quieter now, "I had looked forward to running this place myself one day, but just when I took the reins, something happened, and it's never been the same."

An eerie chill fell upon the room. As if someone had thrown a damp towel over the three of us. The clock ticked louder. The tea turned to ice. My stomach squeezed into a knot.

Suddenly my chair was too uncomfortable to sit in any longer. "Thank you so much for your generosity again," I said, the words peeling through the silence. My eyes darted to the clock. 4 o'clock. If I wanted to get to the newspaper's office before the end of the day, I had to go now. I looked at the elderly couple with a smile and said, "but I must be going. I am applying for a job today and have to get there before the office closes."

"Oh, how lovely," Flora said absently, her eyes still far away. She stood up, re-wrapped the bread, and disappeared into the kitchen once more.

"Good luck, dear," Mr. Clarke said, taking a sip of the cooled tea. "Let us know if you need anything."

With his wife gone, I yearned to ask Mr. Clarke more questions about the inn and about the festival he'd mentioned before they grew still. Why had he stopped speaking, his smile vanishing? And Flora . . . I could never forget those horrified eyes.

But this was my first day here. I shouldn't push it. Besides, I needed to go anyway.

"Thank you. Actually, do you know how I can get to 180 West Street?" I pulled out the newspaper clipping and showed it to him. The advertisement was in the right corner of the fourth page of the paper. It would be easy to miss for most others, but I had to scour each page of every newspaper I could get my hands on in the weeks after Maggie's death. I had to find a job, or I'd end up on the streets.

Then I found this advertisement in the *Brakerton Height Herald*.

It cost more than the other papers, being the leading newspaper for Brakerton Heights, and was hard to get a hold of in my small hometown, but it was worth it. Brakerton Heights was where my mother grew up. I didn't know much about her, but I did know that this was her hometown. It was a ten-hour ride by buggy from Fairbrooke, and Maggie had always refused to visit, no matter how many times I'd asked.

I'd never been here, but it was the last place I had a connection to and the only connection I had to my mother. That and the trunk I got to keep my few possessions in. It had been tucked away in our attic until the day I left. It was bursting with odd papers Maggie had been saving throughout the years, all complete rubbish by the looks of it, but it made me feel closer to them, so I kept it all.

After Mr. Clarke explained the directions to me, I thanked him and said farewell to the both of them, though his wife had still not returned from the kitchen. I put on my hat and tied my scarf to brave the cold outside. As I opened the door to leave, I looked back and wondered one last time if I should stay and talk, but I shook the thought away. *Use this impulse in your reporting, not to berate the people here to help you*, I told myself. Still, there was a nagging feeling deep within me that told me this was only the beginning. I was sure another opportunity would present itself.

Before I could second guess myself anymore, I plunged

into the night, determined not to return until I landed myself a job. There would be plenty of time to learn more about the festival.

I couldn't have avoided it if I'd tried.

CHAPTER Two

I was worried it would take me a while to find the office, but the directions were surprisingly straightforward, and I got there in no time at all, at least I thought I did. I stared at the paper in my hand:

Women writers wanted. It's time to change the present. Write at The Woman Speaks!

I looked up at the sign and then double-checked the address on the paper. My forehead creased. This couldn't be it. The shanty building in front of me looked more like an abandoned, vandalized general store than the office of an up-and-coming newspaper. Its windows were broken and covered with a long, dark cloth, fluttering from the slightest breeze, and the door was gouged and pitted. On top of it was a sign, small but clear:

The Woman Speaks

A thin film of nausea settled in my stomach. This was it. This was the paper.

I looked to either side of the small office. On one side sat a butcher shop, its smells barely contained behind murky glass windows, and on the other was what appeared to be an insalubrious apartment building, the muffled sounds of people talking hummed through the barrier. The only other sound I could hear was the clanking of dishes from an open window on the second floor. I took a deep breath and opened the door, cautiously optimistic and hoping I wasn't walking into danger.

A bell on the top of the doorframe rang as I stepped inside. Shelves of different colored wood lined the walls, paper spilling out of books and threatening to fall onto the ground. Despite the biting air outside and snapping breeze blowing through the broken window, the papers stayed in place, and the room was warm (or at least less frigid than the temperature outside). I looked around and saw no fire. Just four small tables with papers and ink and a woman seated behind two of the makeshift desks.

The woman behind the table-desk closest to the door looked up from a stack of papers. On the spare table beside her stood a tower of blank parchment paper; next to it were two quills and a fresh bottle of ink. That must be their method of producing their magazine. They have to copy it all by hand.

My gaze returned to the woman; she smiled but was clearly confused as she looked me up and down. She had thick black eyelashes and red hair that curled around her face, dropping in swirls below her ears and down the nape of her neck like crimson ribbons. With most of it pinned on top of her head, she looked like a living bouquet of roses. Her expression changed and her smile widened, her once concentrated face lighting up. "Oh my! Are you here for the open position?" She swiftly stood up and moved to the front of her desk to shake my hand. Even through my gloves I could tell her fingers were freezing.

I smiled faintly. "Yes, but am I too late? The ad was posted a few months ago."

She shook her head, her curls bouncing slightly against the shoulders of her dark olive dress. "No no no. We haven't been able to get this spot filled for almost a year."

I frowned. "Why not?"

She looked to the broken window. "Let's just say our idea hasn't been very popular."

"We're actually looking to move our office," a voice came from behind the red-haired woman. The other lady in the room made her way to us.

"We may end up just doing it privately at one of our houses," the first woman said, her eyes sadly studying the broken glass that still jutted in small, angry teeth at the bottom of the window frame.

The second woman smiled, her cheeks dimpling, "I'm Mary." She held out her hand, her own curled hair—blonde and thick—bounced against her shoulders.

"Caroline," I said, taking her hand and shaking it. "I guess this job is a little more dangerous than I thought."

The first woman looked back at me, her eyebrows rising. "Oh, no! We just had one bad encounter with a group of men a few weeks ago. Luckily, Herman at the butcher shop next door came to our rescue, as did Thomas from the bakery. They've been very helpful and help us keep an eye out for any strangers looking for trouble."

Mary nodded with a smile. "Thomas is a good man. We owe a lot to him. He stood up for me in town a couple times, too." A blush crept up her cheeks.

I smiled. "They sound like good people."

"Yes," the redheaded woman said. "By the way, I'm

Agnes. Welcome to *The Woman Speaks*."

The first week went by in a flash. Each day was even more work than the one before. Agnes brought in both old and new newspapers that her husband had scrounged up in town; he had to be as inconspicuous as possible to avoid any trouble for the three of us. She'd explained that it was hard to get their hands on papers because many of the locals wanted to sabotage their efforts at *The Woman Speaks*, even some of the women.

We spent hours upon hours looking through them, searching for something that would point us in some direction—any direction—to stories we could cover. We scoured some articles for leads and read between the lines of others, mining for our own stories to tell. At one point, Mary suggested we put all the papers aside and go out and find stories in the real world. I thought it was a great idea, but Agnes was worried about us leaving the shop unattended during the day and that we would end up wasting time. So, we continued searching the old-fashioned way.

Day in and day out, we searched until our eyes were too tired to see straight. I was surprised at how tiring the work was. I didn't expect working at a desk all day would be so draining; I wasn't used to working like this. I was used to moving around and working with my hands. Being an only child in the creaky house I grew up in, I had to learn a thing or two about fixing things, and that's how it all started. It didn't take me long to realize my aunt either didn't notice the leaks in the ceiling or was too afraid to check the creaks in the attic, so I became the handy-woman around the house and then consequently in town. As young as thirteen, I'd been commissioned to do things like fixing storage sheds or creating one from scratch. I made gifts, fixed roofs, changed doors—you name it, and I probably either made it or fixed it.

I also loved making things for Maggie. When she was close to passing away, I made a teacup delivery system for her so she could enjoy tea while I was away. It was a simple pulley system, and she had to take her tea cold, but she loved it. She had a hard time getting out of bed in the end, but she always wanted her tea. When I was gone, there wasn't anyone around to take care of her, so I did everything I could to take care of her from afar.

Even before she got sick, taking care of Maggie was a full-time job. Even on her healthiest days throughout my adolescence and young adulthood, I could never be away for very long. She wasn't comfortable with solitude and was always afraid something would happen to me whenever I was gone for longer than an hour or two. Unfortunately, we needed the money, so I couldn't afford *not* to leave the house. She didn't work (other than selling knitted hats and scarves in the fall and winter), so once I was old enough to work, I did. I wasn't sure how we got by before I turned thirteen and started bringing in money, but we managed.

I didn't mind it, though. Creating things was cathartic for me. It helped mend the broken walls in my mind and keep the darkness at bay. When I was left to wander inside myself for too long, bad things would happen—terrifying things. Flashes of nightmares and thoughts I wished I could tear from my mind clung to me, and I couldn't shake them off. Before I knew it, I'd find myself engulfed in darkness, hugging my knees to my chest and desperately wishing it would all go away.

Creating and fixing things allowed my mind to focus on

something without having to think. I welcomed the distraction wholeheartedly, especially on the more difficult days.

This new work was different; it wasn't as hands-on as I was used to, but it was exciting. I loved learning. Our library back in Fairbrooke was meager at best and held few new materials at any given time, but I read what I could and when I could. It was one of the only ways I experienced the outside world since I lived such a sheltered existence. When I wasn't creating things or caring for Maggie, I read. I let myself wander to new places and learn as much as I could—experience as much as I could. So, sitting here with stacks of papers, being so accessible to current events and new information, was thrilling, even if it was exhausting.

I sifted through the papers in front of me, reading as much as I could while skimming titles and paragraphs for something exciting to cover. After two hours passed by, I decided I'd settle on anything at all. I hadn't found a thing all week, so today I was determined to find something before I went home. I didn't want to risk feeling like a failure on my first week.

So I persevered. I spent another two or three hours scouring the papers. Still, I found nothing. Absolutely nothing.

"Caroline, have you found anything yet?" Agnes asked. I blinked twice and realized I'd been staring off, unconsciously watching rain dribble through the gaping window.

"Er, no, sorry. I'm still looking."

Time ticked by at an even slower pace, and I thought I might fall asleep, endless streams of words carved inside my eyelids. Thomas' bakery across the street always grew busy at this time of day—when evening was on the horizon and people were on their way home from work. The faint aroma of freshly baked bread, warm and crisp, made my stomach turn in violent hunger. It made staying focused even harder, so I decided to get up and stretch and maybe get some water.

I walked past Mary's desk and reached for the cup beside the faucet in the back of the room. She was working away, unfazed by my movement. I peered over my glass and watched the others work, each one with the same determination and distressed, narrowed eyes as they searched for any stories that could get the town talking and get us on the map. And paid.

I took one last gulp and placed my cup down, taking a deep breath. It was going to be another long hour before I headed home. We didn't get paid hourly or anything like that, but we made the most of the time we had each day, hoping we could one day get actual salaries and start making progress. Mary and I currently received eight shillings a week (from Agnes' husband's pay), which wasn't enough to live off of. Anything additional would be paid upon any commission we could snag, whether it was to investigate soiled crops or finding lost cats and reporting them in our paper. If we couldn't find anything to report on or anything to sell or do, we couldn't keep *The Woman Speaks* going, and we'd all be out of work and out of luck.

I moved back to my desk and readied myself to block out the voices coming in from the other side of the window when something on Mary's desk caught my eye. I reached down to pick it up. "May I?" I grabbed the corner of the paper.

Without looking up, she mumbled. "Yeah, sure." Lines were etched low on her forehead as she sat in deep concentration. I thanked her and slid the paper off of her desk.

I read the byline as I walked to my seat:

Ashdown Manor to Revive Town Festival. Reporters Needed. 50 shillings a week and accommodations.

I set it down and searched for the other article I saw with the same manor mentioned. I found it almost immediately:

Brakerton Heights Herald to cover Ashdown Manor Festival. First One to Brave the Story.

My lips pursed. First one to brave the story? What was that supposed to mean?

"Hey," I said, my voice cracking from lack of use. I moved my finger over the name "Ashdown Manor" as I cleared my throat and spoke again, louder this time, "What is this festival at Ashdown Manor, and why would it be brave to cover? At 50 shillings a week and accommodation, it seems too good to be true."

When I looked up, both women were staring at me, and the room was suddenly still. I couldn't even hear the crowds outside anymore. It was as if a ghost had walked into the room and masked us from the outside world. Finally, Mary spoke. "That's because it *is* too good to be true. That place has a sordid past. No one has come in and out for almost thirty years, other than the family's personal servants, doctors, and grocers."

"Why?" I asked. The two women shot each other a look.

"Well, it's a long story, and I wasn't around for it personally," Agnes said, her eyes studying the hem of her skirt. "Very few people in town were here when it happened."

"But it wasn't that long ago," I said, studying their strange expressions. "Surely there are people who have lived their entire lives here that would have been around for it."

The women gave each other another grim look. "What she meant was . . ." Mary winced as she spoke, as if forcing herself to say the words, ". . . very few people who attended the festival . . . came out alive."

"What?"

The wind rushed in, sending the papers on our desks into a flurried frenzy. Mary and Agnes leapt to their feet and reached for the papers, Agnes catching some floating by while Mary crawled on the ground, collecting ones scattered across the floor. I got to my knees, helping Mary with the stragglers. When I offered them to her, she shot me a dark look, as if this gust of wind was my doing. She got to her feet but didn't say a word.

"That place is cursed," Agnes said curtly, her words puncturing the thickening air. "Anyone stupid enough to cover that festival will not live to give the report." She returned to her seat, her shoulders pulled back in an awkward, stone-like position. Although she appeared calm, I knew she was hiding the true depths of her fear. After growing up the way I did, I could detect fear in someone as easily as I could spot them breathing.

I couldn't help but laugh. "Oh, come on, you two. Don't tell me you believe in that nonsense. There is no such thing as curses. And we can't let everyone think we aren't up for a job like this. It will just give them fodder for what they already think of us: that we aren't serious journalists and can't handle working the way men do. Look—two other papers have already announced that they will be covering the event."

I picked up the article and held it out to them. Neither one of them took it. They just kept fidgeting and looking at me as if I were telling them to storm a haunted house. "Come on! This is a big opportunity. It's the perfect thing for us to cover to show everyone what we're made of.

They'll have to take us seriously when they see us brave this story."

Mary looked as if she were about to cry, and Agnes was staring off with a vague expression, pursed lips, and crossed arms. I couldn't tell if she was mad, sad, or just generally upset by the whole thing. I looked at both of them carefully. "If what the two of you say is true, there may not be many others who will apply. We will stand out. I need to do this."

Agnes' stoic facade broke, and she and Mary looked at me in horror. "Caroline, you can't. It's dangerous," Mary said, her eyes red and glossy.

I gave her a sympathetic smile. "Mary, I'm not afraid. Maybe it was meant to be that I came here. Maybe an out-of-towner needed to cover this for our paper. Since I didn't grow up here, I don't have the same fears you do." As I said the words, Maggie's face appeared in my head. Any other words I was about to say stuck in my throat.

Her anxious mantras repeated in my ears:

Don't get too close to anyone when I'm gone, Caroline.

There are dangers in the shadows.

I've seen them, Caroline. I've seen them.

I shook away the thoughts and kept speaking. "I'm going to do it. If other reporters are going to do it, why shouldn't I? If we don't show up, no one will ever take us seriously. They'll never see us as more than these scared, fragile creatures unless we show them that we can go into battle, too."

I gathered my things and looked out the window. I could feel the beginning of rain's dewy mist on my skin. "It's going to rain soon. I'd better get going." Without looking back at them, I took the papers with the details of the festival, put on my hat and coat, and headed out the door. "I'll see you both tomorrow."

I tried to be brave as I left into the night, but there was a feeling I couldn't shake as I walked home in the frigid drizzle. I chalked it up to the same old fears I'd had since childhood. Maggie was always so afraid, and a lot of it bled onto me. How could it not? She told me danger would stare at me from my bedroom ceiling and that no one could be trusted.

But it didn't stop there. After a while, I started seeing things. Things I couldn't even remember anymore—things that left me terrified. I couldn't place what they were, but I could never forget how they made me feel. Terrified. Alone. Freezing cold.

The clouds rumbled above me, and I quickened my pace until I got to the inn. By the time I ran upstairs and locked my door, I couldn't tell if my cheeks were wet from rain or if I'd cried and didn't realize it. As I changed my clothes, I repeated the same thing I'd repeated to myself over and over again during my youth: "Maggie is just frightened from Mother's death. There are no such things as monsters."

Chapter Three

The mansion was heavier than it had been in years. Every clock was silent, every room filled with unease so thick you could almost reach out and grab it. They were the most dangerous creatures on Earth. Why should they be afraid?

Still, things moved forward. The clocks ticked on the walls, the floors creaked. Everything led to the study, where all three of them nervously shifted. The woman in the group was deep in thought. Her amethyst eyes stared off as countless thoughts rushed through her mind. She absentmindedly moved a sheet of her lustrous black hair out of her face and let it pour down her back like spilling ink.

Everything was off now, their daily lives no longer mundane. The usual comfort of routine and boredom had completely evaporated, and Evelyn couldn't tell if that was a good thing or a very bad one. Nothing was the same, and they knew it never would be again.

"I didn't think there would be so few," she said, her fingers lingering on her lips as she looked at the papers on her husband's desk. He hummed thoughtfully in his chair beside her. She leaned forward, placing a hand on one of his broad shoulders, her face close to his as she craned her neck over the back of his chair. Her brows were heavy against her moon-dipped eyes. No one knew what to say or do.

She continued looking at the papers, her forehead crinkling. She almost didn't hear William move to meet them in the corner of the study.

"Are you really that surprised?" he asked, crossing his arms.

She sighed and looked at her brother in exasperation. "William, what do you want?"

He raised a dark eyebrow and walked over to her. "You know what I want, Ev. I want you to call this whole thing off."

Her eyes widened. "Don't be ridiculous!"

"I'm not the one who's being ridiculous. You *know* this is dangerous. We have been in a delicate state for decades. Why are you opening the floodgates now?"

Her face hardened as she inched closer to him, fury practically steaming from her ears. "You know we can't keep living like this," she said through gritted teeth, "We have been confined up here for far too long. I'll go completely mad if I have to do it any longer, and I'm sure you feel it, too, whether or not you'll admit it." Her expression softened. "What's the point of life if we cannot truly live?"

"Ha!" he barked, shaking his head in disbelief. "Evelyn,

you of all people should know that we don't have the luxury of living actual lives. We just breathe and hope we don't get killed, or worse." His eyes flickered toward the wall, his jaw clenched, and she knew what he was thinking.

After a long, thoughtful pause, she let out a heavy sigh and looked at him. "William, I can't live the rest of my life—whatever you choose to call it—up here all alone. I miss being able to go out and mingle. I've been cooped up here for too long."

"You do get to get out. You and Charles go out on your trips all the time!"

The look of fury returned to her eyes and reflected in the rising volume of her voice. "You know what that's about, William, and don't you dare tell me you truly believe that's the same thing as going out and living!" The last word echoed through the spacious room. The void that swallowed her voice was just another painful reminder that no one ever visited and that they could have no company there.

The three of them stood still, not even breathing their usual, uneven breaths. When it became clear that she wouldn't change her mind, William nodded and backed away. "Alright, Evelyn, but you'll regret this. Mark my words. This won't go the way you're hoping it will."

"William," she said as he left, like a mother disappointed in her child. She hoped he'd turn around and reconsider. Talk things out. But she knew it was no use and that him changing his mind would be a bigger feat than this festival going smoothly. Still, she hoped for both, especially the latter. At this point, it was too late anyway. She'd already made up her mind. William would just have to deal with it. Come what may.

She let out another sigh and pointed to the applications on her husband's desk. "Reply to the ones we've gotten.

Beggars can't be choosers, I suppose."

I looked out the window; it was raining even harder now. The droplets skated down the murky window, leaving a greasy trail sliding down the glass.

The events of the day rolled through my mind. The newspaper. Mary. Agnes. This strange place. My uncertain future. All of it crashed into my mind, and I realized how much I missed my old life. I didn't live an exciting one before this, but at least things weren't so uncertain. So intimidating. Every night I fell asleep worried that at any moment I could be kicked out on the streets and be stranded without food or shelter.

I had no backup plan, either. I didn't know anyone here. Everyone I'd met so far was a mere acquaintance at this point. Sure, I'd been largely providing for myself since I was a kid, but I could always fall back on the help of people I knew. There was always a job waiting for me—always something that needed fixing or improvement. These were skills I couldn't use anywhere else. Not anymore. No one here would hire a woman to fix anything, and it would likely be the same anywhere else. If the townspeople thought women couldn't write anything worth reading, it was unlikely that they would hire one to fix the leaks in their houses.

The whole thing made my blood burn. What made them think women couldn't do these things? How does such ignorance even start? At least working at *The Woman Speaks* allowed me to work toward changing that horrendous misconception. It was something in dire need of fixing—more critical than any leak or creak I'd ever fixed before.

Still, I missed my life in Fairbrooke, but it was gone now. I was homesick for a place that didn't exist anymore, in a time that had long since passed. I missed fixing things and exchanging homemade craft boxes for mouth-watering pastries and freshly laid eggs. I missed watching the dogs running with the children near the house, weaving through trees as they began new adventures in the forest.

Most of all, I missed Maggie. She was a mother to me, and we really only had each other. Fixing things for her and the people in town was a life that I'd loved, even if it was hard for Maggie and me to make friends. For her, it seemed more out of choice, though. I always got the feeling that a part of her never healed from my mother's death. She loved me so much, but I could see that somewhere in her heart, there was a hole that would never be filled. And sometimes those same thoughtful eyes would show something else, though I could never figure out what.

A carriage outside struggled on a dip in the street; the sound, loud and jarring, jerked me back to the present. The homesickness of my old life curled in my stomach like a scared kitten as reality set in: I could never go back to that life. It existed only in my memory now, and there was nothing I could do about it but keep living and keep remembering.

I looked down at the papers I'd brought home, wrinkled and wet from the drizzle outside. This was my life now. This work and these people. I needed to make the best of it.

I walked over to the vanity and sat down, my eyes still scanning the inked letters on the paper: "The terrifying castle that has loomed over us all for so long has finally opened its gates, for those who dare enter its maw."

I put the paper down and looked at my face in the mirror. Despite everything, I couldn't help but smile. The thought of me—a woman—showing up at this castle with a group of men and awestruck passersby gave me a strange sense of satisfaction that only furthered my interest in applying for the position. I would prove that there was nothing to be scared of at this Ashdown Manor, and I'd prove that I could write a story just as well as any man.

I turned around and adjusted my hairpins, readying myself for supper. I hadn't dined with the Clarkes all week because of the late nights I'd been spending at work. As I pinned my hair in place, I heard Mr. Clarke's voice in my head.

I had looked forward to running this place myself one day, but just when I took the reins, something happened, and it's never been the same.

The words were engraved in my mind as if they were my own. I couldn't stop thinking about the look in his eyes. The eerie thickness of the air when Flora fled into the kitchen.

I opened the door and closed it quietly, as if in fear of waking a baby. There is something about a quiet house that makes you worried to make any sound at all, even if you're alone.

The stairs creaked as I descended toward the lobby, but when I turned into the dining hall, my stomach twisted. Mr. Clarke was reading a paper, his bald head spotted and white against the pale light of the room. He turned the page with a weathered hand, adjusting his pipe with the other.

He was alone.

This was my chance.

Ever since that first night, I'd been dying to press him for more details, but there was never an opportunity. His wife was always around, and she had an odd look in her eyes. Something that gave me the feeling that I should tread lightly in my conversations. I'd waited for another chance to get Mr. Clarke alone, but it didn't happen. In the mornings, she was always there, and in the evenings I walked up the stairs alone.

I quickened my pace, my eyes watching for any sign of Flora Clarke, but she was nowhere in sight. This was it. I had to ask him now.

Now more than ever, I needed to know as much as I could about the festival. It wasn't just about curiosity anymore. I needed to know before applying for the job. That was a good reason, right?

I made my way over to him, unconsciously holding my breath until I pulled out the seat across from him. He looked up from his paper. I smiled. "Hi, Mr. Clarke. How are you doing this evening?"

The man grunted, but I could see a hint of a smile beneath his mustache. He took a long puff of his pipe and then folded the paper and set it on the table next to him. "Could I get you some tea, dear? Mrs. Clarke is out getting some ingredients for supper."

"Oh? Has she been gone long?"

He shook his head. "No, she left just a moment ago."

I shifted in my seat. I had to do it now. "Sir, I know this may be a touchy topic, but can you tell me about the Ashdown Manor Harvest Festival?"

The man's mouth closed around his pipe, his hand frozen around its bulbous chamber. He studied the flickering light of a candle on the table, its bright orange glow waxing and waning.

Finally, he took the pipe out of his mouth and placed it on the table, still watching the shuddering of the candle's flame. "Flora and I were childhood sweethearts," he said hesitantly, pausing before he continued. "We grew up with the rolling hills as our playground. We knew Ashdown Manor well enough; mind you, we never went *inside*, but we knew of it, and we weren't afraid of it back then. As kids, we were simply intrigued. We used to make up grand stories about its tenants and what went on inside."

He smiled softly. "We thought it was a magical castle full of adventures we couldn't even begin to fathom. But we tried." He chuckled. "We invented all kinds of things we thought were going on inside, but all we knew was that the people who lived there were the most handsome people we'd ever seen. Flora in particular would watch the ladies of the manor stroll into town during the weeks leading up to the festival. They'd greet people, go to plays, and go shopping. They always looked so glamorous. Flora's eyes just lit up like firebugs whenever the lady of the house came into town."

I tried to imagine it. Flora and Tom Clarke as young kids, playing make-believe along the lush landscape around the city, laughing as they jumped and rolled between each hill, as if playing on the back of a giant, grassy dragon. His raspy voice continued, "I was never allowed to go to the festival. That was when our inn was the busiest. My parents needed all the help they could get. Still, I yearned to go one day. Flora used to go and bring me back caramel apples and little prizes she'd won for me. Finally, when I was about twenty-five, I was able to pass my work on to someone else and was able to go and enjoy the festival myself."

He glanced sideways at me, a wistful smile on his lips. "I proposed to her that night."

"That's wonderful!" I said, but there was something sad in his eyes, and he went on as if he hadn't heard me.

"I was never able to go back, though," he said, his smile fading. "My father passed away shortly after Flora and I got married the following year. After that, I had to run the inn and never had the luxury of taking a night off during that busy season again. Flora went, though. It helped her when things were tough." The last few words were barely audible, and I wasn't sure if he had said anything after that. His mouth had moved, but no sound came out.

His shoulders were tense now, and he had a look I recognized all too well. The look of someone falling deeper and deeper into memories he'd hoped he lost, falling through endless open doors in his own mind.

I cleared my throat in an effort to break the dark spell cast over him. His fingers twitched, but he didn't seem to hear me. "So . . . what happened that has made everyone so afraid then?" I asked. Hearing my voice seemed to tear him from whatever thoughts he was lost within, but he still said nothing.

"What happened at the last festival?" I asked, clearer this time. "What has made everyone so afraid?"

Mr. Clarke closed his eyes and let out a long breath. "That festival was nearly thirty years ago," he said, his voice lower than before. "Flora and I had been married about eight years at that point. It was just as busy as every year before it, but . . ."

He froze again. I wondered if I should have just avoided the topic completely, but if I wanted to be a journalist, I'd have to get used to pushing for answers. No matter how uncomfortable it may be. Still, I waited. I didn't want to prod him further if I didn't have to.

The grandfather clock in the lobby sounded throughout the inn, the gong rattling nearby silverware. I jumped in my seat and realized I hadn't even noticed its ticking or how much time had passed. I suddenly became anxious of Flora's inevitable return. I looked at the clock in the dining area but couldn't remember what time it had been when I'd arrived.

I didn't know how much longer I had before her return,

but I also didn't know when I'd ever have an opportunity like this again. I looked at Mr. Clarke's face, still lost in some sort of nightmare, and I wondered if I'd even have the strength to ask him again if given the chance.

Finally, he spoke. "Flora left that evening. It was another hard year. We had lost another baby, mere weeks before its expected birth." Tears welled in his eyes. "That festival was a refuge for her. She was always able to forget about the world and dive inside. She loved the bright colors, the sweet smells, the warmth of laughter threaded within the crowd. I always looked forward to her smile at the end of those nights. Each year after we lost our first baby took more of a toll on her. Soon, that bright, beautiful smile that I loved so much became more of a miracle to witness.

"I looked forward to that smile of hers every fall. When nostalgia took hold of her heart at Ashdown Manor, she could be a kid again. She wasn't the mourning wife who longed to be a mother. She was little Flora Jane, running along the hills with me, barefoot in the grass."

He leaned forward, his eyes returning to the candle. The intensity of his stare on that wavering flame made me uneasy. There was something off about it that didn't feel quite right. "At about ten o'clock each night, patrons used to start piling back to the inn, drunk on life or cider, or maybe a bit of both. I expected it every year. Some young lovers stayed out past that point, but most people started stumbling in around nine or ten . . ."

His voice trailed off, and his stare remained locked on the flame. "But that night, no one came back. I had about twenty guests that weekend. It was the second night of the festival, so I knew roughly when this particular group of guests might wander back to the inn." He shook his head. "But none of them ever made it back."

Something curdled in my stomach, a cold queasy feeling squirming in my gut. When Mr. Clarke stopped speaking, I asked the question hanging in the air. "What happened?"

The candle's dancing head reflected in his pupils. "Flora never told me. Someone brought her home. Both that woman—an older family friend named Ethel—and my dear Flora wore similar expressions that night, like they'd seen terrible, horrible things happen, which I suppose they did . . . but my dear wife . . . something left her soul that day. When Ethel brought her home, there was nothing in Flora's eyes. Nothing at all.

"She didn't speak for days. I had to spoon-feed her, which was very difficult because she had that same haunted look. I'd help her eat, but I don't even know if she slept that whole week. Every night I looked at her and kissed her forehead before bed, and every morning I woke up and saw her wearing that same expression. Finally, after about a week, she spoke, but she has never told me what happened that night. None of the few survivors have ever freely talked about it, but I saw enough to understand why. A few of us who hadn't been there were asked to help gather and bury the bodies . . ."

His hands began to tremble, and soon his shoulders were shaking, too. Soon his whole body was shivering. He cupped a hand over his mouth, covering it and leaving only his widened eyes undisguised on his face. "We couldn't identify most of them," he whispered through his tremoring fingers. "I wasn't there when they were first going through them, but what I did see . . . was horrifying. I'd never seen anything like it. Those people were *massacred*."

"What?" I said, my heart pounding faster. The room grew even colder, and as I watched his terrified expression, I remembered something. It wasn't a thought so much as a feeling. An experience I couldn't identify but also couldn't shake. With it came a rush of darkness—a wave of something that could easily drown me if I so much as took the wrong step.

What was this feeling?

A flash of light sparked across my mind. I could hear something. Someone. Was it someone crying? A woman? A child? I couldn't see the source of the noise, but there was something else. I was suddenly moving in a void of light with nothing around me but the feelings of darkness and the flurry of unknown noises.

That other noise. I'd heard it somewhere before.

"What's going on here?"

The bright light was gone. I was back. I looked around and saw that I hadn't gone anywhere. Of course I didn't. It was just a thought. A memory. I looked away, trying not to look at Mr. Clarke again. Whatever that was—a vision, a memory, a nightmare—I didn't want to experience it again. I didn't want to go back there.

"Well?"

I looked and saw Flora, scowling and holding sacks of freshly bought ingredients. Her eyes shifted to her husband, and I followed her gaze. Mr. Clarke was wiping his face, his body still shaking, and guilt suddenly washed through me. This was my fault. I could feel the heat rising in my face as I stood up. I reached toward Mr. Clarke, hoping I could assuage his fear in some way, but before I could, Flora snapped, "I think you should go to your room now."

"I'm sorry," was all I could say. I wished I could do more, but it was clear I had done enough. With my head down, I scurried upstairs, hoping and praying that after tonight, I'd still have a place to stay.

Chapter *Four*

Something shifted after that. Things felt different at the inn when I woke up and got ready for work the next morning. I couldn't help but worry that it was more than just fear and guilt building inside me. Sometimes our bodies can feel that something is about to happen, like an animal before a hurricane. Sometimes the feelings prove to be true. Other times, we find that we got all worked up for nothing. I wasn't sure which this was.

Whatever the case, there was nothing I could do about it but move forward and hope I didn't end up on the streets by the next time I spoke to the Clarkes. When I got ready to leave, I looked for them but couldn't find them anywhere. I tried to release the anxiety within me and tell myself it would all be okay and then headed out the door.

Once outside, I could finally breathe. I clutched my bag

to my chest. My application to cover the Ashdown Manor Harvest Festival was inside, and since I still wasn't sure what the crime was like here, I decided to err on the side of caution and keep my bag close. I had to ask a couple passersby where to go, but I finally made it to the post office, paid for the letter, and handed it over to the carrier. When he saw who the letter was addressed to, he raised his eyebrows and asked if I was sure I wanted to send it.

"Yes, I do," I said firmly before exiting the building. I held my head high until I rounded the corner. Once out of sight, I breathed a deep sigh of relief. *I did it*, I thought. *I sent it.* It was out of my hands now. I just hoped I wouldn't regret it.

As I headed to work, I tried not to think about it. But I couldn't escape it. I even caught a conversation or two as I passed shops. It was a long walk to work.

"I heard a few journalists are actually going to do it," one man said in front of the general store. My shoes caught on the cobblestones and scratched to a stop. I didn't want to look at him and make myself obvious, but I listened.

"Yeah, I heard that, too," the man with him said. "It's crazy, if you ask me."

"Oh, most definitely. The lot of them should be tested for lunacy. No one in their right mind would step foot in that murder house."

The words hung in the air, immobilizing me. *Murder house.*

The first man continued. "No one has seen a single Ashdown family member leave that house in years. Does anyone even know who's living there now? Did they all die off?"

"No, they couldn't have. They still have grocers and the like in and out throughout the year."

There was a silence between them, and then the first

man grunted. "Well, I'm not going to that festival."

"Oh, *I* am."

I looked then. The first man—a long, lanky one with the body of a snake and the nose of a rodent—spat tobacco on the ground and huffed at the stout, mustached man to his side. "You're kidding," he said. He looked up and noticed me staring at them. A shiver rushed up my spine. I dipped my face down and strode forward, not looking up until I was well past the store and close to work.

Soon, my thoughts drifted back to my application. I wondered if it looked professional enough. I had very few papers at my disposal, and I wasn't even sure if I was too late to apply, so I had used one of the papers in Maggie's trunk. One of the barest ones. It had a couple of strange markings on it, but it wasn't as littered with them as the rest of them. All the papers' content was nonsensical. Some had odd phrases and fragmented sentences, while others held hastily drawn images of symbols I didn't recognize.

As I went through the trunk and inspected each piece, I realized it was the first time I'd really searched her trunk since leaving Fairbrooke. It had been a welcome distraction after my questioning Mr. Clarke. Part of me had hoped that I'd find a letter from Maggie or from my mother—maybe even a correspondence between the two—but there was nothing. Not even a coherent journal note or grocery list. The only thing I could think of was that these were papers Maggie had used to jot down the static crackling of her mind during the weeks where things were too hard for her to keep it all inside. Maybe she drew how she was feeling or wrote what words would pop into her head.

But why keep them?

Perhaps she was afraid to dispose of them. Throwing her ramblings away would have released the papers into the world where others could potentially find them. She was always fearful of being locked away (a topic often brought up by the people of Fairbrooke). The possibility of someone else misinterpreting her musings could have led to her concealing and hoarding such notes.

My heart ached for her. No one should ever feel that they have to hide their suffering in fear of punishment or becoming an outcast. That wasn't the way the world should work. Maggie was a lot stronger than she knew, too. People who constantly wrestle with their demons end up cultivating a strength others can't even recognize.

Despite her battle, those demons never left her, even during her final days. She thankfully didn't die because of them, but they never stopped haunting her. Whatever part of her snapped when my mother died never returned. I did my best to contain her unraveling while taking care of my own, but I could only do so much. For either of us.

I finally made it to work. The unwelcome stench of the butcher shop was even stronger than usual today. It swept up my nose as the brisk autumn wind cut through me. I stood in the road and looked at the abused office building, wondering what everyone else in town thought of us—of these three women busy working at their makeshift desks, constantly facing opposition and controversy, shielded only by a tarp and a dented door.

Then I thought about my assignment. I thought about Mr. Clarke's terrified eyes and the stories of the massacred bodies and speechless survivors. I thought of the man in front of the general store and his talk of Ashdown Manor being a murder house, while his companion's curiosity would take him to the festival anyway. I tried to shake away the second guesses of turning in my application—of wondering if going to Ashdown Manor was dangerous or not, or if I was stupid for applying—but I couldn't help but wonder.

The questions gnawed at me as I walked to our dented door. Through the shattered window, I could hear Mary and Agnes in a heated argument, and my hand froze on the doorknob when I heard my name. "I think she's being reckless," Mary said. "Caroline doesn't understand what she's getting herself into. She's walking into a lion's den, and she's doing it willingly."

"No, Mary, she isn't. We don't know what's going to happen. We don't know why the Ashdown family is reopening this festival. Maybe they're trying to make amends and start over."

"If they wanted to make amends, they should show their cowardly faces!"

"Perhaps they should, Mary, but that's not up to any of us. All we need to do is support Caroline. She's right, you know. We're a laughingstock to half the city, and we're seen as trollops to the rest."

"But it's her *life*, Agnes," Mary said breathlessly. "We can't let her do this."

There was a brief pause. I didn't move out of fear that I might miss Agnes' reply. "We are in no position to tell her what to do," Agnes said calmly, "or anyone else for that matter. Isn't that one of the missions of our paper? To give voices to the marginalized, and to give us the freedom to choose our own lives?"

Mary said nothing. Agnes continued, "I commend Caroline for what she's doing. She's incredibly brave. I think she'll do a fine job. Her determination and passion will help us finally reach our goals. She'll put us on the map and help all the women in town. She's a hero, even if she doesn't know it yet."

I could hardly believe the words as they met my ears. No one had ever said anything like that about me before. Was I really a hero for taking a small risk to help out an important cause? I figured that was something anyone would do if given the opportunity.

Another breeze cut through me, rippling the window's covering. My hand was still on the doorknob when the women saw me through the window. I was caught. My face turned bright red. *I might as well head in now.*

When I walked through the doorway, Mary's face was as pale as paper. "Caroline, how long had you been there?"

"Long enough," I said with a smile, "but it's okay. I can't blame you. After hearing what some of the others in town have said, I think I'm a little crazy too." Agnes hid a smile beneath her fingers and watched Mary's pale face turn pink.

"I still don't believe in this curse by the way," I added, "I know horrible things have happened there, but that doesn't mean it's cursed." I crossed my arms, still smiling and expecting them to back me up. But neither of them said a word, not even Agnes. I frowned. "Don't you think so? You said you thought I'd be okay, Agnes."

She nodded, face blank. "There may not be a curse," she said, looking up to meet my gaze, "and I don't think it's necessarily dangerous . . . at least I hope it isn't . . . but you should still be careful. You should know that I support you either way, though. If you're uncomfortable even five minutes before, or three days—or weeks—in, it's okay to quit."

"But at that point, it will be even worse than if I never showed up at all," I said. "I have to do this. Everyone thinks we're less intelligent and less capable than men. We need to show them they're wrong." I hadn't realized my voice had escalated until the sound of my pressed words echoed back at me from the walls.

A fierce wind rippled through the window and rattled across the room. The weather was in rare form today.

Agnes' quiet laughter coaxed my mind back into the moment. "See, that's what I like about you, Caroline," she said, "You're a tough one. We need more people like you." The words struck me, just as her earlier comments had. People didn't usually reward my boldness with praise.

"Thank you, Agnes." I smiled again. "I'll do my best to give our readers a good story."

"I'm sure it will help us *get* readers anyway," Mary said, her voice flat, but then she turned to me with a slight smile. "I *am* rooting for you. I'm just worried."

"I know, Mary, it's okay."

"It's just," she continued, "no one has seen the family for decades. They never came out with an apology or explanation. They were never even charged with anything—"

"Well, to be fair, we don't know if they were behind any of it," Agnes interrupted. Mary raised an eyebrow at her, her mouth agape.

"Then what do you *think* happened? The proof is in the pudding: They held a festival where most of the guests died, leaving all the others scarred, and they have never shown their faces in public again." She waited for Agnes' reply. When it didn't come, she continued. "We don't know what kind of people they are. For all we know, they're waiting hungrily for their next victims."

"That's ridiculous!" I said. "We need to give this a shot. I'll be fine. We will *all* be fine. Do you honestly think they'd put this festival on if there was a risk of another massacre? They probably haven't come out again because they're frightened of what people here might do to them, whether they're guilty of anything or not."

Neither of them looked at me, but I could tell they knew I had a point. "And they could have done something at any point over the last three decades—something horrible—

but they haven't, right?" They nodded, albeit reluctantly.

"I suppose you're right," Agnes said.

Mary grumbled before adding, "Maybe."

"Exactly. I'll be fine. There's nothing to be afraid of at this *Ashdown Manor*. I'm sure everything will be all right. A horrible thing happened thirty years ago, or so. That's all there is to it." The confident smile remained on my face for one moment longer before I heard it. My name.

Caroline!

My skin went cold, and the corners of the room started to blur.

Caroline! the voice called again. Neither Mary nor Agnes was saying a word; I watched their closed mouths, which weren't so much as twitching when I heard the voice one more time, clearer now.

Caroline!

The blood drained from my face.

"Maggie?"

As I said her name, the room went black, and despite the gusts of wind that had torn through me earlier, I was even colder now. It felt like I'd been plunged into an ice-cold sea but didn't know how to swim.

All around me was sheer darkness, and I couldn't feel anything but pins and needles at my fingertips and toes, and on every inch of skin in between. It was that feeling when your body succumbs to sleep when the world around you is too cold to bear.

Then I heard something else—like someone yelling through water. I tried to scream out to it over and over again, but I couldn't make a sound.

The voice called out again, closer this time. I still couldn't make out what it was saying, but I could tell that it wasn't saying my name as the first voice had. I listened as closely as I could, but my body was shivering uncontrollably and aching with pain.

A glaring flash blinded me momentarily, and then everything went dark again. Spots splattered across my eyes as they adjusted between the two extremes. Then I heard it again, but this time, I began to remember.

Another burst of light crashed around me, and the sheer horror that splintered through me was unbearable. The light fled once more, but my heart was pounding. I didn't notice anything but the terror forming knots in my body, tensing the muscles in my back and pulling at my chest. My body shook harder, doused with fear. And I waited. I waited to see what happened next. I didn't know where I was or what was happening. I just wanted it all to go away.

Another flash crashed around me, revealing the body of that dreaded creature even closer now. A creature I'd forgotten all about. One I could never escape. It reached its claws out at me, but just as its talons splayed out toward my face, it all vanished. All of it.

I was back at the office. Then darkness cloaked the room, and I lost consciousness completely.

When I woke up, I saw Mary, Agnes, and the Clarkes hovering over me. When my eyes adjusted to the light, I sat up and realized I was on my bed back at the inn. I looked outside. It was already night.

What had happened back there?

"Caroline . . . are you alright?" Mary asked.

I was shivering. After passing out and being here for hours, I was still shivering. I wrapped my body in my arms and tried to meet the gazes of the people around me, but I couldn't do it. The fear was still a sour taste in my mouth that made it hard to be present, and I knew it wouldn't leave any time soon.

The image of that creature crawled into my mind again, and suddenly I was a child curled beneath my covers and wishing for it to leave me alone.

Go away go away go away go away I used to whisper through silent sobs. I tried to muffle my cries, just in case the "Shadow Beast" reached its claws out and pulled the covers off of my head. I imagined it plucking me up and tossing me in its gaping jaws, its daggered teeth blooming out like a demonic flower, ready to eat me alive.

"That . . . that thing," I whispered, my gaze fixed on the window, focusing on every tiny detail of the wood around it so my mind wouldn't wander off again. A technique I learned in childhood. "I haven't seen it in years. I'd forgotten all about it." That's all I could say. I didn't want to breathe more life into it.

It was a myth. A nightmare. As a child, that "Shadow Beast," as I used to call it, tormented me in my dreams. It tore through my nightmares, shaking me awake. That didn't help either, though: waking up. All it did was cast those demonic eyes onto the walls beside my bed, the shadows groaning with fangs too familiar. Its face etched into my mind whether I was asleep or awake.

"I haven't seen it since I was a kid. Why would it come back now?" I uttered, the words barely dribbling from my lips. I had no idea what to think.

As I grew older, and that creature stopped appearing, I figured it had been a manifestation of the fear which came from hearing Maggie's stories, my mind gripping onto the warning tales and spinning them into a new warped reality. Because as I began learning how to cope a little better, the nightmares seemed to stop. At least that's what I remembered. But if that was the case, why would they start again now?

And I was still so cold.

Agnes leaned over. "Caroline, I think you've come down with something. I think you had a fever dream of some kind. You should rest and take a few days off to recover." I looked at her, my eyes probably large and unsettling.

"What happened?" I asked. "Back at the office."

One of Agnes' red curls had escaped her pins and fallen across her forehead. She pulled at it as she spoke. "It was strange. One moment you were talking with us, and then you just . . . *stopped.* It was like your body had been running off the flames of a candle and someone blew it out. Your face fell, your arms dropped. You looked . . ."

"Scared," Mary finished, looking up at me like something tragic had just happened. I hoped that the look had no truth behind it.

The Clarkes stayed by my bedside without saying a word. They looked worried, though, which was pleasantly surprising in a way. Maybe they didn't harbor any bad feelings for me after all.

"Well," I said, forcing a smile, "As you can see, I am perfectly fine. Perhaps you're right, though, Agnes. Maybe I need some rest."

"That's a grand idea, Caroline. You do that. Fevers are no good. We'll leave you to it." She nodded and led Mary out the door.

"Let us know if you need anything, dear," Mrs. Clarke said and smiled softly, though her eyes showed that she was still more than concerned.

"Thank you for your kindness, Mrs. Clarke. I appreciate it," I said. The older woman smiled, and I was suddenly grateful that I met all these people.

As they all left and bid me a good rest, I sat back and realized I shouldn't have let them leave. Soon, the darkness would creep back up my . . .

No. I'm not a child anymore. I have a fever. That's all. I hallucinated and passed out. That's it.

I thought those words to myself over and over again until I fell asleep, ignoring the fact that my skin was ice cold.

I had a nightmare that night. The first one in years.

Chapter Five

"What is this?" he asked, picking up the yellowed piece of parchment. "Did one of you do this?" He shot a glare at his sister and brother-in-law. "Is this a joke?"

Evelyn looked at him, her eyes unblinking as he held up the paper for her to see. Her eyes flickered back to the symbol, and she couldn't look away. That madly curled symbol that watched her—mocked her—telling her that this was all doomed from the start. "No, William. Why would we joke about something like this? Look on the back."

He flipped it over and scanned the words inscribed in smudged black ink. "What . . ." William's voice evaporated. Because there it was. It stared back at him the way it mocked his sister with its intricate lines. Whatever part of him thought he could escape it was terribly wrong.

"We should keep an eye on her," Charles said, his usually stoic self even more solemn than usual. He rubbed his fingers against his brow. "We'll send a letter informing her that her application was accepted." He slid a blank sheet of parchment from a pile on his desk and laid it out in front of William. "It appears the master of the house has one more application to accept."

William grimaced and took the quill from Charles. He dipped it in the round canister of ink on the desk, then paused. "Who are you Caroline Blake?" he muttered, "And what do you know?"

A few days went by, but I couldn't peel the image of that creature from my mind. I couldn't shake the nightmare, or the hallucination, if that was truly what it was. I still couldn't believe it. I hadn't seen it in years. Maybe it was like it was when I was a child—maybe it was a manifestation of my inner distress.

It was probably because I was worried about this new assignment. Everyone was getting all worked up for nothing—out of some blind hysteria. A mass belief in a curse borne from one horrific incident no one wanted to talk about.

My whole life had been riddled with superstition and fear. I was absolutely sick of it. I would face the fears I'd lived with my entire life, as well as the fears of this city, and I'd prove to everyone that there were no such thing as monsters or curses.

I went home at the end of another busy day to find Mr. Clarke sitting at the front desk, drumming his fingers on something in front of him. He watched me walk in with a look of deep unease. That same queasy feeling snaked through me, a contagious sensation around here. I feigned a smile and nodded in greeting. "Good evening, Mr. Clarke."

"Caroline, you have something here," he said quietly.

"What is it?" I asked, my voice catching slightly on my throat. He sighed, picked up the envelope, and made his way over to me. My eyes immediately fell on the letter. It undoubtedly had my name on it. When he handed it to me, I flipped it over and saw the crest of Ashdown Manor, along with the name of the family. The color drained from my face.

I looked up at Mr. Clarke, trying to find the words to say. When they failed to come, he spoke up instead. "Are you really going to do this?"

The grandfather clock in the lobby thumped even louder than usual, filling the space between us. I swallowed, then nodded. "Yes," I said quietly, "I am." He nodded in return, a sort of resigned nod, and then walked into the dining area.

Unsure of whether or not he wanted me to follow him, my feet stayed planted in place. I wasn't sure if I could move right now anyway. My body felt like ice, though it had never really felt the same since that day I passed out at work.

The man shuffled back into the room, holding what looked like a frayed, cream-colored cloth. It was rolled up tightly, and the way he handled it made me feel that there was something inside. He held it out for me to take, so I grabbed it carefully. Something was indeed inside.

When I unraveled it, my hands froze. It was a knife.

I looked up at him, fear and confusion clear in my eyes. He puffed out a breath and said, "Take that with you to the castle. It might prove useful to you." My hand stayed frozen in place, fingers out and palm upright, as if afraid to fully grab hold of the blade. What would it mean if I accepted it? What would it mean if my fingers curled around the handle and I tucked it into my purse?

Mr. Clarke continued, "You may need protection. You don't need to say anything, but please take it with you." Neither one of us moved for about two minutes after that, judging by the crescendoing *thunks* of the clock.

Then, finally, he shuffled away, and for some reason, tears burned against my skin. I closed my hand around the knife, tucked it back inside the cloth, and shoved it in my bag. I grabbed hold of the letter, which had been tucked under my arm, and walked up to my room.

After closing the door, I let myself fall against it, my back sliding down the wood until my bottom reached the floor. I looked at my name on the front of the envelope. So flawlessly written, with swirling curves and thick black lines. I flipped it over and examined the seal—the crest: two ravens and a lion, vines looping around the exterior, outlining the curious animal depictions.

The ravens were floating atop the lion, the feline's paws reaching heavenward, its gaping mouth snarled open. The odd thing about it, though, was that the ravens didn't look like they were afraid of the lion. They looked like they were commanding it, smiling over the lion's vain attempt at attacking them. *What a strange crest*, I thought, mesmerized by its peculiar design.

I reluctantly took the knife Mr. Clarke had given me and broke the seal, cutting the envelope open and releasing the contents inside. A crisp, bone-colored piece of parchment fell into my lap. I picked it up and read it:

Brakerton Heights

September 16, 1885
Miss Caroline Blake,

We are pleased to inform you that your application has been received and accepted. Please report to the front gates of Ashdown Manor at 9 am sharp on Friday, September 18th. Your stay with us will be for a period of six weeks, in which you will accompany a member of the house as we make preparations for the newly re-introduced Ashdown Family Harvest Festival. We look forward to making your acquaintance.

Sincerely,

William Ashdown
Ashdown Family Manor

September 18th. That was only two days away.

I could hardly believe it. I applied for the job, and I wanted it, but a part of me thought I'd get rejected. What was I to do now? I looked out the window as if the dreary weather would offer me my solution. What *could* I do other than wait until the morning for my fate to arrive? Whatever fate that might be.

Chapter *Six*

When the morning of my departure came, I was exhausted. I was awake half the night, both worried about the day to come and haunted by the sound of Flora's whimpers down the hall. I heard them as I fell asleep, twisting and turning. The guilt and anxiety nearly suffocated me. I was awake for so long that I wondered if the morning would ever come. And when it did, what then?

But here it was. My trunk was packed, and I was ready to leave.

The entire day prior consisted of me telling Mary and Agnes the news and getting prepared to leave. They gave me a new set of papers—ones free of Maggie's scratchings—and a quill and pot of ink that would hopefully last my entire stay at the mansion. That night, I ate alone and didn't see either of the Clarkes until the following morning when I passed Mr. Clarke on my way out.

He stopped me and said he'd already arranged a carriage for me, which I was deeply grateful for; it was relieving to know that I wouldn't have to drag my trunk to the edge of town. After I thanked him, I thought he might offer me a quick breakfast or a heartfelt goodbye, but instead, he waited with me in silence as I watched for the carriage.

"Thank you for doing this for me," I said, breaking the silence. "It's very kind." I dipped my hat in a polite bow, but the tension was thick. That same uneasy feeling from before filled the air, and I wondered if I could escape it. When the sound of hooves and wheels on cobblestone reverberated from the front of the inn, I turned to Mr. Clarke and forced a smile. "Well, goodbye. I will see you in a few weeks."

"Do you have the . . . you know . . ." The first few words stumbling over each other as they left his mouth. I froze. When I nodded, he said, "Be sure to keep it on you at all times. You never know when something might happen." My lips flickered up awkwardly at one corner as I tried to force a smile. I tried to say something, but all I could manage was another small nod. What more could I do? I had no voice after that.

The journey to the mansion was steeped in fog. It felt as though I were deep inside a dream but aware that I was asleep. I needed the coachman to help me out once we arrived because I could barely stand up; my legs felt like they were full of water. I almost felt out of my body altogether.

It wasn't until I was out of the carriage that I noticed

how unbearably bleak it was outside. Clouds slowly churned in the sky, dark shades of gray grumbling with distant thunder. The wind pushed against me as I walked along the path to the bottom gates of the manor.

And it was cold. Not just the weather. All of it. It was a feeling in just about everything. Inside me, in the looks around town—those drooping stares, the darting eyes, the hesitant onlookers both too afraid to come close but too curious not to be there at all. And it was in the way Mary and Agnes watched me as they met me at the gates, which stood dauntingly at the bottom of the large hill.

It became harder to breathe as I continued toward it. That caged mouth ready to devour me, as well as the others. Its offerings. We were hogs ready for slaughter, eagerly anticipating the opening jaws at the monster's lips. Why was I walking right into its belly?

I looked around to anchor myself to the moment and not let myself flutter off into the feeling of today. To grasp onto anything I could to keep the tightening of my chest at bay. I focused on the sounds. Muffled voices—grunts from some and panicked whispers from others. The rippling snaps of my coat against the wind.

The smell of the trees soaked into my skin as the wind blew its earthy scent through my nose, and everything vanished. I closed my eyes and pictured myself running through the woods behind my old cottage. Maggie used to encourage me to run outside and get my energy out all the time as a child. *Just don't talk to anyone*, she'd say, eyes hard as rocks, *Don't follow anyone or anything suspicious, either. Just run and play and come back in an hour.* She'd usually let me run out for longer than that, as long as she knew where I was.

I loved it. I ran as fast and as hard as I could in the carefree splendor that only children seem to possess. I loved the feeling of earth beneath my feet, my shoes coming off as soon as I reached stretches of thick blankets of grass. I'd splash in puddles and laugh as the water splattered all over me, pretending I was a baby elephant in the wild.

I was free.

"Caroline?"

My eyes opened, and I was back—back to this dreary, unpredictable day. One of many, I was sure. My shoulders dropped, but I tried to seem upbeat. "Hi, Mary. Agnes."

"Are you ready?" Agnes asked, her gloved hands wringing. Both women wore dark shades today, Agnes in a plain gray smock and Mary in a wool dress with black lace cuffs, as if going to an almost-funeral.

"Yes, I am very much ready," I lied, trying as hard as I could to force a smile. They needed to know I'd be okay. They needed to know that we weren't making a mistake. And by *we* I meant *me*. It was my responsibility to ensure the good name of our paper and that I didn't mess this up. It was my choice, and there was no backing out now.

"Well, be sure to call on us if you need anything at all," Mary said, her matching hat tied in ribbons beneath her chin, "If you need us, we will come right away."

I put a hand on her shoulder. "I'll be fine, honestly." But there was a sinking feeling in my stomach as the words escaped me. I had been so sure of my decision; why was I nervous now?

"All four reporters must report here immediately," a voice erupted from a boisterous fellow with a stocky, bell-shaped body. I looked back at the other women and gave them one last reassuring smile.

"Well, that's my cue. I will be seeing you both in a matter of weeks. Take care of yourselves." With that, I grabbed the handle of my trunk and didn't look back. I didn't want to see their expressions as I walked into the monster's jaws. They were so superstitious. I didn't want them to be afraid on account of me. There was nothing to be nervous about anyway, right?

I stepped forward and stood to the left of the other journalists. With all of us in a row, I was able to look to my right and see the others who would be accompanying me these next six weeks. The man on my immediate right was as plump and red as a tomato. He was a small man, nearly a head shorter than me (and I wasn't terribly tall), with a small tuft of black hair atop his head and a matching mustache beneath a bulbous nose.

In the middle of the three stood a long, lanky man with skin so pale and gaunt he looked ill. His hair was as white as his pallor, and his high cheekbones pointed up with his nose to the sky. His eyes were closed for whatever reason as he awaited further word from the boisterous man who called us forward.

Finally, the man at the far right was as thick as a tree trunk, with wisps of light brown hair forming a thin layer on the top of his head. Stubble dotted his chin, which jutted out beneath pursed lips. His right leg was bouncing, and his hands were crossed behind him. He looked bored. I was about to return my gaze forward when his eyes met mine. When he noticed my stare, he gave me a wink and a full crooked-tooth smile that made my skin crawl. I immediately snapped my head forward and didn't look back.

The wind whipped against us as the unnecessarily loud man at the front inspected a piece of paper, balancing spectacles on the bridge of his nose. "Four coaches have currently made their descent from the manor. They will be here momentarily. When they arrive, you will each be called to ride in the one assigned to you." As he finished his sentence, the gates opened and four coaches appeared, paired with the most beautiful horses I'd ever seen.

"Step forward when your name is called," the man continued. After clearing his throat, he began. "Evan Tucker." The man who winked at me stepped forward, a slimy smile curling up one side of his face as he glanced at me one more time. My body tensed, and I found my hand gripping the handle of my trunk a little tighter. I could have lived my entire life without him looking at me like that again, but now I had to spend the next few weeks with him.

I shuddered at the thought.

When he stepped into his carriage, the next name was called. "Hubert Reelsey." The stout man to my right stepped forward.

"Y-yes, that's me," he said, taking as long of strides as he could toward his designated carriage. Something about the way he acted once catching my eye caused me to believe his stiff, upright posture and attempts at striding were somehow for my benefit.

"Stuart Day." The middle man with the hollow face walked forward. His legs looked like those of a crane as he glided forward and bent his twig-like body into his own carriage.

"And lastly, Caroline Blake." He almost spat out my name as if he didn't want to say it. He cast me an awkward sideways glance when I smiled at him on the way to my carriage. As I stepped inside, I noticed that all eyes were on me.

I tried not to look—the way you try not to look after climbing too high on a tree—but I couldn't help it. I sneaked a glance and immediately regretted it. The last things I saw before climbing into my carriage were the awestruck yet horrified expressions of over a hundred onlookers and the grim expressions of my two co-workers.

Something about the way Mary and Agnes watched me

as my coach crawled up the hill shook me more than anything else had since taking this ominous position. I didn't know what I'd expected. I knew they didn't think this was a good idea. I knew Agnes was just politely encouraging me, knowing full well that I wouldn't back down from my decision. So why were the nerves hounding me now? Why did the looks in their eyes suddenly cause me to wonder?

I tried not to think about it, but part of me knew the answer. Their expressions were obvious and the last things I wished to see; they were something beyond frightened—the hard lines of their mouths and the stiff way they stood there, watching me. But that wasn't the worst of it. What haunted me most was the expression in their eyes—those resigned looks of finality as if someone they loved was being hanged for a crime they didn't commit.

When the carriage stopped, my heart snagged in my chest. *This is it*, I thought, but I couldn't move. I just sat there until the coachman finally came around and asked if I needed assistance. "No, I can manage on my own, thank you," I said, smiling. After taking a deep breath, I adjusted the strings of my purse hanging from my bodice, grabbed the handle of my trunk, and stepped onto the driveway of Ashdown Manor.

I tried not to look at the other reporters. I knew what they were thinking. At least somewhat. Out of the corner of my eye, I saw them staring. The slimy one was smirking, while the other two looked at me and then each other skeptically. Like I was some creature in need of inspection. I didn't want to give them the satisfaction of looking back, so I kept my eyes forward until two footmen at the front of the house came marching toward us.

Then the doors of the manor opened, and more maids and footmen emerged. It was like a beautiful, choreographed performance watching them gracefully flock toward us to welcome us to the estate. After they all took their positions by the pathway to the mansion, the most beautiful woman I'd ever seen glided out through the open doors, a gown of gold silk dripping from her statuesque body. As she walked, a thick veil of black hair trailed behind her. Her lips were full and red like a blooming rose, and her eyes sparkled brilliantly beneath thick, curled lashes, dipping delicately at the sides. I was in awe at the shade of purple around her pupils. I'd never seen anyone with eyes like hers.

"Hello, everyone," she said, waving as she approached us. "My name is Lady Evelyn Bower, formerly Lady Evelyn Ashdown, before marrying my dear husband." She smiled brightly, revealing teeth as white as seashells. "You can call me 'Evelyn' if you'd like, or 'Lady Evelyn,' or 'Lady Bower' if you'd *really* prefer. I just want us all to be as comfortable together as possible. The footmen will take your bags up to your rooms, so feel free to leave them where you are and follow me." She swiveled around and walked back from where she came.

The bright shimmer of her dress was like a beacon for us to follow. I did as she said and dropped my trunk onto the ground. One of the men picked it up before bowing and waiting for me to pass him on my way to the giant arched doorway.

As I made my way there, my three competitors pushed past me. I nearly fell over when the third man, Evan Tucker, knocked me hard against the shoulder. I managed to catch myself at the last second and avoid further humiliation, but when I looked back up, I saw each of them already bowing to Lady Bower one at a time.

I rushed over in time to curtsy and bow without being too noticeably behind the others. "Thank you for having us," I said.

"Caroline Blake, I presume?" she asked, her voice both smooth and melodic.

"Yes, that's me," I said. She smiled.

"We have been expecting you. Welcome to Ashdown Manor." Her smile remained as she turned around and began the tour of her home. I wanted to smile back, but all I could manage was something faintly resembling one. There was something off about her smile. Or maybe it was in the way she said, "We have been expecting you." Whatever it was, it felt off. Not necessarily bad. Just . . . off.

She walked us through her enormous home. It was an 86-room castle with about 50 bedrooms and over 30 additional rooms for various purposes, including dining rooms, smoking rooms, parlors, rooms to entertain for special occasions, nurseries, the servants' quarters, and more. Evelyn even mentioned having an expansive ballroom. I couldn't keep track of all the parts of the house or the history and art in each room. What did catch my eye, though, was one of the walls we passed when we got to the second story. The middle strip of the wall was a highly detailed mural of some sort, and it stretched all the way down the hall, possibly farther.

I missed the opportunity to ask about it, though, and we didn't even get the chance to venture down there. It was apparently the wing of the three family members who resided in Ashdown manor, and none of us were permitted access to that wing. "You are all more than welcome to explore this house," she'd said, "But we ask for our privacy, so please don't go down our wing under any circumstances." She'd smiled and then kept walking.

After about an hour, she led us to a large window at the side of the manor. We were still on the second story, and from this angle, we could see the whole empty expanse that the festival would soon sprout on top of. But the true sight was beyond that. Beyond the hill of the manor was Brakerton Heights.

You could see the whole city from here, and it all looked so small. That "big city" I moved to looked like a pile of toys and boxes from here. I wondered what the Ashdown family thought of us all from up here. Do they look down at us from up on this hill? Do they watch as we scurry around like ants, picking up food and barely scraping by while they live like kings?

"My brother, William, is the master of the house, and as I'm sure you all know, he is the one who answered your letters." Evelyn's voice returned to my ears. I hadn't realized she'd stopped talking until she started back up again, or maybe I'd just stopped listening at some point. "However, my husband and I are equal partners with William in running the house, so please don't hesitate to ask any of us questions. We will all be assisting you in your coverage of the festival." She turned toward the enormous, open window to our right. She walked closer to it, pointing to the ground beyond, and explained that they already started getting the ground ready for the preparations.

"We have workers assigned to all the outdoor tasks. We hired a whole new staff to help this festival run smoothly, including hiring additional maids and footmen to assist you four." She resumed her graceful walk down the hall as she continued. "You have each been paired with someone in the house whom you will shadow and work with over the next few weeks . . ." her voice trailed off as someone from across the hall caught her eye.

"Ah, here my brother is now. William, dear, come greet our guests!" Her voice was melodic as it moved through the room. She raised a hand above her head, as if to coax her brother over.

I couldn't see the man in question; I was in the back of the others, and he was coming from the opposite end of the room. But judging from the fact that he hadn't been there to greet us, and from his silence now, I'd say he was avoiding this very moment. Soon enough, however, I heard footsteps and Evelyn's jubilant laugh. "Ah, William, please greet our guests. They wondered why the lord of the house wasn't there to say hello to them when they arrived."

There was a brief awkward silence, as it was clear that none of us had asked for him, and William likely knew it. "It's a pleasure," he said finally, his deep voice tight with bored insincerity. I tried surreptitiously standing on my toes but still couldn't see him very well. The men in front of me were blocking my view. I liked to think they weren't doing it intentionally, but I had my doubts.

I could only see part of his head and one of his shoulders, fitted in what appeared to be an extremely expensive black suit. Despite how new and crisp it looked, as dark and fine as any suit I'd ever seen, it still wasn't as beautifully dark as the hair that fell softly on his forehead. Smooth and thick, like the feathers of a crow. His fingers moved through it as he continued. "Thank you all for coming. We look forward to your stay." His voice was cavalier, and it was clear he didn't want to be here, which I found odd. Why wouldn't the lord of the manor want to greet his new employees and shake our hands? Wasn't he the one who wanted us here? My acceptance letter had come from him.

"William is very busy," Evelyn said, the words rushing from her lips, "but he will be joining us for supper tonight. Isn't that right?"

There was a small pause before her brother replied. "Yes, of course." He stepped closer in my direction, and I glimpsed his profile briefly before he turned back one more time and added, "I will see you all then, and we'll have a proper greeting. Now, if you'll excuse me." He smiled stiffly, and I wondered if anyone else could tell how little he wanted to be here. He was about to turn away when he saw me.

Our eyes locked. The faux mask he'd worn to feign pleasantries disappeared like smoke. His mouth fell partly open, and for a moment, it was as if we knew each other. As if we always had but had just forgotten. Yet, he also seemed so new to me. Like I'd never seen someone who looked quite like him before. Someone whose eyes looked into mine so unabashedly. Someone whose single glance left me breathless. A rush like white-hot fire burned against my skin, and I couldn't look away. I didn't know what it was about him, but in his eyes I saw something familiar. As if he were a memory or a dream I'd long forgotten.

When my head grew light, I realized I'd forgotten to breathe altogether. I wondered how long we'd been standing there, staring at each other and unable to move. But by the disinterested looks of the others and the chatter of Lady Bower, I assumed it wasn't as long as I'd thought.

I looked back at him, and when I found his eyes still fixed on mine, and he realized he'd been discovered, he quickly turned and walked away. He was out of sight in a flash, but I couldn't tear myself from what had just happened. Did that moment feel as long for him as it did for me?

It was hard to focus after that. We all took a brief break for luncheon shortly after William's departure, but even that didn't help. Throughout the rest of the tour of Ashdown Manor, I couldn't stop thinking about him. Why had he looked at me like that? And why did I care? I thought about the way his eyebrows sat against his narrowed eyes as they burrowed into mine. I thought about the way he rushed away and how just before that I caught him staring at me in the most peculiar way.

I wasn't sure why he left me so breathless, so curious and confused, but I didn't like it. I wasn't here for him anyway. I just needed to focus. *Remember, Caroline,* I thought as I steadied my breath. *Remember why you're here.* I shifted my gaze to the other reporters, who were clumped together in conversation. The tour of the vast manor was at its end, and they were already swapping thoughts.

What do I do? Do I just go over there and start talking? My heart rate quickened, but I moved toward them anyway. The thumping in my chest grew louder with each step. By the time I reached them, I could feel it pulsing through my ears.

I cleared my throat, and the men stopped talking. Each one of them looked at me, eyebrows raised. "I think we've got our work cut out for us," I said, trying to smile despite the pounding in my ears. They just looked at me. The gaunt Mr. Day scoffed, folded his arms, and turned one bony shoulder away from me and resumed his conversation with the others.

The nervous pulsing turned into rage. "Excuse me? What is your problem?" I poked Mr. Day on the shoulder. He turned around and looked at me with an equal amount of anger, as well as disgust.

"Why, you—"

"Leave her alone, Stuart," Mr. Tucker said, and up close, I could see that one of his yellowed teeth hooked over the one next to it and nearly stuck out of his mouth. "Her kind gets all fussed up over everything, but they're mostly harmless."

My mouth dropped open. "You *cannot* be serious."

Mr. Tucker smiled, as if excited by my response. "It's

all right, hon," he said, craning his neck to look me in the eye. "We know all about your little paper and the other ratbags stirrin' up trouble. Don't tell me you really think you're makin' a difference." He chuckled.

My eyes flashed. "Do you really think someone like you has the right to say one way or another what difference we're making?" The smile stayed plastered to his face until I added, "Are you really that moronic?" He snarled at me and opened his mouth to say something else but stopped at the sight of someone coming up behind me.

I turned to see the staff waiting to see us to our wings. Oh right. Evelyn had told us that our maids and footmen would be seeing us to our rooms. When she left, she must have given them the word to come out. "Hello," I said, heat rising to my cheeks. A young woman with long, braided blonde hair stepped forward. She looked to be in her early twenties, or maybe late teens. When she smiled, her cheeks dimpled.

"Hello, Miss Blake. I'm Molly. I'll be your maid for the next little while."

"Hi, Molly. It's good to meet you." I forced a smile, but I was still incredibly frustrated at what had just transpired. As she explained where my wing was and what the evening would entail, I politely nodded and followed her, all the while trying to calm myself down. I had to keep my cool. Those fools would try to get at me in any way they could while I was here. I couldn't give them the satisfaction of my reactions.

I also knew that my reputation was the most on the line out of the four of us. If I got into a fight with any one of them, I'd be an easy scapegoat for their stories and the press. It was horrendously unfair, but it was the ugly truth of the matter, and I had to navigate it as best I could. I had to show them that they didn't have the ability to touch my emotions. They didn't have the right to any part of me.

I could do this.

"This wing is all yours, ma'am," the maid said softly when we finally made it to my wing. "Since you're the only woman here, you get the area all to yourself."

"Being the only woman here is kind of nice then, right?" I asked with a laugh.

"Yes, I suppose so," she said with a soft giggle, but then her walking slowed to a halt. When she turned around, her face was suddenly serious. "Miss Blake, thank you. I know it must be hard having to deal with the others like that and all. I just want you to know we're all rooting for you." She looked up at me with a smile, and my heart pulled in my chest.

This was why I was here.

"Thanks," I said, "I'm rooting for me, too."

Chapter Seven

I could hardly believe my room when Molly ushered me inside. It looked like the bedroom of a queen, or at least what I always imagined one would look like. The walls were draped in warm velvet tapestries—deep quilted reds adorned with rusted golds. The wallpaper perfectly accentuated the rest of the room with gold and red floral designs that fell vertically from the ceiling to the ruddy carpet that sat in a large oval in the center of the room.

Beneath the carpet was a dark mahogany floor, the same wood as the four-poster bed, footstool, bedside table, vanity set, and wardrobe, all of which had their own places at different points in the room. The bed was to my left as I walked in. Its quilt and pillows looked like clouds balanced against a sunset, especially as the dimming rays outside passed through the window and pooled onto the sheets. The bed was set against the wall so that the person inside could sit up and look out the window without getting up. I thought it was strangely placed until I saw that it was closest to the fireplace, which was only a few feet from the foot of the bed.

I didn't think the words to describe such an extravagant room had been invented yet. It was like walking into a storybook, and I was the queen. It was so beautiful and so invigorating to be inside. As I took it all in, I was convinced that I was the luckiest woman in the world. I just wished Maggie could have lived to see it. Although, I wasn't sure she would have stepped foot in a place like this anyway. Any mention of a monster or curse would have had her running for the hills.

As I looked around, I had a hard time believing a curse could dwell within such beautiful walls. A place as breathtaking as this couldn't be haunted, possessed, or cursed. Could it? Yes, appearances could be deceiving, but could it be *this* deceiving?

"Madam told me to leave you to exploring your new chambers," Molly said as I walked about the room, opening drawers and looking at my face in the mirror. "But I will be back later tonight to help you into your supper gown."

I turned around to face her. "What do you mean?"

Her dimpled smile returned. "Are you not used to changing for supper?" At my silence, she continued, pointing to the wardrobe. "Your evening clothes, morning clothes, and sleepwear are all inside there. They are all pieces the lady of the house selected personally."

I wasn't sure what to say. I only had one good dress, two pairs of skirts (which I'd had for the last eight or ten years or so), and two blouses. Trying not to look too excited, I walked to the wardrobe to see what I'd find. But before I could open its doors and inspect the contents within, another maid walked into the room, pulling my trunk along with her. She was an older woman with tanned skin and kind eyes. Her hair was thrown into a messy gray bun atop her head, which jiggled when she stood upright and dusted her hands off as if pulling my trunk from the hallway was a dirty, laborious task.

Placing her hands on her hips and taking a breath, she said, "Hello there, dear. I saw you come in and heard your name was Caroline, is that right?"

I nodded, reluctantly walking away from the wardrobe, looking at it one last time. "That's right. Caroline Blake." When I turned around, the older woman's smile remained, but her eyes had narrowed.

"Caroline Blake," she repeated, her eyes still narrowed as she took another step toward me.

"Um . . . yes?" I stood there awkwardly, trying to figure out what to say next when her face finally softened again.

"You can call me Mrs. Wells," she said. "I'm the housekeeper here."

"What a lovely name," I said, trying my best not to show how uncomfortable I felt. The woman nodded but wasn't looking at me anymore. Her gaze had shifted to the distance.

"Mrs. Wells has been working at the house since she was my age," Molly said, her face brightening, "And she's so kind, Miss Blake. You'll love her." The young maid's face grew concerned as her superior remained quiet.

I walked past Molly and looked at the housekeeper. "Is something the matter, Mrs. Wells? I haven't offended you, have I?" When she looked back at me, I could see her gray-blue eyes with perfect clarity.

"Oh heavens, no, child. Goodness. I just . . . I *remembered* something I thought I'd lost years ago."

"A memory?" Molly squeaked. "Or did you remember where you put your good purse? You know, I thought I saw it in one of the sitting rooms the other day." As the young woman rambled on, I watched Mrs. Wells smile and nod, obviously fond of the young girl and ever-patient.

I wondered if they were related somehow. The way she looked at her made me think they were. And Molly had so much familiarity with the older woman and seemed to have so much insight into Mrs. Wells' life despite being newly hired.

I was jealous a bit. The way Mrs. Wells looked at Molly reminded me of how Maggie used to look at me when I was a child. Or, more recently, at pictures I'd sketched throughout my adolescence—pictures of the leaves from the gnarled tree outside or the rocky bank of a river. Pages she kept and looked at whenever she had a bad day. She looked at them a lot those last few weeks.

"I think we better get going," Mrs. Wells said to the girl. "We have a lot of preparations to make for tonight."

"Ooh, yes!" Molly said emphatically before swiveling back to look at me. "I will be back later to help you into one of your new evening gowns!" My cheeks immediately went pink, and I unconsciously wrapped my arms around my chest.

"That . . . won't be necessary," I said with a small laugh, but Molly wouldn't have it.

"No, that's what I'm here for! I'll be here at 5 o'clock sharp."

I looked around the room until I found a small clock in the far corner, near the wardrobe. It was just as beautiful and ornamented as the rest of the room: a long, mahogany piece with embellishments of gold, like elegant frosting on a gourmet cake. It was only 3 o'clock. I had two hours to kill before the next leg of my day.

The other two curtsied and turned around, saying their goodbyes, before I had the chance to decide what I wanted to do. "Wait!" I called after them, a little too loudly. Their shocked expressions told me my behavior probably wasn't considered very proper. I grimaced but continued, "Um, could one of you possibly spare some time to show me the way to the dining room from here?"

What I really wanted to ask was if I could accompany them. I felt so awkward and useless in this great big house with nothing to do, but I knew it wouldn't be "proper" and that the answer would be a polite "sorry, but no, Miss," so I just ran with whatever came out of my mouth first. It didn't end up being too bad.

Molly smiled, even though I was sure she was wondering how I'd missed that important set of directions on my tour of the mansion. "Of course, Miss. Please follow me, and I'll show you." We stepped outside the room and walked a few paces over to the banister. It wasn't until then that I realized the house was laid out rather strangely. If I walked straight out of my room, I'd run into a wall that stopped at my ribs. Sitting on top of that was the banister, which stretched all the way down the hall and wrapped along the stairs, only stopping at the last step to the floor below.

I found the architecture somewhat odd, but I also didn't have much experience in elaborate mansions. It *was* convenient that the stairs were so close to my room, though. I studied Molly's movements as she pointed down the stairs and turned her wrist to the right once, then to the left, then to the right again and said, "And that's how you get there. I better be off now! Have a lovely afternoon, Miss Blake. I will see you shortly." She bowed, still bouncing like an endless ball of sunshine with braids, and went on her way.

Mrs. Wells smiled and nodded slightly as she said, "Please don't hesitate to ask us anything, dear," and went her separate way as well. I watched the two of them disappear and then let my shoulders drop. *Now what?*

I looked back at my room, made sure the door was locked, took my new key, and then memorized the area around me. This place was like an indoor maze, large enough to comfortably house a small city (and uncomfortably hold a large one). Despite looking at it all day, I still couldn't get over the extravagance. The sheer volume of art and decor alone was enough to keep me stunned, but what really took my breath away was the grandeur of it all, and the beauty. Every piece of furniture or tapestry was tactfully placed in every given spot. Each one created a masterpiece simply by being there. It was like I'd walked into a painting.

I loved it. I loved the feel of the wooden banister as it slid beneath my fingertips on my way down the stairs. I loved the scents of each room. The hallway smelled of pine and cinnamon, and as I descended the stairs, I started catching whiffs of different herbs and spices as food preparations and floral arrangements were underway.

I caught myself smiling, the inside of me giddy to the brim. I couldn't believe it. Even if I walked into the past and told myself one month ago that I would be in a place such as this, I wasn't sure I'd believe it.

One month. It had already been one month since I'd left.

The memory of my last night at the only home I'd ever known sparked before I could catch it and put it out. It shot through me like wildfire. I had cried the whole night before I moved away. Maggie was gone, and I had no other family or friends. I had no idea what to do or where to go.

I both wanted to leave Fairbrooke and wished I didn't have to go. In actuality, I would have hated living there without her. The place reeked of bad memories. Husks of lost friendships and painful chapters of my life were scattered everywhere. Though Maggie and I had a few close acquaintances who trusted and relied on us in town, I didn't have anyone I could ever turn to after she passed. Then there was everyone else . . .

Nope. This was better. Much, much better. And that was the point. I was so scared back then. It had been just over a month since I'd left, but it felt like years. And I couldn't believe the turn of events that had taken place. If someone had told me that day—when I was crying in Maggie's bed, unsure of my future or where to go—I definitely wouldn't have believed them.

But here I was, walking in the halls of this beautiful castle. I tried to let myself be happy—to let myself feel proud of where I'd gotten myself—but for some reason, I couldn't smile.

I stopped in the middle of a hallway, completely lost, despite my efforts. There was no person in sight other than the one in the enormous painting before me—oil on canvas in the Grand Style. It reminded me of a Joshua Reynolds painting.

The large portrait was of a beautiful woman dressed in a brilliant blue gown. It was clear that she was noble, and with her perfectly sculpted facial features and lustrous black hair, she resembled Evelyn. So much so that it was almost shocking. I would have thought that it was a portrait of her if it hadn't looked to be over a century old. Some families had striking resemblances, I supposed.

After looking at the portrait and some more like it for about another half hour or so, I found the way back to my room. It took a couple of tries, but I finally found my way. Once inside, I unpacked some of my things and sat at my new desk. I took out my quill and ink and decided to write my initial thoughts about the manor. I stayed there thinking and writing nothing too substantial until Molly arrived and helped me into one of the rib-crushing dresses Evelyn had so graciously given me.

Then I made the descent to supper.

And I was terrified.

All I could think about was how the other reporters acted toward me earlier—how they spoke to me and how they looked at me like I was some sort of insect or creature. A feeling I wished was more foreign to me than it was.

I shook away those thoughts, and I tried shaking Fairbrooke as far away from my mind as I could. But, as always, it stuck around. It always found ways to stick around.

The closer I got to the laughter erupting from the dining room, the tighter my stomach constricted. *You can do this, Caroline*, I assured myself. *Who cares what they think anyway?*

But it didn't become real until I entered the room and all eyes fell on me. I could feel every one of their stares singeing my skin—some more than others. I tried not to glance at anyone in particular while also looking indifferent. It was a delicate balance of looking relaxed without seeming afraid.

I wasn't sure how successful I was, but I persevered nonetheless because I knew. I knew the other journalists looked down on me. I knew they thought it was a joke that I even showed up. And I knew that I was a stranger here and that I wasn't good at making friends. I knew. But I went in acting like it didn't matter anyway.

That's all anyone can do when faced with this type of situation. When you walk into a room and know there are people there who don't like you, the only person who can get you through it is yourself. Believing you deserve every right to be there, just like anybody else. Then you can walk with your head held high. I knew these men thought I was a joke. I knew they mocked me—both in front of me and behind my back. But it didn't matter. My reason for being here was just as valid as theirs.

I could do this.

I let one of the footmen pull out a chair for me next to Evelyn. "Thank you," I said as he bowed politely and walked away. I took slow, steady breaths before looking up and greeting everyone. "Good evening," I said, managing to keep my voice even.

"Good evening, Miss Blake," Lady Bower said, her nose scrunching with her warm smile. When I met her gaze, her eyes widened. "And look how beautiful you look in that gown. I'm so glad you like it. *Do* you like it? Because if you don't, I can send for some new ones."

I laughed. "No, I'm quite all right. Thank you, though. What you have donated to me was extremely generous and more than enough." I thought back on when I finally opened my wardrobe before supper. There were twelve different day dresses inside, ten evening gowns, and eight nightgowns. Each dress looked unique, posh, and so expensive that I felt nervous just touching the fabric. I decided to choose a black and blue piece with velvet cuffs and tiny bits of lace sprouting from the neckline.

"Don't you think she looks darling, William?"

The mention of his name paralyzed me momentarily, and then I carefully looked up. Not eagerly or bashfully. Just . . . *carefully*.

And there he was, seated directly across from me in a

dark suit and waistcoat even finer than the one he'd been wearing earlier. When his eyes fell on me, something in my chest fluttered.

Seeing him so close made me realize just how handsome he was. I had noticed it when I saw him earlier, but now it was harder to ignore. Up close, I could see the deep caramel brown of his eyes and the smooth clarity of his skin, which rested against the sharp, masculine bone structure of his face. His shoulders were broad, and his posture was perfect. I cleared my throat and crossed my legs, vaguely aware of the pink dusting my cheekbones.

I was determined for William not to notice anything. I was only mildly flustered, after all, and this type of thing didn't usually happen to me. *It must be a first-day nerves type of thing.*

His stoic expression momentarily shifted to a more welcoming one. "Yes, I dare say she does," he said. The words sizzled across my skin like fizzing candy. I toyed with the notion of thanking him but thought it would be better not to say anything at all. So, I just took a small sip of my water and remained silent.

There was a moment where the two of us silently noticed the other before the conversation started back up again. Apparently, Evelyn and her husband had been introducing their thoughts for the festival assignment to the others while they waited for my arrival.

"Oh, and Charles, darling, this is Caroline Blake," she said to her husband. He looked over at me and smiled a wide, ear-to-ear smile that stretched across his face. To my surprise, he was almost as good-looking as his wife and brother-in-law. I wasn't sure how all these striking people got here, but it was definitely worth jotting down in my notes later.

Unlike the more conventional good looks of William

and Evelyn, Charles' features were more subtle. He looked like an average bookworm until you looked into his eyes and found something almost mystical about him. He was thin but broad-shouldered and had frosty blue eyes almost as beautiful as his wife's amethyst ones. His skin was far paler than the other two, but it didn't make him look sick, like it did for Mr. Day. It just made him look almost doll-like. He and his wife looked like two porcelain dolls as they glanced at each other lovingly across the table.

"We are so happy to have you, Miss Blake," he said, smiling and looking directly into my eyes before cutting into his food. Oh right. Food. I looked down at my plate and noticed a diced pheasant, cooked carrots, a large potato, and a thick tea biscuit. Butter and jam were placed conveniently nearby. It all looked delicious.

"I'm happy to be here. Thank you for having me," I said, sticking my fork into one of the carrots. "It's been a pleasure so far, Lady Bower. Lord Bower. Lord Ashdown." I looked at each of them as I said their names, but when I got to William's, his eyes darted to mine, and something moved between us—a feeling like wild static.

"Oh, you are quite welcome," Evelyn said, "but please call us by our first names—or at least try to. I know it isn't proper, but we want to bridge any gaps between all of us with familiarity. I hope that's all right."

I nodded, but the others either grunted or simply continued cutting into and eating their food. When her face fell, I quickly said, "Thank you, Evelyn. You may call me by my first name, too, if you are comfortable."

She smiled softly and squeezed my hand as if to say *thank you*, and then continued with her meal.

No one talked for a while after that. The air filled with the symphony of silverware and the faint sound of music. My ears perked up. "Is that . . ." I searched for the source of the sound and found it: a brand-new phonograph machine. I couldn't believe my eyes—or ears. I had never seen one in person, and I had only heard of it recently. It was a new invention barreling through the world. I'd been waiting for my time to experience the music playing from one myself one day. This day was full of surprises—this being one of the pleasant ones.

I closed my eyes and listened to the soft voices coming through the machine, trying to recognize the song and pick out the tune. I almost got it when Evan Tucker spoke up, his voice immediately causing my ears to want to shrivel up and stop working altogether.

"I'm gonna be the first one to say it," he said, throwing a large piece of pheasant in his mouth. "I'm lookin' forward to gettin' this show on the road. I know everyone out in town's all scared and wants to know what happened last time," he made a mock-grimace and then continued, "but I'm sure this time will be different, right?" He barked out a laugh and then eagerly awaited our reactions. His shamelessness appalled me, which was saying something, considering his actions earlier today.

He gave a slimy, self-satisfied smile at the awkward silence that fell upon the room. Ironically, this allowed me to identify the song on the phonograph (it was "Wait 'til the Clouds Roll By"). I didn't know if anyone would speak up again for the remainder of the evening. It was such an odd thing for that moron to say. It was one of those shocking moments where nobody knew what to do next.

"It . . . will be different this time," Evelyn said finally, her voice much quieter than before. She cleared her throat and looked at her food. Everyone had stopped eating but Mr. Tucker and Mr. Day. "We had nothing to do with what happened last time. And it was . . . truly horrendous, but . . . this time will be fun." She smiled weakly and then took a quick drink of water.

"It will be, darling," Charles said soothingly. "It's apples and oranges. A tragedy doesn't strike twice, right?" He jokingly knocked on the table, but his laugh was a little too forced.

No one said anything to this.

Evelyn took another sip of water.

"I think a lot of people are excited," the stout Mr. Reelsey said. "I know I'm excited to see what happens." When the maids and footmen around the table nodded in agreement, Evelyn looked a little more at ease.

"It will be lovely," I said, giving her a reassuring smile. "I think everyone is either excited or curious. Most people in town won't be afraid when the time comes."

"I, for one, think this whole thing is a mistake," the man across from me said.

"William!" his sister hissed. A small thump came from beneath the table where she hit the leg of his chair. He didn't act stung by it at all. He just shot her a look and continued.

"It's true," he said, stabbing a piece of potato with a fork, "Why don't we address what we're all thinking here?" He gestured his fork like it was rounding up everyone at the table. "We all know that this place isn't the most well-liked house in town. I find it hard to believe that the villagers in Brakerton Heights even claim it as being a part of their community. Yes, horrible things happened here about three decades ago. We all know this, and neither you nor I," he pointed to his sister with his fork and then waved it toward the other guests, "or any of these people, will deny it. Obviously, nothing bad will happen this year, right?" He chortled, making a point to be as loud as possible to get his disdain across. "That's a joke. Do you *truly* believe the townspeople will be quiet and pleasant about all this? I highly doubt they will even come to this blasted thing. So why are we even having it?"

"William, that's quite enough," Evelyn growled.

"We're having it to re-enter our community," Charles said, grinning a little too broadly, "We want to make a good first impression. We don't know anyone in the town, and ever since Evelyn and I got married a few years ago, we found it about time to call this community home."

William laughed again. "And you believed the way to do that was to recreate a famous massacre?"

"We are *not* recreating a *massacre*," Evelyn said through gritted teeth. "We are trying to move past the events that happened and re-establish Ashdown Manor as a place where people are welcome. We want joy in the community."

"*Joy*?" William's voice remained level, but the fury building inside him was evident on his face. He leaned back and chuckled quietly, smoothing out his shirt and taking a drink. "*Joy* . . . Well, I don't think the town will find our festival very joyful."

"You're wrong," I said, and as the words left my lips, I could hardly believe I was the one to have spoken them.

The room fell silent. All eyes were on me.

I sat up and cleared my throat. "I think a festival at Ashdown Manor will give this town exactly what it needs. New life. If you put on this festival and everything goes smoothly, the people in Brakerton Heights can finally move past their fear, and the town will be reborn. It will show everyone that there is nothing to be afraid of and that their future doesn't have to be anchored down by the past."

Evelyn smiled gratefully and reached out and squeezed my hand again. I hoped she believed what I'd said. I meant every word.

As I took another sip of water, my eyes shifted to William. He looked somewhere between shocked, intrigued, and impressed. But he must have quickly realized this because he looked away momentarily, and when he looked at me again, his face was hard to read.

He watched me carefully as he leaned forward, balancing his elbows on the table. "So, what then? You think everyone will come rushing in on the event's opening night?"

"Yes, I do," I said, firmly returning my glass to the table, my eyes staying locked on his. "Judging by the crowd that gathered to watch our departure this morning, I'd say just about every person in town will make an appearance at the festival next month."

"I think you're giving them a little too much credit," he replied, his eyes piercing mine.

"I think you're forgetting human nature. People can't tear themselves away from the curious and the macabre. It's like walking by a horrible accident and being unable to look away."

"So, are you counting on a misfortune falling upon us, Miss Blake?" William teased.

"I'm simply stating facts."

"Well, so am I. People like what's comfortable. They want what's familiar. To them, what's familiar is avoiding us and pretending the massacre never happened."

"How would you know that?" I asked, putting my fork down, frustration starting to bubble inside me. "Have you gone out and asked the people of Brakerton Heights? Have you walked the streets and asked their opinions? No, you haven't. At least to my knowledge, anyway. Because people down there think you're all a myth. The only reason I wasn't afraid or superstitious about this place is because I'm not from Brakerton Heights."

"You're not?" Charles asked, but William interrupted before I could reply.

"So, what you're saying is that the people are afraid of us purely out of superstition and because we don't go around making friends with everyone in town anymore? Is that it?"

"That could be part of it," I said, "but you're missing the point. What I'm saying is that it's been tradition for the people here to be afraid because you all closed your doors after something atrocious happened. And if you truly had nothing to do with it, and you want to start things back up again, that's great. It will give the city the breath of fresh air it needs to heal and move forward."

William didn't say anything to this. He just continued watching me carefully as Evelyn let out an over-dramatized sigh and said, "Oh, Caroline, you have made me feel so much better about this whole thing. Thank you so much."

But my eyes were still on William, waiting for his next move.

"I don't think they'll be satisfied with whatever happens," he finally said. "People love to be afraid."

I cocked my head to the side. "I thought you said people love what's comforting and familiar."

"I stand by that. People can love what's familiar and comfortable for them and also be comfortable being afraid. The people of Brakerton Heights only know fearing us. It would be too . . . *adventurous* for them to move past that."

"Well, perhaps the people need to be up for new adventures then," I said, the words falling like icicles.

His eyes narrowed. "You really think holding a festival that the people fear so much is a good idea? Even though a massacre happened here and neither you nor anyone else knows how trustworthy our family is?"

My head jerked back in surprise. Why would he say

something like that? Something that could paint them as villains. "Well, I would like to give you the benefit of the doubt. Why would I have reason to be alarmed?"

He laughed, exasperated, and said, "Did you not hear what I said? People died here, and nobody knows us. Regardless of how innocent we are or aren't, do you think any of this is a recipe for a smooth event?"

I shook my head, my mouth gaping open in disbelief. "Why must everything be coated in mystery and fear? Why can't people move on from the past and just be happy? Why can't we live peaceful lives, hoping for the best and not cowering in fear until the next big thing happens? Because chances are *nothing* will happen. Why stay afraid?" It was then that I realized my voice had gotten too loud, too intense. Far too intense for someone who was supposed to be objective.

I quickly continued. "No one in your family has done anything to anyone since that day, and from what I understand, none of you actually did anything at all. Right?" I looked at Evelyn, whose face was still as stone, her eyes drilling into her plate, unmoving. I looked back at William. "Besides, you and Evelyn are so young. You would have been babies if you were even alive at all. Why should anyone be afraid?"

The siblings shot each other a quick, unsettling look—William's agitated expression meeting a wide-eyed Evelyn. Before I could analyze it further, they broke it, and William's eyes shifted back to mine.

"All right, Miss Blake," he said, "I guess we'll just have to see what happens." He picked up his glass and took the last swig of water at the bottom before muttering, "It's too late now anyway."

Triumphantly, I sat back in my seat with a wide grin, picked my fork back up, and started eating. After finishing my first bite I said, "That's right, and when you see me again on opening night, I'll show you how right I am." I looked over at Evelyn, beaming over the victory I gave us over her brother, but she just looked back at me sheepishly. "What's wrong?" I asked.

I couldn't tell if she was smiling or frowning as she said, "Miss Blake, perhaps I should have told you sooner, but . . . before you came down, I gave everyone their assignments for the festival." My fork halted. I looked up at her slowly, trying my best to keep my face emotionless. *Don't say what I think you're going to say. Please.* As if already knowing what I was thinking, she winced and continued, "You won't have to wait until opening night to find him. Your partner for the festival preparations is William."

I wanted to scream. *Him?* How was I supposed to work with someone like him? Someone who clearly didn't see eye-to-eye with me? We had completely opposing views on the festival. Wasn't that an important thing to have in common while working together?

The rant could go on and on in my head forever, so I stopped it before it spiraled. I looked at William and put on the cheesiest smile I could muster. "I'm looking forward to it." The sarcasm oozed from my words, and my eyes dared him to retaliate.

Despite the warning in my voice and my eyes searing into his, he smiled. My brows pulled together at his strange response. Why was he smiling? He watched the butler fill up his glass, now with wine instead of water, and as he took it, he looked at me. "As am I," he said, holding it up as if cheering to the two of us.

He looked at me over his glass, and I suddenly found myself fuming. I took a sip from my own and turned my attention elsewhere. It was at this point that I realized I had probably never taken so many sips of water during one dinner in my entire life.

"So, Lady Bower—er, Evelyn," I said, turning my attention away from her brother, "please tell me about this lovely painting above your head." I pointed at a painting hung in a gold-rimmed frame behind her. She smiled, seemingly suppressing a laugh. She nodded and began telling me the long history of the oil painting that depicted a large black horse on the great wall of the dining room.

I watched her intently, nodding at the appropriate times, taking sips of my new wine here and there. Though if someone were to ask me what she'd said, I wouldn't have a clue. I didn't hear half of it, and I secretly hoped she wouldn't notice if I nodded at the wrong time or if I didn't know the answer to a question at the end.

I could feel William's eyes on me, but I refused to look his way. It was hard to concentrate with him staring at me like that, though. Why was he staring at me like that? I wanted to groan in frustration. How was I supposed to focus when someone was looking at me so unashamedly? So intensely?

Still, I kept up my ruse, fiercely pretending I was paying attention to the lady of the house and the others. But, of course, I wasn't. I nodded and kept my face tilted toward them, but all I could think about was William's presence and how loudly my heart was pounding in my ears.

Chapter Eight

The day was here. The day we'd all been dreading. *Even Evelyn has to be dreading it a little*, I thought as I looked out the window. She was out there welcoming the new "guests" to our mansion, a bright smile plastered on her face as if this was some frivolous game with no risk at all. There was no way she wasn't at least a little afraid. She was taking a big risk putting this festival on.

I wasn't sure why she couldn't just keep her head down as she had for the last twenty-odd years, but here we were. I sighed, letting my fingers drum against the windowsill. I wasn't sure how I was supposed to rest easy during all this. Not that I necessarily needed to, but it was a nice notion. Resting in peace.

I squinted, trying to find the woman who sent that

application, but it appeared I didn't get to the window in time. All I saw were the new staff we brought on, the few we've always kept (ones who had served our family for years), and two men whose faces already told me what I was in for. But what was I expecting? They were here to dig up dirt on our family, after all.

That was the only way anyone would have accepted this job. What type of people offered themselves up like this without an ulterior motive? Either these four were extraordinarily greedy, willing to risk their lives for money, or complete and utter fools. Whichever it was, I'd likely not get along with them either way.

But what about the woman? The thought wouldn't leave me. I couldn't stop thinking about the symbol on her application and what it might mean.

I knew I should join Evelyn and meet them, but I was against all of this. It was irresponsible and dangerous for everyone involved, including us. I had no idea what Evelyn was thinking.

"Why not just hold the festival, if you're so set on having it? Why invite these people to stay here for six weeks?" I'd asked her.

But she gave me that same incensed look she always did when I brought up how bad of an idea her plan was. "Because it will show them that there's nothing to be afraid of. We need to convince the people of Brakerton Heights that we aren't dangerous."

"But we *are* dangerous," I'd replied. She'd glared at me.

"We are *not* dangerous, William. You always insist that we're monsters, but we're not. You do know that, don't you?"

I didn't have to say anything. She knew what I thought, and she knew she couldn't change my mind. She never had before. We *were* monsters. No matter how much Evelyn tried to convince herself otherwise, that was the truth. There was no escaping it.

Still, she continued with the preparations, deluding herself into thinking reviving this festival was a grand idea. I tried. I really did. I tried to stop her, but she was determined. And she was the head of the clan. What was I supposed to do?

None of it mattered anymore, though. The plan was already in motion. We just had to hope for the best.

I left the window and paced around the house for the better part of an hour, a million thoughts racing through my mind. I didn't want to think about every possible way things could go wrong from having the reporters here and putting this festival on, but I couldn't help it. All I could do was swat away the thoughts, replacing them with any positive thought I could conjure up. However, very few thoughts came to my rescue.

In the end, my curiosity got the better of me. When I heard Evelyn's voice from down the stairs, I knew I couldn't stay away. I had to know who this person was. Even if I had no idea what symbol stained her application, the fact that she was a woman, willing to risk not only her life but her reputation to come here, was enough to pique my interest.

I swept down the stairs and made my way down the hall. I didn't want to stay long. I did *not* want to talk. I just wanted to see them. Then I'd be on my way.

When Evelyn caught sight of me, she lit right up. With her signature melodic laugh, she called out to me. "Ah, William, please greet our guests. They wondered why the lord of the house wasn't there to say hello to them when they arrived."

I highly doubt that.

I did my best to smile, but I never was good at acting. I

tried my best for Evelyn, though. She was a kind person and was doing her best to make this run smoothly. The least I could do was pretend.

"It's a pleasure," I said, scanning the faces of the visitors. So far, I only saw one gangly fellow, a man with an obnoxious grin on his face, and a small, portly man with a beet-red face. But no woman.

When no one said anything, and the silence became awkward, I was ready to take my leave. But Evelyn could see it a mile away, and she knew I didn't want to be around any of the guests longer than I had to be. So she frantically trapped me. "William is very busy," she said, "but he will be joining us for supper tonight. Isn't that right?"

I suppressed a sigh and forced another tight smile. "Yes, of course." She beamed, pleased at her success. I tried not to roll my eyes as I stepped away. "Thank you all for coming," I said to the others, "We look forward to your stay." I bowed slightly and turned to leave.

That's when I saw her.

She was the most beautiful creature I'd ever seen. Soft brown curls framed her heart-shaped face, spilling purposefully from a small black bonnet positioned perfectly on her head. Her eyes were a striking green that shone like emeralds against her creamy skin.

Her beauty wasn't just physical, though. Not even close. There was something else—something radiating from her. A confidence, an elegance. Something I couldn't put my finger on. Something in the way she held herself—something in her stare, in her stance—was hypnotizing. Magnetic. Powerful. She could have destroyed the world and built it back up again with a single glance, and I wouldn't have been surprised.

I didn't know what I was expecting from Caroline Blake, but it wasn't this. This radiant woman, whose eyes caught onto mine like fire, her full lips parting as she studied me in this strange, captivating moment in time. I didn't know if I should be entranced by her or afraid.

Who is she?

When I realized I'd been staring, I blinked and looked away. Determined to get away quickly, I rushed down the hall and tried my best to avoid any further thoughts of her. But the farther away from her I got, the more I longed to see her again. "What is wrong with me?" I grumbled as I made my way up another set of stairs. I hadn't felt that kind of reaction towards anyone before.

I was suddenly irritated, though I didn't know why, or at whom. Was I mad at myself for being attracted to her? Was I frustrated with her? This beautiful, enigmatic reporter with eyes like seafoam and a mysterious connection to this house? Was she a succubus ready to kill us and devour our hearts? She'd be sorely disappointed if she was.

I made it to my room before I let out a long groan and flung myself on my bed—something I hadn't done since I was probably twelve years old. I knew I should be preparing or working in some way, but I was consumed with thoughts of her. Questions and theories.

I wasn't sure how long I had been lying there, contemplating my next move, but it was long enough for a knock to come at my door and for Charles to step inside. The air immediately shifted, and I knew what it was about.

He seated himself at the desk across from me. Neither one of us said a word until he broke the silence with the last question I wanted to hear right now. "Have you spoken to him yet?"

I shot Charles a look he was probably expecting. "I didn't even want this," I said. "Why must I be the one to talk to him?"

Charles scratched the back of his head, grimacing, as if our conversation was physically painful for him. He looked at me. "Yes, I am well aware of that, but we both know you need to be the one to talk to him."

I ran my hands through my hair, a nervous habit I picked up at some point over the last two or three decades. I didn't speak for a few minutes. I didn't have any words for Charles. I didn't want any of this, and yet here I was, doing more than my share of work.

I finally sighed. "Fine. But not yet. He probably doesn't even know what's going on. If we let him know, something might happen."

"Do you really want to risk that?"

"Yes, I do."

"Still, you should warn him."

"How?"

Charles looked at his hands. He knew that he had no idea what I should say to that man. He knew there was nothing any of us could say to him that would make a difference. There was only one thing he wanted.

"I'll think about what to say," I said, getting to my feet, "but I'm not going to do it yet. There's no point."

Charles shook his head. "You're playing a dangerous game, William. What if he gets out?"

"How could he get out?"

He kept his gaze on his hands, his fingers fumbling together.

"He can't," I said, "and as long as we make sure no one goes near him, we have nothing to worry about. Now, if you'd please," I gestured towards the door, "I'm quite busy."

"You sure looked it when I came in."

I shot him another cold look. "Please leave, Charles. I have a lot on my mind."

My brother-in-law sighed. Well, to our guests he was my brother-in-law anyway. To me, he was just my friend. Someone I respected and cared for. Someone I didn't want to get hurt.

He got up from my desk chair and made his way back to the door. When his hand reached the handle, he paused. "He could ruin everything for us. Everything we've worked for." His voice was low but steady. "I hope you know what you're doing." Then he opened the door and slipped away.

"Me too," I said, the door closing behind him. "Me too."

Chapter *Nine*

The growls grew louder. The air pumping into my lungs stung my throat as I ran, but I kept going. It was closer now. I could feel its hot breath as it nipped at my back. Its vicious teeth slid like ice-hot knives against my shoulders, scraping down my legs. I let out a cry of pain and fell onto the hard ground below. The beast's malformed body eclipsed the trees canopied above me. As it opened its jaws, I let out a scream.

My body jolted upright, and my eyes shot open. As I caught my breath, I realized I wasn't running through the forest. I wasn't lying on the cold, rocky ground beneath that monster. I was safe in my bed. This new bed in this strange mansion. I touched my arms and rubbed my legs, inspecting every part of myself for signs of claw marks or evidence of teeth grazing my skin. But there was nothing.

It was just a dream. A very realistic, terrifying dream.

I knew it would take me a while to catch my breath, so I fell back onto the bed and pulled the covers over me. I tried to think about something else, but I couldn't get it out of my mind. That same creature. The one I'd forgotten about until mere weeks ago, or was it days? I couldn't remember anymore. Time was moving at such a strange pace these days. I felt like I was walking through a carnival, trapped in the tent of warped mirrors, but couldn't escape.

Then the Shadow Beast crawled back into my head, as if it had been dormant in a cave all these years, hibernating until the time was right. And for whatever reason, the time was right now. It found its opportunity and pounced back. How could I rip it from my mind? How could I remove it as I had all those years ago?

What did I do back then, and how could I do it again?

I blinked again and again, focusing on the wardrobe on the other side of the room. Of the vanity nearby. Of the mirror. Of the porcelain brush and sleek mahogany furnishings.

As I focused on my surroundings, my breathing returned to normal, and any tightness in my chest released. Still, I couldn't shake it away. I got up and walked to the vanity set, picked up the brush, and started running it through my hair. I focused on the movements and tried to stay away from the shadowed corners of my mind. I tried convincing myself none of the things that had scared me as a child were real, including the Shadow Beast.

But a part of me felt like something was off about all this. I never believed in the stories Maggie told me, but maybe I should have.

It wasn't long after she passed that memories began to surface. They were splintered deep into my mind like pieces of broken glass I couldn't pluck out. They swirled around my head like the eerie melodies she used to sing to me but I never understood. Memories of darkness. Of swearing I saw something in the corners of my eyes. Nightmares that festered and burned inside my head long after rousing from sleep. Memories of strange places I had no recollection of, as if forced to watch someone else's life through a haunted looking glass.

These days the memories seemed to manifest every time I turned around. Every time I fell asleep or heard a word that triggered something I thought I'd forgotten. Like the creature I could still hear panting in my ears.

There were other images, too, but luckily they weren't paying me any visits today. Perhaps the Shadow Beast had claimed me for now, and they'd have their turn in my head eventually. Maybe it was a territorial creature. It wanted to be the one to torture me.

I wouldn't let it, though. When distraction wasn't enough, I replaced the thoughts with actual memories. Real ones I knew I'd experienced. Ones I had felt against my skin and through my hair. Happy ones.

Memories of my hand in Maggie's as we walked to the market each Saturday, and then her arm looped in mine when she started losing her eyesight. For the whole twenty-eight years I'd been alive, Maggie was my mother. She raised me like I was her own, and with her curled lashes, turned-up nose, and caramel-colored hair, she looked almost identical to my birth mother. The only physical difference was my mother's golden hair and higher cheekbones, the latter of which resembled my own. They were sisters, only a year apart, and as close as any two sisters could be.

A knock came at the door, and I jumped. "Molly? C-come in." I ran my hands along my face and tried to get a hold of myself. I had to get into the proper mindset for the day. I needed to be ready to fight back if Mr. Tucker said anything ignorant again. I had to be brave. I had to be strong.

"Hello, Miss. I came to help you get ready. I also brought you breakfast, as you are needed downstairs in the lobby as soon as possible." She set the tray on the bedside table. Warm, buttered scones flaked onto a plate covered in large slices of ham, two plump eggs, and four thick slices of bacon. I hadn't seen so much food in one tray for breakfast in my life. Did they really eat this much every morning?

"Thank you, Molly. I'll be ready as soon as I'm done." I picked up my fork and not-so-elegantly dove into my food. Each scoop felt like little bites of heaven melting in my mouth. It was the best food I'd ever tasted, which made me wonder if the food the night before would have been better if I had better company (one who wasn't so negative and keen on despising the festival).

I needed to get over that, I supposed, since I'd be dining with William every day for the next month and a half. During dinner, Evelyn had mentioned that our aid in preparing for the festival was the price for getting the opportunity to be so close to everything and receive all the perks we did during our research period. We got the chance to investigate things in a comfortable, up-close manner while receiving top-quality clothes, fine meals, and incredible lodging. We got to write all we wanted and enjoy ourselves. We just had to help out.

Part of our partnership with the members of the house was apparently for us to understand how the festival worked—how it was prepared and how things would go. They wanted us to see exactly what went into making this festival. As Evelyn explained it, I couldn't help but wonder if this was to assure the people of Brakerton Heights that the Ashdown family wasn't plotting anything devious. That they wanted us to watch them closely and vouch for their innocence so people would feel safe coming to the event.

It seemed Evelyn wanted that at least. I wasn't sure about her husband, and William obviously wanted no part in any of it. I wondered why he was willing to help out at all.

When I finished my breakfast, Molly helped me into my clothes and styled everything else. I looked at my reflection in the mirror as she tugged at my dark ribbons of hair and added a touch of rouge to my cheeks, dabbing the rest on my lips. She unraveled a long necklace of black pearls, draped it over my head, and strung it across my neck and down my chest. It glittered subtly in an almost mystical way, blending into my dark green-and-black dress.

It was my favorite of the day gowns Evelyn had given me. It was long and slimming, made of sleek satin, and embellished with just the right amount of black lace. The neckline scooped just above my chest and was trimmed with the lace, which trailed up my neck. When I looked at myself in the mirror when Molly was done, I felt unstoppable. I looked like I had just sprouted from the ocean to conquer the land.

I never cared too much about my appearance. I always found myself plain—someone who easily faded into the background. But now I felt like I was looking at myself for the first time. The confidence that had hidden itself somewhere inside me bubbled to the surface. I was ready to face the day.

"Thank you, Molly," I said, wrapping my arms around her. "I've never felt more myself." The girl was stunned by my sudden affection and laughed as she patted me on the back.

"You're very welcome, Miss. But you mustn't be late.

Lord Ashdown is waiting for you."

My smile faded. *Lord Ashdown is waiting for me.* I rolled my eyes. *I can't wait.* I tried not to think about him so I could form a smile when I turned to my lady's maid. "Thank you very much, Molly," I said, managing that smile. "I will see you this evening." I swung the door open, squared my shoulders, and headed downstairs.

My· heart started pounding about halfway there. *I shouldn't be nervous*, I told myself. *There's nothing to be afraid of. I can handle anything William throws at me. He's probably just a spoiled rich boy who doesn't want to be bothered by outsiders "invading" his home.*

When I reached the bottom of the stairs, I saw him waiting by the curled end of the banister, his arm resting on its spiraled head. I cleared my throat. "Good morning, Lord Ashdown." When he turned around, he stopped for a moment, his mouth opening slightly.

Removing his elbow from the banister, he said, "Good morning, Miss Blake." He bowed, but his eyes followed me as I took my last step from the stairs. When I looked up, our eyes connected like they had the day before.

But I hadn't been this close to him then. His dark brown eyes were even more striking up close, and as the light from outside shone through the windows and spilled against him, I realized his ink-black hair had a slight tint of brown to it. "Please, call me William."

I couldn't help being mesmerized by his appearance and by the richness of his voice. He was even more handsome than I'd thought. But still, why was he being so polite to me? This was a stark contrast to our conversation last night. And I couldn't forget his rude, negative behavior, no matter how good he looked in that white shirt and black waistcoat.

I cleared my throat again and tried not to think about it. "All right, William, then please call me Caroline. Now, where are we going first?"

He watched me with that same expression of either bewilderment or awe. I wasn't sure what it was, but the longer he looked at me, the more I wanted to look away and take a few deep breaths. "Are we going outside?" I asked, realizing I hadn't brought my gloves or coat and suddenly wanting the excuse to get them. "Oh, I'll have to go back upstairs and get them before we—"

"No, we're not going outside," he said, snapping himself out of whatever thought or daze he was lost in. "I'll be showing you parts of the house you might find useful, such as the library. Then we will take things from there." His eyes finally broke away from mine as he turned around. "Please follow me."

I did as he asked, and we walked in silence until we stopped at a large set of double doors at the end of one of the halls. He clutched the doorknobs and said, "I'm not sure if Evelyn showed you the library, but you might find it peaceful in here. It might give you a nice place to write or study." He swung the doors upon, and suddenly I wasn't wondering why he was being so polite anymore.

The room was enormous and stacked with more books than I could begin to count. It was a large, rectangular room, all on one floor, except for one raised level in the back, with rows and rows of bookshelves. I couldn't help but utter an audible "Wow" as I walked past the first row of leather-bound books. They were in pristine quality. Some looked rather old, though. Old, but relatively unused.

I plucked one of the older-looking books from off the shelf, and I heard William's footsteps behind me. "Not many of the books are in English, other than the ones at the back of the room. Luckily, those shelves are next to a desk, for your convenience, if you'd like to study. But I believe those are the only ones." Sure enough, the book's contents were in Latin.

Did they collect books in Latin, or did they speak it themselves? Before I could ask, William turned back around and headed toward the exit. "Now that you've seen the library, we can move on to the study upstairs."

"A study upstairs? Why would you need a study upstairs?" I asked, following him out the doors. "You have a library, and there are desks in the bedrooms." He turned around and looked at me like I'd just said something insulting.

"Why wouldn't we have a study upstairs? All respectable manors have studies, whether or not they have libraries," he scoffed, then turned back around and kept walking.

There's the William I met last night. I bit the inside of my cheek. "I beg your pardon, *sir*, but as you can probably presume, I was not raised in a castle like this, so how was I supposed to know any of that?"

He laughed dryly and continued down the hall, his strides longer and faster now. It took precision for me to keep up without running. "This isn't a castle, Miss Blake, it's a *manor*. Castles house royalty and armies. Manors are nobles' estates."

"Oh, you're right," I said, "How silly of me. How could I mistake this for a castle, with *you* as its master?"

He spun around and stopped so abruptly I almost ran into him. He took a step closer, his eyes narrowing. He was so close to me that I could feel his breath against my skin. "Who do you think you are, Miss Blake?"

"Excuse me?"

"Who are you that you think you can speak to the lord

of the house this way?"

My eyebrows shot up. "*The lord of the house*? Are you that pompous, *Lord* Ashdown, that you feel you must make others aware of how wealthy you are? How you're a nobleman with a manor the size of a town, which *of course* has more than one study and a library." I scowled at him in disgust. "I thought you were discourteous last night, but now I see that you are more than that. You're a spoiled brat who doesn't want anyone to play with his things. A little rich boy who complains about his wealth and that a fabulous party will be held at his estate. While there are so many who starve in the world and work until their hands bleed."

Something burned in his eyes. "You don't know anything about me, Caroline Blake," he said through gritted teeth.

I stepped even closer and said, "Neither do you. So don't you dare look down on me." I gave him one last look that told him just how disgusted I was. And I left. I didn't care what I was supposed to do with him today. I wasn't going to stand for this. I took the next right I could and found another set of stairs. It was much smaller than the other two sets of stairs I'd seen and walked on in the house, and it was tucked away in a corner.

William's footsteps were close behind me, so I didn't have a choice. I walked up the steps, fuming, as he called out my name. "Miss Blake, come back. We have to work on the preparations."

I shot him a look. "Don't pretend like you care about this festival in the slightest. You made your feelings clear last night." I climbed higher.

"Miss Blake," he said, his voice getting more pressed, "You shouldn't be going up those steps. Come down right this instant."

"You're not my father. Don't talk to me like that." I didn't even look at him as I ascended to the second floor, but as soon as I made it onto the landing, something shifted in the air. That same chill that came over me at the office of *The Woman Speaks*. That same chill that crept up my spine nearly every day since. But this time, it was even stronger.

The cold cut through to my bones, my insides shriveling and shuddering as I moved forward. The hallway before me was dimly lit, and there was no one to be seen. Not a maid or a valet, a footman or an Ashdown. Not even a sound. It was like walking into a strange void. A cave dressed up like a mansion.

There was nothing extraordinary about the hall, but it felt like something beyond that eerie chill. Something beyond fear. There was nothing, though. I saw nothing. Until I looked to the wall and spotted a mural. It wasn't on the whole wall. Just the center. But it stretched like a thick ribbon all the way down the hallway, appearing to continue to the other side as the wall hooked to a left at the very end.

I looked closer at the mural. There were pictures of people. Beautiful people. They were all fighting. Maybe gods and goddesses on Mt. Olympus. I trailed my finger over the images. There were clouds. Castles. Animals. So much was going on in this long, winding painting. And there was something about it that felt familiar. Something about it . . .

"CAROLINE!"

I turned around and saw William running towards me. The way he called out to me was loud, but it wasn't aggressive. He was clearly angry, but when I turned to face him, he didn't look it. He looked frantic, maybe even frightened.

"Caroline, what are you doing down here? Evelyn told everyone not to come down here."

I blinked, still adjusting to the darkness shrouding his figure. "What are you talking about?"

"The wing," he said, "This is *our* wing. None of you are allowed down here."

"Oh." I looked around the empty hallway. At the strangely beautiful mural. At the darkness. I frowned. "For . . . privacy?"

"Yes, that's right. We have the right to privacy in our own home, don't you think?"

"But . . . why is it so dark?" My eyes gravitated toward the mural again, but William stepped in front of me, blocking it from my view.

"We like to keep our lives private. We have invited many of you into our home—new servants and you four reporters. And eventually, we will be having family members and guests from different cities and countries running through our halls. All we want is privacy. To ensure that, we keep the area dark. No one is allowed in here but us."

"What about your maids and valets?" I asked, trying to peek around him.

"Of course we let them in, but we only need their assistance a handful of times a day. Very specific times each day. You know this, of course, as you now have a maid of your own." His expression was pinched, but his eyes were still frantic.

Regardless of how much I detested the man, I couldn't let him suffer anymore. "I'm sorry. I didn't know this was your wing. It looks different from this side. I only saw it from the more lit hallway. Where . . . is that by the way?" I turned around and scanned the darkness.

"It doesn't matter," he said, his speech still pressed.

"But we have to go." He held out his arm. "Come, I'll escort you out."

I turned around, spotted his outstretched arm, and crossed my own. "I can find my way out myself, thank you." I strode past him the way I'd come. I suppressed a smile, thinking he'd try and fail to land the perfect retort, but he didn't. I waited another minute or two, but still there was nothing.

When I finally made it downstairs and turned around, I saw him there behind me, but he was silent. His face had fallen, and his eyes were elsewhere. Lines dug into his forehead, leaning heavily against his brow, and he was rubbing the back of his neck. I stopped. "Are you all right?" I asked.

He looked up. For a moment, I saw that same unguarded look, but then his face returned to normal, shifting gracefully into a smug, stoic expression. "Yes, I'm fine. Now, let's go outside. Follow me."

This time, I followed him without a word. Still, I couldn't help but glance back up the steps and wonder what had just happened.

What was down that hallway that he didn't want me to see?

Chapter Ten

I followed him outside without saying a word. I felt guilty. I was a guest in his house, and regardless of how I felt about him, I still should have respected his privacy. I didn't know what was down that hallway, but it wasn't my business anyway.

The air was particularly chilly today, but I couldn't help but note that it was still more comfortable than the cold I'd felt upstairs. I studied the back of William's head as I followed him down the side of the hill, all the while pondering whether his hair was really black or an extremely dark shade of brown.

He stopped, and I had to remind my feet to stop too before running into his back. He turned to his right and said, "This is it." He gestured to the empty field Evelyn had pointed out during the tour of the house. "This is where everything will happen," he grumbled. Giving a big sigh, he crossed his arms and added, "What Evelyn has planned for this year's festival is beyond me."

"You don't know what we're going to do?"

Still looking at the field beyond, he said, "I do not. I wanted no part of this." He paused, then continued a little more softly, "I just want to help Evelyn. There was no changing her mind, so in the end, I decided the best thing for me to do was to ensure the festival avoided disaster as much as possible."

I still didn't understand why he was so against the festival. Did he really dislike people that much? If he was so concerned with how the people in town viewed them, was he afraid this would cause them to be ridiculed? He couldn't be scared of being an outcast. He had to be no more than thirty years old—he would have lived his entire life in this isolation. Was he afraid of the change? Of having to interact with people outside his family?

"What about you?" he asked.

I blinked, wondering if I had missed something. "What about me . . . what?"

"Why are you here?" He asked it so abruptly that I wasn't sure what to say.

"Well," I said, pulling my words together, "I want to show the world that women are just as capable of reporting as men. That we have intelligent minds worth using. That we're equals." I held my head high but braced for verbal impact. Very few men had shown our paper much love, to say the least. And William was an opinionated man and the lord of a grand estate. And I had just blatantly ignored him, consequently breaking the rules of his house. Who knew what he might say—what rant he might fly off on?

I watched his face, but his expression didn't change. He was back to looking at the open field, his eyes squinting beneath the bright but clouded sky. "That's a very good reason to do something brave," he said, and surprise swept through me.

Then he looked at me. "But why *this* project?" There was something distressing in the way he emphasized "this." Almost as if he were pleading.

"What other project would have turned so many heads? Proved our point further?" I asked. "I couldn't pass an opportunity like this up. Besides, I'm not afraid."

He shot a surprised look in my direction. "You're not afraid?"

"Of course not. What's there to be afraid of?" I laughed, but he just stood there, unamused.

He straightened his back and tugged at the sleeves fitted against his wrists. Clearing his throat, he said, "What about your family? Won't they miss you?"

Family. The word hung in the air like an old, soaking-wet sock hung out to dry. Did I have to have this conversation? That I was an orphan with nothing and no one to my name? I tried forcing a smile, but it just came out as an awkward grimace. "Well, I, unfortunately, don't have a family waiting for me. My aunt raised me, and she just passed away."

I could feel his eyes settle on me, but I didn't want any pity. And I didn't want to see any judgment on his face either. So I turned toward the field, just as he had done. "I suppose if someone had to risk it all for the sake of a good cause, it might as well be someone who has nothing to lose."

There was a silence between us, and fear spiked through me. *Did I say too much?*

I looked at him firmly before he could say anything. "But just to be clear, there is nothing wrong with being alone. I'm not some sad orphan girl. I know who I am, and

I am confident that I'm the best person for this job, regardless of my background." My fingers curled into a fist, my nails digging into my skin.

My breaths quickened, and I was ready to fight, but he just looked me in the eyes. "I never thought that, Miss Blake. I can tell you're strong. Besides, there's nothing wrong with being an orphan."

I suddenly felt very stupid. I had spoken without properly thinking. He was the lord of the house. He lived there with his sister and brother-in-law. No parents.

"I'm sorry," I said quietly, but I couldn't help pressing a little. "Where are your parents?"

"Gone. I haven't seen them since I was a child."

"I'm so sorry. Did you get along with them?" I couldn't help but ask. His expression was hard to read, and I couldn't tell if he was angry or sad.

His posture stiffened. "Yes, but they died when I was twelve." He was kicking the ground with his shoe, watching the dirt pile up beneath him, a frown firmly carved upon his face.

"I'm sorry," I said again, worried that I'd overstepped, "I envy you, though. I never knew my parents."

"Oh. No?" He looked at me, but I didn't reciprocate. I looked off into the horizon and hoped the bright whiteness of the sky would keep me from crying.

"No. Though I wish I had. Apparently they were very kind people, but they never met me. My mom died when I was born, and my father died shortly before that. That's why I was raised by my aunt." I could feel his eyes on me, but neither one of us said a word.

"If you have no family, what about your friends?" he finally asked.

I blinked. "My friends?"

"Yes, your friends. What do they think about all this?

About you coming here, I mean."

Something in me sunk. The only two I could think of were obvious: Mary and Agnes. And although I was grateful for their concern and kindness toward me, could I really consider them my friends? I didn't know them beyond surface-level observations—the names of one or two people in their lives, favorite drinks to have when taking breaks, which news stories they were interested in.

They didn't know anything about me. Even if they did, I wasn't sure they'd call me a friend anyway.

But I decided on them. "They think I'm crazy for doing this."

He chuckled. "I imagined so. That's the proper reaction, anyway."

"Why?" I asked, my scowl returning. "Why do you say things like that? Do you want people to be afraid of you?"

He smirked. "It's safer if people are afraid of what they don't know."

"And what they *think* they know? What's *familiar*?" I snapped.

"It's safer if people stick with what they know and don't risk their lives unnecessarily."

"And how are any of us risking our lives? Are you going to hunt me down and kill me, William?"

He took a step back. "What? Of course not."

"Then why should I be afraid?"

He paused, biting his lower lip as he thought. "You should be afraid of things you don't know."

I nearly growled. I was so sick of this nonsense from him. From everyone. I turned my whole body toward him and took calculated steps. "I have been told to be afraid of things my entire life," I said, my voice rising, "And honestly, I'm *exhausted*. From living a life in fear, staying solely where the windows reach so sunlight can break through and keep me from the darkness. What if I want to face the shadows? What if I want to take risks?"

I stepped as close as I could to him so he couldn't look away. "When my aunt died, I let my fear go. I left it back where I came from and moved forward." I kept my feet firmly planted on the ground, but the way he was looking at me made me falter. Why was he looking at me like that? Heat rose to my face.

"I'm not afraid," I continued. "Stop telling me to be something I'm not—warning me and telling me to stick with what I know. Telling me I should have avoided this place, along with the others. Maybe I didn't want to stay where I was. Maybe I wanted to recklessly change myself and alter my life."

"And why would you want to do that?" he asked, his face just inches from mine. I could almost feel the rise and fall of his chest as he steadied his breath.

"Because I want to prove to myself and everyone else that there are no such things as monsters." The breeze flitted by and brushed my hair against my shoulders.

"And what will you do if you're wrong?" he asked.

"Then I will face it head-on."

His eyes stayed fixed on mine, and the air around us changed. Warm and unmoving, like the moment we met. That same sliver of time where everything stood still.

"Then I'll stop warning you, Miss Blake. You appear to know what you're doing." The words sounded more like a warning than anything else. Something dark ignited in his eyes as he took a few steps away from me. "And since there is no convincing you otherwise, I might as well stop trying to sway you with my sordid thoughts on the matter."

My head pulled back. *What?*

He nodded. "We need to start getting things ready for the festival anyway. So, please follow me." He headed down the hill, but my head was still reeling at the sudden change.

I hoisted my skirt above my ankles and staggered down the hill. I stumbled for a bit, but when William turned around and noticed me, he held out his hand. "I can't imagine what it's like walking in those things," he said.

"It's not for the faint of heart, that's for sure," I said, and when I took his hand something sparked between us—like touching lightning but feeling no pain. By the look on his face and the sudden tension in his jaw, I could tell he felt it, too.

"We better hurry before the sun sets."

"Y-yeah, but," I fumbled over the words, my head suddenly light. "It can't be passed four o'clock, if that."

"Well, autumn around here has shorter days than a lot of places. Darkness falls upon this hill around five o'clock."

"But even in Brakerton Heights it doesn't get dark until six or seven."

"Yes, that might be the case down there. But the sun sets a little earlier up here."

We took the last couple of steps to the bottom of the hill. "How is that possible?" I asked, frowning. When we stopped, I realized I was still holding his hand and quickly took mine away. My heart caught in my chest as my fingers grazed his.

He didn't seem to notice. Shrugging, he turned to me with that same cocky smile I'd witnessed too many times over the last twenty-four hours. "Perhaps it's the curse."

I rolled my eyes. "I thought you weren't going to bring that nonsense up anymore."

"I said I wouldn't try to *convince* you anymore. I never said I would stop talking about it completely." He flashed me a smug grin, which only made me roll my eyes harder.

"Just show me what you need to. What are we doing out here anyway?" *You said we weren't going outside*, I wanted to add, but I figured it had to do with the swift change of plans after I visited his wing. So I thought it best to keep the comment to myself.

"We all have different jobs," he said, scanning the field and shielding his eyes from the sun with his hand. "Some of the others will be taking care of some of the building, catering, and other types of preparations. You and I are supposed to plan what attractions will be featured at the festival and where we should place them."

"Why can't I work on the construction? I surely have more experience than the others." I tried not to sound pretentious as I said it, but I wanted to make my feelings known. "I enjoy building things."

William studied my face, a smile forming on his face. A *genuine* smile. It brightened his face in a way that made it a little harder for me to breathe. "If you'd like, I could ask Evelyn to reconsider."

"That would be good," I nodded, trying to conceal my smile, but it broke through anyway. "Thank you. For now, though, we can start figuring out the other details. I'm sure the others will have input as well, but we can come up with our own thoughts and lay it out for them."

"That's a good idea," he said, his tone gentler than before. "Let's put our initial thoughts together and take them to the others."

"All right," I said. I tried to guess the size of the field and how much we could fit on it. "Is this the only area the festival will be taking place?"

He frowned. "Do you not think this is enough space?"

I tilted my head. "Well, it might be, but wouldn't it be fun if we started decorating at the bottom of the hill and had small attractions as the guests make their way up?"

"Yes, that's a fine idea. I like it." A smile broke even wider across his face. "What other ideas jump out at you, Caroline?"

Hearing my name on his lips tripped the words falling from my mouth. "Um . . we could . . . Well, what types of attractions were here before?"

His smile vanished, along with any traces of smugness. In its place was a look that more closely resembled the one he wore in the hall upstairs. When he stopped me from following the mural into the mansion's depths.

His eyes looked as though they were searching something. One of his hands slowly crept up to his head and raked its way through his hair.

"William?" I asked.

He snapped out of it and looked at me. "Sorry, I was just trying to remember what the others had told me." He gave a shaky, forced laugh. "I'm just having a hard time remembering."

"Okay," I said, but I wasn't convinced of his answer. His body had tensed, and something changed in his eyes. It was that same look I'd seen so many times before. What did William have to be afraid of? That's what it was, wasn't it? That look of fear.

I smiled softly and walked closer to him. "It's okay. We can start with the basics."

"You're right," he said, pulling himself from his thoughts. "Let's do that."

I waited until he saw me looking at him, hoping it helped put him at ease. "Okay. So, popped corn and pastries are typically at these types of events, right?"

He nodded. "Especially pastries with cream."

"Okay. What else? I've never been to a carnival or festival, or anything like that before. I've only read about them."

He gave a big sigh. "Let's see. Well, most carnivals have attractions that are meant to shock people. Among these are dangerous animal shows, burlesque shows, and freak shows."

My arms flopped to my sides. "You cannot be serious. I refuse to be any part of that."

He laughed. "I figured you might say that. What do you propose then?"

"A family-friendly event for one. I mean, this event is for only two nights. People used to take their kids to it. I can't imagine kids would have found any of that pleasing."

"Well, they surely wouldn't have been allowed at the burlesque portion, but unfortunately, they would have been allowed to the rest."

I crossed my arms. "How awful. I can't imagine the kinds of parents who would allow their children to look at people with differences and laugh. It's truly atrocious."

"I agree wholeheartedly, which is why you don't have to worry. We want to put on a light-hearted event. Well, Evelyn wants to put it on. I just have to go along with it and hope for the best."

"But you do have a say in it?" I asked.

"Yes, I do, so don't worry. Nothing but family-friendly attractions." He chuckled.

"Great. Well, I think we should set up booths for games, too."

William raised an eyebrow. "Games?"

"Yes, such as horseshoes and guessing games. Games with prizes. Dancing. Oh, will there be music?"

"Music? I don't know. I really don't know much of what's going to happen. My main concern up until this point has simply been to make sure things go smoothly. I didn't have much time or energy to think of what to do or the details of everything."

"We shall just have to ask Evelyn then, right?"

"I suppose, but she's probably up to her ears in preparations of her own right now. So why don't we take note of that and keep thinking?" I nodded and made a mental note. *I'll have to write this all down when I get to my room.*

For the next four hours or so, we brainstormed what could be added into the festival and what could be tossed out. I suggested creating new traditions. Why did we have to stick with what everyone else had always done? Why not create something new?

I couldn't believe the fun I was having talking with him. We talked and laughed, and I realized he was actually pretty funny. Although he was prickly on the outside, I thought that maybe there was sweetness inside him. Like a pineapple.

But as he helped me back up the hill, his smiling face transformed back into its usual stoicism. It was like a curtain of sadness and arrogance had lifted from his face after hours of me pulling the strings, but now they had closed and I couldn't see what was hidden beneath.

A butler opened the door for us as we walked to one of the side doors of the mansion. William whispered something to him and then turned to me. "Thank you for your work today. I will see you at supper." Then he took a sharp turn into the house and hurried up the stairs he'd caught me on earlier.

'Thank you for your work today'? There was something about the way he said it that irritated me. It was strained and too formal. Walking up that hill turned him back into the William I talked to last night. I watched him until he disappeared, wondering what made him this way. What made him so afraid to let go?

I didn't have the luxury of thinking too much on my way to my room because I soon got lost in the labyrinth that was Ashdown Manor. When I asked a maid I didn't recognize for directions, she just shook her head and walked away without saying a word. "That's strange," I whispered to myself and walked up a flight of stairs. That's when I spotted Mrs. Wells.

The older woman was holding a silver tray littered with crumbs and dirty utensils. "Mrs. Wells!" I called out, swooping my arm up in a wave. My voice resounded across the enormous room, and I winced. My hand quickly retreated to my chest. "I suppose that wasn't very ladylike of me, was it?"

She gave a hearty laugh as she reached where I was on the stairs. "Ah, who cares about that?" she said. "How are you today, Miss?"

"I'm quite well, actually, but I seem to be lost."

"That's all right, dear. I'll show you the way. Come on." She gestured with her head and picked up her pace so she could lead me.

"Do you need help with that tray?" I asked.

"Oh, no. I'm not *that* old, am I?" She turned around and winked.

"So, how long have you been working here, Mrs. Wells?"

"Oh, I don't know. About forty years, I think."

I paused before taking the next step. "Forty?"

She waltzed onto the landing and said, "Yes, forty or forty-five—somewhere around there." She smiled at me and added, "It's this way, come along."

I followed her down another hall just as luxurious as the last, her words echoing in my mind. *Forty years.* She had to have been there when the massacre happened. She had to know *something* the others wouldn't tell me. Something the people in town didn't know.

But if she had been here during that terrible event, why would she stay?

I desperately wanted to ask the question, but I thought better of it and asked something else instead. I had already overstepped in my conversation with William earlier. I didn't want to do it again. "Do you have any family here? Is Molly perhaps your niece or granddaughter?"

Mrs. Wells gave her hearty chuckle again and said, "My, my, you are observant. Yes, she is my granddaughter."

"I see. Well, it's wonderful that she can work here with you."

"Yes, I was very fortunate. I don't get out much, and my daughter lives in another city far away from here. But when this work opportunity came up, my granddaughter happily came along."

If her daughter lived in another city, it might have been due to whatever happened here at the last festival. But if that were the case, why would Mrs. Wells' daughter willingly allow her daughter to come along?

"That's lovely," I said, "Was her mother sad to see her go?"

"Oh yes. She didn't want her to come because of the obvious trauma behind the manor's festival, but Molly insisted on coming anyway because she has only seen me a handful of times in her young life, and she'd earn a lot of money, too. It was a two-birds-with-one-stone situation for her, and I couldn't be happier."

That explained it. Molly's mother obviously moved away and was against the festival, but Mrs. Wells wasn't. She even encouraged her granddaughter to come and was happy to have her. She didn't seem worried about the festival, which was a good sign.

"Here it is," she said, stopping in front of my burgundy door.

"Thank you very much," I said. "I need to pay more

attention when I'm walking around this place. I don't want to keep getting lost."

"It does take some getting used to, so don't worry too much about it, dear. Have a good evening now."

She turned to leave, so I quickly said, "Wait!" She stopped. "I . . . I have a question to ask you," I said, my heart starting to pound.

"Oh?"

"Yes, I . . . I wanted to know if . . . if there's really a curse here."

Her body bristled, but her face remained calm. "What do you mean, dear?" Her voice was still cheery and sweet.

I might as well be blunt about it now. "Is this place cursed? Is this festival doomed to be disastrous like the last?"

She looked at me blankly, and I tried to keep the pounding in my chest quiet as I waited for her response.

Finally, she spoke. "No, I don't believe this manor is cursed."

Something inside me lifted. "Aha! I knew it! I—"

"But as for this upcoming festival, I really don't know." I froze. She sighed, nodding. "Yes, I'm afraid there is never really a guarantee things will turn out as planned."

"Then why are you here?" I asked. "Why would you let Molly come if it might be dangerous?"

She tapped a finger against one of the tray's handles. "Well, we can't live our lives in fear, can we?"

My shoulders relaxed. "No, I suppose we can't." I laughed to myself. *At least there's someone like me I can count on here.* "Thank you, Mrs. Wells. Have a good evening." I bowed my head and grabbed hold of the door handle, but as I turned it, Mrs. Wells stopped me.

She leaned into my ear and whispered, "But don't take anything for granted, Miss Blake. Always be ready for the unexpected." She repositioned the tray in her arms and said one more "goodbye" before walking away.

My hand froze on the doorknob. *The unexpected?* What did that mean?

When I finally gathered myself, I entered my room, and as I thought of what the woman said, I couldn't help but remember the expression on William's face as he stopped me in his wing. As I followed the mysterious mural down that dimly lit hallway.

I sat limply on my bed and thought about everything that had happened today. It all crashed down on me at once, and that familiar ache in my chest returned. The words about curses and fear and the unexpected ran through my mind and made it hard for me to think. Then I remembered what William had said outside: *Why don't we take note of that and keep thinking?*

I focused on the room around me and took deep breaths. When things slowed within me, I reached down and opened my trunk. *I have to write everything down. William and I talked about so much—made so many plans.* As I flipped through the trunk, a smile rose on my lips, and William's face entered my mind. That soft, subtle smile that broke through that stony wall of his. We talked and strolled through the field, planning the activities and pretending, for a moment, that we actually got along. For a while there, we did. I heard him laugh.

I had a surprisingly good time with him today, I thought as I gathered some of the less crumpled pieces of paper at the bottom of the trunk. I didn't want to use the new sheets of paper Mary and Agnes had given me for notes that had nothing to do with the story. I wanted those pieces to be used strictly for *The Woman Speaks*. I'd have to use Maggie's papers for everything else.

As I lifted one of the papers from the bottom of the trunk, it caught onto something. I looked down and found that the base of the sturdy box was a plank of wood fitted as the bottom. It had blended so closely with the rest of the trunk that I hadn't noticed it was made of a different material. The difference was subtle, but it was there.

I tugged on the paper one more time, and it ripped. *Of course.* I tried to peel the fragment from under the board when something clattered behind it. My forehead creased at the unexpected noise.

What was that?

I removed all the contents from the trunk and placed them on the floor beside me, then reached inside. I shook the whole thing, holding onto the thin piece of wood at the very bottom. And there it was again. A slight clatter, as if something was stuck behind it.

I knew it probably wasn't wise to break one of the only possessions I had, but I needed to find out what was behind that plank. I planted my feet firmly against either side of the trunk and pulled at the board with all my strength.

A loud *CRACK* broke through the room, and I winced as a splinter dug into my skin. I sucked on it and looked inside the trunk. My mouth gaped open, leaving my finger dangling by my lips.

It was a book. A small but sturdy book. I reached in and grabbed it, running my hand over the brown cover. The pages were yellowed, and the spine was a little tattered, but other than that, it looked almost new. I flipped open the first page, and my heart nearly stopped.

I traced my fingers along the name inscribed inside the cover: Claire Duncan. Tears burned in my eyes. "Mother."

Chapter *Eleven*

As I made my way back to our family's wing, I found myself doing something that was becoming strangely more common over the last few hours: smiling. As soon as I caught myself, I stopped. I needed to remember my place, regardless of how strong-willed and attractive my new house guest was.

I had to redirect my thoughts at least five times before I got to my room. What was it about this woman that I couldn't get her out of my head? Everything about her was such a mystery. She lived a life away from this place, raised by one family member who recently passed. And her parents . . . she'd said she never knew them. That her father died before she was born and that her mother died giving birth to her. What was their story?

The story seemed true, but there was something

peculiar about her that made me question the story's validity. There was something about her that made me question everything. And no matter how little we got along, there seemed to be a middle ground we both enjoyed treading—a space where we let ourselves enjoy the other's company.

After a while outside, she didn't stay angry with me. And I found it nearly impossible to be anything but captivated by her. As soon as we moved past any disagreements, she relaxed. She let herself smile. I let myself laugh. A stupid mistake on my part, but how did it happen to begin with? I hadn't felt that light since I was a child.

The memories from long ago rushed into my mind, and the pain returned. I closed my eyes, safe in my bedroom now, shutting the door behind me. Everyone was safe. And these thoughts would pass. They always did, despite the feelings that accompanied them.

I waited for them to pass, but today they weren't budging. I did everything I could to drive the images away. Those horrible thoughts that piled into my mind, one after another, into a giant, immovable heap. The loss of my family. My best friend. Everything I wished I could keep from my memory returned like a monstrous wave, ready to swallow me up in darkness, reminding me where I belonged.

Then I thought of Caroline, and the thoughts broke apart.

I thought of the passion that bubbled out of her like an angry teapot. The intensity of her stare when she refused to back down. The way her body swayed when she walked. The curve of her waist. The fullness of her lips.

She purged my mind of its darkest shadows, cleansing it with her laugh. She entranced me with her alluring gaze and an indescribable charm I couldn't resist. There was something about her that sucked me in. Something in her I craved.

She was a fiery summer, and I'd been in winter all my life.

In a way, the thought of her was somehow worse than the vicious memories piling in my head. I already knew my fate. I had become resigned to it long ago. I had learned to live with who I was and what I was doomed to. Why did someone like her have to show up and remind me all over again? Make me wish my life hadn't ended before it'd really begun?

I wanted to scream. I wanted to yell in a place no one could hear me. Punch the wall until my knuckles hurt. I wanted to escape—to be free of all of this.

That could never happen, though. I knew it. Evelyn knew it. Charles and the others knew it. They all knew we were monsters. That *I* was a monster.

I wasn't one of the fortunate beings in this world who had the luxury of friendship or love, and there was nothing I could do to change that. I'd stay confined in this lonely mansion like the beast I was until I inevitably turned to dust. Or burned. Or however else our kind chose to die. All I knew was that however it happened, I was destined to do it alone.

I let myself sit on the ground near my door, my hands pulled into my hair just a little while longer. But I couldn't stay here long. The thoughts would come again. The guilt. The self-loathing. The fear. And I had something I had to do.

I wished Charles had let me pretend I didn't have to do this just a little while longer. That I could put this off just one more day. But today was a close enough call as it was. I should have talked to him sooner. I just . . . I couldn't get myself to do it.

But I had to do it now.

I pulled myself up and left my room. Even without a properly beating heart, I could hear the steady throbbing in my ears. The reflex was burned into my muscle memory. What beat beneath my chest now was a slow, cold thing—something not quite alive but still moving.

My shoulders tensed as I reached the stretch to his room. I traced my hand against the wall, studying the patterns leading to the entrance. When I finally found the crease, I lifted the concealed latch and opened the door.

I thought about turning around. Concealing the latch once more and pretending he wasn't there. Lying to myself that I didn't need to do this. But then I thought of Caroline and how she followed this path on her own, blind to where it led. The thought of her finding him snapped me back to doing what needed to be done.

I made my way up the stairs, my shoulders nearly brushing against the narrow passage's walls as I moved. Then I stepped into the room, my shoes echoing against the agonizingly bright kaleidoscope of colors that tiled the floors.

I didn't want to stay here longer than I had to, so I just said it. "Don't speak to our guests." The words echoed through the tiny room, but still, he was nowhere to be seen. The small, oblong room was empty of anything but the long mirror, its expertly carved frame making it look more beautiful than it should have.

I looked hard at the mirror, but still, there was nothing. He had to be here. He had to hear me. There was no way he couldn't.

I spoke louder. "Don't you dare speak to our guests. If you so much as touch one of them, or say a word—"

"What? You'll lock me away?" he hissed, his face finally

appearing—those familiar eyes shooting daggers into mine.

I glared at him. "Just don't do anything."

He shook his head frantically. "You know it wasn't my fault. You know that, right? I wouldn't do anything—"

"Just answer me!" I shouted.

I could see his whole body now. "There's no escape for me here," he said. "You've made sure of that."

I scoffed. "Just know your place and keep your head down. If anyone finds you, don't say a word, or you'll answer to me." With that, I turned around and left him in the dark. Despite everything, I couldn't help feeling a small pang of guilt. But what would my life be like if I wasn't used to living with that feeling every moment of the day?

Before opening the entrance, I placed my ear against the door to ensure no one was out there. No one was supposed to be in this wing, but Caroline had ignorantly made her way here earlier today, so there was no telling what might happen. I needed to remind Evelyn to warn the others about the other entrance to the wing. To tell them that they would be immediately excused if they knowingly trod these halls.

Perhaps that was too extreme. Maybe they'd suspect something then. I growled as I exited into the hall. Why must we go through this headache at all? I didn't even want anyone coming here digging up our secrets. Why was I the one in charge of keeping them hidden?

I was already so tired of the situation—so fatigued at the fear of what might get dug up while our guests were residing under our roof. And this was only the second day of their six-week visit. How was I to keep calm during all this? How could we get out of this without our skeletons coming out of our closets?

Chapter *Twelve*

October 8, 1856

The market was busy today. It's now well past the end of summer, and the air has that crisp sweetness to it that only comes around this time of year. I love when the leaves start changing color and the world looks like it's transformed into a new magical world.

There's something comforting about being wrapped up in layers, or tucked under covers, while the air outside is frigid and bites at any exposed skin. Maybe I'm strange, but I like it.

Mags and I found the most delicious apples at the market. This is the time of year where a lot of products and produce switch out for something that matches the shifting season, so there was a lot more to look at today. New vendors came in from out of town, too. That's what's amazing about the autumn market. New faces with lavish fabrics and goods from all around the country, and perhaps farther.

Sometimes I can save up enough to buy something spectacular, but oftentimes what catches my eye are far beyond what's in my pocketbook. Today, I saw the most beautiful item of clothing I'd ever seen. It was a long, thick scarf with soft pinks, blues, and light purples woven together in the most intricate way. The only problem was that it cost about three times the salary I made as a governess. I had only been working for about a year now, so I needed to save every last coin I earned to leave Brakerton Heights one day.

I long to see all the places I've heard and read about. To reach those places these vendors are from, and beyond. India, China, the Americas. I want to see every country I can. I teased Mags once and told her I'd even be willing to work as a carnival actress the rest of my life so I can be on the road, and she nearly lost it, chastising me (something she does a lot of). I suppose that's what elder sisters are for.

I was running the scarf's fabric through my hands when my sister huddled close to me and said, "Don't look now, but there's a very handsome stranger who cannot take his eyes off of you."

"What? That's silly," I said, feigning indifference but peeking over her shoulder to find the man in question.

She stomped her foot and hissed, "I said don't look!" I had to stop myself from laughing at how serious she looked. It was just a man. Why did it matter so much? Mags can be such the worrywart.

I gently pushed her shoulder and stepped around her. I searched the sea of faces and saw not one of them looking my way. I glared at her. "Oh, you. There's no one looking at me. I can't believe I fell for that."

"I'm not jesting, Claire. Look—oh, oh he's coming this way." She swiveled around and pretended not to see him as he approached. When I looked up and saw him, I felt like an arrow had plunged right into my chest. I know it's a silly, cliche thing to say, but that's how I felt.

My first thought when I saw him was that he looked like he'd walked straight out of a painting. His dark suit was finer than any

I'd ever seen, and his smile shone through the crowd like a shooting star. It was clear he was no ordinary Brakerton Heights townsperson.

As he walked closer, I noticed how incredibly beautiful he was. I had never seen a man who could be described in such a way until I saw him. But at the same time, he also looked strong; I'd never seen such a combination before. With broad shoulders, high cheekbones, and lashes curled over piercing blue eyes, he looked like the prince of a fairy tale. Like a knight in shining armor. Someone who could whisk one away on horseback and ride off into the sunset. And when he smiled, a dimple printed into his cheek.

I was so mesmerized by those icy blue eyes that I almost didn't notice the words coming from his mouth. "Why, hello, madam. Are you enjoying the market this fine day?" Despite the cold, his face looked warm. He didn't appear to feel it at all. Unlike me, whose frosty nose must have been pink and puffy. I could just about die thinking about it.

I tried my best to smile without coming across as eager or nervous. "Yes, I am, thank you. How about yourself?"

He nodded. "Yes, it's a beautiful day. Made even more beautiful by your company."

I nearly melted at his words, my eyes darting to Mags. Over this mystery man's shoulder, I saw her covering her mouth, her eyes bright with excitement. I turned my attention back to him and said, "Oh, that is awfully kind of you to say." As I said the words, I wanted to die. Had I never talked to a handsome stranger before? Well, I suppose I hadn't, but I still couldn't believe I was being so . . . juvenile. So awkward and silly.

My face was growing warmer now, and though I welcomed the reprieve from the cold, I wished it hadn't come like this. But he didn't appear to mind at all. He just smiled at me and said, "Well, it is the truth. May I ask for your name, beautiful stranger?"

The heat was moving down into my shoulders now. I couldn't believe what was happening. Nothing like this had ever happened to me before. I just turned 19 a short while ago, and while many of my peers have already gotten engaged to be married, I have remained single and out of the gentlemen's attention. I love balls but often don't have the time or energy to go. My mother and father both work long days. Mags helps Mother with the dress shop, and Father works hard at the office in the middle of the city. I am a governess, but I work any other hours I can at the dress shop.

All the other mothers in town are ecstatically throwing their daughters at balls and social gatherings, but my mother is under the impression that Mags and I are so perfect someone will swoop us up and take us without any prior meetings. This could possibly have something to do with my father's business and how his partners seem interested in us. But I'd rather die than marry one of those old coots.

But maybe my mother had been onto something. This mysterious gentleman was the most handsome man I had ever seen, and he appeared like a rose in a thornbush. I nodded bashfully and said, "My name is Claire. Claire Duncan." He took my hand and kissed it. The heat of his lips burned through my glove.

"It is lovely to meet you, Miss Duncan. My name is Cassius. Cassius Laurent."

I wish I could remember much of what happened after that, but it's all a fantastic, cloudy blur. What I do remember is that he said he wanted to see me again and that he will call on me soon, as long as that is something I also desired. Of course, it was *something I desired, so I nodded (not too eagerly, of course). He kissed my hand again before turning around and disappearing back into the crowd.*

When he left, Mags returned to my side, shaking her head. "You sure are lucky, Claire."

I turned to her with a grin and said, "Oh, I'm not lucky." I shook my head, still beaming with the widest smile I've probably ever worn. "It's fate." The two of us giggled and rushed home to tell Mother. Her premonition was true. Clearly.

Until next time,

Claire

I set the book down and processed everything I'd just read. I touched the crisp pages. The curled handwriting of my mother. At one point in time, 29 years ago, she'd been touching these pages, too. The paper was so thin I could see the words on the other side of each page. Its flimsy material made me afraid to handle it too much.

As much as I wanted to sit here and read the rest of her words all night, I decided to set it down for now and savor each sentence. I let myself reread the words and run them through my head a few more times before getting ready for supper. When I began reading of this man and my mother's interactions, I had wondered if he was my father. I didn't know much about him, but I was twenty-eight years old, so the timeline would have aligned. However, the name wasn't right. My father was Richard Blake, not Cassius Laurent.

I wondered who this Cassius was and where my father was during all this. I couldn't resist reading just one more, so I flipped the page and started reading the second entry. It was dated only three days after the first.

October 11, 1856

I had a hard time getting Cassius out of my mind after I met him. I was moving through that day and the next like I was out of this world. Like I'd become a spirit blending into the world beyond. Mags could tell I was elsewhere, and she knew why. She'd give me that knowing smile of hers and ask what was going on in my head. I would blush and say it was nothing.

I truly did feel that it was nothing—nothing to dwell on anyway. It was highly unlikely I'd meet him again, but I couldn't help daydreaming about him. He was so handsome. How could I forget someone like him? His eyes looked like precious gems, like the rare ones sold at the market. Perhaps he wasn't real at all. Perhaps he was a magical figurine come to life.

I went on like this for two days, imagining him being this and that. Creating different stories that could explain where he came from and what made him so beautiful. I'd thought he'd only be a fantasy—a magical memory for me to hold in my heart until I eventually got married one day. Maybe it would become one of those fleeting yet powerful moments in one's life that they cannot possibly forget and wouldn't dream of losing.

But then, to my surprise, I came home from tutoring the Welkins' children and was immediately met with Mags rushing out of the house and telling me someone came to call on me. I gave her a peculiar look. "Me? Is it someone Father knows?"

She shook her head and clung to my arm as she led me into the house. "Nooo," she said with a giggle. "Wait until you see who I'm talking about."

I stopped and looked at her. "No. You cannot be serious—"

"I am! Now hurry up before he gets terribly bored and leaves altogether."

The excitement overwhelmed me, but I tried to stay composed. Women are supposed to play aloof in times like these, correct? That's what I'd been told anyway. Whether or not I'd accomplished such composure is beyond me because as soon as I saw him, my jaw nearly dropped to the floor.

Cassius Laurent was sitting in my drawing room, eagerly awaiting my arrival with his hat on his lap and his eyes out the window. My heart fluttered in my chest, but I remained composed.

Apparently, he had never heard of such playful composure because as soon as he noticed me standing in the doorway, he lit up like a candle and said, "Ah! Miss Duncan! I was so worried you wouldn't come."

"Why ever would you think such a thing?" I asked, smiling coyly. I knew a trick or two of how these things were done, and I was extraordinarily grateful for it, too.

"Well, it's just been a while since I'd called on you."

"You . . . called on me?" I looked to my father, who was sitting at a desk in the corner of the room. He shrugged and shook his head like he honestly didn't know what the man was talking about.

Mr. Laurent got to his feet. "Yes, well, I had sent someone out with an invitation to have you over to my family's estate, but perhaps the card went missing somewhere. Regardless, I hurried down here when I didn't hear any word from you. I hope that's all right."

I nodded, a stupid smile likely all over my face.

"Wonderful," he said, "I also wanted to deliver this to you." He handed me a package, which looked more like a blue silk purse than actual wrapping. I untied the ribbon wrapped around it and pulled out a divinely soft piece of cloth that took my breath away as soon as I laid eyes on it. I almost immediately recognized the beautiful thing of intricately woven pastels. It was the scarf I'd been eying in the market—the one far too lavish for my poor pocketbook.

"You bought this for me?" I asked, running my fingers over the soft fabric.

His smile adorably dimpled as he nodded. "You seemed so fond of it. I simply could not resist." I was still marveling at the stitchwork when he walked closer to me. "Miss Duncan, would you do me the honor of accompanying me to the park? With a chaperone, of course." I looked into his eyes, captivated. I couldn't even speak. So I just nodded. He smiled even wider and said, "Lovely. Well, then let us arrange this as soon as possible, so we do not have to wait any longer. I cannot wait one more moment."

I was floating on the clouds for the rest of the evening. He and I arranged things rather quickly and went out with a chaperone within the hour. I think that was Mother's doing. She was positively ecstatic about the whole thing.

He and I talked and laughed all evening. He is so hilarious, and beyond charming. I was so comfortable. I had never had so much fun in my life.

He told me he would only be here for a short while, though. He's here to help his family with the festival. I found out he is part of the fabulously wealthy Ashdown family. A somewhat distant relative, I assume, as he has a different surname, and I've never seen him before now. I wasn't sure, though, and I forgot to ask. I was so swept up in him and in every word that came from his lips.

He says he will call on me again tomorrow, and I don't think I've ever been so happy.

Now, please excuse me while I dream of him until I fall asleep. For the first time in my life, I think my dreams will be dull compared to my reality.

Until next time,
Claire

I read the words over and over again to ensure I'd read them correctly. *Cassius Laurent is part of the Ashdown family.* My mother was so casual with the fact. Well, she was elated, I supposed. She was so young and excited. This handsome man came in and swooped her up, giving her extravagant gifts and charming her out of her wits. It was probably a sparkling dream to her.

I chewed on my lip, thinking the inevitable question that kept repeating in my mind: *What about my father?* The events in the journal took place mere months before I was conceived. Why was there no mention of my father?

She was so wrapped up in this elusive man—a man who was apparently part of this family. I remembered William's words from earlier; he'd said his extended family would be walking through their halls in a matter of weeks. Perhaps Cassius Laurent would be one of them.

I decided that waiting would be my best course of action in discovering who he was, if things didn't become clear in the remaining entries. But that still left the question of my father.

Maggie always told me his name was Richard Blake and that he was a warm, loving, protective man who adored my mother more than anything. He died of influenza before I was born, and my mother died giving birth to me. Maggie said losing my father took too much out of her body and that she couldn't handle childbirth on top of it.

That was all I was told—all I ever knew about him. I was never even shown a picture of him. I'd never seen a picture of my mother, either. Maggie just told me she looked like me with golden hair. Still, I craved to know what she looked like. I yearned to learn more about her, but Maggie would cry whenever I'd ask. Sometimes she'd snap at me and tell me to stop asking so much.

It was clear that they'd been close, especially by these journal entries. It must have been devastating for her to lose my mother. I tried working my questions in as naturally and inconspicuously as possible when Maggie was in a good state, and sometimes I'd get answers. Sometimes I wouldn't. But she never said much about my father. I knew nothing of him, really.

A rock formed in my stomach as I looked back at the journal. Fear crept up my spine. Perhaps my father was not a person named Richard Blake after all.

Maybe the man Maggie claimed was my father never existed at all.

If that were the case, why would she have lied to me? Why would she have taken me so far away from her hometown and given me his last name?

None of it made any sense. Hopefully, it was all my own musings—my mind getting carried away.

Hopefully.

Chapter Thirteen

As Molly prepared me for supper, I couldn't stop thinking of Cassius. Of my mother and the possibility that my father wasn't who I thought he was. I just couldn't imagine Maggie would do something like giving me a false name. A false history.

The feeling in my stomach only worsened the more I thought about it—that this theory aligned with Maggie's curt answers to my questions throughout my adolescence. How cryptic she was about my past and where I came from, and how she tried to shield me from the world.

What happened to her? That was the question I'd had my entire life and never learned the answer to. And now I had even more questions I might never know the answers to.

Molly celebrated how beautiful I looked, moving me closer to the mirror so I could see for myself. I smiled politely but didn't pay much attention to what she'd done. I knew her efforts were a form of laborious art for her, and I wished I could appreciate it more, but so much more weighed on my mind that I couldn't give her a proper reaction.

Everything I'd ever known might have been based on a series of lies. I'd always known that secrets and trauma were a large part of Maggie's background, but maybe it was beyond what I'd comprehended. Perhaps she'd hidden things from me to protect herself from the pain but, in the process, made things worse.

Her past had gored her with so many wounds that they'd always bled onto me, causing so much pain in my life she probably never realized. It took me years to discover I was covered in that blood. But even now, I wasn't sure what to do about it.

Maybe she'd thought the truth was worse than the pain.

My fingernails dug into my palms as I walked down the stairs. I tried not to think about all of it. I needed to focus on supper. I was curious about the journal and craved more answers, but I also needed to do my job. Part of that job was making appearances and being a gracious house guest. And part of it was to uncover what was going on in this very house.

I took steady breaths as I walked into the dining room. Everyone was seated as they had been the night before. I was a little more comfortable in my skin today, though, but I couldn't figure out why.

William was seated across from my spot next to Evelyn. He had changed into a new suit, which was more tightly fitted than the one he'd worn earlier, and it looked even more flattering. It was hard not to stare, but I didn't want to give him the satisfaction, so I just made my way to the empty seat.

As much as I wished I could have said I didn't want to see him there, I could not. He intrigued me. His countenance changed so drastically at different points over the last day and a half, each one a mystery to me. He was arrogant and spoiled, then scared and guarded, and something in between. It was strange.

So, I didn't mind seeing him this time, so long as he behaved himself.

"Miss Blake, how wonderful to see you," Evelyn said in her usual cheery voice.

"It's lovely to see you, too," I said. One of the footmen came by with a silver tray full of food, tipping it so I could take the steamed vegetables inside.

"Tell me, Miss Blake, should I inquire Molly to come to you a little earlier each evening?"

I frowned. "I'm sorry, but I don't understand," I said. Evelyn winced, perhaps realizing she should have pulled me aside after supper and asked such a personal question away from everyone else's ears. She opened her mouth to speak but stopped, clearly still contemplating how to word her next question.

"What my lovely wife is trying to say is that we are eager to see you join us for supper at the same time as everyone else," Charles said, motioning to the servants to commence with serving the next course. Evelyn shot him a look, then looked back at me apologetically.

"I'm so sorry," she said. "I did not mean to offend you. I just wanted to know if it would be helpful. I want you to be at ease and feel free to take as long as you'd like to get ready for our evening meal. I was just unsure if Molly was coming at an early enough time for you to make it here with everyone else."

"I assure you it's quite all right," I said, "though I can ask Molly to come a bit earlier so I can greet you all in a more timely manner. I'm sorry I've been late; she just loves making me up. I must be a living doll to her." She laughed as she plucked food from one of the footmen's trays.

"This is exactly why such serious positions as ours should be done by men," Mr. Tucker said, taking a bite of his potatoes before his plate was even back on the table. I shot him a glare but soon regretted it. His ghoulish smirk ruined my appetite. "Women all just want to focus on their ribbons and the latest developments in rouge."

Mr. Day laughed heartily, Mr. Reelsey soon joining in their merriment, which disappointed me. I'd hoped he'd be different than the others. I rolled my eyes and began cutting into my steak. Mr. Tucker just wanted to get a rise out of me. Best not give him what he wanted.

"How was working with William today, Miss Blake?" Charles asked, taking a sip of his drink. Even from across the table his eyes were so noticeably blue they looked unreal. "I hope he was not too intolerable." He and William exchanged a glance, with Charles trying not to laugh. William did not look amused.

"It was actually quite pleasant," I said, suppressing a smile as I took a bite of the steak. "Though I have to admit I was rather surprised by the development." I cast the same teasing grin at my working partner that his brother-in-law just had, but William cracked a smile when I did it.

"Miss Blake was quite the partner herself," William said, breaking his gaze on me and looking at Charles. "I was in awe at her suggestions." He looked back at me with a smile, and I couldn't tell if he was teasing me or not.

"Really?" Mr. Tucker said with a snort. "Well, I suppose any good suggestion made by a woman is awe-inducing indeed." He chuckled and cut into his food.

"Do not address Miss Blake with such casualties and in such an insulting manner," William said, a loud edge to his voice. Mr. Tucker looked up from his plate in shock. He gaped at William in confusion until he finally laughed.

"Don't concern yourself with tryin' to defend the honor of someone like *Miss Blake*, your lordship. Her reputation is lost in the mud at this point." He laughed again, but William didn't find it funny at all. His hand gripped his knife until his knuckles whitened.

"Do you truly believe the nonsense that comes out of your mouth?" William said, his voice nearly rattling the silverware. Evelyn gasped but said nothing. She was likely on William's side in the matter, but she didn't seem to appreciate the way he was handling it. Her husband just watched, expressionless and motionless, ready for the next move.

Mr. Tucker scoffed. "Why are you defending her? Do you pity her?"

"No, I'm afraid that slight has been assigned to you, Mr. Tucker."

I couldn't help but laugh—a loud involuntary laugh. Mr. Tucker ground his teeth. "Do you not see how unseemly her behavior is?"

William leaned forward. "What is so unseemly about laughing?"

"Not just laughing. That impolite sound she made when she laughed. Not to mention her unladylike retorts. Have you not seen how she treats me? Do you not know that she raised her voice to me?"

"As a matter of fact, I know exactly how she's treated you, and I believe she has shown you far more courtesy than you deserve."

I bit my lip, fighting off a smile. I knew I shouldn't be enjoying this so much, but I couldn't help it. And I was surprised. Why was William so fiercely defending such a scandalous creature as myself?

"Why you—"

"Gentlemen, I believe that is enough," Evelyn interjected, her hand out in front of her to silence them. "Why don't we all just enjoy the food prepared for us?" She shot William a look, but he didn't seem to notice. He just picked up his fork and knife and began cutting his food once more.

"I'm a guest in this house. I will not stand to be treated like this," Mr. Tucker said.

William sighed and placed his utensils on the table. Looking up, he said, "Miss Blake is also a guest in this house. So if you would like to *stay* a guest in this house, you shall address her with the same courtesy as you would anyone else. Actually, allow me to rephrase that. I'd like you to show her courtesy at the edge of your wildest comprehension. Nothing less will do." He glared at the man, showing that he was not joking in the slightest.

Mr. Tucker bobbed in his seat like a fidgeting toddler who was deciding whether or not to continue his bad behavior. Finally, he nodded, his tongue stuck firmly to the inside of his cheek. His eyes fell onto his plate, and he resumed eating, much more politely than before. He didn't say anything for the rest of the evening.

William avoided my gaze whenever I looked up from my plate, but when I'd turn to speak to Evelyn or looked down at my own plate, I noticed him sneaking glances my way. And I'd be lying if I said I hadn't been sneaking glances his way the entire meal as well.

When we were all finished, Evelyn asked if we'd like any dessert. Mr. Reelsey eagerly agreed, but Mr. Tucker seemed to have lost his appetite—well-deserved revenge. I thanked her but declined as well. I wanted to get back to my mother's journal.

Evelyn then asked us all if we'd like to proceed to one

of the adjacent rooms for some sort of entertainment she'd organized for the evening. I knew I needed to be a good guest, but today I had to draw a line and allow myself what I wanted. *I have only been here a couple of days and already I'm sliding in my courtesies*, I started to think but then immediately caught the thought before it went too far. *No, this is different.*

This wasn't discourtesy. It was a unique circumstance. There was an unusual and important issue that I needed to deal with. I'd be a gracious house guest during the days and weeks that followed, but tonight, I needed the time for myself.

"I'm sorry, but I must decline, Lady—I mean . . . Evelyn. I am just so very worn out after all of our work outside today. I assure you I won't decline the next time you so thoughtfully arrange entertainment for us."

She nodded, a sad smile on her lips. "I understand. I do hope you join us next time."

"Of course," I said, bowing and turning around before she could change her mind. I didn't think she would, though. She seemed disappointed, but she didn't strike me as someone to fight about it.

Some of the servants began ushering the others out of the dining room, while others picked up dirty dishes and scurried away with them. I swiftly dodged each one of them until I accidentally bumped into Charles on my way out.

"Oh! I'm so sorry, Lord Bower. Forgive me. I mean, Charles. My apologies."

"Oh, no, please. Forgive *me*. I am too tall for my own good and sometimes don't look where I'm going." He smiled at me, a dimple forming on one cheek. My body went cold. I looked back up into his eyes and almost jumped at the color. That same brilliance that was awe-inducing from across the table was unsettling up close. Was it that unsettling before?

I bowed slightly and said, "I should be on my way." I tucked a loose curl behind my ear and rushed by him. I *must be seeing things. He didn't have dimples before, did he? And those eyes . . . I must be mistaken. I'm worried too much.*

I was too lost in my own head to realize I had taken a wrong turn at some point. My hands flopped to my sides and I let out a groan. "Why do I keep letting myself get lost? Seriously." I kept walking until I found a set of stairs.

I stopped. I knew these stairs. I walked more slowly, mindful of each step, making each one as silent as possible.

"The stairs to the Ashdown family's wing . . ." My hand slid up the banister, and my body followed. With each step, my heart pounded harder. *I really shouldn't be doing this*, I thought, but still I continued. William's terrified face from earlier popped into my mind, but that only made me want to journey down these halls even more. I had to know what was bothering him. What he didn't want me to see.

That immediate rush of cold fell upon me again. The closer I got to the mural, the more it seeped into my skin. But I kept going. I let my hand fall over the images decorated so intricately on the oddly designed stretch of painting. The strip of art started halfway down the wall and wrapped around to the adjacent one. I followed it, turning the corner and stepping even deeper into the wing than I had before.

I listened for any signs of the family, but I knew they were all downstairs. Guilt soured my stomach, but I kept going. There was something down there I had to see.

But as I journeyed down the hall, all I saw was the mural—the mural and a few rooms. The strangest part about it was that there were only rooms on the right side of this portion of the wing. There were five doors all lined up in a row, and on the left, there was nothing but the mural striping the middle section of the wall.

The images in the mural were even stranger. The too-beautiful characters depicted in the painting were at war, surrounded by symbols on a clouded backdrop as if battling in the sky. I looked at it more closely, trying to decipher whatever message was behind it, but none of it made any sense.

It was a peculiar piece of art, if one could call it that. While it looked beautiful at first glance, the more I studied it, the less sense it made and the more disturbed I became.

I sighed. "Well, I suppose I can't go into their rooms and look around, so I should just go—" My evening glove snagged onto something on the wall. I hadn't even remembered Molly giving me gloves, or putting them on for that matter.

I am obviously very out of it. I need some rest. I pulled my glove off and plucked it from the wall. Then I saw it. A crease. A thin line sprouting from the floor and snaking partway up the wall. And a latch, cleverly hidden behind a dark chariot painted on the mural.

I blinked a few times to make sure it was what it looked like. When I couldn't deny that it was indeed the latch to a door, I pulled my other glove off and tied them to my dress with one of the garment's ribbons and let them hang from my hip. I pulled the latch up and tugged on it.

Nothing happened.

I pushed myself against it and tugged again. This time something jiggled. I tried again, pushing up against the wall before pulling the latch out toward me, and then it opened.

A hidden door peeled away from the wall, exposing a narrow set of wooden stairs. The temperature dropped even lower, and goosebumps pimpled my skin. I stepped into the narrow entrance and closed the door behind me.

I thought I'd be shrouded in darkness, but a light shone

up ahead from a small window. I followed it and soon escaped the tunnel-like stairway and entered into an oval-shaped room with nothing in it but a mirror. An eerily beautiful mirror with a large, finely crafted frame and intricate carvings of various symbols etched in each corner.

The room itself looked like the inside of a carnival tent. The floor's bright colors came alive beneath my feet. The tiles were glossy and rich in color, as if created from stained glass, and were made even more brilliant by the light pooling in from the window above.

The symbols on the mirror would have been easy to miss had I not been so carefully studying the mural outside. I moved in closer, reaching out to touch the frame. It was smooth and must have been made of the finest wood the family had at their disposal. Or whoever it first belonged to.

I crouched down and studied the symbols, only to find that they were actually all the same, just positioned differently. I grazed the carved lines with my fingertips. "I've seen this symbol before," I whispered. "But where?"

I moved my hand away and looked at it more closely. The more I looked at it, the more unsettled I became. "Why can't I remember?" My eyes stayed fixed on it, studying each line and which way it moved and curved around the others.

A great *GONG* erupted through the room and caused me to stumble to the ground. I gasped and looked up, worried I'd been discovered, but no one was there.

Catching my breath, I assured myself that there must be a clock somewhere nearby, and maybe the room had thinner walls than it appeared. Regardless, I needed to leave before the Ashdowns returned to their wing. If they found me, I could lose everything I'd been working toward.

I would let Mary and Agnes and all the other women in Brakerton Heights down, and possibly more. I couldn't take risks like this here. Curiosity really can kill the cat.

I got to my feet and looked at the mirror one last time before taking my leave. But something in its reflection made me stop. "Hello?" I walked closer, reaching out and touching the glass. I peered into it for a good minute or two, but all I saw was myself. "I really must be seeing things now," I said, dropping my hand from the mirror and turning back around. "I should go to bed."

I made my way quietly down the stairs. I listened at the door. When I heard no movements or voices, I quietly exited the strange hidden room.

I raced to my room as quietly but as inconspicuously as I could. I thought it best to forget everything outside of the journal today. I should forget about Charles' familiar features and everything else.

I tried to dump it all out of my mind, but I couldn't shake what I saw. Even long after I'd gotten ready for bed and was wrapped in my sheets, I could not fall asleep. I could not pry the image from my mind. It happened so quickly, but I swore I saw it.

For a fleeting moment, I swore I saw the image of a man in that mirror—a face staring straight at me—before disappearing like smoke.

Chapter Fourteen

When I woke up the next morning, Molly was already there, insisting I have breakfast with everyone else and that she help me get ready. I'd told her that I would but that although I appreciated her efforts to help me in the morning and knew that it was the "proper" thing to do, I would much prefer getting ready on my own. I told her she could help me in the evenings before dinner, especially because I would have been working outside all day and could use the help to make my hair look right again.

I tried to explain that I was used to being alone and could use the mornings to gather my thoughts and composure for the day. And while this was true, I mostly wanted the time alone to read my mother's journal—and if I were to be *completely* honest, it was also so I could keep my corset as loose as possible while I worked outside. Ever since I'd arrived, Molly had molded my body into the tiniest corsets and dresses I'd ever seen, let alone worn. If I were required to work, I'd need to be able to breathe.

"Why don't we just try this out and see how it goes?" I said. She looked a bit stung, but I assured her it had nothing to do with her. In the end, she reluctantly agreed and I told her I'd see her downstairs. Though I was grateful for the reprieve from the more bone-crushing ensembles Molly put me in, I would miss the way she dressed me up. She could make me look like a diamond instead of a lump of coal.

But I'd have to let that be a lower priority right now. Why did I need to look like a diamond here anyway? When William's face surfaced in my mind, my eyebrow twitched. I didn't care what he thought. I wasn't here for him.

I sat on the chair at my vanity, debating on whether I should get dressed or read an entry of my mother's journal. I wasn't sure I had time to do both without Molly coming back to check in on me. After I thought about it, I decided it was best for me to get dressed first and then read until I absolutely had to go. That way, Molly wouldn't question what I was doing up here for so long.

I had never put on a dress more quickly in my life. I pinned my hair up in the most convenient way possible while still looking presentable. I might have missed a few strands here and there, but I managed to get it done more quickly than I ever had before.

Reaching in the drawer to the vanity, I grabbed hold of my mother's book, but before I could take it out, a knock sounded at the door. I grumbled in annoyance before taking a deep breath and calling out, "Yes, please come in."

"Hi, Miss," Molly said, letting herself in. "I'm sorry to disturb you, but Lord Ashdown is waiting for you downstairs."

The mention of his name made something in me skip. My hand hovered over the journal's cover, partially frozen in the drawer, as I weighed my options. Why did he want me so early?

I took my hand from the drawer and closed it. When I turned around, I saw that Molly had a lone tea biscuit in her hands. It was even larger than the last one and looked just as good. "I brought this for you so you could hurry and meet him more quickly."

"Why do I have to hurry on William's account?" I huffed, sinking my teeth into the biscuit. It was so deliciously soft and warm I tried not to make any sounds of delight as I ate it. Parts of it flaked off onto my dress, and I brushed it off as I went on, bits of biscuit still in my mouth. "Why is he up so early anyway?" I swallowed angrily and took another bite.

"Well, I'm not exactly sure why he's calling on you so early, but I do know he seems excited by something."

I swallowed a chunk of biscuit. "Excited? What do you mean?" And 'calling on me'? Why did she word it like that?

She played with one of her braids as she thought. "Well . . . I don't know how to explain it. I could just tell. He seemed happy."

"Oh? Did he mention what is making him so happy?" I did my best to look indifferent, but Molly gave me a mischievous grin.

"No, but I'm sure it has something to do with you."

I could feel the heat rising in my cheeks. "I-I don't know what you mean. Why would he be happy on my account?"

She shrugged, that same impish smile painted on her face. "I don't know, Miss Blake, but he was positively beaming and asking if he could call on you early."

I picked at the rest of my biscuit, still feigning

indifference. "Well, I wish you had told me that he was asking to begin with and not that he was expecting me. The two are completely different, and I was hoping to take longer getting ready on my own this morning."

Molly rushed over and held out her hand. "Come on, I'll take that. You should go." She flapped her hand, motioning for the biscuit. I sighed and gave her my half-eaten breakfast. Standing up, I turned to the mirror. I looked a mess. What was I thinking getting ready without Molly? My eyes flickered to the drawer. I looked at it for a long moment before sighing and giving up on the idea of reading any more of it before working today.

"All right. I suppose I'll go if he's truly that worked up." I absently wiped the crumbs off my hands. Molly nodded, giggling to herself as she led me out the door. I didn't know why she was so giddy. I wasn't going out on some romantic excursion with him.

As we walked down the stairs, I noticed she was still quite giddy over the matter, so I decided to set the record straight. "William and I are working partners, Molly. There are no feelings between us. I hope you know that. We have just been forced together by bad luck."

She nodded, but she was in front of me, so I couldn't see her face. "Sure, Miss. I'm sure he had no part in the pairings and that he isn't excited to see you—that he's just excited to work today. Because walking around outside and talking about festival plans is so fascinating to him." She turned to flash a sly smile at me. "Besides, I never said there were feelings between the two of you. You're the one who said it."

I was about to say something when I saw William at the bottom of the stairs. "Don't say anything further, Molly. Please," I whispered. When she didn't respond and we got closer to William, panic swirled in my stomach. "*Molly*."

His eyes were on me now, so I couldn't plead to her anymore. And when my gaze settled on him, I found it harder to think at all. His eyes stayed on mine, and although he looked just as frustratingly good as he usually did, he didn't seem very excited at all. He wasn't even smiling.

"Here she is, Lord Ashdown," Molly said with a bow. "I'm sure she is very excited to see you. She rushed getting ready so she could come down sooner." Heat burned my cheeks even more than before, and I wanted to swat at her. Before I could say or do anything, though, William stepped and offered me a smile.

"Will you please join me outside, Miss Blake? It's a fine day, and I have some exciting news." His dark eyes shone brightly, crinkling at the corners. Maybe he *was* excited.

He held out his arm, but I didn't know if I should take it. Molly was still looking at us, and I didn't want to confirm her suspicions. "Thank you, but I think I'll just stroll beside you, if you don't mind." I tried not to sound rude when I said it, but he looked stung all the same. He tried to conceal it. Not very well, though.

Retracting his arm, he said, "Of course. How could I forget? You told me rather strongly yesterday, so I won't offer it anymore. I was just trying to be polite." The icy edge to his voice cut right through me.

"I know. I'm sorry. Let's . . . just go outside."

We walked through the main doors of the mansion, but I could barely stay present. The questions that had formed over the last day flurried through my mind like a wild storm. When I glanced over at William, I couldn't help but remember the wild expression on his face when he stopped me from going farther down that hallway. And then there was that strange room with the mirror. Was that what he didn't want me to see? Or was there more down that unnervingly cold wing that he wanted me to stay away from?

"Okay, Miss Blake, here we are." He put his hands on his hips and looked out at the field beyond. We were farther away from the house than we'd been the day before, and there was a pile of lumber in the distance, but other than that I didn't see much difference, let alone anything exciting.

"Am I supposed to see something?" I asked, still scanning the area.

He laughed. "Not really. I just wanted to show you some of the materials we will be working with."

I turned to him, confused. "Materials . . . we will be working with?"

"Yes, ma'am. To go along with the exciting news." He looked at me with the beginnings of a smile, his hands still on his hips. "Evelyn has approved your request to work on the structures for the festival."

"Really?" I said, a smile breaking across my face. I looked back onto the field with new eyes and walked over to the lumber for closer inspection.

"Yes, I am very much telling the truth." He laughed again as he followed close behind. I knelt on the grass near the lumber and ran my fingers along the smooth wood. I wondered what type of instruments and tools they had at their disposal, though I assumed they'd have it all. Their mansion was the most massive building I'd ever seen, and judging by their gramophone and other cutting-edge household items, nothing seemed out of reach for them.

"Are you . . . happy, Miss Blake?" he asked. I turned around. His dark eyes were soft and wanting, as if relying on the hope that he'd accomplished his goal.

"Yes, of course. Thank you, William." His smile widened, and as the heat crept up my face again, I quickly turned away. "And please, as I've said before, call me

Caroline."

We spent the afternoon plotting where everything would go and deciding which tools we'd need and how many workers would be required to ensure everything went smoothly.

It was so nice to get my mind working like this again. To prepare for my hands getting dirty and my muscles working like they used to. Just thinking of what everything might look like and envisioning what I wanted was like a dream to me. I couldn't believe my luck—I would get to help design the booths and construct them, and I'd get to learn how to use tools that were far out of my price range. Tools that would make my job a lot easier.

The excitement of everything was more than enough to distract me from my worries, at least somewhat, but I still couldn't stop thinking about my mother's journal entries. And about the eerie chill of the Ashdowns' wing, and of that strange room. That peculiar mural. How was it possible that upon coming here, instead of unraveling secrets and exposing that there was no curse or anything to be afraid of, I was met with more mysteries?

William could obviously tell that I was distracted because there were many times throughout our work that he asked if I was all right. Each time I assured him that I was, but he didn't seem convinced. He didn't press the matter, though. We just continued working until the sun was ready to set.

"Well, I think that should about do it for today. What do you think?" he asked, letting out a satisfying sigh of a day well spent.

I didn't hear him at first. I was thinking of the strange mirror. It looked centuries old, and the symbols engraved on the frame . . . I swore I'd seen them before.

"Miss Bla—I mean, Caroline, is everything all right?"

I snapped myself back into the present, all of his words finally registering in my mind. "Yes, I'm sorry. I have a lot on my mind today."

"I can tell," he said with a half-laugh. "Is there anything I can assist you with?"

Yes, as a matter of fact, there is, I wanted to say, but I knew I couldn't. But I craved answers to my questions—answers to why that mirror was hidden away and why no one was supposed to go near it, if that truly was the case. It was the only thing that made sense. Unless they were hiding something else up there.

"No, I'm okay. Perhaps I just need some rest."

"Okay. Well, I'm here if you need anything." I felt a quick stab of guilt. I wasn't supposed to be snooping around his wing, no matter how curious I was. No matter how much I wanted to know the truth. And here he was being so kind to me.

William was softening to me. Something I could tell didn't happen often. His rigid demeanor and frequent bouts of impertinence told me he was used to keeping others out. It was something I both understood and was curious about.

He and I didn't often see eye to eye, but when we did, I could tell there was something beyond that prickly exterior he so ardently tried to shield himself within. Like an impenetrable suit of armor hiding his true nature. He even went out of his way to make my wish become a reality in preparing for the festival beyond what I'd been assigned.

But I hardly knew him. *He could be up to something.* The words leaked through the cracks in my second guesses, as if a voice somewhere inside me told me I was stupid to believe I could trust him after so short a time.

Everything I'd ever experienced in life told me I shouldn't trust him and that it was okay to keep searching for answers, even in his wing. I had to look out for myself. That's what Maggie would have urged me to do anyway. He and his family might be hiding something. I had only known him for two or three days. Who knew what he was really like? He didn't exactly seem like the warm and fuzzy type.

Still, there was something about him that drew me in. Something about him that was so familiar. In the brief windows where he'd peek out of that spiky shell of his, I could see glimpses of what he might actually be like. That maybe he was a little like me.

But I could just be seeing things. That wasn't such a rare occurrence these days.

No matter how much I convinced myself that spying on William's family was a good idea, I still couldn't help feeling a little guilty. I'd have to push through it, though. What if something dangerous truly was lurking down those halls? I couldn't give up such an investigation just because I met some handsome man who may or may not be someone I could relate to.

When I made it to my room, Molly was in there changing the sheets. I had a brief moment of panic when I saw her going through my blankets. Where had I put that journal?

"Molly, how long have you been in here?" I didn't mean for it to sound so interrogative, so I quickly added, "I am just terribly worn out and would like to rest before supper." I forced an awkward smile, but she just looked at me, puzzled, before continuing to take the sheets off my bed.

"I have only been in here a few minutes, Miss. Mrs. Wells reminded me that I was supposed to have changed your bedsheets already, but I'd completely forgotten. My apologies for that. I am still not used to this position."

"Weren't you a lady's maid before this?" I asked,

walking over to my vanity table to check for the journal.

"Oh, no, Miss. I tended to the children in our village, but I never held a job as a lady's maid before. Getting the chance to work here has been like a miracle to me. I'm grateful for the opportunity." She smiled with such sheer joy that I wondered what her life had been like before this. She seemed to run on sunshine and happy thoughts. A foreign concept to me, but an intriguing one nonetheless.

I wondered if she'd worked all her life and was grateful for the work out of desperation, or if she'd lived a comfortable life with adoring parents and an adoring grandmother.

As if feeling her presence in my mind, Mrs. Wells entered the room, holding an empty basket.

"Molly, have you—ah, Miss Blake. I didn't expect you to be back already. How was your day with Lord Ashdown?" The older woman smiled, but something was holding her back. Like she had heard something awful about me and was trying to conceal it. That couldn't be the case in this situation, though. I had nothing to hide.

"It was very productive, thank you."

"Lovely," she said, then turned her attention to her granddaughter. "Molly, be sure to hurry up and get those sheets to the laundry room so you can come back and help Miss Blake into her dress for supper. I brought you a basket."

"Yes, ma'am," the young girl said, pushing one of her braids back. It slid behind her shoulder like a golden snake. She picked up the basket and tossed the used sheets inside. "I'll see you in a minute," she said to me, then offered a small bow and left the room.

Mrs. Wells turned to do the same, but I caught hold of her wrist before she could leave. "Wait! Um, Mrs. Wells, do you have a moment?" She looked at me like I'd just slapped her. I let go of her wrist and apologized. "I'm sorry. I just . . . I need to ask you something."

She lifted a brow. "Yes?"

I tucked a loose piece of hair behind my ear and pulled out a small leaf that had been tangled inside. I wondered how long it'd been in there as I shook it onto my vanity table and cleared my throat. "I, um, I wanted to ask if you knew someone . . ."

Her face remained the same. "And whom might this person be?" She laced her fingers together and shifted her weight.

I looked at my hands and tried to figure out how to ask. I wasn't sure why I was so nervous, but I was practically sweating. "Do you know a man by the name of Cassius Laurent?" When I looked up, I nearly jumped. Her eyes were wide and her mouth had curled inward, as if she'd been stuck in the desert with nothing to drink.

"How do you know that name?" she asked, her voice low and grave. She seemed like a different person. A frightening person. She walked closer to me, her eyes at level with mine.

I didn't know what to say. I suddenly couldn't remember anything. My legs began to tremble, but I tried to keep still. "M-my mother."

"Your mother?"

"My mother's journal," I quickly clarified. "I read his name in my mother's journal."

She froze. "Your mother?" The lines on her forehead deepened as she took a moment to process this. "What is your mother's name, child?"

My mouth went dry, and anxiety climbed up my body and tugged on my chest, making it harder to breathe.

"What is your mother's name?" she asked again, her voice rising. Her eyes were wild and so close to mine.

The room felt smaller, the air thicker. "C-Claire Duncan," I said. As I said it, my legs gave out on me, and I fell gracelessly onto the floor before I could correct myself. "Er—Claire Blake."

I thought Mrs. Wells would do the normal thing in this type of situation and offer to help me to my feet, but she did no such thing. I supposed this wasn't a normal situation to find one's self in, though. But regardless of whatever social protocol would be appropriate in such a situation, she did nothing at all. She just stared at me as I got back to my feet.

I steadied myself against the bed and looked at her. With her a few feet away from me now, I could finally breathe. "What's wrong?" I asked. "Why do you need my mother's name? Who is this Cassius—"

"DON'T!" The old woman shouted as she turned and pointed at me like a scolding schoolteacher. "Don't speak that name to anyone. Do you understand me?"

The blood drained from my face. I could feel it practically dropping to my feet, leaving me speechless.

"Do you understand me?" she repeated, practically growling each word.

I nodded. As the blood slowly crept back up my body, I said, "O-oh okay . . . but why?"

Two maids suddenly laughed out in the hall. The two of us jumped but remained quiet, not so much as uttering a word until the young women were out of earshot.

Mrs. Wells looked at me sternly and whispered, "Just don't. Please. It's for your own good." The anger—or perhaps flustered shock—in her eyes soon dissipated. "I'm sorry, dear, but I can't say anything more than that. And it would be best if you never bring up the matter again. For your own sake."

With a look of quiet sadness in her eyes, she bowed and

turned to leave. But just before she walked out the door, she turned to me again and said, "By the way, where is your mother's journal now?"

Oh no. No no no. What have I done? "It's . . . I-I had it back at my old house. I couldn't find it by the time my aunt passed away, and I had to move on." The lie was clunky and bad. There was no way she would believe it. But I had to try. I couldn't risk losing the journal now.

She watched me carefully. Worried my face might reveal my lie, I added, "So, I'm not sure where it is anymore. Something just made me suddenly remember the name." I laughed uncomfortably, hoping she'd leave so I could breathe easy.

Her eyes narrowed. "Yes, well, all the same, don't speak of this again. All right?"

"Yes, ma'am," I said, though the words barely made it past my chapped lips. My voice was hoarse.

Without another word, she left, closing the door behind her.

I breathed a heavy sigh of relief and laid back on my bare bed. Even in the now comfortable quiet, I couldn't be completely at ease. Even though she'd left the room, Mrs. Wells was still very much with me. Her face was burned into my mind, and I saw her when I closed my eyes. The way she looked at me, her gnarled finger pointing at me as if claiming me to be a witch.

As if I'd never been in such a position before. As if I had never been accused of sins I'd never committed, or that I was someone—or something—that I was not.

What had happened tonight? That sweet old woman was gone in a violent flash at the mention of Cassius' name. What did he do?

Where is your mother's journal?

Panic tore through me. I leapt from my bed and opened

the drawer to my vanity, checking for the journal. I let out a sigh of relief when I saw it there, unmoved and safe. I decided it would be best if I kept it with me from now on. Judging by the careful gaze Mrs. Wells shot my way when asking for its location, its information might be valuable. But why?

I opened it, its spine making a soft, satisfying crack. I leafed through it until I found the third entry. I was just about to sit back down and read it when a knock sounded at the door.

I jumped back to my bed and slid the journal beneath the mattress. "Y-yes? Who is it?"

"It's me, Miss," Molly said.

"Oh, come in." I stood up and adjusted my hair, hoping I didn't look half as frenzied as I felt.

The door opened, and Molly's prim face lit up the room. "Miss Blake, are you excited for supper? I heard there will be a delicious dessert. Lady Bower told me all about it."

I smiled. "Yes, Lady Bower is kind, isn't she? She makes me feel very welcome. She's very warm."

"I completely agree," she said, "though I wonder what she got into a fight about with Lord Ashdown earlier."

"What?" I stood up and walked to the wardrobe, where Molly was sifting through possible dresses for my evening attire. "What are you talking about?"

"When I was on my way back to your room from the laundry, I heard them shouting. I was very surprised. I'd never heard Lady Bower shout before."

"What did they say? Did you hear anything?"

"Not really, but I did hear that William said he'd be gone for the rest of the night."

Something in my chest spasmed. "Are you sure William will be gone? What did he say?"

She pulled out a long brown dress made entirely of silk

and embroidered with gems and roses made of dark ribbon. "I'm sure," she said as she held the dress up to me. "He said something like 'I know what I'm doing, Evelyn! Leave me alone!' or something. Maybe not the 'leave me alone' part, actually. Not word-for-word, I mean. I did hear him say he knew what he was doing. He was very furious as he said it. And then he said he needed to go somewhere. She didn't seem concerned by that part, though. She mostly just seemed distressed by whatever they'd been talking about before that."

I frowned. I let Molly dress me as her words repeated in my mind. I couldn't stop imagining it. William's face, flustered and angry. That pain that often flickered in his eyes. What had happened? Did she want him to do something for the festival that he didn't want to do? He'd said he knew what he was doing, so that couldn't be it.

"Are you ready, Miss Blake?" she asked, the freckles on her nose dancing like tiny stars. I turned to the mirror and smiled for her benefit.

"Yes, I am, Molly. Thank you. I look wonderful."

She giggled. "Hooray! I'm so glad you think so." She then proceeded to tell me what outfits complemented my looks the most and the discoveries she'd made for how to dress me in a way that accentuated my best features. She talked all the way to the dining room, where she left me to join the others.

When I caught sight of William's empty chair but the still very occupied chairs of the other reporters, I cringed. As I seated myself in my usual spot next to Evelyn, I saw her face light up at my presence. "Oh, Caroline! How lovely it is to see you! William told me you two had a wonderfully productive day."

"Yes, we did. Where is he, by the way?"

She blinked. "Well, he decided to take the night off."

"Oh, well . . ." I was about to politely inquire further when I caught Mrs. Wells passing through out of the corner of my eye. She shot me the same firm glance that she had in my room, and suddenly I was speechless.

"Are you all right?" Evelyn asked.

"Y-yes, I'm quite all right." I looked down at my empty plate and realized supper hadn't even begun. I would be here for at least an hour, and for whatever reason, the thought of being here without William to banter with made me loathe having to be here at all, especially if I'd have to make small talk with everyone else. Especially my fellow reporters.

This was my chance to feign illness and get out of one more awkward conversation today. More than anything, I needed answers. Reading my mother's journal was my top priority tonight.

I opened my mouth to speak when Charles lifted his glass of wine and said, "Miss Blake, be sure to enjoy yourself." His bright eyes peered at me from the other side of the table. "It's a specialty the chef has picked up from abroad. The wine is divine as well. Don't you agree, dear?" He looked to his wife, but something in his manner didn't seem quite right.

"Oh, yes. I am quite excited for the meal tonight," she said, turning to me with a smile. "Do you like duck?"

"I'm afraid I've never had it," I said, which launched her into an anecdote about the chef and his preparation of different types of poultry, and that this recipe was something she'd never tried before. As Charles had mentioned, he'd picked it up from abroad.

She kept talking, but I couldn't get myself to stay attentive to what she was saying. I could tell her husband was looking at me circumspectly. I tried not to look, but I could feel his stare getting heavier by the second.

In a brief, almost involuntary moment, my eyes flickered to him.

And there he was, watching me as he cut into his food, a dimple poking into his cheek.

Chapter *Fifteen*

Chaotic knocks erupted from the other side of the door. It was quick and frantic. The way someone knocks when running from a murderer, or a monster, and seeking somewhere safe to hide.

"Come in," Charles Bower called out as he continued scribbling on a piece of parchment at his desk. The door creaked, and the sound of footsteps clicked toward him.

He sifted through the papers, looking for one in particular. His fingers spread the options out in front of him. It had to be here somewhere.

"Lord Bower, I need to tell you something urgently."

The man kept looking at his papers. He picked up his quill and dabbed it in his pot of ink. "Oh? And what might that be, Mrs. Wells?" He wasn't always this casual with his staff, but he'd known the woman for decades. She was more of a friend than a housekeeper, which was precisely why he knew she had the tendency to worry. He tried to defuse her worries as much as possible, and today would be no different.

"I think I know the young woman here," she said.

His quill froze. "What do you mean?"

"The young woman. I think I know who she is."

His quill scratched at the paper, the ink soaking onto the desk underneath. His eyes landed on one of the papers next to it. He tried to play ambivalent, but he knew he couldn't anymore. He looked over at the grayed woman, hunched from years of hard work and distress. "All right. Who is she then?"

"I . . . I believe she is the daughter of Claire Duncan."

His body went rigid, and the chill that accompanied him both day and night somehow reached an even colder, more numbing temperature.

"Are you sure?" he said, staring straight ahead, avoiding the woman's eyes.

"Not entirely, but she looks just like her, doesn't she? And . . . she inquired about Cassius Laurent."

"What?" He stared at the woman in disbelief, but then his eyes went far away. As if his mind were reaching into a murky pot from long ago, hoping to find something in the dismal pool of things he wished he could forget. As she watched him, Mrs. Wells couldn't tell if he was terrified or excited by the news.

"How does she know that name?" he finally asked, his eyes landing on the orange trees beyond the window.

"She said she remembered reading about it in her mother's journal."

"Where is it now?" he snapped, still looking out the window.

"She said it's at her old home."

"Is she telling the truth?"

"I . . . I'm not sure."

"Well, we'll need to find out for certain."

He stood up, picked up his jacket, and then paused. "Has anyone gone into the cellar?" he asked. "Or our wing?"

"Not that I've noticed, but the cellar is rather hard to get into. I don't think you should worry—"

"Lock it up. Do anything you can to conceal the door and ensure that no one can get inside. You must hurry and do it straight away. Does Evelyn know any of this?"

The old woman shook her head.

"Good. Let's keep it that way."

Chapter Sixteen

The sky was dark, and the clouds were spinning in an angry spiral overhead. The grass was so damp that whenever I slid at a wrong angle, I slipped along the blades and nearly toppled head-first into one of the nearby trees. But no matter how many scratches or sprains I collected, I never stopped running.

The creature's growls and screeches grew closer—each one spiking fear higher and higher up my back and into my head. I couldn't think. I could only run and hope I wouldn't fall.

The snaps were louder now, the ear-piercing wails higher. The familiar clammy lick of its tongue wrapped around one of my ankles and jerked me back, knocking me off my feet. I hit the ground hard before it yanked me toward its gaping mouth and saw-like teeth.

I was so frightened I couldn't even scream. I just closed my eyes and waited to die.

But as I waited, nothing happened.

As soon as I felt the creature's hold release from my leg, I opened my eyes.

I was back in my bedroom at Ashdown Manor, my skin slick with sweat. I sat up with a start and caught my breath. My heart was still pounding from the nightmare—one almost identical to the one I'd had a few days prior.

What's going on? I wiped the sweat from my face and hugged my knees to my chest, slowly catching my breath. *I haven't had nightmares like these for years, and now they're returning in spades.* I wondered if my mind had gotten tired of holding back the demons and keeping them at bay for so long. Maybe now they were all spilling out like a breaking dam.

It didn't make sense, though. Why now?

I thought of the journal. Of the strange mirror room. "No. There are no such things as curses or monsters or demons. I know that now." I spoke the words out loud like a soothing mantra. If I said them out loud, the thoughts could have no power over me. I was sure of it. "Maggie was wrong. I'm just scared because of all the fuss. That's all."

I swung my feet around and slid off the bed. I needed to get ready for the day. I needed to keep my mind off of it. I needed to get the sounds out of my head.

I sat on the chair in front of my vanity and combed through my tangled hair. I took deep breaths with every stroke, pulling each curl back into long, soft waves, freeing them from the beads of sweat that had pilled along my hairline. "There's nothing to be afraid of. You are not a child anymore. Don't be—"

A loud roar thundered through the room. I let out a

small cry before realizing it had come from outside. Composing myself, I set the brush down. "It's just raining, Caroline. Get a hold of yourself."

I left the brush on the table and crawled back onto my bed, spreading the curtains open. Sure enough, it was raining. Hard. Storming, really. There was no way we'd be working today.

I watched the rain pour onto the lawn, soaking the newly stocked lumber. The wind was fierce, shaking the trees in all directions. I wondered if it was always this dreary in Brakerton Heights.

When a knock came at the door, I absently asked who it was, my eyes still glued to the window

"It's just me, Miss," Molly said, just as chipper as ever. Even the rain couldn't dampen her mood, it seemed.

"Come in," I said with a sigh, closing the curtains.

The young maid opened the door with a tray balanced on her hip. With her usual smile, she said, "I heard you hollerin' in here. Are you not used to the rain?"

I grimaced. "You heard that?"

She giggled. "It's all right. It *is* stormin' like the end of the world outside."

"So, is work off today then?"

She placed the tray of eggs, biscuits, and juice onto the bedside table. "I'd sure say so. You slept in an extra three hours as well."

"I did *what*?"

She laughed. "Oh, it's fine. You wouldn't have been able to do anything anyway, though I'm sure his lordship is quite disappointed he won't get to spend the day with you." She flashed me a wicked grin. I took a bite of my eggs and pretended not to notice.

"Perhaps. Although, he did leave last night, right? I don't know where he went, but I'm sure he isn't back already. Where could he have possibly gone for just one night?"

"Oh, he didn't leave overnight, Miss. I saw him come in through one of the back entrances last night. He looked exhausted, actually. Well, maybe sad. It was dark, so I couldn't tell for sure. He looked worn out, I can tell you that much."

I stared at my plate. The eggs wobbled as I poked them with my fork. I imagined William's solemn face as he walked down the hallway and trudged to his wing, the pain of his troubles weighing him down by the shoulders.

"Can I help you with anything else, Miss Blake?"

The fork fell from my hand and landed on the floor, bits of egg scattering at my feet. "No, I'm all right," I said, picking up the fork and pretending not to be as distracted as I clearly was. "I have breakfast and apparently a day to myself. You may go about any business you may have or take the day off yourself."

She tapped her fingers against her hip and eyed me carefully. "Okay . . . Well, if you need anything, please let me know. You can call for me with the bell next to the wardrobe." She pointed to the far corner of the room. Partially obscured by the wardrobe was a thin ribbon with a bell hanging from a piece of wood.

"Has that always been there?" I asked, getting up to get a closer look.

"Yes, but I forgot to tell you about it. Well, I didn't know about it, actually. My grandmother told me. We pushed the wardrobe to the side so you could access it more easily when you were at supper last night. I do apologize for any inconvenience not knowing about it might have caused."

I laughed. "It didn't inconvenience me at all. I'm actually not even sure I'll end up using it anyway, but thank you for letting me know. Be sure to tell your grandmother that I'm grateful for her help as well." The look Mrs. Wells gave me the night before returned, sending shivers down my spine.

I wasn't sure why she looked at me like that or what was going on, but I had a bad feeling about it. A bad feeling that made me wonder if my mother fit into some messy equation. An equation I knew nothing about other than how badly Mrs. Wells didn't want me to know about it.

And if she did fit into it, where did that leave me?

After another minute or so of me assuring Molly I'd be fine, she dismissed herself, and I pulled out the journal from beneath the mattress. I flipped through the first few pages and found the third entry:

November 14, 1856

I know I haven't written in over a month, but I have very good reasons for it. The first one being that I am so in love. With Cassius. With life. I never knew such happiness was possible. Does it feel like this for everyone? Feeling lighter than air and brighter than the sun? I feel like I'm going to burst at any given moment, especially when I'm with him.

We have been spending every day together, morning and evening. Even until the moon is ripe in the sky and it's scandalous for us not to part. We just can't help it. We are so smitten with each other.

Lucky for me, he doesn't have to go to work. We've spent the last few weeks working on his family's annual Harvest Festival. I was originally planning on going with Maggie, as I have every year, but this year she understood that I'd be going with Cassius. She knew how badly I wanted to go with him, so she endorsed the idea wholeheartedly and was completely fine with us going together. She acted as a chaperone for us, but she has been a "chaperone" for us for weeks now, and between you and I, she lets Cassius and I be alone all the time! She simply tells Mother and Father that she is going to chaperone us, but really she goes off to Geraldine's house, or to the library or some such place. Ah! I'm so lucky to have a sister like her.

Anyway, Cassius and I have had a marvelous time together, and at the festival, we played games, ate pastries, and laughed and danced the night away. But the very best part is that what I was hoping would happen DID happen! He proposed marriage to me! That's right, my lovely reader, I shall soon be Mrs. Cassius Laurent. I cannot wait! His aunt even offered to pay for the wedding gown. It will be a stunning gown of pure-white silk, lace trimmings, and frilled sleeves.

I cannot wait to . . .

When I turned the page, I noticed a small brown envelope tucked between the pages. I read the last few lines of my mother's entry before inspecting it.

. . . marry him. I shall be the happiest woman in the world! More details will follow soon.

Until next time,

Claire

I couldn't believe my eyes when I finished the entry. My mother was engaged to this man—smitten beyond words—and she was so risky with him. It was scandalous to be alone with a man even now, but so much more so when my mother was young. I was both amused and surprised at the thought. More importantly, though, was that one thing was now certain: Cassius was my father. He had to be.

I closed the journal and looked at the envelope. It had my mother's name on it in perfect handwriting. I opened it up, and something silver slithered down into my lap. It was a pendant. A small, silver pendant that resembled a key—its bow the curved shape of a heart. "How beautiful," I said, holding the necklace up by the silver chain.

I wondered if Cassius had made this for her or if he'd purchased it at a special shop, custom-made to show his devotion. I unhooked its clasp and placed the slinky chain around my neck. The pendant fell down my chest like dripping silver. "My mother wore this," I whispered to myself, feeling it beneath my fingertips. *And my father might have given it to her.* I smiled, imagining what my mother must have looked like when she received it. Did her eyes light up like stars?

I imagined what it must have felt like for her to have the love of her life give her something so precious and then place it around her neck. I wondered how often she wore it, and the thought brought a giddy smile to my lips. I now had something of her to keep with me always—something she wore that I could wear, too

Perhaps my luck in life was turning around after all.

I looked at what else was in the envelope and found a crisp, brown piece of parchment paper. It was a letter.

My dearest Claire,

It feels as though I have lived a thousand lives of emptiness, walking through each one with sorrow I never even knew I possessed. But then you came along and breathed true life into me. I am now alive in a way I never was before, and I shall cherish this one with everything in me. I shall cherish you with everything in me.

You are everything to me. You are the blood coursing through me, your skin the milk I drink. And your eyes—ah, your eyes—they are the vines wrapping me up in you. I hope to be tangled in them forever. You own my heart now. Completely. It's yours. Take its key and

wear it forever.

Yours completely, heart and soul,

Cassius

The letter was so intimate I almost felt guilty reading it. But *the passion.* This man obviously adored my mother. This man. My father.

I held the letter to my chest, letting the browned paper reunite with the necklace snaked across my collarbones. But my smile soon faded when I thought of how their lives had been cut so short. It wasn't fair that two people so in love had to die before their lives had really begun.

I closed the envelope, tucked it back inside the journal, and returned it to its new hiding place beneath my mattress.

I listened to the sound of the rain letting up outside, the roaring downpour now settling into a pattering dance atop the house. I sat down at my vanity, realizing it had become a source of comfort for me. A routine in this new room, in this new life of mine. It was all starting to feel like my own. I looked at my face in the mirror and let my eyes fall to the necklace. Is this what my mother looked like when she wore it? When the flutters of new love showed in her face?

When I looked back up at myself, I thought of William. The way he guarded himself, and the way I caught glimpses of the rare times he didn't. I thought of the way my heart fluttered when he inched closer to me. The way I felt when he looked into my eyes.

When I noticed my flushed cheeks, I immediately got up and rushed to my wardrobe. What was I doing? This was silly. I didn't feel that way about William.

He was my working partner. Nothing more.

I tried to ignore the burning in my face as I searched for a dress best suited for a rainy day. It was well past the morning, likely well into the afternoon. I couldn't laze in my room all day. Besides, William might have things to discuss with me.

For work. Nothing more.

But the more I thought of him, the more my heart wavered in my chest. The more my stomach flopped and face continued to burn. I groaned, beyond annoyed, snatching a plain black dress with a belt and swinging skirt. Why did he have this effect on me? I put my hand against my face and walked to my bed to finish getting ready.

As I stepped into the dress, I remembered what Molly had said. That William had come in late last night, looking worse for wear. I wondered what could have possibly happened. Where he could have gone at such a late hour, and why he was in such rough shape when he returned.

I pinned part of my hair up at both sides and then turned to leave. *I suppose I'll just ask him*, I thought, ignoring the physical sensations that followed.

I didn't get very far out of my room before I ran into Charles. He was ascending the stairs as I was making my descent.

"Ah, Miss . . . Blake, is that correct?" He scrutinized me, his head tilting to one side.

Why was he looking at me like that?

"Yes . . .? That's correct."

His smile curled to one side. "Do forgive me for asking. My mind is quite fuzzy these days. Are you enjoying your stay?"

"Yes, I am," I said, playing ignorant to his scrutiny. "Thank you. Have you seen William, by chance?"

"William?" He thought for a moment. "Ah, he's likely in the cemetery."

"The cemetery?"

"Yes. He tends to visit his mother on gloomy days."

"Oh. I see. I suppose I used to visit my own mother's grave when things were grim. It just wasn't on stormy days."

"Well, the rain has let up quite a bit. Besides, his mother's tombstone is beneath one of the large oak trees out back. He's protected well enough to stay out there in such weather." His smile softened, but his eyes stayed the same. Why did he always look at me as if he were appraising a portrait?

"Thank you," I said with a bow. "I'll be going then." I didn't want to stay there a moment longer. There was something strange about Charles, and I didn't want to look at his eyes anymore. Not even long enough to ask where the cemetery was. I figured I'd find it easily enough. He said it was out back. I would find my way.

It didn't take me long to realize that I should have asked for help. I wasn't sure how many times I wandered around in the rain until I finally saw the cemetery. Luckily, Charles was correct about the weather—it had tempered drastically since I'd woken up. The rain wasn't the only obstacle, though. The usual misty fog had turned into a thick wall of moisture, making it hard to find my way without getting too lost in the wrong direction.

But I finally found it, and I found him.

William was crouched in front of a large statue of an angel. Its arms were crossed against its chest, and engraved on its pedestal was a woman's name, though I couldn't make it out from here. What I could see, though, was that no dates were inscribed on the stone, but maybe it was a family tradition of some kind. Maybe they didn't want to set a date of life and death, instead believing she lived on, eternal. Perhaps they wanted to symbolize that none of us truly died.

"Hello, William. Are you all right?" I watched for any movement, but he looked like he had turned into a statue himself. He stayed crouched there, still and seemingly lifeless. The only part of him reflecting life was his hair, which was slightly curled from the rain and tousled from the wind.

I bent down to kneel next to him. "William? Are you all right?"

He jumped slightly. "Oh, Caroline. I didn't see you there. What are you doing out here?" He repositioned himself to sit with his legs crossed.

"I was looking for you," I said, and he looked at me, even more surprised than before.

"You were looking for me?"

"Well, I was worried about you in this weather," I said quickly. "What are you doing out here anyway? You are going to catch a cold."

He chuckled, but his eyes weren't in it. Deep lines of sorrow were pushing on his brow. He looked exhausted. It was just as Molly said. He looked both sad and tired, and I wasn't sure why. "You don't have to worry about that. I won't catch anything."

"And why is that?"

"Well, I never get sick, you see. You could call it a curse."

I laughed softly. "It sounds like a pretty good curse to me."

"Maybe sometimes," he said, but he didn't laugh. He was looking back at the tombstone now.

Thunder rumbled in the sky, but the enormous tree sheltering us kept us safe from most of the moisture. I *was* afraid of lightning, though. Hopefully I could persuade William to go inside soon.

He stared at the words on the tombstone. I didn't know what to say. I could read him even less than usual. His eyes were like flint, covering his emotions. They usually indicated some sort of reaction on his part, whether they be narrowed with suspicion or frustration, or alight with those moments of vulnerable happiness.

Today they just sat on his face, lifeless and silent. And for the first time, I found myself unable to reach him in some way. His reactions were too far away from me, and the situation was far too delicate for me to try. So I just sat there next to him, hoping my presence was more of a comfort than an annoyance.

The rain pattered against the leaves, and every once in a while I heard distant splashes or felt the violent rush of cool wind—the kind of wind that births pellets of sideways rain. I opened my silk handbag and took out a thin shawl. I wrapped it around my shoulders and continued to wait. Wait for what exactly? I wasn't even sure myself. I just knew I needed to be here.

After more rushes of wind came and went, the rain started to ease up to a sprinkle.

"My mother loved the rain," he said at last. His eyes stayed fixed ahead, but they were brightening a bit, becoming wistful. "She loved the feeling of it after a hard day's work. It made her feel clean. Naturally, I learned to love it, too, especially on the days where work was even more demanding than usual."

I wanted to ask what kind of work he had to do as a child because the thought of him working laboriously at a young age made my heart sick, but I decided to just let him talk. He seemed to need me to listen more than anything else right now. So I sat and listened as he continued. "She was the strongest person I knew. She had the guts to take on life as a working mother. My father worked in the mines and didn't make much money. We couldn't live off of what he made, so my mother begged for a job here."

He smiled wistfully. "Lady Eleanor, Evelyn's mother, was a kindred spirit to my mother. She was just as kind and just as bold. She didn't need another maid, but she took my mom on anyway. Soon, she allowed me to work here, too."

"But I thought Evelyn was your sister," I said. The wind swept over us, this time softer and warmer as the sun broke through the clouds.

His smile dropped. "After my parents died, Eleanor took me in as her own. I grew up here. Soon, Evelyn became my sister."

I imagined what it must have been like for William, growing up in this enormous mansion after having been poor all his life. It was likely a very small comfort considering the circumstances that brought him here. *I guess he didn't grow up as a spoiled rich boy after all*, I thought sheepishly. My eyes flickered to his.

I leaned forward, hoping he would look at me. I wanted to look into his eyes—for them to lock onto mine as they always did. I wanted to see some of the life come back to them. But he continued staring at the grave.

When it was clear he wouldn't be moving any time soon, I leaned back again. "What happened to Eleanor?" I asked.

His brow furrowed. "What happened to her?"

"Yes . . .?" Did he not know what happened to her?

"Well, I'm not entirely sure, I suppose. She could be living at a relative's house. She may be coming with the lot of them when the festival opens. We will be having a lot of friends and family members filling our halls and rooms, after all." Something about the way he said it made me wonder if there was more to the story, but I didn't press it.

"Have you seen any of your family recently?"

"I don't have any other family," he said bitterly, absently pulling at blades of grass, ripping them from the earth.

"But you just said you will be having family members stay at your home when the festival opens next month." I hoped he didn't think I was angry. I was simply confused.

He seemed to guess as much. He sighed and said, "I don't have any *real* family members besides Evelyn. Other than her, I don't know anyone who's still alive."

A rock formed in my stomach. I couldn't imagine living a life where everyone I'd ever loved had died in my lifetime. It was hard enough that my only family outside Maggie died before I was born, and then I lost her, too. I didn't think I could bear it if I'd known my mother and father's love and then lost it at such a tender age.

"What about Eleanor?"

"Eleanor?"

"Yes . . . Lady Eleanor?"

"Right. She hasn't come in ages, though. As I mentioned, I don't even know where she is."

"At least you have her, though," I said, straightening my legs in front of me. "She loves you, and Evelyn seems to love you. I have no one. No family. No friends—" I stopped as soon as I realized I'd made it about me.

I turned to him frantically. "I'm not diminishing how you feel by any means! I was just thinking out loud. That's all . . . I'm sorry."

"No," he said. "I understand. I know that feeling all too well, though I wish you could be spared from it." He finally looked over at me, and my heart skipped when his eyes met mine, but they were different. Despite his sympathetic smile, his eyes were still somber and listless, his regular gaze still dormant. "Friendships can be wonderful, but when they're gone, the bonds they leave behind are hard to break. Regardless of how things ended."

He sighed and looked back at the ground, his fingers still idly pulling at the grass. "I had a best friend growing up. He was just a little bit older than me, and we did everything together. We ran through these halls and got through life as a pair." His frown deepened. "He was like a brother to me, but I lost him, too." He threw the torn pieces aside, the green strands fluttering in the wind like wild hair.

He started pulling on a new patch of grass and kept talking. "Every time I've offered part of myself to anyone, I've been met with heartache. And everyone I've ever cared for has only been met with pain." He shook his head, his jaw clenched. "That's why I had to stop—stop trying, stop . . . everything." He shook his head. "No one should get close to me. It's better that way."

My heart ached at his words, and I desperately wished I knew how to console him, but I didn't know where to start.

The wind surged by us, shooting into the gigantic tree above. I watched the leaves dance like orange confetti littering the sky, the sound of their mass rustling like the crashing of a rolling wave.

"I wish I could help," I started to say, not knowing where my thought would take me, "but I'm afraid I'm not someone with much positive experience in this matter. I do believe you should open yourself up, though." I bent forward and put my hand on his shoulder so he'd look at me.

When he did, I looked into his eyes. "You can let yourself get close to people, William. It sounds like you have had an atrocious history with such things, but those events weren't the rules of love in life. They were the exceptions. Not everyone you care about will meet horrible ends. Is that what you think?"

He didn't say anything, but his eyes were scanning my face the way that always made my ears burn. "What about you?" he said.

"Me?"

"Yes. What about you? Why aren't you close to anyone? I'm actually rather surprised you haven't recruited a village of followers and friends that bend to your every wish and command."

I laughed out loud. "Why on earth would you think such a thing?"

"Well, unlike me, you don't have a morbid shadow hanging over you."

My smile vanished. "Well, I'm not so sure about that." If only he knew. The voices of those girls often returned to me, poking holes in my thoughts and deflating any budding self-confidence. Whenever I thought of trusting someone new—of believing in myself—there they were.

"In my experience, there are very few people outside of one's family you can trust." I spotted some stones nearby and began stacking them. I didn't want to see his face. I'd never told anyone about this but Maggie. There was never anyone to tell, really. It was one of the biggest reasons I'd left Fairbrooke.

I pressed a flat stone into the dirt and placed an even flatter, thinner one on top of it. "Back in Fairbrooke, I was the strange girl with the sordid past. I was the adopted daughter of 'Mad Maggie,' as they'd call her." I pressed the next stone against the others even harder. "Wicked people," I spat. "They were horrible."

I looked at him. "Do you know what it's like for everyone to mock and taunt the one person you love? And to ridicule both of you behind your backs? And sometimes to our faces . . ." I bit my lip, trying my best to silence any sobs. I didn't want to cry, even though I knew they would be more angry tears than anything else.

I looked back down at the rocks. "We helped everyone who needed us, and they always smiled and thanked us. They even gave us little gifts, like eggs from their chickens or fresh milk from their cows. Pastries, and the like. But they all thought we were strange." I stopped stacking the rocks. "I thought my friends were different," I whispered, "but looking back, there were signs, but . . . I never thought . . ."

I didn't want to talk anymore. The pain was still too fresh. Too real. Even though it'd been years since it happened. But can anyone really get over the betrayal of a friend? Of abandonment? Of being hung out to dry?

"I was stupid," I said, laughing bitterly to myself, "I was too loud and too different to blend in like the others. The girls in town all knew how to behave. How to interact safely, despite the things they thought behind each other's backs. But I didn't know of such rules. If someone hurt me, I said it. If someone gave me a cold shoulder, I would walk up and confront them."

I looked back at William, who was watching me with gentle eyes, and with patience. "I'm sure you have noticed that I'm very passionate," I said with a laugh. "Very daring, you might say. But . . . I've learned how to tame and nurture the strength to my emotions. I'm the same person I was ten years ago, but I've learned what people can use against you. I learned the hard way that unless you go about things perfectly, it can all blow up in your face and no one will be there to help clean up the mess."

I picked up another rock and tried placing it on the others, but the tears forming in my eyes obstructed my vision, and the pile collapsed. "I had a group of friends. I *finally* had a good, tight-knit group of friends." I wiped my face, still looking at the fallen rocks, and suddenly I wanted to crawl under one.

I couldn't believe I was talking about it. Let alone with *William*. Part of me wanted to die at how uncomfortable it could become, while the other part of me wanted to just let the pain explode out of me like a fountain of sewage.

The latter impulse won.

"A new girl moved into town when I was about seventeen. She and I became quite close. We didn't always see eye to eye, but we were good friends. Sometimes, we, in our immaturity, would say things we probably shouldn't have when we were in disagreements, but we always knew the other had a good heart." I shook my head, tears rolling down my face.

"I didn't know anyone could be so wicked. Not her. Another girl in our group of friends. A girl named Rose." As I said her name, my chest tightened and my stomach coiled until I felt sick. I hated when that happened. She was just a person, and it was so long ago. Why did the thought of her still cause this kind of reaction in me?

It was eleven years ago. Eleven.

Time didn't matter, though. That's the secret to pain. They say time helps heal all wounds, but they never say it will go away. There will always be a scar where the wound once was. Even after it's healed, when you touch it, you can still wince. You can sometimes still feel that pain as if the wound were still gaping open right in front of you.

I puffed out a breath and tried not to think. *Don't think about the memories. Just get the words out.* At least the tears had stopped coming. "One time, Rose bragged to all of us that she knew how to manipulate people. That was the first sign. A *big* first sign. I don't know why I didn't see it for what it was. I cannot believe I let someone like that into my life and allowed her to do what she did."

I had to stop to catch my breath. Whether it was the

memories suffocating me or I was talking too fast, I needed some air.

"What did she do?" he asked.

I glanced over at him. "It's a long story, but she turned everyone against me simply because she could." Tears burned in my eyes again. I wished I could fight them back, but it was no use at this point.

I let out a shuddering breath and then let it go. "It started because my best friend Leta and I got into a fight. She and I didn't know how to handle it, so we kind of pushed it aside, trying to bury it in a sandbox that was too shallow for it to disappear all the way. We both knew it was there, but we tried to move on anyway.

"We each went to Rose on different occasions, individually, and expressed our concerns. I, in particular, trusted her too deeply, I think. I didn't want to worry my aunt with such trivial matters. She had enough going on in her life. And I had nothing to hide. I loved Leta. I was just frustrated because she'd hurt me. And I didn't know how to deal with it.

"I didn't know it at the time, but I think my mind was going through a lot. I think I was working through the trauma of my childhood. Of going through everything I did—the way Maggie raised me, the way people treated us, the isolation, having to take care of my aunt from an early age." I sighed. "And my emotions were so big and so deep, I didn't know what to do with them. So, I expressed my sorrows to Rose. I told her that I was hurt by what Leta had done and about some things she had said.

"Rose then told me that Leta did and said awful things that I didn't know about, but none of it ended up being true. At least I don't think it was, because I found out later that Rose told Leta that *I* said horrible things that I didn't say. So I choose to believe Leta, even if she never chose to believe me, too."

I stopped. The pain came flooding back. There were so many times over the last decade that I wished I could turn back time, but what could I have done if given that chance? Would I have pointed out Rose's behaviors to the others? Reminded them of her bragging about manipulating others as if it were something only accomplished persons could achieve?

As I tried to catch my breath, I felt William's hand on mine. He leaned forward and looked into my eyes. His were no longer lifeless; they were lit with a gentle fire, warm and kind. He looked at me like he wanted to scoop up my sadness and take it from my shoulders. Like he would carry it for me so I could smile again.

After what happened with Rose, I was always too afraid to be vulnerable again. But being here with William, I felt like maybe it could be easy again. Because unlike how it felt when I'd talked to Rose that day, here with William, I felt safe. I felt heard. I wasn't confused or incensed. Someone wasn't trying to force anger into me—to stir me into something I wasn't due to things that weren't true.

I felt like I could tell him anything.

I tucked my hair behind my ear, still keeping my other hand safely beneath William's. "Rose gained all of our trust," I said, "and since she was crafty, she convinced the others I said things I never did. And since I was hardly around, as I constantly worked when I wasn't busy caring for my aunt, she won over their opinions. She told them I hated Leta and that I said things I didn't say."

I shook my head. "When I tried to refute the nasty claims, it didn't matter. They had already made up their minds. Who would they believe? Would they believe the girl they were around all the time, or someone like me—a casual friend who was out of sight and out of mind most of the time? Of course, it was easier for Rose to win them over. And I was left alone. I was devastated."

The sorrow and heartbreak I'd been carrying for over a decade crashed down on me, and I let it go. I let the sobs out. I let the pain rise out of me like steam. I let my face fall into my hands and let my shoulders shake.

"I was so young, and life had been so cruel to me," I said between cries. "My heart couldn't take the abandonment. I had never had a good group of friends before, and I never did again." I let out even louder sobs, my face still hidden in my hands.

I felt William wrap an arm around me, and I let my hands fall to my lap as he leaned me into him. The warmth of his body against mine was a surprising comfort to me; it made it even easier to let myself cry into him, my body trembling in the cold and my tears soaking his shirt. I didn't let myself think about it. I just let it be what it was.

I had been carrying this pain for too long, and not just this pain—all of my pain. The pain of my night terrors as a child, the isolation, the ridicule. I loved Maggie, and she loved me more than anything, but life with her was often tough. I could never show fear or sadness to her, or she'd be scared for months on behalf of me.

When I told her about what had happened with Rose and the others, she did her best to comfort me, but she wasn't used to me crying, and fear was always her natural instinct. So, for weeks afterward, she feared someone would come to our house and kill me. She was in agony, no matter how much I tried to calm her down.

After that, I learned to keep it all inside completely.

But now it was all coming out.

The rain kept spilling from the sky, prickling against the tree and leaving pattering sounds as they fell to the ground beside us. The sun was out and the sprinkling was light, but the rain kept falling all the same. It was subtle, but it was there. It was strange and seemingly impossible. Perhaps the sky knew. Perhaps William and I were controlling the weather as it fell in the canopy above our heads. I wondered if it was raining anywhere else.

When I finally looked up at him, he looked down at me with those same gentle eyes. No judgment. No smirk. Just compassion. "I'm sorry," I said. "I . . . don't usually do that." I sat back up and moved back to where I'd been.

"It's perfectly all right," he said, but when I looked at him, he was frowning. "What happened after that?" he asked.

I blinked. "You mean . . . with Rose or with Maggie?" Did I talk about Maggie, or just Rose? I couldn't remember how much I had spoken and what had just been rolling through my mind.

"With Rose," he said, "and the others. Did they ever come to you?"

"No," I said, "Not even when Maggie died. Leta did ask how I was doing one time after Maggie passed, but that was it." I smiled at him sadly. "I guess it was easier to believe Rose and forget about me." My eyes trailed off.

"I don't understand," I said, shaking my head. "I don't understand how someone can be so cruel. How someone like Rose can think it's fun to ruin someone's life. I just don't understand."

"I don't think that's something you will ever understand," William said. "Because you, Caroline, are not cruel. You are not cold and unfeeling." He smiled, an unguarded beautiful smile, and leaned in closer. "I hope you don't mind me saying this, but you are a beautiful person, Caroline. And one day, you will meet people who will cherish you. Who will see you for who you are."

I tried to smile back, but I didn't believe him. I believed

he believed it, but I had never had good luck with friends. In my experience, they were quick to come and quick to go.

"I don't know about that," I said, sorting the stones that had toppled over each other. I began stacking them again. "I've never had a true friend. Even as a child back in Fairbrooke, whenever I made a friend, there was always someone they liked better."

"That might have been the case in Fairbrooke, Caroline, but it doesn't have to be the case here."

I shook my head but smiled at his effort. If only he understood that he, like everyone else, would eventually see me for the odd soul I was and fly away. I was someone who seemed to attract friends like pollen to bees. But once they'd had their fill, they moved on to other flowers. Ones more bright and beautiful.

"It's not the case anywhere," I said, placing another stone upon my pile. "I've always been a friend to the shadows, but nothing else." I tried not to let any more tears fall, but I couldn't help it. No matter how used to abandonment and loneliness I was, it never got easier. The hole in my heart would forever gape open, bleeding out and getting eaten over and over again, like Prometheus' liver.

"I'm used to the pain," I continued. "I know I'll always be someone people like on the surface. Someone who is passionate and driven, but dripping with demons and shadows, even more frightening than the ones my aunt warned me about."

When he didn't say anything to this, I said, "That's why I'm not afraid anymore, William. You have told me time and time again that I should be afraid of curses and everything, but my aunt told me what to be afraid of my entire life, and she was wrong. Monsters, vampires, demons—those are not the enemy."

He looked at me carefully, as if weighing his words before asking them. "Then . . . who is this enemy?" he finally asked.

I frowned. "What?"

"If monsters, vampires, and demons aren't the enemy, then who is?"

I thought about this for a moment, then sighed. "I suppose there are many enemies," I said, "Everyone has their own fears. But to me, nothing is more frightening than suffering through darkness alone. The next most frightening thing would be suffering at the hands of another. There are good people in the world, but there are very, very bad ones, too." My eyes flickered to my broken pile of stones. "And some pretty callous, middle-of-the-road ones, too."

"Caroline," he said. I could tell he wanted me to look at him, so I did, begrudgingly. When he looked me in the eyes, he said, "Your aunt was right. Don't be afraid of being alone or of making friends. Be afraid of what you can't see."

I narrowed my eyes. "What are you talking about."

He flinched. "Well, let's just say that I know curses are real and that you should stay away from them, like the one here."

I rolled my eyes. "Not this again. Please."

"Caroline, it's true—"

"I don't believe you, and you won't convince me otherwise." I started to get to my feet when he grabbed me by the hand.

"Then please," he said, looking up at me, "at least know this: You don't have to be alone, Caroline. Let yourself be free from fear just enough to meet the right people and live a life you can be happy with."

"People are the real monsters," I said, shaking away his hand.

"Well, in my experience, there are a lot of good people in the world. It's just the monsters that tear them apart."

"What do you mean?"

"Some people are monsters, as you mentioned," he said, then shook his head, "But those are not friends. You will meet the right people, and the monsters won't be able to touch you anymore."

"I don't know about that," I said, letting myself sink back onto the ground next to him. "But if that is true, then I suppose I should reflect upon myself and wonder if I'm actually one of them."

"You are not a monster," he said, wiping a tear that had fallen to my neck—one I must have never swiped away. His touch was warm against my cool skin. "And you'll find your way out one day. Out of that cage of fear constructed from your past."

"What makes you so sure?"

"Because no one can be locked in the past forever."

"What about you then?" I asked. "If people aren't bad, then why do you shut them out?"

"Because I am the one who doesn't fit in. Unlike you, I *am* a monster," he said, looking away and retracting his hand. "Everyone who has ever known me has suffered."

"Well, we have one thing in common then," I said. He looked up at me, confused. "We are destined to be alone. Lost in the shadows of our past."

"*No*," he said firmly. "You should leave the shadows. You are so bright, Caroline. You are the torch breaking through the darkness." He smiled and moved closer to me. "Your passion makes your light too bright for some people, but you'll find someone who craves it." His voice lowered as he added, "Someone tired of the darkness."

I couldn't look away from him. His black-brown hair was still tousled from the rain, and his dark eyes were alight with his own kind of fire. Was this what he'd be like if he shed that stony curtain and let himself be free?

"What about you then?" I asked.

His smile dropped, but the closeness between us remained. "What about me?"

"You say I should believe that others will come my way. That I'm some source of light, but you don't believe the words yourself."

"That's because there's no light inside me," he said, throwing away a loose piece of grass. "And even if there was, it would be the kind of flame that attracts moths and burns them alive when they get too close."

His words made my heart ache. Why did he think of himself in such a way? I wasn't always the best judge of character, clearly, but there was something about him that seemed so . . . *good.* "You're wrong," I said, "I can see the light inside you right now, and it's wonderful." He looked at me.

"What makes you say that?" he asked, and in his voice, something shifted. Like he truly wanted to know. Perhaps he'd let me in after all—let me explain why he was allowed to let his guard down and take off that prickly shell of his from time to time.

"You say you have lost others because of your own deeds. If this is true, all you need to do is work on yourself and accept responsibility. Change is powerful and important. If you believe you have made mistakes, all you can do is change them and move forward. Believe you are a worthy friend and try again."

"You don't understand. It's not like that."

"What is it like then?"

He didn't respond. He didn't even look at me.

As I waited, I realized it was silly of me to think I could get through to him so easily, considering I was doing the same thing

"Let's make a deal, William," I said finally. He looked at me cautiously. "If I try to be more open to the idea that I can find a true friend and keep them, then you must do the same. Stop blaming yourself, being trapped by your past, and move forward. And I'll . . ." I winced, "I'll try to do the same."

I reached my hand up to shake his, but he didn't take it. "I wish that for you, Caroline, but I'm afraid I can't promise you the same."

"And why not?" I said, getting irritated now.

He wouldn't look at me. He was back to staring straight at the tombstone in front of him, but now his shoulders were starting to shake. The tense feeling of irritation lifted from my shoulders. Something was wrong. I was about to put my hand on his shoulder when he turned to me, his eyes red and glossy. "Because my mother and father died because of me. And my best friend . . . Augustus . . . He suffered because of me. I can't just let that all go."

I didn't know what to say, but I felt ashamed. I shouldn't have assumed his wounds were exactly like my own—that they could even be approached the same way. I couldn't imagine the pain he must carry—the incomprehensible weight on his shoulders.

"Then let me help you," I said quietly, reaching over to rest my hand on his shoulder. Tears began spilling down his face, but he didn't look at me.

"She died at the last Harvest Festival. I saw it happen. My mother. I just . . ." He lifted his hands to his face and tried not to cry. He silently shook, but no sound came out. After a moment, he continued, his hands still pressed against his face. "I begged her to go with me. So I could see the others and see how everything turned out. To get pastries and have fun. I just—" He broke down crying then, and I ignored any questions I had and just leapt forward and held him.

I rested my head against his, but he immediately forced himself to compose. He sat up straight and dried his eyes. "I'm sorry. I shouldn't be making such a fuss. It's not proper." But his body was still shaking.

"What isn't proper about showing one's feelings?"

"Well, a man shouldn't—"

"A man shouldn't cry? What? Men don't have feelings?" He avoided my gaze, but I didn't let him off easy; I grabbed his face in my hands and looked straight at him. "It's perfectly acceptable for you to cry."

At first, he looked into my eyes so intently that I thought he would listen to me and let himself cry, but then he took my hands off of his face, straightened his back, and readjusted his shirt. Looking away, he said, "It's fine. I shouldn't burden you with such things. My troubles are of no concern to you."

"You are mistaken, William. They are of great concern to me." He finally looked back at me, so I leaned forward and gave him a firm look. "So you can choose to either let me comfort you when you're in pain, or you can be in even greater pain and I shall worry about you anyway."

He watched me for a moment and hope spread through me. I wanted to see more of his heart, and more of that happy fire that lit in his eyes. And I wanted him to let himself cry—to let himself mourn. I wanted him to open himself up to the world. To me.

But he just shook his head and got to his feet. "I'm sorry to have concerned you, Miss Blake, but I am perfectly fine. These things don't burden me often. I was simply sentimental today." His shield was up, his tough exterior back in place.

"I find that hard to believe," I said, taking his hand as he offered it to help me off the ground. I didn't let go of it when I got to my feet. Instead, I looked up at him and said, "Let me help you, William. Please."

From this close, I could tell his eyes were still red—that he was still fighting it all back. But he just said, "There's nothing to help." His voice softened as he added, "but I do hope you can realize how valuable you are. How worthy of love you truly are."

The words settled inside my heart, soothing my aching chest, more than I'd like them to. I didn't want this friendship, or whatever it was, to be one-sided. I refused to believe his words until he believed them himself.

"I hope that for you, too," I said. Our hands were still intertwined, and we were so close to each other I could smell the rain soaked into his skin. He looked at me with such fondness that I didn't know what to do with myself. I just knew I didn't want it to stop. I hated how much I loved it, but I wasn't willing to let it go.

"Maybe one day," he said, his voice steady, our eyes still locked. "But I cannot accept your invitation for your help, Caroline. You will live a much better life if you stay away from me."

"No, that's not true, William. Can't I decide for myself what I do and don't do?"

He didn't say anything, but I could tell that despite what he claimed, he didn't want me to leave. He leaned in even closer, and his warm breath against my skin made me forget the cold completely. He was so close to me that I couldn't even look into his eyes.

My eyelids fluttered close, and my heart raced beneath my chest. "I can't let you get close to me," he said, but his free hand wrapped to the small of my back.

It was getting harder to breathe. "Why not?" I whispered back.

I felt his lips get closer to mine, but then loud laughter burst out from behind us. Startled, I jumped back and turned around, letting go of his hand. Two male workers were gathering wood for the hearth in the field nearby. They were laughing heartily about something, blind to our presence. What would it be like to be so unencumbered by the stress of life? To be able to laugh so freely and openly, even while you work?

"Oh, it must be getting time for supper," I said quickly, smoothing out the wrinkles of my dress and catching my breath. My face was hot and flustered. I didn't want to meet William's eyes.

"Right. We must get going then," he said. I nodded, still not looking at first, but when I almost ran into him, I saw that he was holding his arm out to me.

I quickly looked to his face and noticed that those stony curtains of his were parted a little more than usual. His tender smile and the light in his eyes made me hope that things would be different after today, if even just a little bit.

I smiled back and took his arm, letting him walk me inside. Neither one of us said a thing, but there was an unspoken kinship between us now. An unspoken spark of hope. We didn't need to acknowledge it. We both knew it was there.

Perhaps the world wasn't such a lonely place after all.

Chapter Seventeen

Two days had passed since William and I saw each other at the cemetery. When we'd gotten inside, the maids and footmen were aghast at how soaked to the bone we were. The funny thing was that we hardly even noticed. They wondered why we were smiling as much as we were. I think they thought we were crazy. Maybe we were. Just a bit, anyway.

We had discussed such serious matters. Such heartbreaking memories. Why did we feel so light? Why did I feel like I'd been cleansed by more than just the rain?

Although Molly immediately helped me get dry and brought me new clothes, I ran a terrible fever the next morning. I was in and out of consciousness the entire day, dizzy and limp. Almost every time I fell asleep, I either dreamt nothing at all or had nightmares show up like exhausted songs playing over and over again in my head. Reliving the dreams felt like the twisting of a dull knife on top of my fever.

But sometimes I was lucky. Sometimes I dreamed of William, and in those dreams, I lacked the inhibitions of my real life. I let myself wrap my arms around him, and I let myself trust him without holding back. In one of them, he leaned in to kiss me, that same sensation of warmth against my skin that I'd felt in the cemetery. He was so close to kissing me in one of them that my heart was still racing when I woke up. If only I could have stayed asleep for just a few more minutes.

When I woke up the next day, my fever had broken and I was feeling much better. From the window, I could tell the day was well underway and could even hear workers cutting lumber outside. I wondered where Molly was but assumed she'd let me sleep because of my state the day before.

I slowly got out of bed, testing out my limbs to see if any of my aches or pains had lingered from my fever. *So far so good*, I thought. I cautiously stretched and then drew a bath for myself to take things easy.

But I couldn't stop thinking about him. And I loved it. I hated that I loved it, but I loved it all the same.

I loved that smile that broke through that brooding facade. I loved holding onto his arm when we strolled back inside, dripping wet. I loved that I was comfortable talking with him and that we were both so alike yet so different.

With William, I didn't feel so alone anymore. The world had more color and the fields had more flowers. I had more hope that people could be like me. That *he* was like me. I just hoped the feeling would never end.

I tried not to think about that. I tried not to give life to the nagging voice in the back of my mind that said *You know this won't last forever. It never has before.* "It's different this time," I wanted to tell that part of myself.

But William was so adamant about not getting close to anyone. Logically, he was the last person guaranteeing lasting friendship, or anything more. But there was something between us that told me otherwise. Something I couldn't let go of.

No matter how many times he'd told himself not to get close to anyone, he had still found solace in me. I could feel it. I could see it in the smile he wore on the way back to the mansion. I could feel it in our connection.

We fit together like the two lost pieces of a puzzle that had fallen through the cracks. We'd been abandoned by the bigger picture—those pieces so perfectly molded together—forever feeling alone, not realizing that somewhere in a nearby corner, beneath thick coats of dust and scattered crumbs, there was another one just like us.

Perhaps those mismatched pieces could fit together.

The thought fluttered in and out of my mind, but I tried to push it out. The more of myself I ever gave to others only gave weight to a greater fall. I'd always been left scraped and marred, the pain growing a little more each time. Did I really want to risk that again?

And this time, I knew the pain would be far greater than it had been in the past.

With William, it was more than friendship. The way I felt for him cut so deeply into me that I couldn't get it out, and even if I could, I didn't think I'd want to.

And that terrified me.

The fall after such a leap could cause damage outside my experience; the recovery could be immense, the pain everlasting. And with Maggie gone, I had even more to lose.

I let my arms fall to my sides and looked at myself in

the mirror, studying my face and wondering how much more pain I could take in my life before I broke beyond repair.

I picked up my mother's necklace and clasped it behind my neck. I wondered what it would be like to get advice from my mother. What would she say? Judging by her journal, her heart was a passionate bomb ready to burst every time the man she loved looked her in the eye or held her hand.

What would she say to me now? "Let yourself jump," I imagined her saying. "You won't know how good life can be unless you open yourself up to it. Do you want to live in your lonely corner the rest of your life, afraid to break?"

I hadn't let myself jump in over ten years, but maybe now I should try. Maybe I should risk falling in the hopes that I'd soar even higher. If I did end up falling, I'd always been one with a knack for repairs anyway. If anyone could fix the damage, it would be me, right?

I groaned and slumped into my seat, my face falling into my hands. "What do I do?" I grumbled.

Someone knocked at the door. "You can come in, Molly," I said. *That girl must listen for my every move*, I thought. The young woman opened the door. I could see her trademark smile from her reflection in the mirror.

"Good morning, Miss. Ah, you look lovely. How are you feeling today?"

"Thank you very much, and I'm doing well. I'm feeling much better. Thank you for asking."

"Oh good," she said, placing a hand over her chest in relief. "I'll tell Lord Ashdown right away. He's been beside himself ever since he found out."

"Oh?" I said, my heart rate picking up. "What did he say?" I played with the chain of my necklace, pretending not to care one way or another.

"It was quite annoying, actually. He wouldn't stop bothering Mrs. Wells and me. We would come to tend to you, and he would ask about you over and over again. He kept saying it was his fault that you were sick because you were both out there in that dreadful weather all afternoon a couple days ago." She flashed me a look. "What *were* you doing out there anyway?" That mischievous grin of hers returned.

"We were just talking, Molly."

She made a sound of disappointment and frowned, her shoulders slumping forward as she plopped herself on my bed.

"What did you think we were doing?" I asked, raising an eyebrow.

"Nothing," she grumbled. She pulled herself back off the bed as quickly as she'd flopped onto it and said, "Well, you should go see him anyway. He'll be relieved you're not dead." I couldn't help but stifle a laugh as the girl padded away, clearly very disappointed at the lack of drama that happened between William and me.

I caught myself smiling. He was worried about me. Beside himself, she'd said. "I suppose I'll let the man out of his misery," I said before Molly closed the door behind her.

I sprung to my feet and grabbed one of my smaller purses—another glamorous perk of living here—and tied its string around my wrist.

I didn't know what the future looked like, but I could enjoy today. That would have to be enough. For now, at least.

I was barely downstairs when he came rushing over to me from down the hall. "Oh, Caroline, are you all right?

I'm so sorry. I told you I don't get sick, but I should have thought about you!" He put his hands on my shoulders and inspected me, looking me up and down, and then he put a hand on my head to make sure I wasn't still running a fever.

I wiggled away and said, "William, please. I'm quite fine." I turned away so he wouldn't see my face. Blushing was becoming a regular occurrence for me. I couldn't risk him seeing anything.

"I'm sorry. I got carried away. I was just so worried."

When I turned back around, I saw just how pitiful he looked. His hair was disheveled, and the buttons on his waistcoat weren't aligned. I smiled sympathetically. "I'm really fine. It was just a cold."

When he wouldn't smile back, I said, "Why don't you make it up to me by giving me a tour of the garden out back? I saw it on my way to the cemetery and was quite taken with it. I would love a formal tour."

"Of course," he said, his mouth finally turning up into a smile. He held his arm out for me to take, and my heart skipped, my mind returning to the other night. After everything that had happened in the cemetery, he still wanted me to stay. He still wanted to be with me.

I tucked my hand in the crook of his arm and breathed in the moment, savoring the rush of feelings swirling inside me. I wanted to soak everything in and remember it piece by piece.

As we made our way outside, he asked, "Did your recovery take long?" He was frowning again, the lines on his forehead deep with concern. "I hope you didn't suffer too much."

"Oh, no. I was sick for about twenty-four hours or so, and I was asleep for most of it. You needn't worry so much, William. I'm not so fragile, you know."

"Yes, I am aware. Your ferocity is one of the reasons I

forgot you weren't invincible."

"Well, I'm sure you'll remember it now," I said with a laugh. "You looked scared half to death when I came down the stairs."

"I *was* scared half to death. I thought I'd killed you."

I laughed harder. "*Killed* me? What on earth do you think happens when people get colds?"

"I don't know! All I knew was that you couldn't even speak for yourself, let alone eat or move around. I was terribly worried."

I tried not to smile because he had clearly been legitimately worried, but I couldn't help it. The thought of him being so flustered over me made me giddier than it should have. "Well, I'm grateful you are so concerned for my wellbeing. I will try to be more responsible."

"Very good," he said, chuckling.

"But I hope you know that I'd show you the same courtesy of being overly anxious and far too worried, so please do not do anything reckless, either," I said, smiling up at him. I watched for his reaction, but when he didn't say anything, or even smile, I didn't know what to say. Had I said something to offend him?

We were almost at the garden now, and I was getting worried that I'd said something wrong. But then he said, "Okay." He looked so serious, his voice steady. "I'll try my best. But, Caroline?" He stopped walking, and I would have fallen if he hadn't been holding my arm.

"Hm?"

"I need you to be careful."

"Whatever of?"

He turned to face me, but he didn't meet my eyes. I waited anxiously as he gathered his thoughts. Why the sudden shift in mood? As the wind swept over us, it brought with it the sweet perfume of the flowers in the garden. I closed my eyes and tried to identify which flowers made such a concoction, distracting myself from the anxious tension between us.

"Caroline?"

I opened my eyes. "Yes?"

His face was still serious. He placed his hands gently on my arms and looked in my eyes. "There will be times where I look like I've been through hell and back. Where I look absolutely dreadful. If you will be watching me with such a close eye, I just wanted to tell you not to worry."

I sighed with relief. "Oh William, you scared me. I thought you were going to tell me to never speak to you again." I laughed. "You don't have to worry so much. It's okay for people to care about others. Don't you want someone to care about you?"

He was still frowning. "Not if that someone gets pulled into it." He looked at me as if pleading me not to jump into a fire after him.

I looked at him just as seriously, but with a reassuring smile. "People who care about other people will worry for their wellbeing. There is nothing wrong with that."

"It is if something bad happens to them, too."

"What could possibly happen to me for worrying about you?"

"I can't say," he said, letting go of my arms.

I shook my head. "Then don't say it. Don't worry about it. Let me worry. It's healthy."

"I don't know about that," he mumbled.

I rolled my eyes. "Well, I'm going to do it whether you like it or not, just as you did with me." I took his arm and looked up at him. "Do you really think I'd endorse the notion of you being in a twist over my fever for an entire day and a half? Absolutely not!"

He smiled. "I suppose."

"Exactly. Now, let's stop worrying so much, all right? Let us simply enjoy this garden. Now, tell me about these plants."

He eased up a bit after that. He led me along and told me about the hyacinths and chrysanthemums, the roses, the lilies, and an entire area devoted toward growing perfect vegetables. "How divine," I said, bending down to inspect a group of growing tomatoes.

"Do you like apples, Miss Blake?" he called out to me. I turned around and saw him a few feet away, plucking an apple from a tree.

"As a matter of fact, I do," I said, brushing the dirt of my skirt and joining him. When he handed it to me, I thanked him and took a bite. Its ruddy color was almost purple and its taste was sweet without being bitter. It was perfectly crisp, with just the right amount of juice. "This is so delicious," I said, my mouth full. I took another bite, and he just watched me with a smile.

"I'm glad you like it. The apples here are the best in the country." He reached up and examined one on its branch. "I think our spot on the hill gives them the right amount of sunlight."

"Despite the early sunsets?" I asked, taking another bite, remembering the first day we worked together.

He let go of the branch. "Yes. Despite that."

I tossed the apple core to the side of the tree, secretly wishing I could eat another. "Thank you. That was delightful. What did you want to show me next?"

I walked closer to him and caught sight of his mis-buttoned waistcoat again. Should I say something? Or should I let him go about the rest of his day like that?

"Um . . . Well, actually, we have seen pretty much all of it. What do you say? Should we head back in? Or did you want to work?" He smiled down at me, and though I smiled back, I decided to let him in on his waistcoat situation.

I stopped walking when I got close enough that our shoes almost touched. "Hold on a moment," I said, reaching out and touching the top button. "Your buttons are in disarray."

"Oh no, I—"

I shook my head. "It's all right," I smiled brighter, hoping it set him at ease. "I think it's charming, especially since it happened on my account." I played with the idea of unbuttoning it and straightening out the situation for him, but I figured that would be a little too improper, so I let go of his clothes.

He turned around and apologized for his appearance. I kept waving it off, but he didn't stop until he had completely straightened himself away.

"Would you please just loosen up a bit?" I asked him, still grinning so he knew I was teasing. "It's a beautiful day, and we are in an enchanting garden. But you won't do anything but worry today, will you?"

I stepped forward and poked a finger to his chest. "You cannot worry anymore today. I shall not allow it."

He suppressed a grin. "Oh?"

"Yes," I said firmly, "No more worrying. About anything. We will be carefree. We won't work today. We will just play."

"Play?" he said, raising an eyebrow.

I laughed. "Yes! Play! Let's let our worries go like we're children!" I stepped back and spun around to demonstrate, but he just looked at me, baffled, with one eyebrow still raised.

"Let's be carefree like the wind. The way we all lose somewhere before adulthood. Now. Close your eyes."

"Close my . . . eyes?"

"Yes. Right now. Go on!" I motioned for him to cover his eyes and then waited for him to do it. When he did, I said, "Now, count to twenty, and no peeking!"

"What is happening right now?"

I laughed as I ran away. "We are playing. Remember? No cares today. No worries. Now count!"

He finally got the message because I heard him counting as I hid behind one of the trees. He wouldn't suspect me here. It was too obvious. *There's no way he'd look somewhere so obvious. He—*

"Are you even trying?" he asked. I deflated when I looked up and saw him leaning against the tree.

"Yes! I mean . . . I was just . . . warming up!"

"Warming up?" he asked incredulously.

"Yes! Count again!" I shooed him away and he did as I said. When he started counting, I made my escape. As I ran around, looking for places to hide, I realized the garden was an awful place for hide-and-seek. The only places to hide were behind the trees. And that obviously didn't work out for me.

When he finished counting, I fell to the ground and hid behind a nearby bush. He was obviously going to find me, so I needed to think of something fast.

I stood up. "New game!" I said. I took off my shoes and hid them behind the plants. "You need to switch places with me and stand right here. Then, I will hide behind one of the trees. You'll count as usual, and then you will choose which tree to find me behind. If you choose right, you win. If you don't, you'll have to keep searching until you find me."

"That isn't much different to the game we were playing before," he said with a laugh.

"That's true, but this time you have to catch me!"

"Catch you?"

"Yes! So, even if you guess which tree I'm behind, I can run away. And if I make it back here, by my shoes, before you catch me, then I win." I put my hands on my hips triumphantly.

He laughed "Well, if we're being carefree as the wind I don't see why not."

So we proceeded with my plan. He traded places with me, and I hid behind one of the trees. I chose one far enough away where I could hear him coming, but not so far away I couldn't run back.

When he finished counting, I pressed my back against the tree and stood as still as I could. I even tried to slow my breaths, which didn't work. I just couldn't believe that the wind wasn't whipping by the one time I needed it to.

But no. There were no noises to muffle the sounds of my breathing. Or the sound of my soft yip when a beetle crawled over one of my toes. I silenced a squeal as I felt its creepy legs move over the rest of my foot before it made its leave. When it had been gone for a few seconds, I let myself breathe.

After another minute or so went by, I realized I hadn't heard William counting in a while, and I hadn't seen him yet. *I must be winning*, I thought, quite proud of myself. I didn't know this game was actually going to work out.

Right as I thought those words, William swung around to the back of the tree and said, "This one! AH! I got you!"

"What! No! There's no way you randomly chose the right tree!"

"You better get running, Caroline."

I scowled playfully and ducked beneath his arm and started weaving through the trees. Unfortunately, I made the mistake of checking over my shoulder to see where he was. As I turned around, I tripped over the roots of one of the trees and tumbled to the ground, William falling along with me.

When I opened my eyes, I looked over and saw him lying next to me. He turned to look at me, but a leaf was stuck to his head, and I burst out laughing.

"Laugh while you can," he said, "Because you're about to lose—"

I quickly jumped to my feet and gathered my skirt so I wouldn't fall this time. But before I could escape, William jumped up and grabbed hold of my arm. "I won't let you escape that easy!"

I turned around and my back fell against the tree. "Ah! That's not fair!" I said, laughing, my head falling back against the trunk. "You have to count first!"

He laughed and started to stay something when he lost his grip on the tree and fell against me. And though he immediately caught himself around me, his hands on either side of me, his body stayed pressed against mine. I felt the muscles of his arms tighten around me. The rise and fall of his chest. I looked up at him, knowing that once I did, I wouldn't be able to look away.

When our eyes met, heat rose to my chest, and my heart stopped beating altogether. I couldn't ignore the slight movements of his body. The way he smelled like spice and cinnamon and man. The way he looked at me so breathlessly.

I wanted to speak, but I couldn't. His eyes flickered to my lips and my body turned to liquid. One of his arms wrapped slowly around my waist, the other one moving up my arm, his hand catching my face.

His forehead rested against mine, and my mind went blank. My heart picked up again, beating harder and faster than ever before. And as I felt his breath on my lips, my eyes fluttered close. And as his lips grazed mine, something sizzled like white-hot lightning up my skin.

And then he kissed me, and I thought I escaped life altogether. As if my soul had propelled right into the sky. That all my life I'd been confined to my body, locked away from reaching the stars, but William had the key.

His hands rushed over me, and I surrendered to his touch. The more he kissed me, the more I craved the taste. I wrapped my arms around him and let him kiss me even more deeply, becoming drunk by his dizzying elixir.

As I let myself get lost in his spell, I knew I couldn't deny my feelings anymore. I wanted him. And I wanted to want him. I didn't want to go back to living my old half-life. I didn't want to live a riskless life with no costs and no benefits.

I wanted him. I wanted this. I wanted to live.

Soon, our kisses grew farther apart and the spinning world around us went still. When he slowly pulled away, he left a hand on my face, as if unable to stop touching me. I opened my eyes and looked into his. Those dark eyes that had once vexed me were now soft and unguarded. He looked at me like I was the most precious creature to have ever existed. Like I was his and only his.

With the dizzy madness of his kiss still fresh on my lips, I smiled and whispered, "What are you thinking?"

He smiled and traced my lips with his finger. "Just that I want you."

"You want me?" I repeated, my whispers barely audible.

He nodded. "I do. I want you." He trailed his finger down my neck, then down my arm, and then laced his fingers in mine.

Then he wrapped his arms around me and pulled me into an embrace. "I want to keep you. I want to forget everything and run away. I want to be carefree with you for the rest of my life."

Tears welled in my eyes, and my voice caught in my

throat. I couldn't speak, but even if I could, I didn't know what I'd say. Because there was something sad in the way he said it. Like the desires of his heart could never be granted.

When I didn't say anything, he swept my face into his hands and kissed me again, and I let myself get lost one more time. I didn't know what would happen after this, but for right now, this was enough.

Chapter Eighteen

For the first time in three decades, I could taste the meal served to us that night. I hadn't been able to taste most foods since I was a kid, before I'd changed. It was as if tasting Caroline's kiss had awakened a human part of me that had been dormant all those years. It was horribly reckless of me, but I'd be lying if I said I regretted it.

We always caught each other sneaking glances between spoken words at the table every evening, but today it was different. Today, it felt intimate. She had ignited a fire I had long thought extinguished. A brightness that had been locked away in the sea of shadows that made up who I was. She'd brought me back to life.

As if I hadn't been craving it since I'd first laid eyes on her, I wanted her even more now. In more ways than a monster should. And in ways only a monster would. When I felt her warmth beneath my fingertips, the part of me I hated most urged me to sink into her skin and make her mine. To taste her blood.

Which was exactly why I couldn't let this go any further. Despite how I felt about her. Despite that I was falling in love with her—something I thought I'd never experience. Something that made me want to push her away even more. I couldn't risk getting swept up in her again. I wasn't sure when that part of me would take control.

Though I'd never had a problem controlling myself before, the overpowering feelings I had for her made me worry about the risk. And yet, I still wondered. I still debated with myself on how much of a risk falling in love with her really would be. If I had never lost control—never bitten a human before—then I was free, wasn't I?

How foolish. I couldn't lie to myself long enough to truly believe that. And even though I knew that I was no good for her, and that I didn't deserve the love she would give me, I still wanted to love her. Even if I didn't allow her to love me in return.

When I saw those sad eyes in the cemetery—when I saw how bent and broken her heart had become—I wanted to mend it. I wanted to take the shattered pieces that had splintered off over the years and paste them back together again. I wanted to purge her body of shadows and clean her scrapes and bruises. I would carry her the rest of her life if I could. As long as she didn't love me back.

How could anyone break a heart like hers? Why did she have to suffer the way she had?

I yearned to take her wounds and heal them, even though I couldn't do the same for myself. I just couldn't stand the pain I saw in her eyes. Someone so vibrant and strong shouldn't have to suffer. And there was so much more pain beneath the surface. I was sure of it.

What other poisons plagued her heart? What was in there I couldn't see?

I knew I shouldn't allow myself to care, but I couldn't help it. I couldn't fight the longing to save a life like hers. If one of us had to escape the darkness, it should be her. If I couldn't help myself, I should let her stand on my shoulders and make it out of here alive. Before it was too late.

However much I desired such a thing, there were pivotal questions that remained. Questions I tried to deny but burned their way through the whirring thoughts of my mind anyway: Did I even possess that kind of power? And did I even have the right to try?

I was a walking field of shadows. I had no right to help someone conquer theirs. Everyone I had ever grown close to had gotten hurt in one way or another. I had to watch my own family be ripped to shreds before my eyes.

And since then, I've been denied closeness and lost the only friends I had.

I froze again, wishing it all could go away. The memories. The pain.

When Caroline had talked of the pain brought on by friends, I couldn't help but think of Augustus, though that was a completely different situation. Just like everything else, I was to blame for that.

The pain seared right through me. The pain, loss, and betrayal I'd faced throughout the years had eaten me alive. I had constant parasites sucking whatever life I had left in me.

I pulled my mind away from the images and resisted the urge to excuse myself from the small crowd gathered in the awkwardly large room. Supper was over and Caroline was gone. Evelyn had lured the other guests into the parlor because she arranged for special entertainment—a violinist she heard was particularly skilled in a nearby village. Caroline had said she wanted to spend some time alone in the library, so she left a bit early. As soon as she was out of my sight, reality started sinking in.

So there I was—stuck tormented in the parlor—and all I wanted to do was to stop thinking. For all the thoughts to go away. The thoughts about the loved ones I'd lost. The thoughts about the life I'd lost and would never know. And even the thoughts about Caroline—perhaps *especially* the thoughts about Caroline.

No more thoughts. No more daydreams of what I wished I could do for her. What I wished could happen between us. I tried to hammer it into my mind: *you cannot help her. You cannot love her.* But the more I thought about her, the less I was convinced I could stay away.

But I had to. I *had* to.

I breathed a heavy sigh and leaned against the wall, closing my eyes and listening to the hauntingly beautiful piece coming from the violin. There was still one more thing about her I couldn't ignore. One peculiar thing I didn't understand: despite what Evelyn, Charles, and I thought, Caroline didn't seem to know who we were, or what we were and what our people had done.

Surely it was ignorance that made her treat us so kindly and look at me with those beautiful green eyes. That she kissed me back like she wasn't afraid of turning into one of us herself. But if she really didn't know anything, why did her application bear that symbol? That emblem only our kind knew about.

This couldn't have all been by chance. I had a hard time believing anything about her arrival here was simply by chance. But if she didn't know the truth about us, and it wasn't by chance, how did she come to walk through our doors? Could there be such a thing as fate? If there was, hers would be an unlucky one. A dark fantasy even worse than her dismal past. Far worse.

It would be best I watch her then. Keep her close but not too close. To ensure her safety. I'd keep her safe for the remainder of her stay here and then make sure she left safely. And that she didn't stay.

I groaned at the thought. How was I supposed to accomplish such a task? Everything she did and said was so intriguing to me. Her mind was a universe—a beautiful enigma—that I craved to learn from. Her heart was something I yearned to understand.

I longed to keep her, regardless of who or what I was.

But I couldn't. I was dangerous. A beast. Someone who brought the darkest fates to those around him. It was a hard truth I couldn't ignore. I couldn't have her—I couldn't keep her. No matter how much I wanted to.

When everyone started clapping, I was torn from my stupor. I started clapping, too, and tried my best to act like I'd been paying attention.

"My next piece will be A—"

"Aye, I'm going to stop ya right there," a gruff voice interrupted the performer. I rolled my eyes when I realized it was the insufferable Mr. Tucker. "I've had enough listenin' to your scratchings for one day. If you wouldn't mind, I'd like to excuse myself."

As the man stood up and left, Evelyn quickly said, "Don't mind him, sir. Your playing is fantastic, and I'm sure the rest of us are all enjoying ourselves." She looked around, pleading for everyone's nods with her helpless expression.

I nodded and said, "Please continue." When the man nodded back and began playing the next piece, Saint-Saëns' Violin Concerto in B Minor, Mr. Tucker made his way to the back of the room. I felt his eyes linger on me as he stopped at the door, and when I looked over at him, a slight chill crept up my spine. I half-expected him to say something, but when he didn't, I looked away and did my best to ignore him. After a few seconds, he left the room.

Chapter *Nineteen*

I tried to keep my mind on my research. I was here for a reason. I needed to find out everything I could about the man who could possibly be my father. I needed to find out who I was and to make sense of the entries in my mother's journal. I pulled out a book from one of the shelves in the back of the library, inspecting its contents.

But I couldn't stop thinking about William. About the way my body buzzed when he'd kissed me, my mind melting into a dizzying cocktail of warmth and fizzing lightness. The way my heart shuddered in my chest, and my legs turned to gelatin. I'd never felt anything like that before. I'd been blind to the knowledge that such a feeling existed. William had opened my eyes, and I wasn't sure if I could go back now—that I could go back to seeing things with the dull vision I'd unknowingly been seeing the world through before.

But he wanted to stay away from me. He'd made that clear the other night. It was an impulse I very much understood, but where did that leave us now? Would we forget about the kiss—about each other—and pretend there was nothing between us?

I didn't think I could do that. I didn't think I could go back to the way things were before.

Up until now, I had become so accustomed to loneliness. It was a fate I'd resigned myself to, as it had been a constant presence in my life since I was a child. I was convinced there was no one out there for me. That I would never belong.

But in William, I saw that a life without loneliness was possible. That there was someone I could connect with after all. Someone I yearned for. Someone I wanted to trust.

But there was no future for us, so I needed to forget about it. I needed to move forward and focus on my work here.

I picked up another book and sifted through its contents, trying to keep the thoughts at bay. But I couldn't stop them from coming. I thought of William standing up for me at the supper table when Mr. Tucker was putting me down. I thought of his arm around me as I cried. I thought of his breath against my skin. The way he tasted in the garden. The way he looked at me like I was the most spectacular person in the world. Like I was someone he cared for.

I snapped the book shut.

Life could be so cruel. And the past was hard to break free of. So, despite how much William and I might want to be together—to spend time together and possibly even fall in love together—it might not happen. In the end, our fates were ours to choose. We were the ones who could decide whether to keep it or let it slip through our fingers.

I tried to distract myself again. I walked through the stacks of books at the back of the room, hoping for something that could point me to answers. I pulled out a faded green book, as heavy as an armful of bricks and coated in dust. *I need to focus. William can wait.*

I took a seat at a table in the far corner in the back of the library. Being hidden away like this made me feel safe somehow. The quiet made me feel still. I couldn't even hear clocks ticking. No laughter. No talking. It was just me.

Perhaps I could leave everything behind. Perhaps I could stop hearing William's light laughter fill my head. Perhaps I could stop wondering if I should trust him and if he'd let me in. Perhaps I could stop thinking altogether and just read.

I opened the book and decided to try. I coughed as speckles of dust rose from the pages. I waved them away and skimmed the words for something that could aid me in my search. I'd been looking for about half an hour now, but I couldn't be sure. There were no clocks in the library. I thought it was odd, especially considering how many clocks were in the rest of the house, but I also thought it was a bit magical—like time stopped when one entered the library. I'd been searching for anything that might point to the events of the last Ashdown Harvest Festival—any news clippings, any instructional manuals, any guest registers, or anything at all.

So far, I hadn't been very lucky, but I was hoping this mildew-scented book might have *something*. It was written by one of the family members. The woman William had mentioned in the cemetery: Eleanor Ashdown. I flipped through the pages and looked for Cassius' name. There were no newspaper clippings, as I had hoped there would be—I thought that maybe there would be news coverage on the 1867 festival my mother attended. But no such luck. However, toward the end of the book, I did see something familiar, though I wasn't sure where I'd seen it before. I just knew that I had.

It was a symbol. A thick, inky spiral coiling like the tail of a snake, its head dripping down like liquid onyx. A venomous question mark. "I've seen this somewhere before," I whispered, narrowing my eyes and leaning in for a closer look, "but where?"

"There you are."

I jumped and looked up. "You scared me—" When I saw who it was, I scowled. "What are *you* doing here, Mr. Tucker?"

As if he'd been hoping for this type of reaction from me, the lecherous man grinned. "Isn't it obvious? I wanted to see you," he said, taking a few steps closer to me. My heart turned into a heavy lump in my chest.

"Well *I* don't want to see *you*," I said icily, "so you best be on your way."

His smile cracked into a sneer. "What if I don't want to?" He paced slowly around the desk, and my body went cold. Nausea and fear swirled through my stomach.

"Why are you really here?" I asked, still scowling. I stood up and got ready to leave, picking up my dinner gloves and the green book, all the while hoping he didn't notice my legs beginning to shake.

He took another step closer to me, and I took a step back. He kept walking, and I kept backing away until my shoulders hit the shelf beneath the window. He didn't say a word. He just crept closer, his tongue slithering across his lips. I repeated my question, each word drenched in distaste. "*Why* are you *here*?"

His tongue pushed against the side of his mouth as he

looked my body up and down. Taking one of my loose curls between his fingers, he said, "I wanted to know if you're always this fiery."

"Get your hands off of me," I said, smacking his hand away. He stumbled back slightly, so I took the opportunity to push him with every ounce of strength I had in me. He fell against the desk and cursed under his breath as I rushed by.

"GET BACK HERE!" he yelled. I didn't look back. I just kept running, weaving around the tall bookcases. My breathing was getting strained, and I was too disoriented to remember which way I needed to go to find the exit. Moving in any direction was better than none right now, though, so I turned to my right and got ready to sprint when a sweaty hand caught hold of my arm.

Fear shot up my throat like broken glass. He pulled me against him and tightened his grip. "You're vile," I said, trying to shake myself free, "Let me go." Tears stung my eyes.

"You need to learn to shut up," he barked. "It's about time you show me respect. You always look down on me."

I wished I could tell him just how disgusting he was and that the way he treated me warranted no respect. He treated me no better than a sewage rat and acted like I should be licking his boots. And that was before I knew he wasn't a harmless pig. He was an angry boar who wouldn't leave until he got what he came for.

"Let me go," I said again. "What could you possibly gain from this?"

My whole body shook as my words hung in the air. I tried to formulate a plan of escape. My legs were free. If I could figure out how to wriggle out of his grip, perhaps I could lose him in a dark corner . . .

"I don't have to have a reason to take what I want." His

reply slid into my ear like a poisonous worm. I didn't know what else to do, so I started to scream. It was a loud, glass-shattering scream, but it only lasted half a second. As soon as the noise left my lungs, Mr. Tucker slapped a hand over my mouth and slammed me against one of the stacks of books.

A ringing sounded in my ears. The room was spinning, but I managed to get to my feet. He cackled at my futile efforts and pushed me back to the ground and pinned my hands against the floor. My head fell back with a bang. I tried kicking my legs, but he just pinned them down, too, jabbing them with his thighs. Panic flooded through me and I wanted to cry, but I had to keep trying.

Now that my mouth was free, I tried screaming again. As soon as the noise left my mouth, he lifted his hand behind his head and got ready to swing it at me. But it stopped. Someone had grabbed it. When his body jerked off of me, I saw William, whose eyes were black with fury. He pulled the man off with one heaving motion and punched him right in the jaw, propelling him into the tall bookcase opposite me.

I watched as the enormous case fell backward and hit the one behind it, and that one doing the same with the next, causing a domino effect across the room until the whole library was shaking. William took the man by the collar and punched him again. And again. And again. He kept beating him over and over until Mr. Tucker's body stopped trying to fight back.

"William," I said, my voice hoarse, "William, stop! You'll kill him."

His arm stopped, but he didn't look away from the nearly unconscious man beneath him. He panted heavily, blood trickling from his knuckles to the floor. "I *want* to kill him."

"No, you don't," I said, "You'll never be able to live with yourself if you do."

"I don't know if I could live with myself if I don't," he said, but he let his arm drop. "But I suppose if he dies, his suffering will end far too soon." He got to his feet and pulled Mr. Tucker up with him. He tossed him to his feet, and the man staggered until he regained his balance.

"You'll regret this. I'm not afraid to take this up with the law," the man said, though the quiver in his voice said otherwise. William's violent glare deepened, and he took a step toward him. Mr. Tucker quickly covered his head and hunched forward, whimpering in anticipation.

William walked over and took the man by the collar. "I'll wipe the floor with you if you take this to the police, so I hope that's a promise." The man kept shaking, cowering in William's grasp.

"William, what on earth is going on?" Evelyn asked as she rushed in, her golden dress billowing out behind her. Her husband followed close behind. Evelyn gasped. "William, what did you do to our guest?" Her hand rose to her mouth.

"This *guest*," he said, shaking Mr. Tucker, "tried to take advantage of Miss Blake. Charles, come here and take him." He tossed the man in disgust. When Charles caught Mr. Tucker by the back of his now bloodied shirt, his muscles tensed at the sight of it.

As soon as he was free from my assaulter, William turned around and rushed over to me. He fell to his knees and took my hands in his. "Are you all right?" he asked softly, his dark eyes searching my face.

"I think so," I said. He let out a deep breath.

"Can you walk? Or shall I carry you?" he asked, his voice still gentle. Pink dusted my cheeks at the thought of him carrying me. It was tempting but not necessary, so I shook my head.

"I'm okay. Just shaken up. And my head hurts a bit." *Because he threw me into the books*, I wanted to add, but I thought that if William heard exactly what had happened, he might actually kill the lecherous reporter once and for all.

He cupped a hand to my face. "I am so sorry this happened to you. I will make sure nothing like this ever happens again." He looked into my eyes, and the rock that had formed in my chest fell away, the choking fear that had caught hold of me fading completely. I played his words in my head again, wondering how he intended on keeping me safe. I didn't know how he would, but I liked the thought of it.

"Okay," I said, and I smiled. A relieved, thankful, genuine smile. He saved me. He cared for me. I wanted him to see how grateful I was. That I felt safe with him and that I would always be grateful for what he did for me today. "Thank you. For everything."

"Of course. I would do anything to protect you." He brushed the hair from my face, running his fingers through it and smoothing it out so it wouldn't fall back into my eyes. My heart fluttered as he did it, as he cleansed my hair from having ever been touched by the vile Evan Tucker. "Let's get you to your room," he said. "Here, grab hold of my arm and I'll help you up."

I looped both my arms in William's and let him help me to my feet. I reveled in the warmth of his bicep as he led me out of one of the only bookcases still standing. My smile faded when we rounded the corner. The library looked like a battlefield. Old books and expensive furnishings had been destroyed and thrown about like a tornado had spun through the room. Brand-new light fixtures were ruined, antique tables were snapped in half, and all the books were either torn or mangled as they lied in piles across the room.

Through the carnage, I could see the others. A butler and two maids had arrived and were dressing Mr. Tucker's wounds. One of them had apparently called the family's doctor and were expecting his arrival within the hour. Charles and Evelyn Bower were giving instructions on what room to put him in and what the next course of action should be. On our way out, William glanced over and said, "Mr. Wilson, treat his wounds so he survives, but don't treat him too kindly. Okay?"

"Yes, my lord," the butler said, his shoulders rigid. Everyone was avoiding our gaze but Evelyn, whose lavender eyes followed us on our way out. She probably had no idea what to do, and perhaps she was wondering if this would be the first of many catastrophes that would befall those entering their mansion this year. Whatever she was thinking, she seemed most concerned about William. Her stare was burned straight into his back, so much so that I could feel it as it grazed my shoulder. There was no way he didn't feel it, too. He just didn't look back.

William spent the entire night sitting outside my door. I wondered if he even slept, or if his back ached, or if he got hungry. If he had, he didn't complain. He just stayed on watch and made sure no one came to touch so much as a hair on my head. Though if any of the other reporters or servants had seen the state Mr. Tucker was in when he'd returned to his room, they wouldn't have let the thought so much as cross their minds. And I highly doubted Mr. Tucker would come back for another try.

When I awoke in the morning, William was gone, but

Molly informed me that he did, in fact, stay outside my room the entire night. "He didn't leave until he personally saw Mr. Tucker being dismissed from the mansion this morning," she said as she brushed my hair. I let her get me ready that morning because William had insisted I take the day off to recover.

I wasn't sure how I was going to spend the rest of the day, but I knew this would use up at least an hour. "Where's William now?" I asked, picking up my mother's necklace and stringing it across my neck.

"That's so beautiful!" Molly said as she watched me put it on. "Where did you get it?"

"It was my mother's," I said fondly, "I found it among her things recently, and I can't bear taking it off."

"I can see why," she said, inspecting it closer.

Feeling vaguely self-conscious, I coughed and said, "So, William . . . you never told me where he was."

She removed her gaze from my necklace and put the brush back in its drawer. "That's because I don't know where he is," she said, turning to find a suitable dress for me to wear. When she opened the wardrobe's doors she said, "But I heard he went into the woods east of the mansion. Perhaps he's letting off steam." She flashed me her devilish smile. "He was quite worked up, you know. All on account of protecting you." She giggled, then sighed. "I wish I had a man like that."

My face burned. "He's not *my* man. He's *a* man."

She grabbed a dark gray dress with black ribbons. "Yes, a man who's madly in love with you."

The ruddy shade on my cheeks darkened. "He is not in love with me. He's just a close friend."

She shook her head and handed me the dress. "Right. A friend who knocked a fellow out cold for a casual acquaintance."

My eyes widened. "Did he really knock him out cold?"

She laughed. "No, he seemed able to walk at least. Anyway, I better be off. Enjoy your day, Miss Blake." She curtsied and left the room.

Did William really do that because he loved me?

I thought of the fury in his face when he jerked Mr. Tucker off of me, and then the gentleness in his eyes when he knelt down to see if I was okay.

I shimmied into my dress and was silently grateful this one was both dark and didn't require someone to lace up the back. I could walk around the house without drawing attention to myself. After last night, I didn't want to show my face to the others. I knew I didn't do anything wrong, but I didn't want any more attention than I'd already gotten here. I wanted to slip by unnoticed without looks of concern or whispers coming from the servants and other reporters. I also didn't want Evelyn to coo over me and ask how I was doing. The only person I did want to see was apparently gone.

I sighed and fastened the velvet buckle on the waist of my dress. What else could I do today, with William gone? I slumped onto the bed, but then the thought occurred to me. The blatantly obvious thought of my mother's journal. I'd been so wrapped up in what had happened that I'd completely forgotten the reason I'd gone to the library to begin with.

I reached under my mattress, grabbed the book, and flipped through its pages. When I reached the beginning of the second entry, my hand froze. It was gone. The rest of the second, all of the third, and whatever came after. It was all gone—ripped clean out.

Panic flooded through me. I flipped through it over and over, repeatedly saying "no" and then silently wondering who would have done such a thing, and why? No one even knew about it. How—

Mrs. Wells.

Molly had said she and Mrs. Wells had checked on me throughout the day when I was feverish. I remembered the old woman's face when she told me not to ask about Cassius again, and when she asked how I'd found out. I closed the book, opened my trunk, and buried it inside. When I fastened it shut, I grabbed my dark cloak and left the room. I had to get to the bottom of this.

As I walked the maze-like halls of Ashdown Manor, I kept to the darkest corners, the most unused wings, to avoid anyone's unwanted stares—and even more unwanted questions. Unfortunately, in doing so, I inevitably got lost again. And since I kept to the most unused wings, I had no one to ask for directions.

I didn't know how long I was wandering the halls, but it was long enough that I started getting worried that I wouldn't find my way back at all and that no one would find me for some time. I knew William would scour the building for me if he found I'd gone missing, but who knew when he'd be back? He'd also likely ask why I was wandering around like this to begin with. So I just kept walking.

After I passed the same room three times, I decided to just trace my steps back and then go down a completely different wing altogether. I followed its narrow hall, and the farther down I walked, the more empty the walls became. Paintings disappeared and no rooms were in sight.

An uneasy feeling crawled up my skin, cold and unnerving. My heart rate sped up. I tried to ignore the pressing question in my head and the answer that worried me. Surely I wasn't in William's wing. How could I possibly stumble upon it a second time? Or was it a third time now? Either way, the coincidence would be far too great.

But then I saw it. The mural. Jutting out of a fork in the hallway and extending out in front of me. The cold feeling inside my body intensified, its numbing chill rushing through my limbs like icy lake water. I walked closer, feeling the wall next to me to make sure I was still here—that I hadn't somehow transcended reality, my body a thing of the past. That's what it felt like here. That stale, lifeless chill.

A logic-warping breeze pushed me deeper into the wing.

And there it was. I knew exactly where to open it this time. That strange pocket in the hallway.

I knew I shouldn't go inside. I knew I should leave the wing immediately and respect William's wishes of privacy. But the pull was too great, and the mural too familiar. Maybe it was all right if I went in one more time. It wasn't as if I meant to enter their wing after all. I could just check it out this once—this last time.

Before I could convince myself it was a bad idea, I tugged on the hidden handle and crept inside.

It was just as I'd remembered it. The carnival-colored tiles, the high ceiling, and that enormous mirror with symbols in every corner. My eyes narrowed as I walked closer. *Wait a minute.* I studied the symbols, now realizing they were all the same—just positioned differently, some upside down, some sideways—except the one in the middle, which looked exactly like the symbol that was inscribed at the back of that library book.

"So you're back," a voice said from behind the glass. I jumped, and my sharp intake of breath snagged in my throat as I fell to the floor. I looked toward the source of the voice and saw an image of a man. I didn't see myself in the mirror anymore. Just him.

He had hair so dark that I could barely see it beyond the

darkness behind him—so pitch black it almost looked blue. A *dark* blue—not the river-like cyan blue that shone from his eyes. His nose turned up slightly, and his cheekbones mirrored Charles' in height and sharpness. He had a boyish look about him, and he wore a loose, white work shirt, unbuttoned in the center, that billowed over his fitted black pants.

I couldn't speak. This wasn't a mirror at all. It couldn't be. Someone was inside. "Who are you?" I finally asked, the words coming out ragged.

He laughed softly. "I think I should be asking you the same thing." He sat down and crossed his legs, a gentle smile spreading across his boyish face. "I haven't had a visitor here in quite some time. Well, a *new* visitor anyway."

I still couldn't manage a word. It took me all the composition I had just to ask who he was. He cocked his head to the side. "Your face . . . It looks so familiar. Have you come here before?"

"W-Well, yes, but you know that already, don't you? You just told me that I was back."

He nodded and said, "Yes, that's true, but I meant before that. I didn't get a good look at you then. I had only caught the side of your face and the back of your hair."

"I'd hardly call stumbling into this room visiting. I just investigated what I saw."

"You just happened to stumble into this hidden room where I've been locked away?"

I crossed my arms, but I was still so dumbfounded I didn't know what to do. "Yes . . . that's right. I assure you I didn't know you were here. Do you not believe me?"

"I'm sorry, I didn't mean to offend you. I've been in here quite some time. It looks like I've forgotten how to talk to a woman." He chuckled and scratched the back of his head.

How to talk to a woman? Was he trying to flirt with me? "You still haven't told me your name," I said, standing up and steadying myself. My knees wobbled, but I told myself there was nothing to be afraid of. Yes, it was odd that a person was behind what looked to be a mirror in this secret room, but he seemed harmless, and I didn't think he could get out.

"And you still haven't told me yours," he said, watching as I moved closer. I reached up and touched the mirror with my fingers, then pressed my hand against the glass. *Yes, it's solid. There's no way for him to get out.*

"It's Caroline," I said absently, tapping my knuckles against the mirror.

"Hello, Caroline, I'm Augustus."

Chapter *Twenty*

My heart nearly stopped. "Augustus?"

"Yes . . .?" He raised an eyebrow, a smile creeping up his face.

"Augustus." I repeated, "William's Augustus?"

His smile vanished. "What are you talking about?"

"William—he . . . He told me about his good friend Augustus. About how . . ." My voice trailed off. I wasn't sure if I should say any more. William surely deserved his privacy, even though I was imposing on it already.

"He told you what?" the man asked, his casual manner stiffening.

"Nothing. Nothing really." That was partially true anyway. He barely told me anything about Augustus—just that he was his friend and that he'd caused him great pain. I looked back up, studying his eyes. What happened between those two?

He looked away, and neither of us said anything. What could I say to him? I had so many questions, but I wasn't sure how to ask them, or what was okay for me to say. I didn't know this person. Surely there was a reason he was in there, right?

He bent forward to look at me closer and squinted. "Are you sure you've never been here before?"

"Of course I'm sure," I said, shifting my weight, "Why do you keep asking?"

"Because you look familiar."

"Well, I'm sorry, but you don't," I said, and he laughed. "Fair enough."

"Augustus . . ." I repeated his name, more for myself than for him. I just couldn't believe it. This was the Augustus who was William's former best friend. Why didn't he tell me he was here?

"Yes?" he said again.

I looked at him and decided to just come out and ask him. "What happened between you and William?"

He sighed as he sat down and leaned an elbow against his bended knee. "You really don't know?"

I shook my head.

He sighed again. "I don't really relish the idea of living through that particular memory, so why don't we just leave it as William and I were dear friends and something got in the way, and he decided he should put an end to it?"

"That—that doesn't make any sense," I said, shaking my head. "He's torn up about—" I stopped myself again. Better not say too much.

Augustus made a *tch* noise. "Oh, I'm sure," he said sarcastically, "I'm sure he's really torn up about what he did to me." He made another *tch* sound and shook his head. "The man's a beast."

My stomach jerked. "William is *not* a beast," I said, my voice a little too loud.

He raised his eyebrow again. "What did you say?" He looked almost amused.

"I said he's not a beast."

He laughed one bitter bark that shot out like a bullet. "Don't joke like that," he said, resting his face against his hand. "You may actually convince me that you're serious."

"I *am* serious. William is a good man," I said.

He studied me for a moment. "You're in love with him, aren't you?"

My face went bright pink. "I am *not* in love with him! He's just . . . a good man. That's all." I looked away. I knew if he looked in my eyes, he'd see I was lying. Molly was hard enough to ward off. I didn't need him challenging me, too.

He rubbed his forehead and groaned. "I sure hope you're telling me the truth." Blood pounded in my ears. Maybe it was time to leave.

"I assure you I am," I said, still avoiding his eyes, "But I—"

"What is that you're wearing?" he interrupted, slowly getting to his feet. He craned his neck forward and said, "I recognize that pendant."

I clutched the silver hanging from my neck. "What? You do?"

He nodded and looked closer. "Yes, it's from a painting my father created years ago."

"Your father?" I squeezed it tighter against my chest and turned slightly. I was starting to get uncomfortable with all the staring.

When I looked back at him, his expression had changed. His eyes were wide, and his lips parted as his mouth dropped open. "You're the woman in the painting," he said. He blinked a few times and then looked closer.

"I'm the what?"

He squinted again, as if that helped him analyze my every feature. Then he shook his head. "No. You're not her. Her hair was brassier than yours. Maybe even golden."

"Golden . . ." I whispered, pushing away any speculations. "Who was this woman in the painting?"

"She was someone my father was quite smitten with. I never met her personally. I just know about her. She became quite famous among us. He claimed he loved her, but it was a bit more of an obsession, if you ask me."

"Your father?" The blood pulsed even harder in my ears, and it was getting hard to hear myself think. "W-Was your father a painter?"

"I suppose you could say that. He didn't have a declared profession. He just did as he pleased." He rolled his eyes, apparently not amused by his father's laissez-faire lifestyle.

I thought back to the letters. *Lucky for me, he doesn't have to go to work*, my mother had written. "Was he an Ashdown?" I asked. It was hard to hear my own voice over the pounding in my ears.

"Eh, kind of. He was a distant relative, you could say. His surname wasn't Ashdown, but I suppose technically he was one. Like the Bowers of this house. In a different clan, though, of course."

"Clan?" I shook my head. "What do you mean he was in a different clan?"

He stared at me, either shocked or horrified, or perhaps a bit of both. "You mean you don't know?"

My heart had been beating so quickly that it started to slide off pace. The unequal rhythm paired with the thumping in my ears made me feel faint. I tried steadying my breaths. "Don't know what?"

He looked at me carefully, as if deciding whether to tell

me whatever it was I didn't know. And I waited. And waited. It was getting harder to breathe steadily, so I asked again. "What is it that I don't know? Tell me." When my voice came out as more of a shout, I added, "Please."

"Are you sure you want to know?"

"Yes. Tell me."

He let out a long breath and then looked me in the eye. "Do you promise you won't be afraid? Do you promise you can handle it?"

Well, I wasn't until now, I wanted to say, but I just nodded. "Yes. I promise."

He leaned in closer, his face almost hitting the glass barrier between us. "Have you noticed anything strange about this house? Anything off?" His voice was lower now.

I thought back on everything. The beautiful rooms, the lavish décor . . . but nothing seemed out of the ordinary. "I don't know what you mean." But then I remembered the painting on the wall. The one of the woman who looked exactly like Evelyn but had been painted in another time.

"Have you noticed anything . . . different about the Ashdown family?" I thought of Evelyn's beauty. Of William's striking looks and how youthful he looked for his age. His declarations of being dangerous.

All I could do was nod.

The corner of his mouth twitched, as if starting to smile, but his eyes were still serious as they stared right into me. "That's because they're not human. They're vampires."

The thin hairs on my neck pricked up, and the blood drained from my face. "What? Vampires?" I shook my head and let out a shaky laugh, "There's no such thing."

"I assure you there is."

I shook my head harder, my heart rattling in my chest. "No. No, there's not." Maggie's lullabies filled my head. She always sang songs and recited lyrics about the dangers of demons and shadows, monsters and creatures, and even vampires. There was one she sang all the time that focused on vampires. It was the most unnerving one of them all. I could still hear the haunting words as if she were singing to me now:

In the night, they will hunt and will play
Their twisted games, and the hunt
Will go on until they've stolen
All your names.

They won't stop until they're free
To do whatever makes them bite,
So you better hide away
Or they'll eat you in the night.

And you'll never fly away.
Fly away.

My heart skipped in mismatched steps again, and the room around me started to spin. This couldn't be true. William wasn't a—

But I thought back to the cemetery. When he told me that his mother was a servant of the house before the festival and that he was, too. That was almost thirty years ago, but he looked thirty himself. I had thought that maybe he looked young for his age.

I thought back on all the times William warned me to leave. I thought back on the Clarkes' terrified faces back at the inn, and the way Mr. Clarke had told me that everyone at the festival had been massacred. What could cause such brutal destruction was surely not human.

"This," I muttered. "It was this." I looked up at

Augustus. "This is what they wanted to hide, isn't it?" I said, but he didn't meet my gaze. His face had fallen, his eyes lost somewhere else. My breathing picked up again, and it became so shallow that the familiar pinch of anxiety pulled at my chest.

I shook my head. "No. No, that can't be. William wouldn't do anything like that."

"Anything like what?"

I shot him a glance. "Kill people."

He looked at me, stung. "I never said he killed anyone. I said he was a vampire."

"What . . .?"

He crossed his arms. "As much as I dislike William—hate him, actually—he didn't *kill* anyone."

I shook my head again, and it started to get dizzy. "I still don't understand."

He smirked. "Perhaps it's better that way." I tried to focus on my breathing. This couldn't be happening. "You shouldn't trust him," he said. "He may have never killed a person, but he's done a lot worse. He's a dangerous man, Caroline." He stopped. "No. He's not even a man. He's a beast. Just like my father."

"Your . . . father? The painter?"

"Yes. The arrogant, selfish, obsessed fool. That man was a monster. The worst kind of vampire." I winced when he said the last word. The venom I'd always heard behind it stung from a wound I thought had healed. My thoughts turned to my mother. She was in love with an arrogant, obsessed vampire. What did he do to her? Did she suffer? Did he drain her of her blood and tear her apart? How did she meet him? None of this made any sense, but maybe I didn't want it to.

My stomach knotted in my belly. I felt sick.

"What was your father's name?" I asked, a new ringing

finding its way in my ears.

"Cassius Laurent."

The name echoed across the spinning room. The elusive man I'd read about—that I tried to learn more about. The man who might have been my father. But that couldn't be true. He was a vampire. Vampires weren't . . . living beings. "How did your father . . . How was Cassius your father? He was a vampire, right?"

"Yes, he was, and so am I."

My stomach turned again, but I tried not to react.

"How did your father come to give you life if he was a vampire?"

His fingers tapped against his leg. "Well, there are two ways a vampire can have children. One way is the more gruesome way, and not technical. When a vampire bites you, you become part of his or her clan unless you swear otherwise. The other way is more aligned with the natural way. Two vampires can create a child in the mother's womb, despite the obvious . . . complications." He looked at me grimly. "My parents had to seek the proper help, get the proper *medicine*. The proper incantation and sorcery. Then they could have a child together."

"Do you age like a human then?" I asked.

"No, it's the same as with those who are bitten. I only age to around the ages of my parents."

I thought about this a moment—about how odd it was that such forms of conception were even possible. That any of this was possible. "What happened to your mother?" I asked.

He bit down on his lip. "My father killed her when he became obsessed with that woman—Claire." When my body twitched at the sound of her name, he looked at me and narrowed his eyes. Something flashed over them. "You're her daughter, aren't you?"

"Yes," I whispered, studying the tiles on the floor, "Yes, I am."

He sighed. "There are also ways for vampires to have children with humans."

My heart stopped. "What are you saying?"

He gave me an apologetic smile. "I'm just saying that it's something that is possible. That's all."

I stared at him blankly, paralyzed. I shook my head. "I couldn't be . . . He couldn't."

"I never said you were. I was just saying it's a possibility."

I couldn't think about that possibility. I couldn't think about any of this. I didn't want to.

I changed the subject. "William said he was a boy when his mother and father died. About twelve, I believe."

"He was. He and I were friends." His eyes looked off wistfully, but then he frowned. "But that was short-lived."

"But how could he age? My aunt always told me vampires couldn't age."

"A common misconception among mortals," he said. "We are immortal; but as I mentioned, we can age. When a human is turned, they age to whatever age the vampire who turned them was. William was dying. Bleeding out. Eleanor Ashdown turned him, so he aged to the age she was."

"So, someone could be an elderly vampire?" I asked, but he just smiled, amused.

"No," he said with a chuckle, "No. Someone who was older when getting turned by a younger vampire can reverse slightly. However, older people don't have the ability to turn. Their bodies are too frail for the transformation."

The transformation. But . . . All of this still didn't explain what happened to my mother. I opened my mouth to ask, but I couldn't get myself to. Not here. Not now. I wanted to see her first. I wanted to find this painting and see for myself if Augustus was telling the truth. I couldn't trust him so blindly.

My thoughts shot to William, and my heart ached. Had he been lying to me all along? And had he really done things worse than murder?

"There's something you must understand," Augustus said. I looked up at him. "Vampires can be dangerous in love. When vampires turn, everything in them intensifies. Not just their physical strength, but their emotions, too. Their passions get deeper, their fantasies wilder. Everything they feel gets amplified. Love. Lust. Hate. Obsession."

He pointed to my necklace, and the paralysis took hold of my body again. I clutched the pendant until my fingers turned white. I tried not to think of what fate my mother might have reached—how much suffering she'd endured. "But he loved her," I said.

Augustus shook his head. "He claimed to love her, but he was just a mad fool, lost in an unruly obsession."

I couldn't wrap my head around all of this. Why did Evelyn want to hold the festival, risking hundreds of people's lives? Did she really believe herself to have such control? Did William?

I remembered William's protests about the festival. He didn't think it was a good idea, so that made him good . . . right?

My eyes stung. "But one can love without obsession. Those two things don't necessarily equal each other. Surely not all vampires become obsessed over actually loving someone?"

I thought of the way William looked at me when he asked if I was all right. Of the way he smiled at me. The way he kissed me.

The way he kissed me.

My heart sank. Thoughts I desperately wished to keep away sprung to my mind, and I begged them to leave me alone. *William isn't like Cassius. He's a good man.* I tried to press the thought into my mind, but it wouldn't stick, and each time I inhaled, a sharp, quiet cry escaped my lungs. *This isn't happening*, I told myself. *This has to be a dream. Another bad dream.*

"I suppose I don't know," Augustus said, "But what I saw was enough to make me never want to touch something as powerful as love."

"But one cannot live without love," I said, blinking at him through teary eyes, "What kind of life is that?" But as I said the words, I realized how little I even knew about it—how little experience I had in it.

He snorted. "Do you fancy a life with William or something?"

The words hit me straight in the chest. "Why does it matter?" I asked, my hands now in fists at my sides, nails digging into my palms.

He leaned against the glass. "You still don't get it, do you? He's dangerous. You'll regret getting close to him, if that's what you're intending to do."

You're wrong, I wanted to say, *he's not dangerous*. But how could I know for sure? All I knew was how he made me feel. But how many times had my blind leaps of faith served me well in my life?

I couldn't even think of any. The only person who had never betrayed me was Maggie, but I was starting to realize that even she didn't tell me the truth. All she did was lock me in a cage of fear with no way out. She warned me of the shadows but didn't teach me how to spark a fire to escape.

"Why should I trust you?" I asked.

He smirked. "I guess you don't have to, but why would I tell you all this just to lie to you? I have nothing to gain or lose. Look at me. Look at where I am. If you don't believe me, go and ask William yourself." He shook his head and laughed bitterly, his eyes drifting to the distance. "But he won't tell you anything." Then he met my eyes. "You'll stay away from him if you know what's good for you. Your mother didn't stay away from my father, and look what happened to her."

Fire shot through me. "How dare you speak of my mother like that. You don't know anything about her!"

"I likely know a lot more than you, considering I know exactly how she died."

My blood turned cold, and my stomach was even more nauseous. This conversation was becoming unbearable. I couldn't stay any longer. "I'm not ready for this," I thought angrily, not realizing I'd said it out loud. A tear escaped down my face.

"For what?" he asked. "The truth?"

My body was shaking. "For someone to tell me who I should and should not believe," my voice was rising rapidly, "and to tell me he knows more than me about my own mother. That you know how she died—"

"I do know how she died!" he said, his voice getting louder but still not matching mine. His breathing grew heavy, but his eyes stayed burrowed into mine. He took a deep breath. In a more controlled voice, he continued, "I'm sorry. I shouldn't have said that. I'm just . . ." He frowned. "I just don't want anyone else to get hurt." He looked up at me over his dark lashes. There was great sorrow in his eyes. A different kind of sorrow than the kind I saw in William, though I couldn't place my finger on why or how.

I nodded and took a deep breath myself. I wanted to tell him it was all right, but I would just be lying. There was only one more thing I wanted to ask him. "Tell me how my mother died."

He flinched, like someone had come up and slapped him on the back. The room felt even colder, and I silently wondered if I'd freeze to death if I stayed too long. Were vampires only comfortable in the cold?

"I'm sorry, but I can't tell you that," he said finally.

My eyebrows drew together. "Why not?"

"Because . . . you might never . . . be the same if you knew." I stared at him, completely lost at what to say. "I'm sorry," he said, "but some secrets are better left buried."

Voices came from outside, and panic instantly spiked through me. "Oh no!"

"Go," he said, nodding his head toward the door. "Quick."

I didn't have time to think of anything else, so I swept across the tiny room and started down the narrow stairs. Before I fully made my descent, Augustus stopped me one more time and said, "Just think about what I said. Please."

My hand stopped on the wall leading to the entrance. At first I didn't reply. I just continued down the stairs. But then I turned to face him. "Where can I find that painting of my mother?" I asked.

There was a pause before he answered.

"Around back near the servants' quarters," he said, "There's a door leading to a cellar. Walk down that corridor and head to your right. There, you will find things the Ashdown family, including the Bowers, have locked away. Things they don't want anyone else to see."

"Okay," I said faintly, avoiding his eyes. I paused, sniffing as a tear slid down my cheek. "I'll see for myself which one of you is lying." Before he could respond, I fled down the stairs and left the hidden room, sealing its entrance behind me.

I felt like I was about to vomit. My head was pounding, and I could barely walk. I didn't want to be anywhere near this wing anymore. A lump formed in my throat as I fled to my room as quickly as I could without looking back. I silenced any sobs that tried crawling up my throat and fled as quickly as I could. I knew it was risky not to check who could see me, but I didn't care anymore.

I wanted to go to the cellar immediately, but I knew now wasn't a good time. Not in the state I was in. I felt like I'd just made it out of a harrowing journey, lethargic and barely breathing.

I needed to lie down. I'd have plenty of opportunities to get to the bottom of everything. But for right now, I just wanted to sleep. I didn't want to think of William and wonder if everything between us was a lie. I didn't want to know if Cassius was my father or if he killed my mother.

I just wanted to close my eyes and think nothing at all.

Chapter *Twenty-One*

The sky turned black as smoke covered the mansion grounds. I couldn't see anything. I could only hear screams—screams and horrible, terrible, unnatural sounds, like the roar of a lion mixed with the screeching of a crow. Then I saw flashes of things I couldn't make out. My heart raced. I looked everywhere I could, grasping at the smoke, but there was nothing I could do to stop the screaming. They were getting closer, louder—suffocating me and ringing in my ears.

I woke up, gasping for breath and caked in sweat. My hair was stuck to my face, and my skin was burning. I had fallen asleep in my clothes.

"Miss?"

I jumped. "Oh, Molly, I didn't see you there."

"I'm the one who woke you up," she said slowly,

studying my face.

"Oh." I wondered what would have happened if she hadn't woken me. If I had been lost in those screams any longer.

She tilted her head and looked down at me. "Are you okay? You look frightened. And very uncomfortable. Why did you fall asleep in your clothes in the middle of the day?" She leaned forward and placed the back of her hand on my forehead. "Are you feeling ill again?"

I gently swiped her hand away. "No, I'm fine. I just had a headache." Although my headache was gone, I wasn't any less flustered than when I'd fallen asleep.

"Would you like for me to draw you a bath?" she asked. I knew it was probably a good idea, considering my current state, but sitting in a tub, vulnerable and alone with nothing but my thoughts, was the last thing I wanted to do right now.

"No, thank you, though. What time is it, by the way?"

"It's about five o'clock, Miss. Are you hungry? I believe Lord Ashdown is bringing in something delicious for supper soon." My stomach sunk at the sound of his name. What was I going to do? Was it best to confront him? But even if I did, how would I know if he'd answered honestly? If he'd been lying all this time, he would have proved to be an excellent liar by now.

As the thoughts caved in on me, I decided there was no time to think of him yet. I needed to go to the cellar. I needed to find out if Augustus was telling the truth.

"No, that's okay. I'm not hungry, Molly, but I fancy a walk outside, so I'll be off to do that, if you don't mind. First, I'll get changed, though, but I can do it myself." I laughed nervously when I realized I was talking much more quickly than normal, my words tripping over each other as they fumbled out of my mouth.

She looked at me quizzically and said, "Okay, well let me know if you need anything."

"I will, thank you. You best hurry. Actually, I'll come with you." I helped her out so that I could leave as quickly as possible and get things underway. I was afraid of what might happen if my mind was left to wander right now. I didn't want to find out.

I practically pushed Molly out of the room and scurried down the stairs, hoping she wouldn't realize I hadn't stopped to change my clothes. My heart pounded as I took each step, skipping two or three beats at a time as I rushed down the winding staircase.

I looked around and saw no one but froze when I saw the front door. I remembered William smiling at me, excited to tell me the news that I would work on the construction aspect of the festival. That excitement couldn't have been fabricated.

He was so sad when I'd first come here—anger and bitterness overtaking the pain inside him, protecting his scars. He was so insufferable, too. But slowly, he started opening up. I saw him truly smile. I saw him cry. He couldn't have faked all of that, could he? No one was that good at deception.

Then I thought of Rose—of her feigned friendship. The twitch of her mouth when she denied knowing a thing and turned things on me. *This is different*, I told myself, thinking back to his protection of me in the library. That wild look in his eyes when he saw what Mr. Tucker was trying to do. That couldn't be faked. He cared about me.

But then I remembered how he kept beating him and beating him, even after the man stopped flailing. Was that borne of obsession or affection?

I made my way to the servants' quarters and then around the back, as Augustus had told me. Sure enough, there were two large cellar doors boarded up near the back. My brow furrowed. Why was it boarded up? I looked around to make sure no one was watching and then curled my fingers around the first of the three wooden planks sealing the doors shut.

I heaved and pulled, but it wouldn't budge. I put my hands on my hips and looked at it from various angles, then tried again. I put my foot against the bottom of the doors and pulled as hard as I could.

My fingers slid off the wood. "Ow!" I waved my hand in the air before inspecting it and finding a splinter wedged into my finger. "Perfect," I grunted. I looked back at the entrance. There was no getting in there now. I needed to come back with something to pry the boards off with, and I'd have to do it when no one would see me.

I looked around. It was a beautiful day, and the sun was ready to set. Why was it that the first thing to pop into my mind was William? That exciting jolt I got every time I'd go back down to meet him—whether it was in the morning or in the evening after only parting briefly between work and supper. I was attracted to him like a moth to a flame. Would he burn me if I got too close, just as he'd said?

I took one more look at the cellar doors and then stalked back towards the servants' quarters. I was about to walk past the kitchen and into the hallways leading to the main part of the house when I noticed Mrs. Wells. She was talking with the cook. She wasn't in her room.

I looked around for another way into the servants' quarters, sneaking beneath the windows and swerving past the cellar doors and over to the other side of the house.

Nothing.

I let out a puff of air, which sent a loose lock of hair fluttering from my face. I leaned against the gray walls and let myself slide against it until I was on the ground. I was so tired. Mentally and physically. I couldn't remember when I'd eaten last, but even if I were offered food right now, I felt too sick to eat it.

I let my eyes close as two swallows sang in a nearby tree. My mind was creating that familiar fog of drifting to sleep when I heard my name.

"Caroline?"

I looked and saw William. I let in a sharp breath, which made me cough. He frowned in concern and leaned down to offer me his hand. "Here, let me help you," he said, cradling the small of my back and helping me to my feet. My heart jerked as he smiled at me, and even after everything that had happened today, I felt like jelly in his arms.

"I'm all right," I said, backing away swiftly and releasing myself from his grip. His arms hovered in the air where he'd been holding me.

"Okay," he said, his brows knitting together. His eyes found mine as he said, "Caroline, are you sure you're all right? I've been worried about you all day. I had figured you'd rest."

"I did rest a bit," I said quickly, only briefly glancing in his direction and then turning my gaze to the swallows. "I'm quite well."

An awkward rift formed between us, a void too uncomfortable to possibly go unnoticed. I thought that there was no way he couldn't feel it, but when I looked at him, he didn't look uncomfortable at all. He looked wounded, and I had to resist the strong urge to soothe him—to give him a safe place to turn to, as I'd told him I would.

I wanted to fulfill that promise I gave him—that he could cry and that I'd worry, and that he could come to me and I'd be there—but what if he wasn't being honest with me? He never even told me what he was.

He reached out to touch me, but I jerked away.

"What's wrong?" he asked, and the pain in his voice made me want to cry. "Did I do something to offend you?"

I didn't know what to say. I didn't know if I should talk to him—confront him and ask him everything. But what would he think of me? He'd told me not to venture into his wing, but I had anyway. Then again, he might have only wanted me to avoid it because of Augustus. Because there was a skeleton still alive in his closet.

"If it's about last night, I'm so sorry." Without meaning to, I looked at him in surprise. He continued, "I was an ogre, blind with rage. When I saw what that . . . that *animal* was trying to do to you—" He shook his head, his jaw clenched, his eyes lit with fury "—I lost my head. I shouldn't have been so reckless. You deserve protection, and he deserves a lot worse than what I did to him last night, but it still wasn't right for me to go that far. If I scared you, I sincerely apologize."

He looked at me with such softness in his face—such tenderness in his eyes—that for a moment, I forgot everything else. And when the memories of Augustus surfaced, I couldn't help but poke holes in his accusations against William. William was someone who shut out the world and those around him, but here he was begging for my forgiveness for something he did while protecting me. That wasn't something a "beast" would do.

It's possible he's changed, I thought. *Perhaps he isn't who Augustus remembers him to be.*

"It's all right, really," I said, reflexively reaching out to touch his arm but then stopping and pulling it back. "I'm grateful for what you did. You saved me. Thank you."

He smiled back, but his eyes weren't in it. It was clear that I'd hurt him, but I didn't know what to do about it. I didn't know if I could trust him. But what if I could? The internal struggle raging in my head was driving me mad.

I couldn't see him anymore. Not until I figured this out. "I'm sorry, but I really have to go," I said, turning to leave, but he caught me by the arm.

When I looked back at him, I saw the pain in those soft, dark eyes. "Are you really all right?"

I gave him a tight, wooden smile and said, "Of course. I'll see you at supper." And then I left before I could change my mind.

At first, I'd thought he'd follow me, but when I turned to look, he wasn't there. My heart ached. The William I knew was kind and full of scars. I had promised to help him heal, not wound him further.

As I continued walking, I looked to my left and saw the kitchen. It was empty. *The servants must be getting everything put out for supper*, I thought. *This is my chance.*

I crept through the kitchen as quietly as I could, despite how empty it was. I couldn't risk any mistakes. As soon as I moved past it, I tip-toed around to the hallway leading to the servants' quarters.

I peeked into each room, trying to find which one could be Mrs. Wells', but unless I were to go into the dressers in each one, I wouldn't know whose room was whose.

"Miss Blake?" I turned around quickly, pressing my back against one of the doors. It was Molly. "What are you doing here?"

"I'm just looking for Mrs. Wells," I said, forcing a laugh. "I, um, I have a note for her."

Her eyes landed on my empty hands. "Where?"

I forced out another laugh and said, "Oh, silly me. I must have forgotten to grab it." She eyed me like I'd gone insane. "But, um, which door is hers so I can drop it off when I come back?"

She pointed to the door at the very end of the hall. *It's a good thing I didn't comb each room*, I thought. "She's in the last door at the very end. I'm sharing it with her while I'm here." She beamed, her smile stretching beneath her freckles, then leaned in and whispered, "It's the biggest room."

"Wow! That's really great, Molly. Well, thank you. You can go on and do whatever it is you need to do. Sorry to keep you."

I turned to go when she said, "But I'm supposed to come see you now, Miss. It's almost supper, and you're still in that dress you slept in." My heart pounded. Any moment now, Mrs. Wells could show up and I would lose my opportunity to search for the stolen journal entries.

"Right. Okay. Well, why don't you get everything ready upstairs and I'll meet you? I just need some time down here to think before I come up." What a terrible lie. I watched in hopeful agony as I waited to find out if Molly would let me go, whether or not she believed me.

She stared at me quizzically but said, "Okay . . . If you insist . . . I will see you shortly." She made a face to herself at how strange I was being and then left. As soon as she rounded the corner, I turned back around and made my way to the end of the hall.

When I opened the door, I made my way into a room with minimal furniture, two four-poster beds, and a fireplace. Molly was right—it was a lot larger than the other rooms. Probably twice as large. I supposed Mrs. Wells had earned it since she'd been working at the mansion for most of her life.

I scanned the room for her dresser and went there first. I felt guilty as I went through her things but tried to remember that she probably went through mine, too. She was the only one who knew about the journal and was the only one, other than Molly, to go in and out of my room when I was sick.

It had to be in here somewhere.

I went to the bed next, checking under the mattress and between the sheets. I turned to her bedside table and opened its single drawer. As I reached my hand inside, I heard an angry voice behind me. "What are you doing in here?"

I swallowed down any fear or nervousness and flipped around. I had nothing to lose by being bold now. "Where are the rest of the entries?"

The old woman shook her head. "I can't tell you that."

I clenched my fist. "Yes, you can! And you just admitted to it!"

"It's for your own good, Caroline. Stop searching for answers that are better left in the dark."

"Nothing is *ever* better left in the dark. You had no right to rip those out. You went into my things and stole part of the only connection I have with my mother. I didn't know her, but that journal had her thoughts. She touched those pages. She wrote her deepest feelings on them. When I read them, I felt like she was talking to me." My voice broke as tears stung my eyes, but I swallowed that down, too. "How could you?" I whispered.

"You don't understand, Caroline," she said, her gray hair bobbing as she shook her head.

"What don't I understand? That you were on Cassius' side?" I thought of what she'd said—about how she'd been here for decades. I shot her a look. "You're one of Cassius' followers, aren't you? That's why you won't let me see those pages."

Her eyes widened, and she staggered closer to me. One of her withered hands pressed against her bed as she steadied herself. "What? Who told you—"

"You know Cassius is my father, don't you? You've known all along—"

"What? Cassius isn't your father, Caroline."

"How would you know?"

"Because I knew your father. Don't—"

"How? *How* did you know him?"

"He was my son," she said, and the room went quiet.

She was lying. She had to be.

"No," I said, falling back against the bedside table. Her mouth was still in an angry, hard line, but her eyes were turning red.

"Your father, Richard, was my little boy."

"But my mother was in love with Cassius," I said, trying to make sense of everything. My mother was in love with Cassius twenty-nine years ago. I was twenty-eight. There was no way my mother met someone else in such a short time. She was smitten by the man.

Mrs. Wells stared fixedly on the table behind me, her eyes sharing that same faraway look I'd seen in so many others recently. A look of peering into the past—a past that shouldn't be revisited. A look I saw a lot in Maggie growing up. She would just sit in her rocking chair and look far away, as if she'd left the present completely.

"She *was* in love with Cassius," she said, still not looking at me, "but your father loved her very much. He'd loved her since he was a child." The corners of her mouth rose up in a smile. She looked at me then. "Your father's sister was best friends with your mother and aunt. The three of them were inseparable. Richard, being just a year and a half older than Geraldine, was always around when her friends came over."

I frowned. If the three of them were so close, why hadn't Maggie told me any of this herself? The old woman continued, a wistful twinkle in her eyes, "Richard teased them when they were children, and oh, how your mother would get so incensed by his antics." She chuckled, "But, as they all bloomed into young adults, Richard realized his feelings for Claire weren't the feelings of a pestering older brother. He confided in me that he was in love with her, but he was shy, and he was afraid of rejection."

"Then what happened between my mother and Cassius?"

She sighed and stood upright, smoothing a wrinkle in her skirt as she went to the fireplace and knelt down to start a fire. She threw in a couple of logs and continued. "Your mother was infatuated with him—with Cassius. He was handsome, rich, and extraordinarily charming. He knew how to get what he wanted." She took a match from a box next to the fireplace, lit it, and tossed it between the logs. "She was head-over-heels smitten by him. Poor Richard watched her, utterly heartbroken. He kept going back and forth between deciding if he would tell her how he felt or if he should just let her be happy with Cassius and try to move on."

She smiled as she kindled the fire. "But he knew he could never stop loving your mother. He'd never loved anyone the way he loved her, and I think he knew that even if he moved on and got married to someone else, there would always be a part of his heart that would never stop beating for her. And that a hole would form where hers was supposed to fit—a hole that would never go away."

She let out a heavy sigh. "I worried for him. I didn't want to watch his heart break and slowly crumble throughout his life, so I told him to confess his feelings for her. He wouldn't, of course, at least not until Cassius started . . ." Her voice trailed off. The fire cracked as it came to life. She watched the flames as they slowly ate at the logs.

"Started what?" I asked, part of me wishing I'd never have to learn the answer, but I knew I needed to know. I had to find out what happened. I walked up behind her and crouched next to her. Orange reflected in her eyes as she stared into the flames.

"He became obsessed. He wanted her so badly, but he was very controlling. She had to do whatever he said, and he treated her like a glass figurine he'd like to place on a mantle and stare at when he pleased. He started saying things that frightened her, and he would get carried away when he kissed her."

The fire's warmth burned against my arms as I listened. The more Mrs. Wells spoke, the more my heart broke for my mother. She must have been so scared. Judging by her journal entries, she was so young and naive. She must have felt like the rug had been ripped from beneath her feet. "She saw him as a fairytale prince," I said, thinking back on her entries.

"She did at first," she said, nodding, "but she soon discovered he was the dragon. The beast who wanted to capture the princess, whether she liked it or not."

I pulled at the strings on the bodice of my dress and tried to wrap my head around everything. Cassius wasn't my father. My father really was a man named Richard, a humble blacksmith who loved my mother with all his heart, just as Maggie had told me.

A great wave of relief washed over me, and I was almost able to breathe again, until my mind went back to William. Back to Augustus and everything that led me to doubt William's true nature. His true intentions. "Are vampires' emotions heightened?" I asked. "Is that why he easily became obsessed and dangerous?"

The fire had completely consumed the logs now, taking up almost the entire space of the fireplace. Its heat was too great to sit in front of, so I stood up and waited for her reply. "Yes," she said, "and it can be very dangerous." She looked at me then, and I could tell there was something else—something she wanted to say.

But she just looked away again—looking one last time at the rolling flames before she got up and walked to her dresser. She knelt behind its weathered base, reaching behind it and pulling out the familiar yellowed pages of my mother's journal. My breath caught in my chest, and I didn't know what to say. So when she handed them to me, all I could say was, "Thank you so much."

"Don't thank me yet," she interrupted, a little too harshly, then smiled apologetically and said, "Just . . . read them, and I'll tell you the rest." When I smiled and nodded, she touched me softly on the cheek. "My dear granddaughter. I never thought I would see you again."

Granddaughter. I was so wrapped up in what she was telling me that I completely ignored the obvious fact right in front of me. She was my grandmother, and Molly was my cousin. I couldn't believe it. "I have family," I said, a grin breaking across my face, but then it dropped.

All my life, I had had more than just Maggie. I had a grandmother who knew about me. A grandmother who never visited. A grandmother who let me live that life as an outcast, taking care of an aunt who should have been taking care of me.

"Yes, you do, and I've always loved you."

I looked at her, studying the lines on her wrinkled face. If she loved me so much, why had she never come?

Anger simmered inside me, but I tried to remain calm. I needed answers, not a confrontation. At least not yet. "You said you never thought you'd see me again, but I've never seen you before."

"I helped your mother give birth to you," she said, her

face pulling tighter together. "Maggie and I both helped."

"What? Wouldn't you have gotten sick?"

She stared at me. "Did I get sick?"

I nodded slowly, thrown off by her question. "Maggie said my mother died in childbirth after losing my father to influenza. Didn't she have it, too? Maggie was never clear. She said it was because the strain of losing my father was too hard on my mother, but I could always tell there was something she wasn't telling me. I thought that maybe she was also sick."

Mrs. Wells' confused stare turned to one of surprise before she lifted a hand to rub her forehead and temples. "I can't believe Maggie never told you."

"Told me what?"

Pain pulled at her face even tighter, and I could tell she didn't want to say what she needed to. She swallowed, and after a shaky breath, she looked into my eyes. "Your mother was killed by Cassius, Caroline. So was your father."

Horror struck through me, and the feeling of nausea returned. "S-so she didn't die in childbirth?"

"Well, she *did* die in childbirth," Mrs. Wells said quietly, "and she *was* deeply grieved by the loss of your father, but he only died a few minutes before she did. Maybe even seconds. Cassius . . ." Her voice trailed off again, and her muscles tensed. "I don't want to get into it, but he . . . I-I can't say it. All I will tell you is that your father died fighting for you, and so did your mother." She gave me a faint smile and whispered, "Even though they never met you, they loved you very much."

I didn't know what to say. It was all too much, and I just felt like sobbing—and I wasn't even sure what I'd be sobbing for. For all of it, I supposed. For the death of my parents. For the knowledge I now had about my existing family. For the pain my parents had to go through and what Maggie had to go through. *Oh Maggie*, I thought, tears finally falling in hot trails down my cheeks. *You must have been so frightened. No wonder you were in so much pain for so long.*

I looked down at the yellowed papers in my hand and wiped my face so the tears wouldn't soil them.

The first entry was dated four months after the last one and was scribbled in more frantic, hastily drawn letters. I took a deep breath and started to read.

March 5, 1857

I know I haven't written in a while, but in truth, I am afraid. I don't want to write what's happened. I'm embarrassed I let myself get tangled into this love so easily—so blindly—not even realizing what it truly was.

Cassius doesn't love me. I didn't realize that until I got so frightened that I fled to my one true friend, other than Geraldine and Maggie. Richard. He has been my friend since childhood, and all along I'd been blind to his love for me. I didn't realize love could start as a slow warmth simmering in my heart, ready to bubble into something greater. I thought it came in like a rush of fire. I didn't realize until I started to burn.

I regret ever forming an attachment to Cassius. He terrifies me. I even thought about throwing this journal into the fire so no one ever had to know. But I wanted to remember. I wanted to remember how easily someone—anyone—could be fooled. I wanted to remember myself so I never got swept away blindly again. I didn't realize what love was until I felt Richard's warmth—his arms around me and his thoughtful whispers of comfort.

I don't know if anyone will ever read this, but if they do, I hope they know that what I had with Cassius with infatuation, but what I have with Richard is love. I know Richard. And although I didn't instantly see sparks the moment we grew up into the people we are now, as he did, it doesn't mean our love isn't any less passionate or real. It's more real. What I had with Cassius was a short, dangerous spark sizzling its way into kerosene. If Richard hadn't come and put out the fire before the explosion, I might have never escaped.

It makes me feel horrid, and I'd rather not think about it if I can help it. But I want to explain what happened. Perhaps so that if anyone reads this, they can understand. And maybe it will even help others avoid the same mistake.

I won't go into great detail, but I will give a brief depiction of the events that led me to where I am today.

It started shortly after the Harvest Festival's conclusion. I was enjoying my time with Cassius, and I was sad that he would have to go back to where he came from. He assured me he wouldn't go without me, which made me happy at first, but then things changed. The more time he spent with me, the more desperate he became. I am not sure if that's the right word to describe it, but that's the word that comes to mind when I think of it. He looked hungry when he saw me. Like he was starving. Like he had stopped eating and would only be satisfied if he gobbled me up instead. He started following Maggie and me on our trips to the lake when we'd go swimming. He would watch me everywhere I went.

When I caught him following us to the lake, I yelled at him, embarrassed. He yelled back at me and told me I should know better than to take off my dress where anyone could see me. He gripped onto me so tightly that my arms ached afterward. I wanted to cry. I didn't think anyone would see me. Maggie and I had been swimming there since we were old enough to go on our own. At the time, I didn't realize he was the one in the wrong. He made me feel ashamed.

"I'm sorry," I said. He tossed me away and ordered me to pick up my clothes and put them back on and follow him to town. I did as he said, but he watched me as I did it. I felt so violated, but he kept saying it was just because he loved me and he was doing it for my own good.

Maggie didn't like what had happened and warned me to back away from Cassius after that. I lashed out at her and told her she was just jealous because he was interested in me and not her. She looked so hurt, but I didn't know what to do. I felt that I'd be betraying Cassius if I apologized to her. He was to be my husband; I had an allegiance to him.

So I kept seeing him, and he kept getting worse. The last straw was when he got angry at me for smiling at the man who sold us fish. I was only doing so politely. I always smile and thank the vendors at the market. That explanation wasn't good enough for Cassius, though. He yanked me into the forest and hit me across the face. When I broke into sobs and crumpled to the ground, he bent down and kept telling me he was sorry. He even started crying, too, and said he hated himself for hurting me. But I didn't care about his feelings anymore. After that, I hated him, too.

I ran away from him but didn't want to go home. I didn't want my parents to worry. The only other place I could think of was the Wells' house, so I ran there as fast as I could. I thought I had lost Cassius, but he had been watching from afar the whole time. I didn't know this until later.

When I got to their house, Richard opened the door. I fell into his arms and sobbed. He closed the door and asked me what had happened. His eyes lit up like an uncontrollable fire when I told him what Cassius had done. He was about to go out and fight him when I begged him to stay. "I don't want you to get hurt, too," I said, still crying, "And I just want someone to hold me. Please."

"Of course," he said, falling to his knees and wrapping me in his arms again, "I'm here for you. It's all right."

I stayed there all day, and that's when I realized what love really meant. It wasn't frenzied excitement with extravagant ribbons and perfect smiles. It was feeling warm. It was feeling safe. Of course, in the weeks that followed, Richard and I fell deeply in love, and we are now in our own frenzied state of excitement, but it's different. It doesn't make me feel small. It doesn't make me feel used, or like I'm a prize horse to be stroked and admired whenever the rider pleased.

It was the excitement of being free. Of not holding back because you know the other person won't let you fall.

Richard makes me feel safe and excited. He makes me happy. Not just giddy—though I feel that, too—but truly happy. When I'm with him, I'm full of peace.

But even Richard can't take away all the danger in my life. Cassius won't leave me alone. He still tries to follow me into the market, and when I go to Richard's house or walk home from work I can see him watching me. Richard has started escorting me everywhere. When he started, Cassius left me alone at first, but last night he came to Richard's house while I was there. Mrs. Wells answered the door, but Cassius burst right through and screamed for Richard to meet him outside.

Richard told me to hide and that he'd be right back. I crawled beneath Geraldine's bed, but I didn't have to wonder what was happening outside. I could hear it all perfectly from the window.

"You can't keep her from me," Cassius hissed. "She deserves someone better than a blacksmith."

"What would you know about deserving her?" Richard shouted back. "All you've ever done is hurt and scare her."

"She'll come back to me. I'll never stop until she does. I'll come by every day and night if I have to."

"You'll have to go through me, you disgusting piece—" I heard a punch and Richard yelping. I pushed myself out from beneath the bed and ran outside.

"Richard! Please come back in!" I yelled, but when I saw them, I gasped. He was bloodied, and Cassius looked like he was about to bite him in the neck. "GET AWAY FROM HIM!" I screamed, and my voice echoed through the trees. Cassius immediately turned his face into a frown, tears pilling against his eyelids and then falling down his face. He dropped Richard and came rushing to me.

"Oh, Claire," he cried, skidding to his knees and taking my hands. "Please take me back. I can't live without you. You deserve someone better than him."

"There is no man better than him," I said, twisting myself free of his grasp and running to Richard. Luckily, he was okay. A little battered but conscious. He told me he was all right as I helped him up.

Cassius watched as we went back into the house. Richard led me inside and then turned toward Cassius as he started to close the door. "Stay away from her!" he yelled, then slammed the door shut and locked it. Then he held me as I cried. He was hurting because of me. Cassius hurt him because of me.

This was all my fault.

I stayed there all night, wrapped in Richard's arms as he fell asleep. I couldn't sleep, though. Cassius was outside crying all night. His bellows and sobs could be heard through the trees. I couldn't get past the guilt. Perhaps I'd led him on. He seemed so sorrowful. Perhaps I had hurt him and drove him this way. When Richard woke and I told him how guilty I felt, he assured me I'd done nothing wrong. He assured me Cassius was an evil man.

"I know. I know," I'd said, but I couldn't help but feel like somehow some of this was my fault. His eyes were so somber when he came to me. He looked so heartbroken. I just didn't know what to think anymore. Logically, I knew he was evil, but I felt so guilty when he cried. It made me wonder if somehow I had caused all this.

Her letter went on in that circle of thought for another page or so. The tug-of-war of her wondering if her guilt was from doing something wrong, while recognizing logically that she wasn't doing anything wrong.

I set the pages down. *Oh, Mother.* I sighed, rubbing my eyes, my heart squeezing in my chest. *You feeling sorry for a man who had done such awful things simply because he was crying and breaking down in front of you wasn't a sign that he was a good person. It was a sign that you were—that you had a conscience that felt sad when others suffered—and nothing more. It didn't mean you did anything wrong.*

I kept rubbing my eyes, the distress of it all crashing down on me. *I wish I could have been there. I wish I could have looked you in the eyes and told you that it wasn't your fault.*

I flipped the page and read the final paragraph of the entry:

Regardless of anything I may or may not have done, Cassius is a wretched man who hurt my beloved Richard. I know he'll never leave us alone if he thinks he has a chance with me. I'll show him that isn't possible and cut him out of my life for good

Until next time,

Claire

There were no more entries after that.

I set the papers down and let it all sink in. "What happened?" I asked in a hushed whisper, blinking away tears.

She tenderly placed a hand on my back. "They were very much in love," she said, "They eloped shortly after she wrote this, and they went away for a while. When they came back, she was pregnant with you." She rubbed my back softly, and my chin quivered as I swallowed the emotion welling in my throat. "They loved you," she said. "Very much."

I couldn't hold it in anymore. I began to sob—loud and hard. The kind of sobbing that happens when all feels lost—the kind where it feels like your soul is peeling from your body and it all starts to hurt. I cried and cried until nothing else came out. I must have cried for close to twenty minutes before my body gave up on producing any more tears.

When my sobs turned to silent hiccups and shuddering

breaths, Mrs. Wells took my face and turned it gently toward hers. "I know this is hard to hear. That's why I thought it would be better for you not to know at all." She smiled weakly, and I stared at her, numb. She let out a heavy sigh and said, "But as it seems you managed to learn some truths yourself, I wanted to make sure you stopped before you reached dangerous waters." Her eyes turned hard, and her expression shifted to one of warning. "Now, I don't know how you came to know the truth about this family, but you shouldn't speak of it to anyone else. Do you understand me?"

I nodded, but my heart wasn't in it. I felt hollow. My mother and father were killed. They were so in love, and they were killed by a deranged immortal man who claimed my mother's life as his own. I couldn't even cry anymore. I felt like I'd cried out every ounce of water in my body and would forever be a dried, empty husk.

"Come, child," she said, hoisting me up, "Let's get you to your room. I'll tell the others that you aren't feeling well enough to go to supper. Just rest." She held onto me as she took me to my room.

I was in a fog the whole way there and didn't snap out of it until I heard Molly's voice. "Miss Blake!" I looked up and saw her gleeful, freckled face. Her smile dropped. "Are you all right? Grandm—I mean, Mrs. Wells, what happened?"

The old woman smiled at her granddaughter and said, "Miss Blake is just feeling a little under the weather. Can you please tell the others she won't be joining them tonight?" Molly nodded, still frowning.

"I'm sorry you've been so ill lately," she said. "I hope you get well soon, Miss."

As she said it, I no longer felt it was appropriate for her to be so formal with me. I'd let her keep up the formalities because I could tell it made her feel important in her role, but perhaps it was time for her to call me by my first name. She was my cousin, after all. I no longer felt that such a formality was proper anymore.

"Please, call me Caroline," I said with a smile. She lifted a brow.

"Why?"

"Um—please go tell Lord Ashdown that Caroline isn't feeling well. I will join you momentarily," Mrs. Wells pasted a fake smile on her face, and her granddaughter nodded and left to do as she was told. I looked at the older woman with a confused expression of my own. Before I could ask her anything, she said, "Please don't tell Molly about any of this. At least not yet. We can tell her about your connection after the festival, but not until then." She smiled sadly.

"Why?" I asked.

She shifted uncomfortably. "Because I don't know what will happen at the festival . . ." she whispered, and my body went cold again. "I don't know if anything dangerous will happen, but I do know that there will be plenty of vampires arriving the day before the festival or so." She flashed me a serious look. "Stay away from them as much as possible, okay?"

I nodded, but I didn't know how I could make such a promise. How was I supposed to stay away from people I didn't know were vampires? Surely there would be more family members than just vampires attending the festival and staying at Ashdown Manor. Though I suppose I couldn't be sure of anything anymore.

Well, I *was* sure of one thing: I had enough vampire talk for one night. So I asked the only question I could: "If you are my father's mother, why isn't your last name 'Blake'?"

Mrs. Wells fumbled with the keys tied to her waist.

"Maggie must have given you a new last name to conceal your identity from the rest of us," she said, "but 'Wells' was your father's real last name."

My thoughts again turned to my aunt and all the pain she had suffered through. So much so that she didn't want any of it to reach me. She wanted to shut everyone else out. I just wished she hadn't. I wished she had told me the truth.

"Thank you," I said, too tired to ask any more questions, "but I think I'm going to lie down now."

She took my hand in hers and gave it a squeeze. "All right, dear. Sleep well." She opened her mouth to say something else but must have thought it better to just leave things like that because she closed it again and then got up and left.

When the door closed, I let the darkness of the unlit room engulf me. Once again, I didn't want to think. I just wanted sleep—to enter a realm of nothingness so I didn't have to be in so much pain anymore. I didn't want to think of the terrible fates of my parents, or of William or Augustus or anyone else.

So I took off my clothes, slid into a nightdress, and crawled into bed. When sleep didn't come immediately, I cried. The thoughts of my parents and the fear that plagued Maggie all those years broke my heart. And the fact that the only thing I wanted to do right now was go to William and have him hold me made my heart break even more. I didn't know what was true or real anymore, but at this point, I didn't care. I just wanted the pain to go away.

Chapter *Twenty-Two*

I woke up in the middle of the night, my heart racing, but I didn't remember dreaming anything. I hadn't woken from a nightmare this time, but when I touched my face, it felt wet. I'd been crying. Was I crying in my sleep?

I wiped my face and curled into a ball on my bed. The air was still, and the only sound was the soft crackling of the fire near my bed. I wondered who had started it and if it'd been Mrs. Wells. Er—my grandmother. That would still take some time getting used to, but I was supposed to pretend I didn't know anyway, so I was better off still referring to her as Mrs. Wells.

The distant hoots of an owl were the only other sounds at this time of night. I wondered if vampires slept at all. I'd always heard they'd burn in daylight and that they would sleep until the sun set, but that had proved to be untrue. The most I'd ever noticed was when William seemed agitated when the sun had poked out through the clouds for an hour or two during one of our afternoons outside, but he didn't burn.

I sighed as I thought of him. "What should I do?" I whispered to myself, hugging my legs to my chest. A big part of me wanted to trust him. He had protected me, and he'd stuck up for me at supper before that. He always seemed so kind to me. Even when he was grouchy to everyone else in the world, he'd turn to me and smile.

My father made my mother feel safe, and that was how she knew it was love. William wasn't like Cassius. He wasn't obsessive and demeaning. But still . . . Augustus had said he was dangerous. He told me not to trust him. And he'd been right about my mother and Cassius.

Then I remembered the painting. He'd said there was a painting of my mother in the cellar—in a place the Ashdown family kept their secrets hidden from the world. I had to get down there. I needed to know more about Cassius. More about the Ashdowns. More about William.

I swung my feet from out of my sheets and slid off my bed. I groped around the darkness in search of something to light and take with me—a candle, an oil lamp, *anything.* I moved around the pitch-blackness that was everywhere but the fireplace until I felt the familiar waxy touch of a candle, long and thin. I shuffled to the fire and bent it near the flames. Once a spark had grabbed hold of the wick and the candle came to life, I grabbed my cloak and tossed it over my shoulders, slipped on some shoes, and headed out into the hall.

All the lights were off in the house, and when the realization came over me that I could have turned on my own light to find the candle, instead of feeling around in the dark, it became clear how frazzled I was. I hoped going to the cellar would rid me of this state rather than make things worse.

I was about halfway down the hall before I remembered the cellar doors were boarded up.

Great.

I had to think fast.

My first thought was to go outside and search for a tool near the lumber. We had gotten a new shipment in a day or two ago, so there should have been plenty of tools to choose from. But then I remembered how bitterly cold it was outside. I didn't particularly relish the idea of keeping my candle lit in the frosty wind while I fumbled around in my shift in the middle of the night. *Especially after what happened last night*, I thought, shuddering.

The flame of the candle danced as I thought, and then it hit me. *The fire iron.* I went back into my room and grabbed the sharp stick from the fireplace. With both items in my hands I realized I needed a candlestick or candelabra if I planned to navigate through the house and around to the cellar.

"This is becoming a great ordeal," I muttered to myself as I searched for what I needed. Finally, toward the back of my wardrobe, I found a solid gold candlestick with the Ashdown family crest on it. I planted the candle inside, grabbed the fire iron, and resumed my journey to the cellar.

When I crept outside, the wind bit at me with a nasty chill. It was even colder than I'd imagined, especially in such a thin garment. I closed the small side door I had sneaked out of and ran hastily to the servants' quarters, all the while panicked that the light in my candle might blow out at any moment.

The fear I'd get caught took the edge off of how cold I felt, and after a while, I surprisingly got used to it. Or maybe I was just numb. Either way, I was able to make it to the cellar doors without losing my breath, or my candle's flame. I inspected the boards that were still stuck in place and tried to figure out how to tear them off without waking up the servants.

I set down my candle and grabbed the fire iron. "Here goes nothing," I said and stabbed the sharp end into the top of the three boards. I wiggled it around quietly, digging it throughout the wood until fragments of the boards started falling into the grass. I did this to all three, working my way down until the wood deteriorated enough for me to rip the rest off by hand without causing too much noise.

Planting a foot on the cellar doors, I grabbed hold of the wood and pried it off, piece by piece, until I could easily open the iron doors and get inside. As I paused to catch my breath, I felt grateful that years of helping my neighbors fix their homes had made me deft with tools and strong enough to do this. I picked up my candle and swung one of the doors wide open. Inside was a large entrance lined with stairs, like stone teeth stacked in a gaping mouth.

The passageway was much larger than the one leading to the mirror room, and much easier to navigate within. Once I was deep enough inside, I turned back and closed the door behind me. The great big *BANG* that echoed after the door slammed shut made me aware just how depthless the dark void in front of me was. The candle was small, but luckily the light illuminated my path enough for me to see a few steps in front of me, as well as the walls around me.

I expected it to be much colder than it was in here. I'd figured that an old cellar in the middle of autumn would be harsher than the snapping wind outside, but it wasn't. I supposed the lack of wind helped, though the air in here was damp and smelled of mildew. It formed droplets on the walls, which I only noticed when I placed my hand on one to swing around the first corner.

I wiped my hand on my nightdress and tucked my cloak more tightly around myself. The area I walked into was a labyrinth just as dark and seemingly endless as the stairway had felt. From what I could tell, I had three options, as the corridor split off into three separate branches. Augustus had told me to take my right, didn't he? Or was that the way here?

Something dripped from the ceiling onto my head and caused me to shriek. I instantly bristled, blanching as my voice bounced from wall to wall until it disappeared. I braced myself for whatever came next. But nothing happened. No footsteps came barreling through the corridors. No yells or shouts came in response. Just empty quiet, and the occasional drip of condensation.

I moved to my right and searched the darkness. Eventually, I came upon a mountain of boxes. Smooth, well-crafted crates too perfect to be full of rubbish. So I made my ascent. I picked up the first box and tried getting inside, instantly regretting leaving the fire iron outside. Luckily, I was used to working with my hands and making boxes of all shapes and sizes. As soon as I figured out how the boxes were constructed, I was able to open each one with ease. The only thing wrong was that nothing was inside—nothing but old clothes and unused knick-knacks.

Sweat was pilling along my hairline as I dug deeper into the heap. *It has to be here somewhere.* Hopping between stacks, I searched and searched until my hands hurt. The splinter from earlier was still wedged in my finger and started puffing the skin around it.

I leaned my back against one of the crates, sitting on a stack of three. The sun would come up soon, and I had nothing to show for it. Someone in the house would notice the broken wood outside the cellar doors, too. What would I do then?

Maybe this was a waste of time, I thought and then sat back up and decided to look in a couple more crates before heading back to my room. As I slid down the boxes, something flat caught my eye behind one of the stacks. It was a thin, dark-green rectangle poking out from behind the maple-brown crates. I walked closer and leaned around to grab it. As I felt the smooth, linen texture, I immediately recognized that it was a painting, and my heart skipped.

Quickly, I moved the crates forward and pulled the painting out from its place against the wall. When I turned it around, I gasped. *This woman . . .*

"She looks like me," I said, my eyes glistening and my hand covering my mouth. "I can't believe it."

There was absolutely no doubt in my mind that this was her. This was my mother. She was beautiful—much more beautiful than me—but the resemblance was undeniable. Her long blonde hair fell over her bare shoulders like the unraveling of fine silk. It poured in soft curls down to her hips, coiling just above her lap. Her almond-shaped green eyes were striking against the dark olive backdrop of the room she was sitting in. Her eyes looked just like mine, and her hair was just as long and wavy.

But she had something I did not. There was a sweetness to her. A guilelessness that came from being pampered and sheltered. From a life without struggle. Her cheeks were plump and pink, her waist long and narrow.

While there was this sweetness to her, there was a shocking contrast of sexuality as well. Her lips were pursed, almost smirking, and her dress was slipping off her shoulders and pulled up and over her knees. The flouncy skirts fell over the arm of the red embroidered chair she was lounging in. Her arms were relaxed—one on her lap, the other on the chair.

She looked free and uninhibited.

I was shocked at her boldness in posing in such a way. Like she didn't have a care in the world. But at the same time, it was unsettling. And the more I thought about it, the more my stomach twisted at the thought of her trusting Cassius so wholly. She let him paint her in such a vulnerable way—in a seductive way that could have ruined her in society. Did she realize that at the time? Had she known that but let herself fly into his open arms without a care in the world?

She trusted so easily. And as soon as she realized her mistake, she tried to escape, but it was too late.

The pain returned to my chest, and I had to rely on my will to continue on in order not to feel sick again. I scanned the painting for the artist's name. I needed to find out if Augustus was lying. I didn't want it to be true. I didn't want to trust Augustus' words. If this was true, what did that mean about William?

But my eyes landed on the white signature that showed up so prominently on the hem of my mother's falling gown: Cassius Laurent.

I couldn't help feeling sick now. I dropped the painting and fell back onto one of the crates. Tears formed in my eyes, and my shoulders quaked. I gripped my nightdress and tried not to think—tried to close everything off because I was so sick and tired of thinking. But it wouldn't stop. It wouldn't go away. The noises and thoughts and everything. Everything. The fears. The speculations. Wondering who was lying and what was real.

My hands clasped my head and pulled at my hair as I held in a scream. *Leave me alone*, I wanted to shout to the darkness swelling in my mind. *For once in my life, let me be*. I started to cry when something broke through the silence outside of my head. Something was here.

I listened for another sound, sitting as still as I could, as if moving would cause me to miss the next sound. When I heard a loud crash, I jumped and let out another reflexive yelp. Then came another crash and a low rumble.

A wave of fear rippled through me. The damp cellar was enormous and far too dark for me to know how to navigate through it if something were to happen. What if someone was here? What if someone tried to hurt me again?

Since I found what I'd come for, I figured it was as good a time as any to leave. I quietly slid off the crate and tried tip-toeing to where I'd put my candlestick.

The crashes were getting louder, as if they were getting closer, and as I approached the other corridors, I heard something else. It sounded like the clinking of a chain. *What . . . is that?* When I looked toward the source of the noise, I saw a shadow writhing on the wall.

The air was suddenly even more cold and damp than before. The blood slowly drained from my face, and my eyes widened in horror at the shape coming into view on the wall in front of me. It moved closer, forming more distinct shapes and edges with each clinking of its chain.

"No," I whispered, frozen in place. Tears formed along my eyelashes, but I was too afraid to blink, so they just sat there, blurring my vision until I finally squeezed my eyes shut. "You're not real. You're not real. This isn't real." I chanted it to myself over and over again, just as I did when I was a child.

But the sounds only grew louder, the growls more distinct, and when I finally dared to open my eyes, the shape on the wall was clear.

As soon as I saw it, I screamed, my voice breaking through everything else. I couldn't think anymore. I couldn't hear. I couldn't feel. I just screamed, and it was like all the pain and fear inside me came together and erupted out of me in a single, glass-breaking shriek.

As soon as I stopped, I collapsed onto the floor, as if all my energy was used up in that one moment of sheer terror. Like every part of me gave out. The gears stopped turning in my body, but my mind kept racing. And when my head thudded against the ground, my vision blurred, but the sounds kept coming.

The Shadow Beast was here, and it was coming for me.

"No!" I cried into the cold, damp ground. "No."

I whimpered, desperately wishing I could move. The shrieks of the beast were getting louder, and the room was getting warm. I gasped shallow breaths as I sobbed. This creature that haunted my nightmares would finally win.

Maybe they were never just nightmares to begin with.

I sobbed into the floor, begging for escape, but my legs wouldn't move. When I opened my eyes, I saw why the room was getting so hot. My candlestick had fallen onto the crates, and they were slowly going up in flames, one by one. And I was at its center.

The creature bellowed louder, and the fear in me swelled.

This is it, I thought as I cried, limp and cold on the burning floor. *This is how I die.*

Great bursts of light belched from the crates as the fire climbed higher. The familiar pinching pain in my chest grabbed hold of me, clutching my lungs like the demons from Maggie's stories. I managed to pull my body inward, curling myself into a ball as I cried and waited to die.

I wished I'd lived a more remarkable life. That I'd done something I could be proud of and leave this world knowing I'd made a difference in at least one person's life. But I couldn't even do that. I was alone. Would anyone even mourn for me after I died?

Something snapped above me, like the breaking of wood, and I braced myself for impact. When nothing happened, I opened my eyes and saw figures move above me. I shrieked again and covered my face, sobbing.

When my body rose from the ground, panic tore through me, and I tried to push myself away from whatever had grabbed hold of me. "Let me go!" I screamed. "LET GO OF ME!"

"Shhh, Caroline, it's all right," a voice said, and pulled me in closer. I gasped in a ragged breath before opening my eyes. William had picked me up and was carrying me out of the cellar. He turned around and shouted to whoever had come with him, "Make sure to lock it up once you put out the fire. I'm not coming back."

Someone said something back, but I couldn't make it out. My ears were still ringing, and I was shivering uncontrollably. When sobs escaped my mouth again, William pressed his forehead against mine and whispered, "It's all right, Caroline. It will all be okay. I'll get you in from the cold."

My chest still burned, and the pain clenching all the muscles in my body wouldn't relax. I let out more sobs as he carried me to my room. If I had been in my normal state of mind, I wouldn't have even thought of letting myself cry on him like that. But I'm glad that I did.

He held me close and hushed me softly until we reached my room. The warmth of his chest and the steadiness of his breath helped calm the storm raging in my mind. He opened the door with one hand and held me with the other, my arms wrapping around his neck. He moved through the doorway and then kicked the door shut and brought me to my bed.

My sobs had turned to whimpers, but I wasn't ready to let him go. My fingers pulled at his white nightshirt and I leaned in to stay with him. But he didn't move. I looked up and saw him smiling gently. "I wasn't going to leave you," he whispered, stroking a hand through my hair. "I was just going to place you in bed and kneel right here beside you."

I buried my face in the crook of his neck, my head falling against his shoulder. "No. Stay with me. Please."

His hand ran along my back, brushing over me in long, soothing motions. "I can't do that," he said finally, though I could tell there was some reluctance in his voice. "It wouldn't be proper."

"I don't care." I sniffled. My brain felt like it had turned to mush, and my head was killing me. "I don't care what anyone says or sees. Do you?"

He shook his head slowly. "No, but I just want what's best for you."

"Then you'll come in with me," I said, letting my head drop back onto his shoulder. "Please."

He didn't say anything, but after a second or two, he stood up and sat down in bed next to me. "All right, but I'll leave as soon as you want me to," he said, then pulled himself beneath my covers and wrapped his arm around me. I was still in my cloak, and he was still in his shoes, but we didn't move. I just let him hold me and listened as my breaths started to slow and my body calmed.

He buried his face in my hair and I couldn't help but smile. He always found me when I needed him most. I wondered why that was, how it was possible.

When I felt well enough to turn around, I flipped over slowly and looked at him. I smiled weakly, and he smiled in return. "Feeling better?" he asked.

"Not enough for you to leave."

"Well, you need to at least get comfortable and get in something warm. Let me take off your cloak for you." When he reached to take it off, my eyes widened and I slapped his hand away. “Ow, what was that for?”

“I’m sorry. I just . . . I’m only wearing a nightdress.”

Even in the dark, I could see his face redden. “Oh, I’m sorry. I’ll leave so you can—”

I grabbed his wrist. “No. I can’t be alone right now. Please.” My eyes glistened. The pain in my chest returning. “Please stay.” I said again, quickly, “Just look away and I’ll take it off.”

“O-okay,” he said, his cheeks still flushed. “Let me know when I can turn around.” He rustled to his other side, and when I knew he wasn’t looking, I slid the cloak from off my shoulders. As it moved against my knees and fell to the floor beside the bed, I remembered the painting of my mother. How confident she was to show her own shoulders and be in control of her own skin. My nightdress wasn’t half as sultry as that dress she wore. So why did mine feel so revealing?

I looked down at the fabric. It was a loose, white cotton dress, thin as paper and barely hitting my knees. The only sleeves were thin, ribboned straps that wrapped over my shoulders and laced into the back. Perhaps it was a little more revealing, but it surely wasn’t sultry. Still, the thought of William seeing me in it made my face burn.

After I pulled myself back into my blanket, I reached for him, covering myself with part of the thin sheet. “I’m ready now. Can you please turn over?”

“Of course.” He turned around and scooted a little closer. When his eyes met mine, he smiled, but I could see the worry in his gaze. He leaned forward and stroked my face. “Now, are you all right?” I closed my eyes and let myself be warmed by his touch. Were vampires always warm? I’d always thought they were cold. But William sure wasn’t.

Then the thoughts started coming back. Piling in one

after another—the Shadow Beast, what happened to my parents, what might happen to me. My hands shot to my temples and I took in a loud, sharp breath. My eyes squinted shut. *Why was that thing here?* Each time I inhaled, my breaths got a little louder. I tried to stay calm, but the images in the basement kept coming back.

When I started to cry, I felt William's arm wrap around me. He pushed me against him and held me to his chest. "Shhh. It's all right. You're safe. I'm here." I let his voice pool over me like warm milk. "I'll always keep you safe," he whispered, "I told you that, remember?"

I did remember. I remembered the way he fought for me. The way he stayed outside my door all night to make sure no one would ever hurt me again. And I remembered the way I hurt him earlier, before supper, when I pushed him away and left him alone. He didn't even see me after that until he found me in the cellar.

I opened my eyes, guilt building in my stomach. "I do," I whispered. "You must have been scared when you saw me."

"Shh. Don't worry about me. I'm just glad you're okay Just let your shoulders relax and focus on breathing."

I did as he told and steadied my breaths, my body warm against his. Then I remembered what my mother said in her journal entry—that love is about warmth and happiness and feeling safe. *Richard makes me feel safe*, she'd said. *He makes me happy.*

William moved a lock of hair from my face and tucked it behind my ear as he stroked my head and held me close. The world felt different whenever he held me. It felt like I could feel music and taste spring. When he touched me, it felt like the sun.

When I'm with him, I'm full of peace.

My eyes fluttered open. And as I looked at this man,

with his irresistibly dark eyes watching me in quiet curiosity and concern, I realized my mother was right about love.

Maybe it was from all the crying, or maybe it was because he was here with me, in such a vulnerable place and time, but I decided to be bold. "How do you feel about me, William?" I asked.

He blinked. "What?"

"How do you feel about me?"

He chuckled and said, "I think you need to go to sleep."

"No," I said with a smile, then softly placed my hand on his arm. "Please. Tell me."

His eyes stayed fixed on me, and I suddenly became aware of how sweet his breath was on the tip of my nose and how close his body was, his legs brushing against mine. "Caroline, I—" He blinked, his mouth slightly open, and my heart fluttered in my chest. But he couldn't complete his sentence. He closed his mouth and thought for a moment. "Well," he said, "I feel very strongly about you."

I raised an eyebrow. "You feel very strongly about me?"

He smiled softly. "Yes, of course."

"Well what does that mean?" I asked with a quiet laugh.

"Well . . ." He started, trailing off. I watched him gather his thoughts, studying every curve of his face, and he smiled when he caught me looking at his mouth. I turned bright pink, but he pretended not to notice. "You are very brave," he said finally. "Do you know that?"

"What?"

He stroked my hair, letting his hand fall down my back. "You are a brave person. I cannot believe you went down there all alone. Every time I turn around you do something to surprise me." He laughed. "Although it's reckless, I find it very admirable."

I couldn't help but smile. "Do you really mean that?"

He nodded. "No matter what you've gone through, you

keep going. That's the bravest thing anyone can do. Sometimes it's the hardest thing to do." His smiled faded, and his fingers fell between my shoulder blades. "It's hard to move on from traumatic experiences. To live each day knowing what you know, feeling what you feel. Memories can be terrible things, especially when you've gone through moments you wish you could forget." He paused before quietly adding, "You are incredible, Caroline Blake. And I envy your strength."

My breaths came out in quavery waves, and I was surprised I could breathe at all. Every time his fingers brushed against my skin, my whole body turned to water.

"I may not be as strong as you think," I replied.

He looked at me more firmly. "You are stronger than anyone I've ever known. I've been hiding from my darkness and wanting to run away from my past all my life, just like you. But the difference between you and I is that *you* broke free. You tore off the chains holding you back, and you stormed into the umbra. Into the unknown. I have never seen such bravery in my life." His voice was soft and smooth, like warm honey melting on my tongue, and I could tell he meant every word.

I wanted to believe him. I really did. But how could I after tonight? After what happened in the cellar. "But I'm a coward," I said, "I screamed at what I saw down there. Then I cried like a child."

"Only the brave ones let themselves cry," he whispered. "The kind of cry that can cleanse you from your deepest pains and fears."

"I wish I wasn't so afraid," I whispered, wiping away the tears forming in my eyes, but then his fingers trailed down to my chin and landed just below my lips.

He tilted my face up so my eyes met his. When the softness of his gaze locked onto mine, everything else faded away. "If it were up to me, you'd never be afraid again," he whispered, and something in my heart sparked. He followed his hand as it trailed over my bare shoulder and down my arm. His fingertips danced in flutters against my skin, like the faint brushes of falling leaves.

Then his expression changed, his eyebrows creasing together in thought. After a minute or so, his eyes returned to mine, but they weren't soft like before. They were heavy with that familiar flicker of pain I so often found there. "I've never known happiness," he said. "It had always been taken from me whenever I thought I'd found it. Eventually, I stopped trying, and I found I didn't even know what it looked or felt like anymore. I couldn't even remember what it felt like to be anything but hurt and confined. I didn't know what freedom felt like. To have nothing holding me back."

I watched him carefully, wondering why he was telling me this. There was something vulnerable in the way he formed each thought—each word—and I knew that whatever his reason for it was must have been important. So I listened. "For years, I'd longed for something to fight for," he said, his voice trembling slightly. "I needed light to crawl out of the dark. I needed someone to tell me it was okay to cry and that I wasn't a monster for the people around me meeting fates outside my control." His eyes flickered back to mine, and he stopped.

"Then I met you," he said with a smile. "When I saw you, I was in awe, and the more I got to know you, the more enchanted I became. Your fierce passion and determination astounded me . . ." His words trailed to a stop, and his smile faded.

He looked back up at me and continued. "My life has been so full of pain. I didn't see the point in trying to be happy, but then you walked into it. You've given me the courage to fight my way out of the hole I've been stuck in for so long."

His hand fell into my hair, and he gently wrapped his fingers up in it, pulling me in gently by the back of my head. "Your bravery bleeds into me, and your fear reflects parts of me I thought belonged solely to me—darkness I didn't know existed beyond my own body. For the first time in my life, I knew I wasn't alone." His fingers trailed slowly down my neck. "And you've given me that something to fight for. The light I've been searching for. You've given me hope."

I didn't know what to make of all this. But what I did know was that I yearned for him and that no matter what anyone said, he was good. I could see it so clearly. And I could feel the pain and longing. This wasn't a man who would willingly lock someone away with no remorse or reason. I didn't know what had happened in his past, but what I did know was that he hated it. That he felt such deep guilt that it ate away at him, carving him from the inside out.

I wished I could tear open the source of his pain and let the darkness inside spill out onto the floor and fade away. I wish I could see that pain drain from his eyes and enjoy the ease he felt in his renewed happiness.

His voice fell into a whisper. "Caroline, I'm in love with you," he said, and the words burned like a warm fire in my chest. "I'm so deeply, *deeply* in love with you."

The words fell into my ears in a dizzying rush. "You're in love with me?" I whispered, barely able to speak.

"I am," he said, his eyes and smile so soft and adoring it made it hard for me to blink, not wanting to miss even a second of it. But then his expression shifted, the corners of his mouth dropping and the inside of his brows turning inward. Tears formed in his eyes. He tried blinking them away and keeping his voice leveled as he continued, "But . . . I have no right to catch that light you so effortlessly radiate. To hold onto you. To live a life where I let myself be happy." His gaze went past me, haunted and strained. "All I've ever brought to the world is destruction."

My heart ached as the pain grew on his face. The pain in this man who seemed too good to be as monstrous as he, or anyone else, claimed him to be. I lifted my hand to his face. "I have a hard time believing that's true. You are so good to me."

But his expression didn't change. That haunted look remained, tying his face in a sad, strained knot. His voice lowered. "I couldn't save them. Even after I turned, I couldn't save them. My kind has taken everything from me, and I'm one of them." I tried not to react—tried not to show my surprise. But at first, I couldn't believe it. Did he realize what he'd admitted to? That he was different. That he had turned.

The more I looked at the pain in his eyes, the clearer it became that he hadn't meant for it to slip and that he hadn't even realized he'd done it at all. He was simply vulnerable, wrapped up in whatever tragedies happened in his sordid past. I let my hand trail down the side of his face, wishing I could help him—that I could take the pain away, even just a little.

But that haunted look still plagued him. "I just sat there and watched like a coward. Everyone I've ever cared for has either been thrown away from me or killed." His eyes were still far away, and his jaw was clenched tight. I recognized that look—that pull to the past. That nightmarish pain. He saved me from mine tonight.

My hand stilled on his face. When a tear escaped onto his cheek, I wiped it away. "I know what it's like to see the ones you love slip away, but if something happens outside your control, how could it be your fault?"

"It's more complicated than that. I . . . I'm just a monster," he said, avoiding my gaze.

"How?" I challenged, and he met my eyes, surprised.

"I'm not what you think I am, Caroline."

"Then what are you, William?" I asked. There was no edge to my voice. Just desperation. I knew he wasn't a monster. I knew the way my mother knew. William wasn't like Cassius at all. He wasn't who Augustus swore he was, either. He was nothing like his father—that violently obsessed man. Nothing at all.

He looked at me in horror, his hanging open as if ready to speak but unable to make a sound. Like he was scared of what I might think. Scared of letting me down or driving me away. He had tried so hard to warn me not to stay, to make me afraid and to chase me away. But now, it seemed that was the last thing he'd ever want. As if now he had something to lose.

I smiled and let my fingers fall to his chest. "William, I know you're not human." Before he could respond, I quickly continued. "My aunt always taught me about vampires and witches, and creatures of the night, but she never mentioned that you were so human. That you were so much like me." His eyes stayed on me, his expression changing to another look I recognized. One I'd carried with me a lot lately. A longing for love.

"All my life, the shadows have known me by name," I said, "I was never like the others. I was never normal. But now, I'm starting to believe I was never supposed to be. And there is nothing wrong with that." I leaned in closer and whispered, "So you don't have to be afraid of what I think. But if you want to know what it is I *am* thinking, it's that I'm not afraid of you. You don't have to be afraid of losing me. Because I love you, too."

His lips parted, and his mouth momentarily twitched up into a smile but then fell again. "You don't know . . . You don't know everything I've done."

"I don't care about your past. What matters to me is who you are now. If you let me in, I promise I won't run away." I leaned in closer. "Just be honest with me," I whispered. "Trust me, and I promise I'll trust you, too."

But his eyes kept searching me in wonder, as if expecting me to disappear at any moment. Or perhaps wondering if this moment was happening at all. I leaned back and cupped his face with my hand again. "I'll help you through it. Whatever it is. Just like you've helped me."

When I smiled, and it was clear that I wasn't going to fade away, he finally smiled, too. Really, truly smiled. His eyes fell to my lips, and I suddenly felt even warmer, my skin hot to the touch. And when he leaned in, I let myself succumb to his embrace. Then he kissed me, and my body lit up like a firework.

He kissed me deeply, hungrily, and moved to hover on top of me. I released myself from his kiss just long enough to brush the blanket off of me, and when I did, his eyes drank me in.

His gaze fell to my legs then slowly drifted up my body, but before he reached my eyes, he leaned down and kissed my hand. He kissed his way up my arm and over my shoulder before sinking down into my neck, and for the briefest moment, I felt the sharpness of his fangs graze my skin. A surge like lightning rippled through me, but I wasn't afraid. I knew I could trust him. So I reveled in the quiet invulnerability of his mouth as he trailed along my collarbone, a warm tide of tremors surging through me at the warmth of his breath against my skin.

When his lips once again found mine, I pulled him in closer and kissed him even deeper, feeling his tongue against mine and enjoying his hands against my skin. I fell and let my body move with his—let him control every part of me. Every inch he touched came to life. The power he had over me was immobilizing, as if my body yearned for him to reign over its desires—to pull me in every direction on his own personal whims.

The thought should have made me buckle or panic, but it didn't. I wanted him. I wanted him to have every part of me. I wanted to feel his hands dance across my skin and for his lips to perpetually hunger for mine. I wanted him in the rushing of my blood and the movements of my breath. I wanted him to hold me when I cried and take me and keep me locked away in a secret place only he and I knew about. I wanted the world to be ours and ours alone.

He ran his fingers through my hair and every part of me fell apart in the best possible away. He broke me out of a shell I'd been unknowingly trapped inside my entire life. One of pain. One of fear. But it was gone now. Like a shackle cast off forever. I was free.

When the striking intensity made its decline, and our lips gradually drifted apart, the warm glow he left me with muddled my mind and made my eyelids grow heavy. "Will you stay here tonight?" I whispered.

He fell next to me and took my hands in his. "Of course," he said, kissing my fingers. "Whatever you desire." Another wave of warmth poured through me, so I leaned forward and kissed him one more time before turning around for him to hold me. He wrapped me up in him, his body so perfectly curled against mine.

In his arms, warm and calm, my eyes fluttered shut. My mind was finally quiet. No more living nightmares flashed before my eyes or made my chest tight. I was at peace, finally able to fall asleep.

I was safe.

Chapter Twenty-Three

The next morning, I woke up well rested and free of nightmares for the first time since arriving at Ashdown Manor. I didn't wake up with shallow breaths or an aching head. I was at peace.

When I turned around, I reached for William, but he wasn't there. He must have left sometime after I'd fallen asleep. I supposed I still didn't know if vampires slept. I turned around and let myself bask in the glow of such a glorious morning, the sun bathing me as it spilled through the window. The thought of William's lips on mine settled in my mind, warming my skin. His taste was like candy in my mouth that I longed to savor.

Did everyone know love felt this way? That it fizzled in your veins and made your whole body soar? I couldn't tear my thoughts away from him—the way his fingers felt when they grazed my skin, the way his eyes looked into mine, transfixed and powerful, as he expressed his true feelings for me. How he held me close as I fell asleep. I closed my eyes and let out a carefree hum, stretching out on my bed.

Thinking about him wasn't enough, though. I needed to see him. I sat up so quickly that my mind became hazy, and I wondered how much of my light-headedness came from my thoughts of William. As I got ready, I was so grateful that I'd told Molly to stop helping me in the mornings. I could go straight out and see him. My hands slowed as I buttoned up the fitted jacket that had come with the dress I'd chosen.

Molly is my cousin, I reminded myself in wonder, and a familiar sense of anger brewed in my blood that I'd never known—that my own grandmother had never told me I had family still alive and well. That I had a pampered cousin doted on by our grandmother but hadn't known either of them existed.

I tried not to think about it. Today was about William and me. The first day since revealing our feelings to each other and deciding not to hold back anymore. The hopeful beginning of a new chapter in my life. A happier chapter. One I'd reread over and over again as I grew old.

As I grew old.

My heart sunk at the thought. William would never grow old. Where did that leave me—leave us?

I tried not to think about that, either.

"Today will be a good day," I said into the mirror as I inspected my outfit. The ensemble was the darkest black I'd ever seen in a dress and fell in a series of billowy dark petals swinging to my ankles. The top was fitted tightly against my arms and went straight up to my neck. It couldn't be worn without the jacket in this weather, so it was a good choice for an autumn day like today. I was happy with my choice. It was a lot more flattering than some of the other dresses I'd chosen to fling on over the last few days, and it was surprisingly easy to breathe in.

I leaned forward and pinched my cheeks to give them some color and decided to pin up the front sections of my hair, leaving the rest flowing down my back in a series of chestnut waves and loose curls. This was the longest I'd probably ever spent getting ready, but I wanted to look perfect. I frowned at the slight puffiness of my eyes from crying last night, but that would go away soon enough.

As I swiveled to the side and made sure I looked good from every angle, a knock came at my door. "Hold on, Molly," I called as I decided whether or not I'd wear my necklace today. I put it up to my high-collar and decided against it. No one would be able to see it anyway. The knock came again, and I groaned. "I'm coming, I'm coming." I walked over and swung the door open. "I was—" My body sparked. "William, what are you doing here?" I looked around, but Molly was nowhere in sight.

He cupped my face and the back of my neck and pulled me into a kiss. My mind numbed, all thoughts vanishing into the air. His arm moved to my lower back, steadying me as I let myself get weak with the intoxication of his lips. When he pulled away, he kept his face close and smiled. "I have a surprise for you," he whispered and kissed me one more time before letting go. I stumbled back dizzily.

"Oh?" I said, a smile rising on my face.

He nodded and held his arm out for me to take. "Yes, now follow me and don't ask any questions until we get there."

I laughed lightly. "All right," I said, looping my arm in his, the other hand meeting his forearm. "Then lead the way." He smiled at me just like he had the night before—that same carefree smile that crinkled the sides of his eyes.

It was like a weight had been lifted from his shoulders, and in this moment, the pain I'd seen in his eyes before wasn't there.

My smile widened, and I knew the pain was gone from mine as well. Though I was aware it would be a long road of healing, I knew I wouldn't have to do it alone anymore. We had each other now. We could pull each other up and over every bump and every mountain we faced and simply hold each other on the hard days.

I held tighter onto his arm, breathing in his masculine scent as he led me down the wide staircase and through the familiar set of enormous front doors. Servants were there to open them for us, but William pushed his way through himself, keeping me close behind on his other side. He thanked them anyway. Once outside, the chill immediately bit at my nose, but I didn't care. Somehow, I felt warm, and the cloudy sky felt bright.

I thought he'd lead me to the site of the festival, where we were supposed to be helping build the booths and plan attractions, but he passed the small group of men busy working on the construction and kept going. "Where are we going?" I asked.

"I told you not to ask any questions until we got there," he said with a coy smile.

"All right, I suppose I'll trust you," I said with a laugh.

"Good," he said, then softly added, "You can always trust me." I wanted to say something, but the sincerity in his face and the tenderness in his voice left me at a loss for words. So I just nodded, still smiling.

Soon we reached the woods near the house, and he led me through the mouth of the opening, the trees obscuring our view of the sky above. I wanted to ask what we were doing here, but I remembered I just had to be patient and wait until we got wherever it was we were going.

The trees were vibrant shades of orange and red, and the smell of pine reminded me of Christmas. I loved autumn, and today it seemed to have arrived in full swing. In just a few weeks, the festival would be here. There would be a sea of pumpkins for all to choose from—they'd been growing for some time now, and even more would be brought in—crisp apples dipped in gooey caramel, and games to enjoy until the dewy mists of twilight fell upon the hill of Ashdown Manor. I had never been to a festival before, but I was sure this one would be fantastic. I had great company to enjoy it with.

We kept walking for some time, our shoes crunching against fallen leaves, squirrels dodging our every footstep, scurrying away at our unexpected descent into their homes. I breathed in the air around us, my arm still clinging to his. I took in each small moment, hoping to keep them safe in my head forever. Every once in a while, I'd look up at him and smile, and feeling my gaze upon him, he'd return it, and we'd walk like that for a while, unafraid to fall.

I'd never been so content in my life. I couldn't even feel the cold.

In the near distance, I saw a good-sized Whitehall rowing boat resting near a large pond. It was remarkable. I'd never seen one in real life before. I saw a picture of one in a newspaper once, but that didn't do it justice. At least not for this one. The long white body looked like a ribbed seashell large enough for us to hop inside and ride.

The size of the pond was impressive as well. It was more of a small lake hidden away in a magical pocket in the middle of the woods. As we approached the water, I observed its glassy surface, washed with beautiful strokes of mossy greens and marbled blues, and I wondered if mermaids were hidden underneath. I had fallen in love with a vampire, after all. The existence of mermaids was no longer out of the realm of possibility.

"What are you looking at?" William asked as he took two oars out of the boat.

"I was just looking," I said, crouching down and squinting to see if I could find anything moving beneath the murky glass.

"There are plenty of fish in there, if that's what you're looking for." He gave me a knowing grin as he unraveled a rope that had been coiled in the boat. When I looked and saw the way his eyes looked at me so endearingly, like I was an innocent little doe, I scowled.

"I wasn't sure if there was something more supernatural than fish in here."

He laughed. "I'm not teasing you. I think it's rather adorable." He held his hand out for me to take and then helped me into the boat.

"What's so adorable about me looking for mermaids?"

He put the oars back in the boat and stepped inside. As he sat down, he shrugged. "I don't know. I just love how open you are to the world—to the possibilities of the abnormal." He smiled and then pushed us off the land and into the lake.

"Is it so surprising?" I said as we glided into the vastness of the water.

"No, I suppose not," he laughed, rolling his cream-colored sleeves up to his elbows, "And it's one of the things I love about you." Love. The word sent waves through my body, still as unfamiliar to me as the water beneath my seat.

My cheeks burned as I watched him roll up the rest of his sleeve, and I suddenly realized I'd never seen his bare arms before. He wasn't wearing his waistcoat like he usually did, and he had taken his jacket off at some point while I was distracted by the water. He was just in his light, loose-fitted shirt that fell slightly down his chest and his usual dark trousers. The way his arms moved as he rowed the boat enraptured me, each muscle tight and working as we glided deeper into the wooded lake.

When he glanced back at me, I shot my attention to the sky, hoping he hadn't noticed me studying his body so closely. The trees whirled into the sky like watercolors on a clouded canvas. They spun together in a mesmerizing dance as our boat bounced across the water, and I was grateful for the momentary distraction.

"I suppose you have already guessed this is part of the surprise," he said, still rowing but turning to look at something behind him.

"I had assumed it was at least part of it. Is there more?"

He was focused on something coming in behind us. I leaned over to look at what it was and nearly capsized the boat. As the water splashed at our feet, I said, "I'm sorry, I'm sorry! I was just trying to see what you were looking at."

He laughed again, and I loved how carefree it was. "It's quite all right, Caroline. Don't worry about it. Just try to sit still." He chuckled again and then said, "And I've been looking for our destination."

"Our destination?"

"Yes. I wanted to show you something I've never shown anyone before." The boat stopped against a small island in the middle of the lake, if you could call it an island. It was a tiny spot of land no bigger than a typical dining room (a regular dining room—not an Ashdown family-sized dining room)—a small, grassy rectangle in the middle of the water. Other than some sticks and rocks, there was nothing on it, and there was definitely nothing remarkable about it.

He stepped off the boat and took the rope, tying it to a

thick wooden rod someone had obviously wedged in the land for this exact purpose. "Did you put that there for us to dock here?"

He smiled as he finished tying the knot. "I actually put it here quite some time ago." He leaned in to grab my hands and help lift me onto the little island. He held me against him longer than he needed to for me to safely step out of the boat, but I loved every second of it. He ran his fingers along the back of my neck and kissed me softly on the lips. "Come sit with me," he said, lacing his hand in mine.

We only took about two steps before sitting down, as the island was barely long enough to walk on to begin with. I looked out onto the water and rested my head on his shoulder, breathing in the scent of the lake against the trees.

"I used to come here all the time when I was a child," he said. "My life stopped when I was twelve years old. I lost everyone the day of the festival, and I barely had anyone to begin with. Things were hard, and I didn't have much companionship. The only time I ever tried to have friends, I only got in trouble. I wasn't supposed to mingle with the human kids, but I was twelve, and I wanted people to hang around and play ball with."

I sat up and watched him speak, his eyes looking down into the water. A fish shimmied beneath a cloud of algae. "I was dangerous," he continued. "I was newly turned and full of potent feelings I wasn't used to yet. Still, I wanted to spend time with kids my age. I started sneaking around and playing with other kids. When the others found out, though . . . well, they put a stop to it, to put it simply. And I was alone again. I was in pain and alone, with no one from my human life and no life ahead of me. So I'd come here and explore." He gestured to the trees around us.

"This was my playground. I pretended all sorts of things, imagined so many alternate lives. And when I found this little island, I had another stage for my stories.

"Sometimes I was a pirate—the fish in the water my sworn enemies trying to take my treasure. Sometimes I was a king who was hiding away to avoid his responsibilities." He chuckled wistfully. "And of course, I didn't have a boat readily available at the time, so I became quite the swimmer. I knew how to swim already, but my longing to reach this little patch of land practically turned me into a merman of my own." He winked at me. "Imagine that. Part vampire, part merman. Would you love me then?"

I laughed. "Of course." I turned to him with a smile, and he looked into my eyes with that same wistful look.

"Well, I had a hard time loving myself back then. I suppose that's still something I struggle with." He picked up a small pebble and tossed it idly into the water.

I took his hand so that both my hands were in his. "Then it's a good thing you don't have to struggle alone anymore."

He kissed my forehead. "Thank you, Caroline. You'll never be alone, either." He tilted my chin up toward him. He searched my eyes, and in this lighting, near the water in the canopied forest, he looked even more breathtaking than usual. I nodded absently. "I mean it," he said. "I'll come to you wherever you are, whenever you need me. I'll be there."

A smile broke across my face. "You're good at that." I said. "How *are* you so good at that, by the way?"

He raked a hand through his hair and sighed. "It's both a blessing and a curse."

"What is?"

He took his hands from mine and shifted his position on our little grassy stoop. "Well, vampires have unique abilities. Each one a little different, just like with humans and their own inherited abilities or skills. The unique attributes of vampires, however, are a little different." He picked up a pebble and turned it over as he spoke. "Vampires can hear extraordinarily well, just like a bat. Though contrary to popular legends, we do not turn into bats." He chuckled. "That would be something, though."

"How did that myth come to be then?" I asked.

"I think it's because we share some common traits with bats. People find us dark and ominous, predators who hide in the shadows and only coming out after dark."

"But you come out during the day all the time."

"Only this time of the year," he said, looking up at the sky. "Though it can always be tricky, no matter the season. If the sun is high in the sky and the clouds are parted and no longer obscuring its blaring light, it can be quite intense. So even on days when we are out together, I can sometimes be irritable because of it. If that has ever occurred, I apologize." *That explains it*, I thought. *They don't burn.* I'd noticed him getting agitated during sunnier hours outside, maybe only once. I just thought he was prone to headaches or something of that nature.

"So . . . You can hear extremely well, you can be outside but mostly when it's not sunny, and you are . . ." *A predator.* I couldn't say it. I didn't know how to say it, but the question needed to be asked. I took a deep breath, but before I could ask, William put his hand on mine.

"You don't have to worry about me hurting you," he said. "Evelyn, Charles, and I only feed off animals, which is what vampires are supposed to do, according to the Council. Some get away with it the way any murderer would, though a vampire sneakily killing a human with no witnesses is a lot harder to catch."

"The Council?"

"Perhaps I should stop talking. I don't know what the rules are for talking to a human about such things." He tucked a piece of hair behind my ear and kissed my cheek. "I wouldn't want anything to happen to you," he said softly.

"I understand, but I still have so many questions."

He nodded. "Yes, go on. I'll answer whatever others I can. I may need to hold off on some, though. I promised I would never lie to you, and I intend on keeping that, but I also want to keep you safe. So we need to be careful. I'm not the only one with good hearing."

The thought of another vampire listening in on us sent a shiver down my spine. "I understand," I said again, exhaling carefully. *How should I word things then? How far can they hear?*

"I'm sure we're safe out here," he said, my fearful expression giving me away. "There's a reason I used to come out here so often. It's away from prying eyes and listening ears. But still, since it's you at stake, I want to be as cautious as possible."

"Okay. Well, you don't have to answer all my questions today, but there are a few pressing ones I'd like to know." The wind whistled around us, skating on the lake and vanishing like a pixie through the trees. I wondered what other magical creatures existed in the world that I didn't know about. But I had to focus on the task at hand. "You heard me when I was in danger . . . so . . . do you listen to me *all* the time?"

"No no no. I wouldn't intrude on you like that. We still respect others' privacy—at least the respectable ones of us do—but sometimes there are noises we can't ignore, and sometimes we are more sensitive to certain sounds over others." He traced his finger along the lines of my palm. "For me, I have become quite sensitive to the sound of your screaming. I could hear it clear across Brakerton Heights if you were in danger."

"Oh yeah?" I said, biting back a smile.

"Yes, of course." He laughed. "I'm quite smitten with you, you know, so don't act so surprised." He tilted my chin delicately toward him again and kissed me. "And there are a few other things that are connected to why I am so sensitive to your cries. One is that vampires have heightened emotions, as well as other senses, though we lose the sense to taste human food when we turn—at least not very well anyway." I thought back on all the days they'd eaten supper with us.

"Is it difficult to pretend to enjoy food at the table then?"

"It can be, but it's not too bad. It doesn't taste disgusting to us or anything. It just doesn't really have any flavor." He exhaled heavily. "Ah, but I miss enjoying food." He stretched himself out along the grass. "It's one of the things I miss most about being human."

"At least you don't have to go hungry," I said, lying down next to him and wrapping my arm around his stomach.

"Well, being a vampire living off animals alone is a special kind of hungry that I don't particularly enjoy."

I looked up at him with a frown. "So, it's true then?" I asked. "You also crave human blood?" My heart pounded unevenly in my chest, a strange occurrence that had been happening a lot lately.

He turned onto his side and met me at eye level. "You don't have to worry about that, Caroline. I would never kill anyone." He ran a finger along the side of my body, moving it along the dip of my waist. "Especially not you."

I could almost hear Maggie's words in my head—the words she would have spoken if I had told her I was in love with a vampire who promised not to kill anyone: *Can you really trust a vampire's word?*

It didn't matter what Maggie would have said. I made the decision to trust William. I wouldn't let my past hold me back. I touched the side of his face and smiled. "I know. I believe you."

He kissed me on the tip of the nose. "You make me the happiest man in the world. I hope you know that." He looked at me, tenderness emanating from his hypnotizingly dark eyes. "I don't deserve someone so perfect."

I let out a laugh and rolled onto my back. "Perfect! I can't say anyone has ever said *that* to me before."

He lifted himself up, leaning against his forearm. "I really mean it," he said. "You are so perfect to me."

My face softened, and I sat up to face him. "Well *you* are perfect to *me*. So, it appears we are equals in perfection."

He rolled his eyes and flopped back onto his back. "You can be quite hilarious, you know that?" He stayed looking at the sky, and the seriousness in his tone made my heart ache. I rolled over and crawled on top of him, my hands on either side of his head as I looked him in the eye.

"I mean it, William." I let my body rest on his, scooting down so my head could rest on his chest. "Maybe we are two sides of the same coin, you and I. While you longed for someone to find you in the shadows and help you find your way out, I was there all along. We just didn't see each other in the darkness. Perhaps I didn't know it then, but I'd been waiting for you all along so we could escape it together."

I wasn't used to saying such bold things, but ever since last night, I felt brave. William helped me feel brave. I hoped I made him feel brave, too.

What was love if not helping each other out of the dark? That was the kind of love I was falling into. The kind of love I wanted.

Slowly, he sat up, and my body slid slowly to the ground in front of him. He looked into my eyes. "Could you really love something that came to you from the shadows?" he asked.

"You didn't come to me from the shadows," I said. "You saved me from them."

For a moment, he just looked at me, and we just sat there together, face to face, completely vulnerable. The darkest and most scarred parts of us were out there for the other to see, and we should have felt scared, but we weren't. We knew we were safe. We knew that no one else in this world could understand us the way we understood each other. No one else's souls fit together so perfectly, like those puzzle pieces left behind but complete together. It was like we were finally home after being away for a long, long time.

He moved in closer to me, his hand sliding around my waist. He placed his forehead against mine, and I couldn't see his face anymore. My eyes closed. "Are you real, Caroline?" he whispered so quietly I could barely hear him. "Or is my mind playing cruel games with me and this is all a dream?"

My heart raced as his lips moved closer to mine. "I have been wondering the same thing about you," I said.

He laughed softly. "Well then if we *are* in a dream, let's stay here forever and never wake up."

My lips parted to speak, but I was so aware of his hand on my waist and his lips brushing against mine that I couldn't speak or think of anything anymore. Then he leaned forward and kissed me—the kind of kiss that gets better the more it goes on—with every taste, every movement. I moved my body over him, my hair falling around him, and we kissed longer, deeper, until we rolled into the water with a jarring splash.

I tried to grab hold of something, but my hand kept slipping off the rocks along the shore. Then I felt a hand grabbing mine and was pulled from the lake. I coughed out the water I'd accidentally gulped down.

"Are you all right?" he asked, but I just laughed, and the more I thought about what had happened, the more I laughed. And the more I laughed, the more he laughed, too. Soon, he and I were lying on the grass, drenched from head to toe, laughing until our sides hurt. Laughing without anything holding us back. Laughing like nothing and no one else mattered at all. Like it was only us.

"I'm all right," I said when I could finally breathe. "I can swim fine. I was just startled." I let out another laugh, and he came up beside me.

"I'm glad you're well," he said, a smile still broad on his face. "I was worried I'd lose you."

I smiled, my nose crinkling. "No, you're too late for that," I teased. "I'm already yours. You can't lose me now."

He brushed the wet strands of hair from my face and smiled. "Well it looks like I'm not too late then, am I?" He pressed his lips to mine, and I sunk into his spell. "There's one more thing about vampires that makes me so mad about you."

"Yeah?" I whispered, trying not to plunge myself back into his lips. "And what's that?"

He pulled back a little more so he could look into my eyes. "Vampires only fall in love once." His eyes looked at me so bare and unguarded as he waited for my response. Like he wanted me to know that he wasn't holding back.

I didn't know the right words to say, but I knew that I loved him and that I only wanted him.

"Then it's good that I only want to love you, too," I whispered, and his lips parted into a handsome smile that made me weak all over again.

Then I noticed his fangs. I had never seen them before. They were subtle, but they were there. I lifted a finger to one of them. "Why is it that I've never seen your fangs before." He closed his mouth, and I laughed as I took my finger from his lips.

"I try my hardest to keep them concealed," he said. "I thought I was doing a good job, but it appears I let my guard down."

"What do you mean?"

"I can conceal them, retract them in a way so they look more human, but you—" he pulled me against him and kissed me "—you are making me too flustered to remember." He smiled again, and when I could see his teeth, I gently pressed my fingers against his fangs.

"I think they're rather cute," I said.

One of his eyebrows arched, but an amused smile crept across his face. "You think they're cute?"

"I do."

He laughed. "Well that makes one of us."

"Well, what if I had them? Wouldn't that be cute?" I asked, then instantly wishing I could take the words back. I was about to panic at the thought of him worried about turning me, but then he laughed, not a worry on his face.

"Yes, that would be cute," he said, getting to his feet. "Now, come. We must go. You'll catch a cold again if you stay in your wet clothes like this. Let's head back to the house." He smiled down at me as he took my hands and helped me to my feet. I didn't even have a chance to steady myself before he swept me up into his arms and carried me to the boat.

He helped me get seated safely but didn't extend the same courtesy to himself. When he tried to get in, he lost his balance and fell on top of me, water splashing into the boat as we almost capsized again. I laughed and wrapped my arms around him.

"I'm terribly sorry to have fallen on you, ma'am," he said in a faux gentlemanly voice.

"Why, not at all, sir, I rather like this arrangement."

We laughed and kissed until we decided it was truly time to go. Then we enjoyed every moment that came after, reveling in the bliss that came with being together as he paddled us to shore. Once on dry ground, he took my hand, and I wondered if I would always be this happy. If life would always be this sweet.

Then we walked back through the woods, neither one of us able to stop smiling all the way back to the house. I barely even noticed the cold.

Chapter Twenty-Four

William swung the mansion's doors wide open and led me inside, both of us beaming and lighter than air. When my shoe slipped on the tiled floor, he caught me, and we both started laughing again, giddy the way people are in the throes of new love.

"What is happening over here that is so funny?" A woman's voice rang in from around the corner. I turned and saw Evelyn, her usual cheery self gone. Her face was tight, her mouth rigid. She did not look amused.

"Oh, I'm sorry if we were loud," I said, shifting and almost slipping again. William stifled a laugh, which made me stifle one, too.

"Well why were you loud?" she asked.

"Evelyn," William said, "We were just laughing."

But she didn't smile. She didn't so much as blink. She

just stood there, a perfect statue with arms crossed tightly across her chest. "Why are the two of you so wet?" she asked, her voice like bullets. "It isn't even raining out."

Something was off. I'd never seen her like this before. I wondered if something happened.

"We fell into the lake," I said, but as the last few words left my mouth, I saw William shaking his head discreetly, and I realized I was probably supposed to keep it between us.

Her eyes bulged. "You took her out into the forest? William—"

"Evelyn, everything is all right, and if you don't mind, I'm going to take Caroline to her room so she doesn't catch a cold. Besides, I think you're frightening her anyway."

He took my hand and wrapped it into his arm and rushed up the stairs with me.

"What was that?" I whispered, realizing shortly afterward that if Evelyn wanted to hear me, she could.

He sighed. "I don't know, but I'm sure I will have to find out later and deal with it then." He opened my door and led me inside, closing the door behind us. "And don't worry, she won't listen to us. She and I are both so well-practiced in selective hearing that we don't even remember we can do it most of the time." I nodded, but I was still worried. Why was she so angry at us? I'd never seen her like that before.

"It will be okay," he said, tipping my face up. "I'll sort it all out. It will be okay." He smiled and then kissed me. "Now, go on and get undressed. I'll inform Molly so that she can assist you."

"Okay," I said softly. "I'll see you soon." I forced a smile until he was gone, then I let my face fall. I couldn't get Evelyn's expression out of my head. She was always so happy. Why did she have that angry look in her eyes, and that stiff posture?

I tore the first layer of my clothes off and draped them over my vanity table. It didn't take long for my lighter mood to return, and I laughed at the beautifully odd turn of events that had transpired today—at the clothes I so perfectly curated now crumpled in a sopping pile beneath my mirror. I caught myself smiling and decided that I'd focus on happy things instead. I wouldn't think of Evelyn or why she was so angry. I wouldn't think of Augustus and his ominous warnings. And I wouldn't think about what I saw last night. That couldn't have been real, could it? I had imagined it like I always had.

There I was again, thinking about my demons. I needed to relax—to let myself be happy and free for once in my life. I didn't want to ask any more questions that would cause me grief. I didn't want to see Augustus. I definitely did not want to go back into the cellar to see if I really had seen the Shadow Beast. I didn't even want to learn anything else about my mother, my father, or their deaths.

I just wanted William. I just wanted peace. For once in my life, I didn't want to let myself be bogged down by questions and fear. I just wanted to live.

I was struggling to find the string to my corset when Molly knocked on the door and asked to come in. The real struggle was dodging Molly's questions about William and me and what had happened today and why I came in so wet. When she wouldn't stop pestering me, I said, "Fine. Ugh. You are relentless, Molly." Although I was frustrated, I couldn't help but feel giddy at the opportunity to at least tell *someone* about William and me. "I won't tell you what happened, but I will let you know that Lord Ashdown and I *are* romantically involved, but please don't make a fuss about it."

I was right to wait as long as I did to tell her because

she squealed for the remainder of her stay in my room. Even as she laced me up into my new, dry corset, she squealed. "Molly, please! My ears are ringing," I complained, but I couldn't help but smile. Here I was, sharing secrets about love with my cousin and basking in the sunlight that had finally spilled into my life after so many years under stormy clouds.

When William knocked on the door, Molly practically leapt into the air to unite the two of us. And when I saw him standing there in the doorway, with his newly pressed suit and that smile that made my heart turn in a thousand directions, I finally felt home.

The next few weeks went by in a dizzying flash. William and I spent every waking moment together that we could during the day. His sister and brother-in-law had gotten rather strict with our schedules, though, so he and I could only see each other during our working hours. Evelyn had also found our excursion in the woods improper and told us that if we wanted to go out together again, we needed a chaperone. She added that even with a chaperone, she didn't think it wise for us to go back into the woods that far.

The newly placed restrictions were frustrating, but William and I didn't let it dampen our time together. We constructed the booths for the festival together, ate every meal together, and we even got to spend time sampling food in the market together, which consisted of me sampling food and him pretending he could taste it, too.

If we wanted to see each other outside of those restrictions, we had to get creative. It didn't happen often, but about once a week, William would manage to sneak out when the others were occupied and come to my window to take me to the garden where we'd first kissed. I always looked forward to those nights. We'd lie in the grass, soaking in the moonlight, and kiss beneath the stars where no one could find us.

Other than that, there was only one night where William and I saw each other after working hours. It had been a lovely day, and I hadn't had nightmares for weeks, but then it happened. That same horrific nightmare where I ran away from the Shadow Beast—where it almost got me—and I saw and heard flashes of panic and destruction. Things I had never seen before. William heard me crying in my sleep and came right away. He held me and soothed me, just as he had that night I'd thought I saw it.

Every time I wanted to ask him about it, I swallowed the words and held them back. I had told myself that I wouldn't worry—that I wouldn't let myself wonder if what I'd seen that night was real or imagined. I didn't want to look into the shadows yet. I was having too much fun in the sun. So I just let him hold me and pretended everything would be okay.

The morning after he'd soothed me to sleep that second time, I didn't let myself think about the nightmare or anything that came with it. I just focused on the festival's preparations like I had all the days before.

The festival was in a matter of days, and we were all busier than ever when I received a letter from Mary and Agnes. I gasped when I saw their names inscribed next to the name of our paper. I hadn't recorded a thing. Nothing of use to our paper, anyway. "How could I forget the reason I came here?" I said to William as we walked to the supper table that evening.

"I honestly don't know," he said with a laugh.

"Should I tell them I've had too much fun to remember

and that they should just come and see for themselves? I had written a couple of weeks ago and told them what to expect, but maybe I should update them." I greeted the others and took my seat at the table.

"Did they ask you for an update?"

"Well, no."

"Then what is there to worry about?"

"Who is worrying about what?" Evelyn asked in her sticky-sweet tone—a more saccharine version of the cheery tone I'd been used to until William's and my trip to the lake.

"Oh, I'm not worried," I said, "I was just talking with my friends from *The Woman Speaks*. I'm trying to persuade them to come."

She grabbed my hand and smiled. "Oh, do invite them. You've been working so hard out there—all of us have."

I forced a smile and took my hand back to cut into my venison. "I did invite them. They are most excited about the ball."

Evelyn nearly choked on her water. "What? The ball?"

William frowned. "I swore we talked to you about this, Evelyn. Caroline had thought about having a ball on the opening night of the festival this weekend. Wasn't that a grand idea?" He smiled at me, and my heart fluttered. I would never grow tired of seeing him look at me like that.

"Charles, do you remember the mention of a ball?" Evelyn asked her husband.

He cut into his food and shook his head. "No, I don't remember that, either."

My stomach turned. "Oh no. We must have forgotten. What will I tell Mary and Agnes? They already put it in our paper!"

"It's all right, Caroline, I'll take care of it," William said and looked to his sister. "It's an easy enough thing to pull together, isn't it?"

Evelyn's eyes were wide with horror. "No, William, I don't think it is." She groaned and massaged the bridge of her nose. "But I suppose we should get started on throwing things together if the town already expects it."

I let my fork fall onto my plate. I wasn't hungry anymore. I felt awful. "This is my fault. I'm so sorry," I said.

William shook his head. "No, you came up with a brilliant idea. There shouldn't be much work in adding a ball to the opening ceremony."

Evelyn sat back in her seat and looked at her brother in exasperation. "Well then you can be in charge of it, William." She grumbled something under her breath before closing her eyes and taking a deep breath. When she opened them, she said, "I'll tell Mrs. Wells that we need a decorator right away, and the maids will need to clean up the ballroom. The festival is in two days, and we haven't had a ball there in—"

"A very, very long time," her husband finished, laughing awkwardly, and Evelyn froze, then smiled tightly and poked her fork into her food.

"Well," William said, "It's settled then. We will host a ball, and everyone will love it."

Evelyn nodded. "I'm sure they will, if we can pull it off."

"We'll be able to pull it off," he said, popping a carrot into his mouth. "And it will be the most talk-worthy part of the festival." Then he turned to me and added, "And it will all be thanks to Caroline."

Evelyn and Charles shot each other a look across the table, but William didn't notice. "I suppose we should get to work right away," I said, excusing myself from the table.

"Yes, you're absolutely right," he said, his eyes following me as I walked to the door. He tossed his napkin on the table and excused himself, too.

Right before he left, Evelyn grabbed him by the arm and glared up at him. She whispered something before he shook himself free of her grip and walked away.

"Let's go," he said, taking my hand and leading me down the hall.

"What's wrong?"

"Nothing is wrong."

"I *know* something is wrong. I saw the way you looked at Evelyn and the way she looked at you. What happened?"

He stopped. I studied his face but couldn't see a hint of anything one way or another. After another moment, he looked at me with a smile and lifted my hand in his to kiss it. "Come, my darling, let's plan a party the world has never seen."

The day that followed was a lot more than William and I bargained for, and we started to realize why Evelyn was so distressed about throwing a last-minute ball. There was a lot more to it than dancing and decorations. We had to arrange for a caterer and ensure everything aligned with when the vendors and workers at the booths would start welcoming guests. Evelyn had some of the servants go into town and pass out invitations, letting the public know that if they showed up an hour earlier, there would be a commencement ball. She made sure the invitations clarified that this portion was optional and that the guests may go to the bottom of the hill and enjoy the more traditional Harvest Festival attractions.

By the end of the night, I was exhausted, and I knew the following day would be even worse. We would have to help get everything organized both for the ball and for the rest of the event. We still needed to string up some of the decorations outside and get everything prepared in the ballroom.

That night, I buried myself in my blankets and breathed a sigh of relief. My bed had never been so comfortable. William ran his fingers down my arm and smiled at my apparently adorable human exhaustion. We'd decided that since tonight was the last night before the festival, we earned the right to spend some extra time together before he had to go back to his room.

He drew invisible shapes on my shoulders, working around the straps to my nightdress. I loved feeling him so close. My whole body was sore from all the walking and decorating we had to do from morning until well after supper. It was a welcome comfort for William to lie with me like this.

I just tried not to think about the inevitable—that in just two days I would be gone and we would have to figure out what happened next. Each time the thought surfaced in my mind, I would push it away and focus on the loops and curls skating across my skin.

"I should have just told Mary and Agnes that there would be no ball after all," I muttered as he drew the shape of a butterfly on my shoulder blade.

He leaned forward and kissed it, and my skin warmed against his lips. "No, I think we did the right thing. You wouldn't want your paper to gain a bad reputation from misinformation while it's still getting off the ground." He put his head against my pillow and slid his arm around me. "Besides, dancing with you will be the best part of this festival."

I smiled and turned around to face him. "You're right. I'm sure it will be fine."

He kissed me on the forehead. He opened his mouth to

say something, but the sound of horses drew his attention to the window. His smile immediately vanished as he sprung up and moved to the other side of the bed, peeking through the curtains to see what was going on outside.

His mouth dropped open. "Oh no," he muttered. The sound of wheels bumping against cobblestone thrummed through the window. "I thought Charles said they weren't going to make it." He closed the curtains with a sort of growl and pushed himself off the bed.

"What's going on?' I asked, but his mind was elsewhere as he flung his jacket back on. When I repeated the question, he looked at me with concern.

He came back to kiss me, and after he had, he peered down into my eyes. "Don't go anywhere near those people, all right? They're very dangerous."

"Who? What people?" I knelt up and scooted toward the window. When I peeled the curtains open, William quickly lunged forward and closed them.

"Please don't draw attention to yourself," he said. "Do you have something to protect yourself? Actually, never mind. I don't think there is anything you could do." He quickly raked his hand through his hair, a nervous habit I'd noticed over the last few weeks, and slid back off the bed to put his boots on.

I crawled out and walked over to where he was crouched by my vanity table. When I looked up into the mirror and caught a glimpse of myself and myself alone, my stomach wrenched. *Oh right. No reflection*, I reminded myself. I supposed that was one alleged trait Maggie had gotten right.

Although I knew so much about William and his kind, I always seemed to forget he was a vampire when we were together like this. He was so gentle and kind—not at all what I'd expect from someone who lived off drinking blood.

He swiped his hand through his hair again and got to his feet. He kissed me one more time and said, "I have to go. Don't look out the window, and if you need me, call for me."

"All right," I said quietly, watching him open the door.

"I'll see you in the morning," he said, forcing a smile. I forced one back and waved as he left, his coat nearly catching in the door as he rushed into the hall.

The sound of the door closing was matched by more wheels clattering outside. Horses whinnied, and I could hear people talking. I looked at the closed curtains. Who was there, and why did William want me to avoid them?

Mrs. Wells had mentioned something when I talked to her that night, which felt so long ago now, but all she'd said was that I should stay away from the vampire guests as much as possible. Did that mean some of them were more dangerous than others, or did it simply mean I should be as cautious as possible with all the guests? Either way, the advice was far too vague for me to follow it through adequately.

Though judging by the way William left in such a frenzy, it was safe to say that I should stay away from whichever guests were out there right now.

I heard more voices—shouts, though not angry ones from what I could tell—and I was dying to look outside. How was I supposed to know who to stay away from if I didn't know what they looked like?

I slumped back in my bed and resisted the urge to look outside. Other than the commotion out front, the night was a lot quieter than I'd thought the night before the festival would be. For a while, I toyed with the idea of getting up and writing part of an article for *The Woman Speaks* about my time here, but I couldn't get William's face out of my head.

He looked so shocked. Frightened. Who had come that he wasn't expecting?

I tossed and turned all night, wishing there was something I could do for him. I only had two more days here, and it was slowly killing me inside. I had tried to avoid the thought as much as possible and focus on the time we still had together, but I couldn't avoid it now. In this sleepless night with him occupied elsewhere, I couldn't run away from it.

When I thought of a life without him, my stomach constricted and I wanted to cry. I had unknowingly searched for him my entire life. Could I really leave him now? Could I go back to that bland, gray, stormy life after dancing beneath a new vibrant sun?

He and I always avoided the subject, but as the days passed, we both knew it was an elephant in the room we couldn't evade forever. We never spoke about it, though. We didn't want to. All we wanted was to stay together and never wake up from this dream. No matter what.

In my heart, I knew we would find a way to be together, but in my mind, I didn't know how it was possible. Almost as painful as the thought of losing him was the knowledge that without me here, the pain would return to his eyes, that prickly shell would fall back around him, and he might never feel free again. And I knew he loved me too much to admit that. And I loved him too much to tell him I needed him.

As much as I didn't want to need anyone, I needed him. I needed his arms around me and the softness of his lips. I needed his spirit. I needed that carefree magic that fell upon us whenever we were together. I needed the passion that bound us together, and I couldn't handle the thought of having that yearning for him but never seeing him when

I looked for him. I didn't want to go back to a life in the shadows—not now that I knew what it was like to bask in the sun.

But there was nothing I could do.

I tucked myself tighter in my blankets and tried to sleep, but my mind kept going back to it all. I thought about how painful it would be if we had to part and how unbearable it would be to live a life without him, knowing that that carefree spirit that had once embodied us both, binding us together, was gone. That the darkness would swallow us up again, but this time we wouldn't have each other to find our way out.

All because he was a vampire and I was a human, and we weren't supposed to fall in love.

But we *had* fallen in love.

There had to be something I could do. Anything.

Then it came to me.

I whipped off my blanket and slid out of bed. *William has saved me over and over* again, I thought, tossing my cloak over my shoulders and grabbing my partially melted candle on its candlestick. *It's time I did something for him in return.*

As much as I wanted to believe that everything would be okay and that no matter what, everything would work out, the truth was that I had absolutely no idea. I didn't know what our lives would look like two days from now. So, if the worst were to happen, I wanted to leave William with at least some solace. If he could never be by my side again—never feel my reassurance or hold me when the darkness returned—I wanted to leave him with something to drive away his demons.

I had to try something. The thought of him suffering would tear me apart for the rest of my life. So I fastened my cloak and left my room, letting the darkness welcome me once more.

I didn't know if it would work, but I had to try. After everything William had done for me, it was the least I could do.

Chapter Twenty-Five

Night had once again fallen over Ashdown Manor. The air was silent, and you could hear the slightest creak or squeak if it were to ring out through the halls. The eerie stillness was made worse by the fact that droves of unfamiliar vampires now filled the rooms in the manor—beings who didn't sleep and could hear every little sound far better than someone like me.

The cold gripped me, and my heart skipped in that odd mismatched pattern. Maybe it was the nerves of it all.

I gripped the candlestick tighter and tried to silence my breaths. I didn't know how well the new vampires would be able to hear me, since William mentioned every vampire had different enhanced abilities. Erring on the side of caution was my best bet.

I followed the gray walls, now adorned with alabaster

and ruby tapestries and decorations, welcoming all to the manor for the festival. Since the guests would be led through these halls to the ballroom, Evelyn wanted their experience to be an awe-inducing attraction of its own. Anything less than the most lavish decorations wouldn't do. So the manor looked even more like a castle than it usually did.

It was surreal to think that soon, the Ashdown Family Harvest Festival would finally commence. Guests would arrive through the bottom gates and enter into a long stream of booths full of handmade delicacies and accessories, all of which led to the main activities. There would be horseshoes, games and music, and even entertainment put on by a local troupe of actors. On top of it all would be the assortment of treats and baked goods I was most looking forward to.

And, of course, there was the ball, which would be the opening attraction—a short commencement ceremony, as William and I didn't have the amount of time we should have allotted for such an event.

My stomach twisted at the thought of him again. At what would happen after the last guest left on the final day.

But there was no time to think about that now.

I steadied myself against the banister as I took the back set of stairs to William's wing. And even though I was here to help him, I still couldn't help feeling guilty. I wasn't supposed to be here, but I had to come one last time. I needed to get through to Augustus, for William.

The farther I walked down the hallway, my hand sliding against the mural, the more nervous I became. Nausea rippled through my gut, and my skin got icier than usual. I was just about to round the corner when I heard William's voice, and I immediately jumped and flattened my back against the wall.

"What are we supposed to do then, Charles? You know they can't be trusted. You know where their loyalties lie."

"They made an oath. Their word can be trusted. Besides, they're family."

"They are *not* family."

"Don't be in such haste to judge them, William."

"You cannot be serious," William said with a loud, sardonic laugh. "Are you forgetting what they did?"

"No, I have not forgotten, but they made oaths in front of the Council. Besides, we put away any threats."

"We put away *one* threat. Everyone else either died that day or gave false oaths, and now you're welcoming them back with open arms. They'll probably try to fulfill Cassius' legacy."

My muscles tensed.

"They won't do that. Besides, what do you expect us to do? Lock away anyone who could pose as a threat?"

"We don't have to give them a chance to recreate that massacre."

"That won't happen."

"How could you possibly know that?" William hissed. "Have you thought this through at all?"

"I hardly think you're one to talk about responsibility," Charles said, his cool demeanor finally gone.

"What is that supposed to mean?"

"I'm talking about you and Miss Blake. You know how reckless it is for one of us to fall in love with a human, let alone act upon it. You know what happened last time this sort of thing happened."

"This isn't like that and you know it. I love Caroline."

"And what will happen in the end between the two of you? Will you turn her?"

"N-no of course not."

"Then what? How will the course of your relationship

go? Tell me, have you thought *that* through at all?"

"I can still be with her without—"

"You're walking a very, *very* dangerous line, William, so before you try to preach to me about responsibility, why don't you take a look at your own choices first?"

Neither of them said anything after that. I just heard the slamming of a door, followed shortly by the quiet closing of another. My heart sank, and I couldn't hide the pain any longer. William and I might never see each other again after all this. Could I really live with that?

No. I couldn't think about that now. I had to do what I came here to do. I waited until I was sure they wouldn't leave their rooms before I slunk around the corner and rushed to the secret room. Pushing up on the handle to the hidden staircase, I rushed inside and shut the door quietly behind me.

As I ascended the steps, my legs started trembling. I tried not to think, other than of what I was going to say. I supposed I hadn't thought this through very well.

I walked up to the mirror and called out to him. "Augustus?" I said as quietly as possible, wondering if William would be able to hear my voice from across the hall.

His face appeared in the mirror in front of me. He looked at me in surprise. "Oh, it's you. I didn't know you'd ever be back to see me. Your name is Caroline, right?"

I nodded, my hands clutching my cloak. "I just wanted to talk with you before I left this place. I don't know if I'll ever be back, but I wanted to ask you something." My stomach twisted, but I squinted my eyes shut and went for it. "I wanted to ask you to forgive William." I quickly opened them again and saw him raise an eyebrow.

"You want me to do what?"

"I-I want you to forgive William for whatever he did to

you." I stayed firm, refusing to break eye contact. I wanted him to know how serious I was. "He's been destroyed about what happened between the two of you. Whatever it was, he is remorseful to the point of breaking. He has held so much pain and guilt for so long. He thinks he's a monster. I just—I just want him to be okay when I leave."

As he watched me, his frown deepened.

I quickly continued. "If I have to leave, I want to know that he'll be okay. Can you do that please? Whatever happened between the two of you happened decades ago. I just . . . I want you to help release him of his pain. Please. I want him to smile when I'm gone."

He laughed, his tongue pressed to his cheek. "You want me to forgive him?" I nodded, which made him laugh more. "So, tell me if I understand you correctly. You want me to forgive William for imprisoning me here for all of time just because you want him to smile. Is that right?" He glared at me, waiting for my response.

"He . . . what?" *No. He was lying. He had to be. William would never do something like that.* "You're lying."

He crossed his arms. "Is that so? Well what does it look like, Caroline?" His voice rose, and I winced, hoping no one would hear us.

I looked around the tiny oblong room, the dark walls and colorfully tiled floor. There was nothing here. I knew that. Just this man in this mirror. My eyes fell on him. "He trapped you?" I whispered, unable to believe the words as I spoke them.

His eyes stayed locked on mine as he nodded. "William was my best friend. No, we were closer than that. We were brothers." He sighed and slumped to the floor like he'd done the last time I was here. I joined him on the ground, moving forward so I could hear him more easily. For a moment, he smiled wistfully, though his eyes were still sad.

"We played together after he turned. We were the only friend the other had—I, an unnatural child brought into the world through dark means, and he, a young, newly turned vampire."

He chuckled softly to himself. "We used to play in the woods together. We used to run along the hills out back. We did everything together. It was the only way we stayed sane as the world crumbled around us. My father was on trial for what he'd done. I was hollow, sick. My mother was dead, my father was detained, and I was here. William was all I had."

His smile dropped and his gaze fell behind me. "What happened?" I asked.

Pain pulled at his face and something in his eyes changed. "He grew older, slowly aging into the man he is now. His emotions were heightened, only growing stronger as the years went on. Finally, fear took hold of him. It gripped him so tightly he couldn't think clearly anymore . . ." His voice trailed off, and the soundless room became unbearably quiet. "He was afraid of me," he whispered, his eyes still staring far away. "He was afraid I'd turn into my father, so he arranged with the others to put me away."

I shook my head slowly. No. William wouldn't do that. He saw the light in me. He wouldn't seal someone's fate so cruelly based on a foreboding feeling. That wasn't like him.

"He couldn't have done that. He wouldn't have."

But he just kept speaking. "He was starting to get angrier and angrier with me. He'd find things in me that weren't there. And he lied—he lied to the others to ensure I'd get locked away. He called me a threat."

My skin chilled, and I heard William's voice in my head. *We put away one threat.*

Augustus' eyes found mine. They were stained red now. "He's done terrible things, Caroline. Don't trust him. I did, and look at what happened to me."

"No, William loves me. He wouldn't do anything to me, and he wouldn't do this to you, either." My head kept shaking. It couldn't be true. William didn't have it in him to do something so cruel.

But then I remembered the way he'd cried in the cemetery and the pain and guilt in his eyes. That was why I'd come here, after all—to free him of his guilt. Only now, I wasn't so sure he could obtain such a luxury.

I still couldn't believe it. I knew William. He was kind. Adoring.

"No, you're wrong," I said, "He wouldn't do that." I closed my cloak tighter and got to my feet. "I know William."

"You're blinded by love."

"No, I am not." I turned and walked away.

"Believe what you want," he said as I got to the stairs. "But even if the good side of William has you right now, his dark side will come out eventually."

My hand slipped on the wall by the stairs. I saw William's smile. I saw the curved handwriting of my mother's letters, and then the frantic ones when things started to turn sour. "You're wrong," I said, fighting back tears. "You're wrong." Without looking back, I rushed down the stairs and left the room.

I fought the urge to cry as I ran through the hall, but one sob escaped as I turned the corner. After that, it all came pouring out. I ran with the now burnt-out candlestick clutched in one of my hands. Tears flooded my eyes and gushed down my face all the way to my room.

When I got inside, I threw off my cloak and pulled myself in bed, hoping my cries could be muffled in my pillow so William wouldn't hear me and try to hold me until I stopped. I didn't think I was ready to face him yet.

Not like this. Not yet.

I needed rest. I'd figure out the rest in the morning. Only two more days. We only had two more days.

"William, can I come in?" Evelyn asked after two knocks on the door.

I'd been pacing about my room, still reeling from the nerve Charles had to cast any accusations on me after what they were doing. If I was putting us at risk for loving Caroline, what were they doing, letting the remainder of Cassius' goons flock back in droves?

"William?"

"Yes, fine, come in."

When she opened the door, she had that same hostile look on her face she'd had when I brushed her off earlier. When she'd grabbed my arm on my way out of the dining room. *What are you thinking?* she'd asked in a hushed grumble under her breath so no one else could hear. Her eyes had darted to Caroline before turning back to me. I didn't dignify her with a response, but it seemed I'd have to now.

"Can I sit down?" she asked.

"Do what you please," I said, picking up the flowers I'd picked for Caroline before returning to our wing. Perhaps that was what gave Charles his ammunition to throw blame at me.

I had the flowers all sorted in groups, each one a memory from our late-night meetings beneath the stars in the garden. The green stems were so full of vibrant life, the pastel petals perfect and beautiful. Each one made me think of her. I arranged them so that the colors were patterned just right. I wanted to show her how much she meant to me—that our times together have given me the life I'd always wanted.

As I studied them in my hands, my eyes trailed to the bottom of their stems, where I'd ripped them from the ground, halting their growth and stopping their lives. Was that her fate, too? Could I really risk her meeting such a fate?

I turned the newly assembled bouquet in my hands.

"William, we need to talk about you and Caroline."

"No, Evelyn, we do *not* need to talk about Caroline and me." I put the flowers back on my dresser and folded my arms as I looked at the woman I'd claimed as my sister. "I will only say this one more time: I love Caroline, and I would never hurt her. Nothing will happen."

Her mouth fell open, aghast. She leaned forward on the foot of my bed, across from where I stood. "William, you know the risk—"

"What risk?"

Her eyes widened. "Oh, no you don't. You know very well what the risks are of you getting so close to a human."

"Do I? Or do you think everyone is at risk when they fall in love with a human?"

"We've only known one vampire who fell in love with a human—"

"Yes, and you invited his whole brood into our home. Did you think about *that* risk? Did you?"

She shook her head. "Don't change the subject. You know they took an oath—"

"Who cares about that bloody oath? Do you really think they'd honor that?"

"They have to! You know what could happen if they don't—"

"And what if Cassius were to return?"

She laughed. "That's impossible."

I narrowed my eyes. "Is it?"

She walked over to me and didn't stop until she was too close for me to dodge her piercing glare. "If you want to concern yourself about Cassius and his followers, focus on what you could learn about what happened back then."

"I know what happened back then. I saw the destruction myself." I lowered my voice. "And you have let that clan back into our house after what they did that night." I moved past her and went to the door, opening it and gesturing for her to leave.

Her scowl burned into me as she walked to the door. She stopped to look at me. "You really need to learn how to forgive. Many of these vampires weren't even there. The clan is different now."

"You don't know that."

"Actually, as a matter of fact, I do. Charles and I have done business with them for many years."

"If you want me to trust you, then you should trust me, too. Stop scolding me about Caroline and focus on keeping your precious guests in line." I opened the door even wider. "I hope you have a backup plan in case things go wrong."

She sighed and stepped into the hall. "Of course we do, but you need to move forward and not let what happened that night color how you feel about them now. Don't let fear and hatred rule the rest of your life. Do I need to remind you just how long that is?"

"No, you don't," I snapped.

"Good," she said, then her face softened. "Then don't forget it. And be careful. With Caroline. Please." She smiled weakly and then left for her room. I let my head fall back as I sighed.

I couldn't believe it. Our home was filled with traitors and their friends, and Charles and Evelyn had the nerve to throw accusations my way. I walked to my dresser and looked at the flowers again. Those flowers—so recently alive and soaking in rays of light, blooming and growing like all the rest, then ripped from life.

Was I a monster for wanting Caroline?

I picked them up and walked back to the door when I heard something. I frowned. Was that . . . I rushed to the doorway and looked toward the noise. My stomach dropped.

"Caroline?" I whispered, but she didn't hear me. Her hair fluttered behind her as she rounded the corner. There was no denying it. It was her. *What is she doing here?*

Something uneasy settled in my stomach, crawling up my body and clawing up my chest. I shook my head. She'd promised to never come down these halls. She knew how important that was to me—how important it was for her to stay away. To stay safe.

I looked at the flowers, and my cold heart twisted. I threw them back into my room, slamming the door behind me. I watched as they flopped in sad heaps onto the floor.

Suddenly things weren't so clear anymore. Maybe I didn't know Caroline as well as I thought I did. But maybe I had no right to know either way.

Chapter Twenty-Six

The Day of the Ball

William

I tried to distract myself for the rest of the night. I hadn't hunted in weeks, which usually didn't bother me, but I could feel it now. I hadn't even realized it had been that long, but I hadn't gone out since Caroline's first week at the mansion. It seemed like a lifetime ago.

Just as the case had been then, today I mostly needed the distraction over the actual hunt. I needed to get away and clear my head.

I left without telling Charles or Evelyn. I left without seeing Caroline. I just ran, and I went as far away as I could, utilizing all the strength and swiftness that came with being one of my kind. I went until I found a group of elk in a clearing. I wasn't sure where I was or how long I'd been out, but it was of no concern to me. I didn't want to think. So I let myself hunt until daylight burned heavy rays against my skin.

This was the first time I felt too sick to enjoy hunting. My heart felt like it was in pieces, and I wasn't sure where it stemmed from—Caroline's possible deceit or the possibility I may never see her again. I let myself fall to the ground, shaded beneath a tree, and catch my breath. I chuckled bitterly at the irony that I still breathed. We were no longer humans when we turned, but we weren't quite dead, either. We just became monsters, slowly decaying and turning into something extremely hard to kill.

As the sun reached higher in the sky, my thoughts turned to Caroline even more. How I missed her, how I felt sick when I thought of losing her, and why she was in our wing. Maybe she was trying to warn me about something. Maybe someone had hurt her. When that last thought came, anger seared through me like a hot blade. No one had better hurt her, or they'd have me to answer to the moment I stepped foot back in the mansion.

The anger soon turned to worry, and the inevitable passing of time made me long to see her. She was probably busy preparing for everything. I couldn't stay out any longer. As much as I wanted to forget everything, I could never forget her, and I longed to see her to the point that it was starting to hurt. So I left, retracing my strides the way I'd come until I spotted our home. The manor of the family I was named after. My prison.

When I jerked open the back door near our wing, I almost ran into Evelyn. I pushed past her. "I'm not speaking to you," I said when she tried to catch me by the arm.

"William, you—"

I whipped around. "No. I will not talk to you about any of this. I'm going to get ready for the festival. Where's Caroline?"

She put her hands on her hips and let out a heavy breath. "She's helping the servants get ready for the ball. You were out most of the day, do you know that? And you reek."

"Thank you for that, but as I said, I am about to get ready for the festival. So, if you'll excuse me." I pushed past her and went to my room. *Good. Caroline is safe*, I thought as I readied myself for a bath.

I got ready for the ball in a fog. I was happy Caroline was all right, but I was angry with myself for missing out on so much time with her during the day. But the question still remained: Why had she been in our wing?

As I dried off and got dressed, I turned the various possibilities around in my head, but all my thoughts would just return to the fact that she was snooping around behind my back. And I wondered if there was anything else she wasn't telling me.

I whipped my tie around my collar and chastised myself. *No. I'm sure she has a good explanation for all of this. I just need to ask her.*

But the thought made my stomach sick. How was I to bring up such a matter to her? What would I say?

Maybe I shouldn't say anything at all. Perhaps it's best to just enjoy our time together. We would soon need to figure out our next steps moving forward—steps I was confident neither one of us knew how to take.

When I finished putting my suit on, I wished I could look in the mirror—one of the disadvantages of being a vampire getting ready for a special event. I checked the clock. It was almost five o'clock. The guests would be here any minute now.

I grabbed my jacket and threw it on as I made one final decision: No matter what happened after tomorrow, I wouldn't let Caroline slip through my fingers. I couldn't. I'd rather die than go back to the life I'd been living before. I just wasn't sure what I could do about it. Or what I *should* do about it.

It took me a few tries to find the ballroom, as we had more than one and I wasn't used to visiting any of them, but once I got there, I was amazed at how beautiful everything was. Caroline and I had worked so hard to get things ready, and it appeared she executed the plans splendidly with the help of those we so hurriedly hired.

The massive room looked like walking into a bright golden jewelry box. Great arches dipped across the walls, each one adorned with glittering tapestries of various colors, like sparkling gems. The place looked spotless, and people were already lining the walls—unfamiliar vampires and humans alike, all with eager faces and dressed as nicely as their pocketbooks allowed.

As more townspeople from Brakerton Heights walked into the ballroom, I suddenly remembered I was in charge of talking with the musicians. I was supposed to give them the word to start their ensemble. I looked around the room, walking from one end to the next. Just as I saw the long neck of a cello, a large frame blocked my way.

"Excuse me, sir, but I must tell the ensemble to begin their . . . I know you." The man's face was smug, and it sat in the middle of a head large enough to use as a weapon. His shoulders were massive, and I realized I'd seen him somewhere before. As I looked up at him and studied his face, I remembered.

That day so long ago.

"How are you doing?" he said, his mouth twisted in a sinister curl across his massive face.

I shook my head. "I'm sorry, but have we met? I swear we have."

He chuckled. "We most certainly have."

I frowned and was about to reply when I saw Evelyn gesturing for me to follow her to the musical ensemble. I turned back to the man. "You'll have to excuse me." I nodded in a bow and turned away. Something about him sent a wave of unease tumbling through me. I didn't like it, but I had no time to think about it.

When I gave the musicians the cue, they took their instruments in their hand and began playing.

"What took you so long?" Evelyn asked under her breath, hiding her face from everyone else with the large gold-frilled fan in her hand.

"I had some things to take care of," I said, scanning the room for Caroline. Within the sea of brightly colored dresses, waving fans, and luxurious suitcoats, she was nowhere to be seen. I turned to my sister. "Do you know where Caroline is?"

She shot me a look behind her fan. "Are you really asking me that?"

"Please just tell me."

She sighed and then smiled as some of our guests walked by. "I last saw her going up to her room, but that was hours ago. I don't know where she is now." She fluttered her fan as she greeted more guests, swiveling in her golden gown that matched the glittering ballroom walls, her black hair tied back into a knot at the base of her skull. She smiled and said "hello" to another passerby before looking back at me with a fake smile. "Be careful, my dear brother, and try not to cause any problems tonight. All right?"

I rolled my eyes, but before I could say anything else, I saw her. Walking into the ballroom dressed all in scarlet.

Caroline. She turned and glanced about the room, her dark hair falling softly against the curve of her face and rippling past her shoulders. She opened her feathered fan in one swift, elegant motion as she walked into the crowd of shimmering golds, sapphires, and coattails.

Before I lost sight of her, I rushed into the crowd, dodging the elegantly dressed townspeople who were coming in by the dozens. When I finally spotted her again, a man was holding his hand out to her and asking her for a dance. I watched her as she formed her reply. She began saying something but then looked to her side and saw me.

Our eyes locked in that way they always did—in that mesmerizing, trance-like state where everything else faded away and the world and time itself became ours. She turned her body toward me, and I stepped closer. She was so beautiful. A goddess who could bring Aphrodite to shame, dressed in crimson cloth that curved in rose-like petals from her cinched waist all the way to the floor.

Her cheekbones had been dusted with the faintest hints of rouge, and her full lips matched the deep red of her dress. She made the last few steps to meet me, and I bowed to her and offered her my hand. "May I have this dance?" I asked.

She looked up at me with those glorious green eyes and said, "Of course," but the way she said it was almost breathless, like she'd just run all the way here. I smiled as she placed her gloved hand in mine, then wrapped my other arm around her waist, my hand pressing gently onto her back. The musicians finished their previous piece and started the music for a waltz. "Are you ready?" I asked, my voice barely audible against the clamor around us. But she nodded, our eyes still locked.

I took a step forward and led her in our dance. As the music filled the room, I heard less and less of it. I couldn't stop looking at her—couldn't stop thinking of her. Couldn't stop breathing in the sweetness of her perfume or the current flowing in her veins.

Every time I wondered how I should ask her about being in my wing, or about what our future might look like after the festival, I couldn't think of the words to say. I couldn't think at all. I couldn't focus. My attention was on the way she was looking at me. On the way her body was pressed against mine. The way her eyelashes curled over her seafoam eyes. I could feel the patters of her heart and the snags in her breath as she moved closer.

I threaded my fingers in hers and moved her closer to me, our faces almost touching, our eyes never parting. Her mouth opened slightly and I suddenly wanted to do nothing but kiss her—right then and there in the middle of the ballroom. But I knew I couldn't—or at least I shouldn't—but when she looked up at me her eyes flickered to my lips, her breath warm on mine.

How could I possibly forget about this woman? About the mysteries embedded in her soul or the way her eyes caught fire when I touched her, when I kissed her and held her close.

I moved the back of her hand to my mouth and kissed it through her glove, and she watched me, ever breathless, as my lips moved away. When her eyes flickered down to her glove, she let go of my arm and started taking it off, pulling it off finger by finger. Before she got to the last one, I pulled it off, the cloth falling from her hand and into mine. I leaned down and kissed her newly gloveless hand, trailing my lips over her skin.

I pressed my lips against the inside of her wrist, then looked up at her as I threaded our fingers together, closing her hand in mine. I moved closer again and put my head on hers. "I love you," I whispered. "I hope you know that."

She looked up at me, and the tears in her eyes sent a ripple of fear through my body. "What's wrong?" I asked. As the words left my mouth, I noticed something strange about her wrist. When I looked down at it, she pulled it away.

"I have to go," she said, a tear falling down her cheek. Then she turned around and rushed for the exit. I did the only thing I could do. I ran after her.

Caroline

I had a hard time falling asleep the night before the festival. I tossed and turned, and I couldn't get what Augustus had told me out of my mind. And I had a nightmare. The worst one yet. The Shadow Beast was so close to me I could feel the sharpness of its teeth cut through my skin. I woke up sobbing and covered in sweat, rubbing the spot it had gouged me in my sleep. It hadn't carried over to the real world, of course, but I swore I could feel it all the same.

I looked around frantically, but William was nowhere in sight. It was just me, alone in the darkness like I had always been. I hugged my legs to my chest and let my face fall onto my knees. The sobs came harder, tensing my body to the point of sheer physical pain and exhaustion, all the while hoping that I'd look up and William would be there, ready to hold me. But he never came

When I eventually fell to my side and the crying stopped, I wondered what my life would look like two days from now. Would I be back at the inn, living my whole life knowing that the other half of my soul was out there but that I could never be with him? Would I have to live the rest of my life bleeding in the shadows with no one to help bandage me up again?

I cried most of the night, falling asleep in that odd space between night and day, when the birds have begun chirping but the sky is still black.

When I finally woke up, I had missed breakfast and was running late to get everything done. I welcomed the long list of tasks I had to complete before the ball. It gave me time to get out of my head before the festival started.

As I walked through the ballroom that day and helped everyone get set up, I wondered where William was. He had vanished completely, and though Augustus' words kept gnawing at my skull, I still desperately wanted to see William's face. I had decided to trust him, so I needed to trust him—I needed to ask him what exactly happened between the two of them.

But part of me didn't want to say anything. I still didn't know if tomorrow would be our last night together. Did I really want to spend some of my final hours and minutes with him rehashing the past?

"Are we going to have fireworks at the festival tonight?" Molly asked as she tightened the laces on my corset, pulling me from my thoughts.

I smiled. "I believe so. I heard someone talking about it."

"How romantic," she cooed. When she finished tying the lace, she turned around and saw my necklace—the silver pendant Cassius had given my mother. She gasped. "I had forgotten all about this! You haven't worn it in ages. It sure is beautiful." She looped it around her fingers and watched it shimmer against the light on the wall.

"I suppose it is," I mumbled. I hadn't worn it for weeks. I didn't even want to touch it. The only reason I hadn't thrown it into a fire was because it felt almost too sacred to destroy, having been worn by my mother. But I knew I couldn't keep it. Every time I looked at it, I thought of her being killed by the man she swore she loved—a man she once trusted.

"Here, you should wear it tonight," she said, handing it to me. I shook my head and spooled it back into her hand.

"I don't want to wear it tonight. Please put it in my things for me. Oh, and when you do, can you please bring out that new satin rouge that woman brought by the other day?"

She looked at me like I'd said something scandalous. "You bought that? Wow, I didn't know you had it in you."

"What does that mean?" I said with a laugh. "That woman was invited by Evelyn personally. She had an entire trunk of new cosmetics that are all the rage around Europe and America."

She nodded as she handed the glass box to me. I'd never worn makeup until I came here. It wasn't seen as very respectable until recent years, and I never had the money for it anyway. But tonight was special. As long as I didn't overdo it, I thought it should be fine.

No matter what our futures held, I wanted William to remember me tonight. I wanted to dance with him and forget everything else—our pasts and our futures. I wanted to stay planted in the moment and remember every second of it so I could watch it over and over again in my mind for the rest of my life.

I sat on the chair to my vanity as Molly pressed the powder up my cheekbones. As I watched the rosy pink dust speckle my cheeks, I saw something odd. It looked like a flutter in the mirror, like my body had shimmered, flickering like a light. I blinked once or twice before looking again, but it kept happening.

"Molly, do you see that?" I asked, pointing to myself in the mirror. She bent down and smiled.

"Yes, you look so beautiful, Caroline. William is going to eat you up."

My cheeks reddened, darkening the rouge a thousandfold. "Oh hush, Molly," I said, trying not to laugh.

She sighed. "Ah, well I have a good feeling about tonight." She picked up my hand. "Come, let's get you into your dress."

As she pulled it around me, fastening all the beautiful layers of scarlet and crimson ribbons, I said, "Why is that?"

"Hm?" she asked as she laced up the back of my dress.

"Why do you have a good feeling about tonight?"

She turned me around and finished setting my hair, her cheeks dimpling with a smile. "I think I may get a man of my own tonight." She giggled again.

I laughed. "Well I wish you the best of luck in whatever happens."

"Thanks," she said with an airy sigh. "Now, we should probably get down there. We're running behind."

We finished getting ready, and she helped me down the stairs. I wasn't used to wearing such a corset as this. Of course, they were all atrocious, but this one seemed even tighter than usual, but maybe I was just nervous. Maybe it wasn't the corset making it hard for me to breathe.

I could see the ballroom now, and my heart skipped rapidly in my chest. I was just about to panic when Molly said, "Oh, I forgot something. Here." She handed me a beautiful silk, red-feathered fan.

My eyes widened. "Wow. Where did you get this?" I asked.

"It was one of the fans Lady Evelyn left out for you to use tonight."

I inspected the folded contraption and marveled at how stunning it was. I'd never owned a fan like this before. The only one I'd ever had was one a friend gave to me—it had been a hand-me-down. She got a new one and no one else wanted the old one. Still, I thought it was lovely and kept it anyway, though I never had the chance to use it. I had never made it to a ball.

Now here I was at the ball to end all balls in a dress I never could have afforded, with a fan that likely cost more than the house Maggie and I had lived in. I wasn't sure why, but when Molly handed it to me, it gave me an extra boost of confidence—just the amount I needed to walk through the ballroom's entrance and let myself be enveloped in the night ahead.

The moment my feet hit the marble floor, I opened my fan with a soft snap and smiled, fluttering it like I'd seen the women do back home—the way I used to flutter the pretend fan I'd made from paper when I was a child. That little girl would be so happy to know that one day she would hold a real fan, one made of silk and ivory, and go to a party in the most beautiful dress she could have possibly imagined.

Even though I'd been here for weeks, I sometimes still couldn't believe it was true—that any of this was real. That these golden ballroom walls were real. That this dress was real. That William was real.

When a man came up to me, I immediately looked for William's face only to find it was someone I had never seen before. "Oh," I said.

He laughed awkwardly. He was a husky man with dirty blonde hair and a scruffy beard. Judging by his clothes, it appeared he was one of the townspeople, rather than one of the vampires who had ended up being a lot easier to identify than I realized they would be. Their clothes were the finest I'd ever seen, and they had an air about them. "Hi there, I was wondering if you would care to dance." He held out his hand, but I wasn't sure what to do. I didn't want to spend time with anyone but William here, but I wasn't sure if I was allowed to turn someone down for no reason.

"Well . . ." I started, glancing to my side, and then I stopped. It was him. And he looked incredible. His suit was finely tailored and fit him so impeccably I couldn't help but study every inch of him. The sleeves went down to his wrists and hugged his arms just enough that I could see the muscles beneath without it being too tight. His white dress shirt underneath went up to his neck and made him look regal, and his black satin tie was tucked in a perfect knot. He was like a dream walking toward me, looking at me the same way I imagined I was looking back at him—with that same sense of urgent longing. We wanted each other, and we wanted each other now.

We were so unified and enraptured in this stare that all he had to do was hold his hand out for me to take, and once my gloved hand fell into his, I was his. "May I have this dance?" he asked.

I couldn't speak. It was as if all the words in the English language were wiped from my mind. Finally, I managed to whisper, "Of course." He smiled and wrapped his other arm around my back as the music shifted into a song of slow, melancholic movements, each note a quiet symphony compared to the song we made on our own simply by being together, caught in each other's gaze.

He leaned in and quietly asked, "Are you ready?" The bass of his voice rumbled against my chest. I nodded, still unable to speak. I would never understand how this man had such great power over me. I never thought someone could make me feel this way. When I left Fairbrooke, I was ready to take on the world alone and be thick-skinned, as I always had been. But then I met William, and every part of me wanted to melt in his hands. I wanted him to smile at me like he was now, forever.

We moved along the dance floor, and the sweet scent of his freshly cleaned skin brought back the memory of our day at the lake. That day we fell into the water, kissing beneath the trees. That seemed so long ago, but the memory was still very much alive. Our connection was electric, bringing life to the area around us, surging through our touch. I couldn't look away from those dark brown eyes that looked into mine with such affection, and like I was going to vanish if he looked away.

As he pressed himself closer against me, my body followed. The room was still filled with music, but I couldn't hear a thing. I was so lost in William that I could hardly even blink. And the more we swayed together, the more I wanted him to just wrap me up and take me far away—where no one could find us and we could live happy and free forever. Just the two of us.

When his mouth curved up into a smile, my eyes fell to his lips, and the overwhelming urge to kiss him knocked the wind out of me. When he noticed, he looked down at mine, too, and then down to my hand. He looked at me before leaning down and pressing his lips against my gloved hand. The warmth of his breath sent hot shivers up my arm. I wanted more.

I slipped my hand away so I could take off my glove, and as I plucked each finger of the cloth away, William took it and slid it off my arm completely. As it fell into his hand, the heat rose to my cheeks, and suddenly every inch of my skin was white-hot. He took my hand and moved his lips against my skin, kissing the small space on the inside of my wrist.

My body was burning, and my head was light, and I couldn't take it anymore. How was I supposed to pretend like everything was okay? How was I supposed to ignore what Augustus had said and the fact that I may never get to see William after tomorrow night?

I couldn't live this day not knowing what the future held. I couldn't pretend to be okay anymore. The wave of worries I kept pushing down came bursting through my mind with incredible force, and I couldn't hold it back any longer. I dropped my arms and looked up at him, my eyes glistening with tears. "I have to go," I said, and before I could change my mind, I ran.

I tried to fight the tears, but they started spilling down my face one by one. I cried as I burst through the doors outside the ballroom, throwing myself into the chilly night. I didn't know what to do or think anymore. All I'd gotten since I came to Ashdown Manor was more questions and more secrets to unravel, and I was suffocating under all of it. I couldn't handle the unknown anymore—the unknown of the past or the future.

"Caroline!" he called out to me, but I just wiped my face and kept walking. I was so confused by everything, and I couldn't bear to look at him. The more I looked at him, the more I wanted to stay, but I knew I couldn't. I didn't belong here. I didn't belong anywhere.

"Caroline, wait!"

"Stop following me, William. Just go back inside."

He caught me by the hand. "I don't want to go inside without you."

I didn't turn around. I couldn't. "No. You need to."

"Caroline, what's wrong?" He walked around to face me and lifted my chin toward him. "Please tell me."

When his eyes met mine, I couldn't stop the tears as they fell down my face. "I'm tired of all the unknown!" I cried, "I'm tired of not knowing what will happen after tomorrow, and I'm so tired of all the secrets. I'm tired of being in the dark." I took a shaky breath. "I want you to tell me everything."

"What do you mean?" he asked, "Tell you everything about what?"

I sniffed and wiped my face again, taking a breath and looking back at him. "I want to know what you did to Augustus."

His head jerked back. "What?"

"And I want to know why that beast was in your cellar. And I want to know what else you've been hiding from me." Needles pricked my throat each time I took a sharp breath. I stared at William and lowered my voice. "I want all the secrets out in the open, and I want to know where we go from here."

He looked at me, stunned, and took a step back. "You could see that?" He shook his head. "This doesn't make any sense."

A breeze hit us, and with it came the sound of more guests arriving at the bottom of the hill. All the lanterns were lit, and the vendors and hired hosts were stationed at their booths.

I looked back at William. "What do you mean?" I asked him, but he just stood there staring at me, baffled.

"Are you talking about the bat in the basement?" he asked, and the sudden realization hit me like a tidal wave.

"You mean . . . the Shadow Beast is a kind of bat?" The bewildered look on his face deepened.

"You can see it," he whispered, more to himself than to me. "How is that possible?"

Music started at the bottom of the hill—the strumming of guitars and mild thumping of drums overlapping with the lighter sounds of violins and cellos coming from the ballroom inside.

"And what about Augustus?" I said, my voice hoarse.

His eyes darted back to mine. "What about Augustus?"

My legs started to shake, but I couldn't turn back now. I needed to know the truth. "He said you locked him away—that you doomed him to his current fate. Is that true?"

His expression was almost blank as he continued to stare at me, completely lost and confused, but then his narrowed eyes widened. "Caroline, what are you talking about?"

I frowned. "I'm talking about what you did to Augustus."

"That's precisely what I mean. What are you talking about?"

"I'm talking about Augustus! The man who was your friend!"

He shook his head, his eyes still wide. "No. No, Augustus was my best friend growing up."

"Yes, I know. You were like brothers, and then you—"

"No, Caroline," he said, panic rising in his voice. "Augustus died the same night as my parents."

"But . . . I've been talking to him."

"Where?" He asked, softly grabbing hold of my shoulders. "Where have you been talking to him?"

"In . . . that mirror in your wing."

Horror flashed across his face. "Caroline, that's not Augustus. That's Cassius." The air went still, and my skin turned to ice. All those moments he had claimed that his father was a madman, obsessed with my mother, it was him. He tricked me, just like he'd tricked her.

"Caroline, what did you tell him?"

"What do you mean?"

"What did you tell him?" He pressed, louder this time.

"I-I don't know. I just talked to him about my mother. He said his father was Cassius and that he'd been in love with my mother."

His mouth dropped open. "Your mother was Claire Duncan?" He backed away from me, shaking his head in disbelief. He ran both of his hands through his hair. "Your mother was Claire Duncan," he repeated. He started laughing—a kind of half-laugh, half-cry. "That's why the emblem was on your application . . ." He paced around until a thought struck him. He turned around suddenly and asked, "Caroline, did you give him anything?"

"What? No, of course not. How could I?"

He shook his head frantically. "Did he ask you to bring him a key of some kind?"

"No, of course not, I . . ." Then it hit me. The necklace. *What is that you're wearing? I recognize that pendant.*

That wasn't a pendant on the necklace. It was a key.

"No," I whispered, "No no no . . ." *But nothing happened*, I rationalized. *I didn't give him anything, so it's fine.*

"What?" William asked, "What is it?"

I looked at him, relief starting to wash over me. "I do have a key, I think, but it's safe."

"What? Where is it? Did he see you with it?"

I nodded reluctantly. "Yes, but it's all right. I have it—" I touched my hand to my chest, reaching to pull the necklace out of my dress, but it wasn't there. Horror settled in my stomach like cold, curdled milk when I remembered I hadn't worn it in weeks and that I'd given it to Molly earlier that evening. I thought of her fascination with it and her declaration of finding a man tonight. "No," I whispered, "She couldn't have . . ."

"*What*?" William's eyes were frenzied. "Where is it now? Where's the key?"

Before I could answer, a dark plume of smoke burst through one of the open windows at the top of the mansion. It shot into the sky and covered the stars with sheets of black. Giant claps of thunder roared overhead, and blood-red lightning splintered across the sky.

Guests screamed from inside the house as the lights flickered twice and then burnt out. Frozen in terror, I listened to the screams, both inside the house and down at the booths, where some of the arriving townspeople gaped in horror at the unnatural smoke choking the sky. Another red crack of lightning broke through the darkness, and a loud roar rattled across the mansion grounds.

"Oh no," I whispered. "What have I done?"

Chapter Twenty-Seven

28 Years Prior

The grass was so drenched in blood that it left a metallic taste in William's mouth as he walked back to the house from the woods. The odor was just as putrid as the day of the massacre two weeks before. The pain since that day had been unbearable. Every hour or so, William coughed up a clot of red and black blood, the color so dark and unsettling that it made him want to vomit.

He was turning. "He's turning more slowly than usual," the woman had said, though he wasn't sure what she'd meant by that. He just knew that his body felt cold and hollow, and it hurt almost every time he moved a muscle. Every time he walked.

But he had to—he had to escape the prison this castle now was to him. Any chance he got, he'd slip away and sneak into the forest, no matter how much it ached his little body to do so. If he stayed inside like he was supposed to, the images would come back, and that was more painful than the feeling of broken glass rattling beneath his skin.

He hid there whenever the others were occupied. He'd hide there for hours as they listened for him and searched everywhere for him. But they were monsters. Their family killed his. He couldn't trust them. So he hid, and he watched his veins blacken as his blood chilled, his skin still warm. He didn't know how it was possible, but it seemed he could change the temperature of his body with his mood. He didn't seem to have any power over it, but it was there. If he was angry, it boiled; if he were sad or afraid, it turned to ice. He didn't know what it would be like when he was happy, though. That emotion hadn't come close to him since he was bitten that night, and he wasn't sure he would ever feel it again.

"William!" the woman called out to him in distress. "William, please come inside!"

"No!" he yelled, his voice cracking, scaring a flock of crows that had gathered in a nearby tree. He buried his hands in his bended knees, his back resting against a large rock near the lake. "Just leave me alone."

The woman crouched down, a long sheet of black hair falling to the ground beside her. When he looked up at her, his eyes red and welling with angry tears, she smiled, her bright purple eyes glittering against the water. "I am not your enemy," she said, her voice like velvet.

"I don't believe you," he said, trying his best to fight back tears. *Twelve-year-olds do not cry*, he told himself. *Don't let her frighten you.*

Her gentle smile remained. "Well, that is quite understandable. You have been through a lot, but just remember that I am not the enemy."

"You sunk your teeth into me!" he spat, tossing her a glare. "You took away my life."

"I *saved* your life," she said, her smile dropping to a frown. "You were bleeding out. You were slowly dying. If I had left you there, you would have died a slow, agonizing death."

His face fell back to his kneecaps. "You should have let me die."

She sighed and sat down next to him. The air rustled through the leaves, and a bird hopped next to her before taking flight into the sky. She looked out onto the water. "It's beautiful here," she said. "I understand why you come."

"You don't know anything about me."

"Well, I know that you are in miserable amounts of pain, so why don't you come with me inside and I will do my best to remedy the situation?"

He looked back up at her, shooting daggers into her cheerful face. "I don't need your help. You've helped me enough already."

Her body stiffened, but she wouldn't let her frustration show. Her smile remained strong. "Well, William, I would very much like for us to be friends."

He laughed bitterly. "That makes one of us." He wouldn't budge. He refused to move. No one would make him leave. He didn't want to be one of them—a creature like them. That was what he convinced himself, anyway. He wouldn't settle for anything less than death. Being immortal and stuck with the images of his parents and best friend being murdered in front of him was a hell worse than death. By far.

When Eleanor saw that the young boy had made up his mind, she sighed and stood back up. "Well, I will be waiting for you in the house. If you'd like to take some time for yourself out here, then feel free to do so. Just don't wander off the mansion grounds and come straight inside when you've had enough wallowing for one day."

He rolled his eyes and looked away. "Okay, thank you. Goodbye." His sarcasm was worse than his bite, she told herself as she left for the house. He would be back inside soon enough.

When she had left, William suddenly wished he hadn't driven her away. Speaking to someone—anyone—kept his mind away from the images of his mother getting ripped apart. Of his father bleeding out. Of Augustus wailing in agony as he crumpled to the ground.

It was his fault they had died. He was sure of it. His mother hadn't even wanted to go to the festival, but he'd begged her. And of course, his father went, too. And his family wasn't complete without Augustus, who was a year older than William and had been friends with him his entire life. William was an only child, and Augustus was the only boy in a family with five girls. They were each the brother the other didn't have.

They did everything together. They played ball with the other boys in town, they got into trouble sneaking sweets from Augustus' parents' bakery, and they even worked together. Well, Augustus helped him with his work in the field because William hated it. He wanted to play games and create things. He didn't want to plow fields and plant crops. So, Augustus helped him, and when he did, working in the field wasn't so bad.

Augustus was always there for him. He would stand up to bullies for William, even taking a punch or two to make sure the younger boy made it out with all his teeth. That brotherly devotion was why he went to the festival that night. It was why he died.

William couldn't get the scene out of his head. His

friend stood in the way of a vicious attack by a boulder of a man—a raging ghoul the size of a small house—so that he wouldn't get hurt. So Augustus got hurt instead, before falling lifeless right in front of him.

Now, next to the lake, William wept. He didn't care what twelve-year-olds were or weren't supposed to do. He cried until his aching sides split even more. "It's my fault they died," he told himself. "It's my fault."

When night fell and the tears had drained from his eyes, William decided it was time to go back inside. His body throbbed even more than before, and he blamed it on crying. He thought about that woman—Eleanor. The head of the Ashdown family clan. She had brought back the prisoner in charge of the attack that night of the festival. She brought him back with a councilman, and the two adult vampires spoke of the man's fate.

William wondered if this vampire in the cellar was truly as frightening as everyone claimed him to be. Could one clan leader really wield so much power? So much manipulation?

Maybe it was a morbid kind of curiosity, or maybe he wanted to confront the man who caused his whole life to jerk to an indefinite halt, but he wanted to see him. He wanted to see this master villain of vampires for himself.

So he crept into the cellar and followed the path he'd seen Eleanor take the day before. He walked through a series of paths before finding the man sitting next to the giant beast. A man with thoughtful eyes and a youthful face. Was this really the evil mastermind the adults had been talking about?

As he crept closer, the man heard him. The bat turned to him with a snarl, and William gasped as the creature bounded toward him.

The man whistled and yelled some sort of incantation,

and the creature stopped. The dark-haired prisoner looked at William with his icy blue eyes. "Hello there," he said, a soft smile appearing on his face. "What's your name?"

William folded his arms against his chest. "Why should I tell *you*?"

The vampire sighed and sat back in his smoke-like prison cell. "I suppose you don't need to tell me anything, but you can if you'd like. I'm pretty lonely down here."

"You deserve to be lonely after what you did," he spat.

Cassius nodded. "Perhaps, but they likely didn't give you the full story."

William gave an exaggerated laugh, attempting to mask his fear. "I'm sure," he said, his signature sarcasm oozing out of him.

"You don't have to trust me," the man said, "but I'm here to listen if you want to talk."

William thought about this for a moment. He thought about the constant slew of images that rotated in his mind every moment of every night and day. He didn't even have sleep to rescue him from his agony anymore. He just had himself and his thoughts.

Talking was the only thing that got him through, no matter how much he hated it. When he looked at the vampire smiling in his cell, he wondered if he should talk to him. He wondered if he really was guilty of everything the others had said he was. "You don't look like much to me," William scoffed. "I doubt you did anything. You look pathetic."

Cassius raised a brow. "So, would you believe me if I told you that they are casting blame upon the wrong man?"

William frowned. "What?"

Cassius smiled, a dimple appearing on his cheek. "I wasn't behind any of this. I was just an innocent member of my clan. I was an easy target because of some tension that had been building between the Ashdowns and me. I didn't kill a soul."

William pursed his lips, his eyes studying the prisoner. Was what he was saying true?

When the images of the boulder-like vampire returned, William shook the thought out of his head, grabbed his skull, and fell to the ground.

"What's wrong?" Cassius asked, but William could barely speak. He couldn't get past the images. But when the older vampire asked again, William let himself unravel some of the pain. He didn't care if this vampire was guilty or innocent. He just wanted it to go away.

So he talked about how his parents were slain. "I saw them—their limbs falling to the ground. Their blood and their bones . . . and my friend . . . Augustus." He clapped a hand over his mouth and sobbed. He sobbed until he choked on his own breaths. Wiping his face, he said, "They were all I had. And now they're gone." He shot Cassius a glare. "And it's your fault. You should be killed for what you've done."

Cassius shook his head, frowning, his brows heavy against his eyes. "No. It wasn't me. As I told you before, I was merely a bystander. I didn't do a thing."

William watched him a second longer before saying, "I have no way of knowing if you are lying or not."

Cassius sighed. "Yes, that's true, but what you *do* know is that your pain is too great to keep inside." William looked away, but the vampire continued. "So you should talk to me anyway. Tell me about your parents. What were they like?"

William shook his head vehemently. "I don't want to talk about them. There's nothing more to say anyway."

Cassius waited until the boy looked back at him to smile and say what he wanted to next. "Then tell me about your friend," he said gently. "Tell me about Augustus."

Eleanor looked all over the mansion grounds before deciding to search the house for the boy. She recruited the aid of the handsome councilman who had brought Cassius back to the house with her. "Have you found him yet?" she asked, but he shook his head. Panic tore through her like the slash of a thousand knives. *Where could he be?*

Then the black blood drained from her face and she ripped down the hallway and down the flights of stairs. She rushed outside and threw open the cellar doors. Panicking the whole way there, Eleanor saw exactly what she was afraid to: the young vampire talking to the prisoner as he awaited his trial.

"Stay away from him!" she yelled. "Stay away from him!"

But as the boy turned to face the leader of the Ashdown family clan, the prisoner reached through his bars and grabbed him by the sleeve. "You won't let me get trapped in there, will you?"

William stared at him with wide, fearful eyes. "What are you talking about?" he asked.

"Don't listen to him!" Eleanor cried. "He is a master of manipulation. Come with me." She held out her hand, but Cassius just tugged harder on the boy's sleeve.

"They want to pin this whole thing on me. I didn't do this. I swear. Do you want me to get locked inside that mirror forever? What about your parents? What about Augustus? Don't you want them back?"

"Don't listen to him!" Eleanor shouted as she got closer. "He's the reason your family died. Don't let him trick you."

"SHE'S LYING!" Cassius cried as Charles walked down the steps and moved toward him.

The councilman looked at the boy and said, "She is not lying. Please step away so we can get him ready for departure." William nodded slowly, but he was still unsure of what to do. This vampire had been so amiable to him down here. Could he really be the one behind such destruction?

Two more vampires in the Ashdown clan came down the stairs to assist Charles and Eleanor in carrying out the man's punishment. The blonde councilman turned to the prisoner. "Cassius Laurent, the Council of Shadows has found you guilty beyond the point of probation or exile. You are to be confined in the Shadow Realm for the rest of your life."

Cassius' face twisted in horror. "You can't do that! No one has been sentenced to that for centuries!"

Charles nodded. "Yes, that's true. You should feel very proud to have broken that streak." He scowled at Cassius and told the others to take him upstairs.

The evil man screamed as they took him away. As they led him up the cellar steps, he looked back at William in tears. "Don't let them do this to me! Don't be like one of them!"

William's stomach sunk. "But . . . they say you killed my family."

"I did no such thing!" Cassius screamed, but the others just pushed him harder up the stairs. As the four men walked out of sight, leaving only Eleanor and William alone in the cellar, Cassius called out to the boy one last time. "Don't become one of them!" he yelled. "They have themselves to blame for what happened. I didn't do a thing!"

Then the cellar doors slammed shut, and even from

where he stood, this deep inside the underground labyrinth, the sound resounded thunderously in William's ears.

Eleanor looked at the boy with worry deepening the lines etched between her eyebrows. "It wasn't your fault that your family died," she assured him. But he wasn't convinced.

"Don't worry," he said, "I don't believe that he's innocent."

"Good," she said, placing her hand on his shoulder.

"But he's right."

She frowned and looked down at him. "What?"

His eyes burned, and his body ached again as the images flashed across his mind. "It was my fault they died that night. It was all my fault."

Chapter *Twenty-Eight*

More smoke burst through the mansion's windows, but it was different from the red-and-black smoke hemorrhaging chaotically into the sky.

"The house is burning!" someone yelled from inside, and a wave of screams roared through the ballroom as over a hundred guests pushed their way out into the night.

"This is what I was afraid of," William said quietly, staring into the smoke, "but I still can't believe it's happening." He pulled his attention away and looked at me, grabbing hold of my hands. "Go hide in the forest," he said, looking into my eyes. "Please. Go as far away as you can. Okay?"

More screams erupted from the house, accompanied by the sounds of glass breaking and things being thrown around the halls. I shook my head. "No, I'm going with you."

William frantically looked back up at the smoke, then back to me. "I have to go. Please get out of here." He let go of my hands and began pulling off his suit coat as he ran back to the house. "Hurry!" he said, but I followed him, running as fast as I could to keep up.

"No, I'm coming, too!" I said as we ran to the front doors.

"Caroline, you could die! GO!" He ran faster, but I pumped my arms harder and followed close behind.

"I'm not letting you go alone. This is my fault."

He made a sound like a growl of defeat and took my hand. "Then stay with me and don't leave my sight. It looks like Cassius' followers are causing problems inside. But we need to make it to the mirror." I nodded and kept running, but the longer we ran—through the doors, up the stairs, down the halls—the more my head throbbed and my body ached.

I wasn't able to pay much attention as we ran, but William looked around constantly, watching for danger. As we approached the mirror room, we had to stop for William to fight a vampire that must have been left to guard the hall. He had been facing away as we approached, obviously distracted by the screams and sounds of destruction coming from the ballroom and down the hall. The wild look in his eyes changed to fury in an instant as William growled, swinging his fist impossibly fast. The man tried to dodge the blow, moving like a shadow, but his moment of inattention gave William the advantage, and he went down in an instant.

"Well that was lucky," William said between heavy breaths. "But we need to hurry so we don't run into another one. We may not be so lucky next time."

We peeled down the hallway and rounded the last

corner to the family's wing. By the time we made it to the mural, my head was practically splitting in pain, and a ringing had made its way into my ears.

When William opened the latch leading up to the mirror room, I doubled over in pain. "What's wrong?" he asked, bending down to check on me.

"I don't know," I said, my voice strained. "Help me up please." I gave him my arm, but he picked me up instead and took me up the stairs. I leaned against his chest as the pain moved through my body, sweat beading down my face.

It only took him a second to get from the door to the mirror, and when he saw Cassius, he gasped. I turned to see what was going on, using a lot more strength than I should have needed to in order to turn my head. My lungs instantly constricted at the sight in front of me.

Cassius was outside of the mirror, grinning ecstatically at us with Molly limply flopped against his body, bleeding from the neck. He was holding her with one arm tight across her chest, just beneath the source of the blood.

"Molly!" I gasped, pushing myself off William and collapsing onto the ground. When I hit the floor, the ringing in my head intensified.

Cassius laughed. "You can have her," he said, tossing her beside me. William managed to catch her before her head slammed against the tiles. My eyes followed the trail of blood oozing onto the floor. Her eyes fluttered open. She was still alive.

"Caroline," she wheezed, her lips cracked and white. "I'm so sorry."

Tears fell down my face, and I tried to shake my head, but the pain was too great. "Don't apologize to me," I whispered. "But . . . why did you do it?" She coughed, and I reached out to stop the blood leaking from her punctured neck. I pressed my hand gently against the wound and quickly said, "Don't speak. It's okay."

She coughed again and then focused her eyes on me. "He tricked me," she said faintly. "He told me we could—" she coughed again, and I felt a rush of her blood spill between my fingers, sticky and hot.

My stomach turned. "Don't speak anymore," I whispered. "He's good at fooling people."

I looked up to see what was going on above us, only to see William scowling at Cassius, ready to pounce, while Cassius beamed at him like he was having the time of his life.

"Why did you do this?" William asked him.

Cassius laughed again. "Why *wouldn't* I do this?"

"That's not what I mean," William hissed, moving closer to him. "Why would you hurt her? And how did you plan all this?"

The smaller man grinned up at him. "That's a secret." He winked, and William picked him up by the shirt and pushed him hard against the mirror, but before he could ask any more questions, Cassius slipped from his grasp and punched him in the stomach. William toppled to the floor.

I watched helplessly in a crippled heap, every inch of my body now pulsing in pain. I didn't even have the strength to gasp. William pushed his way back to his feet, and someone else came barreling up the stairs. When William turned to see who it was, Cassius hit him across the face again.

"Get Caroline and Molly out of here!" he called to the person on the stairs as he tried to land a punch on Cassius, but the man moved past him with an amused smile. Another wave of pain surged through me—this one even stronger than the last—forcing my eyes shut.

"Can you walk?" I looked up and saw Charles holding

Molly, his hand pressed against her wound. I nodded through the aches in my neck. I had no other choice. I planted my hands on the floor and used every ounce of energy left in me to get to my feet and move. "Let's go," he said, and I followed him down the stairs, wobbling as my vision blurred from the pain.

My body kept hitting the walls as I worked my way down. I stumbled on the last couple of steps, running into Charles. He didn't seem to notice. He opened the door to the hall and looked back at me. "We need to find your grandmother. Quick."

"You . . . know?" I managed to ask. He repositioned Molly so that he could grab my arm.

"Yes, but she can explain when she sees you. Now hurry. Grab onto me."

"Explain what?" I asked wearily, but he didn't respond. I had no energy to ask again, so I did as he said, wrapping both of my arms around his, my body burning. He sped through the house, and I wondered if he was listening for her. Judging by how quickly we found her, I figured that to be the case.

"Molly!" Mrs. Wells cried out, lunging toward my wounded cousin, but Charles stopped her.

"Take Caroline," he said. "I'll tend to Molly's wounds, and don't worry—I'll make sure she doesn't turn."

I yelped at another surge of pain and fell to the floor. "What's happening to her?" she cried, looking to Charles.

After a brief pause, he quietly said, "I think it's happening."

They whispered something to each other, but I couldn't make it out past the thumping in my ears. The next thing I knew, Mrs. Wells was hoisting me up and walking me down the hall. "I'm taking you outside," she said. "Eleanor can help. Er—Evelyn."

"What?" I asked, the pain pulsing through my head.

"Lady Bower. She doesn't know about you. I . . . I told Lord Bower, but Evelyn . . . We thought it best she didn't know."

"What are you talking about? And . . . Eleanor?"

"Her name used to be Eleanor, but she changed it a little while ago, as she prepared to be someone else to reenter society in Brakerton Heights. We've all been calling her Evelyn over the last few months, but for decades I called her Eleanor. Sometimes it's easy to forget."

Eleanor. That woman who was like a mother to William—who had cared for him and his birth mother before her death. It was Evelyn.

"We need to find her in the woods," she continued. "She brought the people in town down there. As many as she could, anyway. Someone recognized her from all those years ago when she made it to the bottom of the hill and called her a witch. Many people left after that. But the place is still in chaos. Just like it had been back then."

I strained to keep my eyes open, but a jolt of pain struck through my body. "What did you not tell Evelyn about me?" I managed to ask.

"Who your mother was. Who *you* are."

I wheezed, wishing I could ask more, but the pain was too great. My eyes fell shut again, and I resisted the urge to curl my body to withstand the pain.

Cold air suddenly hit my face like a wall of frosty wind, and I knew we were outside. My lungs spasmed as the smoke followed us. I coughed until my body shook. When we finally made it to the woods, Mrs. Wells placed me on the ground and leaned me against a tree. My skin was boiling, but my blood was cold. She placed the back of her hand on my forehead and wiped the sweat sticking to my hair. I opened my eyes and saw her looking down at me in concern.

"Why does it matter who I am?" I asked, blinking the sweat from my eyes.

She knelt down next to me, watching sadly as I grimaced in pain. She pulled me into her embrace and stroked my head. "I should have told Evelyn who you were."

"*Why*? Because of my mother?"

She paused briefly, and all I heard were the distant screams of the people below. I tried to see them, but when I moved my head, the pain got worse. "No," she said. "Because of what happened when you were born—what we thought might happen but never had. At least not until now."

My face scrunched together. "What are you talking about?"

"We didn't think it would happen. We'd thought it was impossible to begin with."

"*What are you talking about*?" I repeated louder before wheezing and letting my head fall back against the tree.

"You're turning into a vampire, Caroline. I think you have been your whole life."

My eyes shot to hers, and I just stared at her, shallow breaths cutting into my chest. "What?"

She smiled sadly and stroked my hair as she spoke. "I helped deliver you when you were born. Maggie was there, too. Cassius had infected your mother when she was pregnant with you. He wanted to turn her into a vampire and force her to live a life alone, as he thought she was dooming upon him, as vampires can only fall in love once." She let out a deep sigh. "He killed your father, but his anger and desire for your mother overtook him, and he accidentally killed her in the process of turning her."

Something rattled in my ears, but the pain was stagnant.

As I listened to my grandmother, I hoped the pain would soon ease up. "She went into labor as she was dying," she continued, "Maggie and I helped her to the side of the house. Your aunt held onto your mother, and I grabbed you. But when you were born, I saw a familiar flash in your eyes—the flash that falls upon vampires when they're hungry, and when they first begin to turn. Over time, they learn to recognize the cues before the moment of inevitability occurs and can act to subside the effect by hunting. But you were just a baby, and I swore I saw it."

I shook my head. "But I'm not a vampire. I have a reflection, I eat, I'm normal . . ." But as I said it, everything fell together. The nightmares I'd had my whole life. My ability to see and sense things in the shadows. The chills that appeared on my skin whenever I entered William's wing. The shimmering of my reflection. My uneven heartbeats. Even my slowing pulse.

I shook my head again. "No. It doesn't make sense. I would have aged much more quickly than this. I would have become a vampire a long time ago."

But my grandmother shook her head. "Apparently not. You have all the symptoms of turning. Back then, Evelyn and I had discussed the possibility that you'd soon turn into a vampire. We weren't sure what would happen, but we decided it best not to tell anyone, other than Charles, and to just keep an eye on you."

"But you didn't keep an eye on me," I said, the pain finally starting to break and ease up.

"I tried," she whispered."But Maggie wouldn't have it."

"What? N-no . . ."

"She didn't want to believe the possibility that you could turn into a vampire. I told her I wasn't even sure it would happen because it had never happened before, at least to Evelyn's and Charles' knowledge. No one knew of any pregnant women being killed in such a way that would allow the venom to make it to the baby. When I said I just wanted to check up on you, Maggie got angry. She said she didn't believe me and told me to leave. But I think deep down she knew it could be true."

I thought of all the times Maggie warned me to stay away from other people as much as possible. To stay away from the shadows. To never leave Fairbrooke. She wasn't just trying to keep me away from dangerous creatures and unfamiliar faces. She was trying to keep them away from me.

"But why . . ."

"I tried to see you every year until you were about three, but each time she told me to go away. The last time I went, she threatened to ruin my life in any way she could unless I left for good. She said I should never try to see you again. So, I had no choice but to stop trying. It broke my heart, but I couldn't go back."

"No," I said, coughing as a rush of smoke drifted in from the manor. "Maggie wouldn't do such a thing."

"She would if it meant protecting you," she said, and when I looked up into her eyes, I saw the compassionate smile of a grandmother. She placed my face in her hands and said, "She loved you very much, and even though I never really got to know you, I always loved you, too." Then she kissed me on the forehead and held me against her chest.

As she stroked my hair again, she said, "She never even told me your name." Her hand stilled on my head. "We decided to move forward, Evelyn and I. It appeared that you weren't a vampire and that you would never become one. So we thought that was that, and we tried not to worry about it. That was one of the reasons Charles didn't want to tell her who you were; he didn't want her to worry and to open that wound again."

She sighed, but a veil of sadness fell over her face. "I thought you were safe from ever being turned, which helped on the harder days, but it appears I'd been wrong all that time."

I didn't know what to say. There was nothing *to* say, really. I just needed to accept that I was never meant to be human. I was never meant to be normal.

"So, why is it happening to me now?" I finally asked.

"You may have been transforming all this time. Perhaps the venom was making its way through your bloodstream slowly because of how it reached you in the womb. The only other thing I can think of is that Cassius leaving the Shadow Realm reawakened the transformation process, or at least sped it up."

"The Shadow Realm?" I asked, my mind reeling.

She nodded. "That's where all vampires' shadows go after they turn. It's why they don't have reflections—their reflections are in another realm. It's what keeps them from being human, from living a mortal life."

"But—" I couldn't finish my thought. A rush of pain pulsed through me, coursing through my body more powerful than ever before.

Then the pain jerked to a halt, leaving me completely, like the quick crack of a whip.

In its place came an overwhelming rush of strength and raw power so potent I could hardly feel my body. The longer it raced through me, the better I felt.

"Is she all right?" I opened my eyes and saw Evelyn. My body was flat on the ground, each limb growing stronger by the second. Then everything inside me changed. Like someone had flicked a switch inside me. Like something in me came alive.

But it was overwhelming, too. Part of it was more

intense than I was ready for. The emotions surging through me felt physical. Like I was falling off a mountain with nowhere to land. "What's happening to her?" Evelyn gasped, but it was clear she already knew the answer.

"She's turning," my grandmother said. "Her transformation is almost complete."

"Is this because of William?" she asked, fury in her voice, but Mrs. Wells shook her head.

"It's because of Cassius."

"I don't understand," Evelyn said, staggering back.

"She's Claire's daughter."

"What? No." She looked at me. "That's not possible. She's . . . she can't be . . . She's the baby?" She walked closer to me, leaning over to stare into my eyes as if to examine me. Then her face dropped, realization washing over her.

"Yes, she's my granddaughter."

"But why now? I—"

"I think Cassius leaving the Realm triggered Caroline's body to complete its transformation, almost like his venom had been revitalized."

"Where are William and Charles?" Evelyn asked, and then a realization hit me, too.

There was nothing holding us back now. There was nothing standing between William and me. I was a vampire. If we made it through today, I could be with him. I could be with him.

Despite everything else going on around me, I smiled.

The other two women were lost in a hushed conversation about what to do next. But I knew what I wanted to do.

I got to my feet and examined myself. I felt incredible. All the pain was completely gone. It felt like life was surging through me, giving me limitless amounts of energy. Every imperfection on my arms vanished, and I assumed the same went for my face. Any blemish, wrinkle, or scar was likely wiped away.

I moved between the trees, testing my new body and ensuring I was strong enough to run back to the mansion to help William. After I moved around a bit more, I decided there was no more time to lose. I felt ready. I had to go now.

"I need to go see William," I said, and as his name left my lips, my heart ached for him. "I need to go."

"No!" Mrs. Wells and Evelyn said in unison.

I frowned. "What? Why not?"

"We have to stay here. We have to keep you and everyone else safe," Evelyn said.

"There is no way I'm going to let William fight Cassius alone in there," I said. "I have the ability to help now."

"No, you don't," Evelyn said. "You don't know what you're up against. You are newly turned. Stay here and help me hide everyone."

"But William is alone! Charles took Molly somewhere to help stop her bleeding. William is—"

"William can take care of himself, Caroline," Evelyn snapped. "Just help me get everyone out of here."

I glanced back at the manor and then looked to my right at the people running into the woods—the people who had chosen to trust Evelyn and follow her out here. As much as I wanted to fight—as much as I wanted to leave and help William—I knew she was right. I needed to help.

"All right," I said, moving back through the trees, and as I spoke, I noticed the sudden sharpness of my teeth. When they pricked the inside of my lip, something shivered up my spine. But I turned my attention to the townspeople who were shaking behind the trees. "All right, everyone. It will be okay. We just need to stay calm. We should go farther into the woods. There—" My voice was cut off by a loud screeching, accompanied by thunderous stomps and rushes of wind.

My slowly beating heart nearly stopped altogether.

"I know that sound," I whispered. Slowly, I turned around to face the source of the noise. I just hoped I was wrong.

But it was there, snapping its jaws and running toward me like it always had, but this time I was wide awake, and there was no escape.

Chapter Twenty-Nine

Cassius looked at me with that smug look he always wore when he thought he'd get his way. I noticed it that night as a boy—when he tried to trick me into letting him go, into believing in him. "You'll stop at nothing to escape. What did you do this time? Trick the girl into falling in love with you?" I lunged at him to strike, but he was too fast and jumped out of the way.

"That maid?" he asked with a chuckle. "That was easy. She practically begged me to take what I needed." He swung at me, but I blocked it and elbowed him in the face.

He yelped in pain and then laughed. "Why are you so angry? It isn't a major problem that I've escaped, is it? I just want freedom like everyone else." He smiled as he said every word, like he was toying with an animal.

"Don't even try to play your games with me, Cassius.

I'm not a child anymore. I've seen you here for decades. I know how evil you are. What could you possibly gain from causing all this destruction? What do you want?" I kicked his chest and sent his back straight into the wall.

He scowled at me, his coy demeanor finally fading. He stood up and spat black blood out of his mouth. The near-dead blood of our kind. He jumped forward and punched me in the jaw before I could move, and the unexpected pain was something I hadn't felt in a long time. The whole lower portion of my skull felt like it was going to crack.

"I won't stop until I finish what I started." He swung at me while I was still straightening myself up, but I was able to move away at the last second and avoid further damage.

"What?" I asked, breathing heavily and watching for my next chance to attack.

"Caroline is Claire's daughter," he said, his wicked smile returning. "I won't stop until she's dead." He walked closer to me, his smile stretching longer across his face with every step. "I will rip her up piece by piece until she's nothing but bloody ribbons."

Blind rage flashed through me, and I couldn't think anymore. I just wanted this vile creature to die. To go extinct. I grabbed his shirt and punched him across the face. Once. Twice. Three times before his shirt ripped and he ricocheted against the wall, falling back onto the floor.

Before he could get up, I leapt on him and rammed my fist into his face over and over until my own blood started breaking from my almost impenetrable skin.

I refused to stop hitting him until I was sure he was dead.

"Go! Quick!" Evelyn yelled, pushing me back in the

direction she'd just come from. "Take the guests deeper into the forest. Hide with them. Tell them not to scream or it will find them—and tell them not to move."

My legs were shaking. I couldn't voluntarily move them an inch. All I could hear were the noises—the ones that had pierced my worst nightmares for as long as I could remember. The ones that repeated in my head like a twisted stage play rehearsing in my mind forever.

"GO!" she yelled again. Her pushing finally worked; I found myself staggering toward the others, then picking up my pace. Soon, I found them. There were about fifty of them, all either frozen in place or trembling uncontrollably, stifling cries and awaiting whatever would happen next. Screams were still making their way up to us from the bottom of the hill.

I needed to get these people moving, but they just sat there, waiting. They didn't know what they were waiting for, just that it was coming, and they felt powerless to stop it. I could see it in their eyes. They kept looking around in different directions, quaking in fear.

With no more time to think, I looked at them and gestured into the forest. "Let's go! Follow me." I ran through the woods, not looking back other than to make sure they were close behind. The only spot in these woods I thought to go to was the lake William had shown me. It was the only place I knew. I just prayed it would be deep enough in that we would be safe—that these innocent people who risked the festival's reputation wouldn't have to die the way they suddenly feared they would.

When I finally saw the water glittering in the distance, I looked back at the others. "There's a lake up ahead! There are rocks and thick trees around the sides—find a place to hide and don't move. Don't say anything. Something is coming. Just find a place to hide and don't make a sound."

I held onto the trunk of the closest tree and watched each of them find somewhere to hide. When I saw their faces, a pain squeezed in my chest. There were mothers holding onto their children, their hands over their mouths so nothing could escape their tiny lips. There were elderly people, young lovers, farmers, businessmen. All these people's lives had changed in a matter of moments, and now they were likely wondering if they would make it through the night.

Once everyone had stilled, I looked back at where we'd just come, but I couldn't see anything but smoke coming from the house. It poured out over the trees like an upside-down hourglass draining its sand into the blood-red-and-black sky. Fear gripped me, and I longed to know what was happening with William and what was taking him so long. The house was burning up, and he was nowhere in sight.

My stomach twisted at the worst possible explanation. "No," I whispered, desperately shaking the thought out of my head, begging it to release its grasp on my mind. *He can't be gone*, I told myself, but the uncertainty was suffocating. The possibility that I might never see him again was strong, and I couldn't take it.

I had to get back there. I had to leave these woods and make it back. But what would happen to them? I looked around at the villagers, each one cowering behind anything they could, whether it was a tree or a boulder. Some of them had even sunk their bodies halfway down into the freezing lake water. If I was this afraid, being able to stand a fighting chance in my new form, I couldn't imagine the paralyzing fear coursing through any of them at this very moment.

I couldn't let anyone get hurt. These people trusted Evelyn enough to follow her into the woods. The ones at the bottom of the hill had tried to escape. From what I could tell just through the voices and screams, and muffled shouts and breaking wood, there were allies amongst the vampires in attendance, and they were doing their best down there as well.

I had to stay here. I had a responsibility to these people. This was all happening because of me.

People were dying because of me.

That eerie, familiar screech fractured the air around us, crippling us in place. We didn't know what to expect; we just wanted to make it to sunrise.

Its cries grew louder, and suddenly I was six years old again. I was crying in my bed, begging the monster to leave me alone. What did I do back then? *What did I do back then?*

The screeches grew louder. I dug my fingernails into the bark behind me and forced my body through its trembling, turning my head so I could see what we were up against.

The air was suddenly dry, my throat tight. I couldn't breathe. I couldn't speak. Its body was materializing through the trees. It was ripping its way through the branches, flapping large wings I'd never seen before—wings I didn't know it had. Then I saw its face—all ridges and teeth and tufts of hair—the face of the monster I'd always feared. The creature that tormented me my entire life. My worst nightmare.

It was here, and I couldn't do anything about it. I couldn't even move. Even with my newfound power and the knowledge that if I ever had a chance at killing it, it was now, I couldn't muster the strength to leave, to be brave. To do anything about it. Its features were too real, too terrifyingly familiar and clear—razor-like teeth and black drool seeping from its snarling mouth as it swept its way toward us.

I whipped back around. "Don't move," I whispered, loud enough for the villagers to hear but hopefully not loud enough for the beast to have heard, too. My head pulled back when I noticed their expressions, unchanged—still scared senseless, but not any more scared than they'd been before the beast's body came into view.

What's going on? I thought, analyzing their expressions. They were sitting in their stations, whimpering, and looking around like they didn't know what direction the snarling screeches were coming from. *Why can't they see it?*

"Caroline!"

It was Evelyn, she was running through the trees, holding onto her tattered skirt, her black hair wildly whipping behind her. "Caroline! Don't let the creature see them! They can't see it! Only we can!"

I looked back at them, the anxiety building in my chest. "What are they going to do then?" I asked, my voice hoarse and loud. I looked back at her.

"They just need to hide. I'm going to need your help after all. Come here, quick, and hold out your hands like this!" She held her hands in the shape of a diamond and readied her body in a firm stance against the creature, holding it up toward its face.

It was so close to her. How was I supposed to get that close? I would be walking right into its mouth—the teeth that had been sharpening in my dreams, waiting for this day. "HURRY!" she screamed.

I took a deep, shaky breath and ran toward it. I focused all my attention on it, making myself stare into its ugly, red-eyed face. It opened its enormous mouth and showed layers of sharp teeth, but I kept going. Tears fell down my cheeks, and they felt hot against the frigid night.

I watched it carefully, never taking my eyes away from it, despite how much I wanted to.

I was sick. I was terrified. But here I was anyway—mirroring Evelyn's stance, standing up against the Shadow

Beast. Standing up to my lifelong bully.

"Repeat this incantation," she shouted to me through another ear-piercing screech from the beast. She began reciting something in Latin that I didn't understand, but I did my best to repeat it. After two or three times I finally got it right, and the beast started quivering.

But then it roared at us, angrier than before, and not any less capable of killing us.

"It's not working!" I said, pushing my hands harder into the air, as if that would cause the incantation to work more effectively. It didn't do anything.

"I know!" she cried back, but it was hard to hear her over everything—the roars and snaps of the Shadow Beast, the screams and destruction at the bottom of the hill, the thunderous rumbling in the air, the cracking of the burning mansion. "But this is all I know to do. These things aren't meant for this world. Cassius used a conjurer to release it all those years ago, and we haven't been able to destroy it or send it back to the Shadow Realm."

I looked back at it in horror. "If you haven't been able to kill it after all these years, how are we supposed to do it now?"

"I think only Cassius can destroy it!" she yelled through the noise, "But we have to try!"

I looked up at it just as it held out one gnarled talon. Before I could do anything, it gathered me into its claws and squeezed me in its grasp. It let out a loud, triumphant cry as it flew higher into the air. I wondered if it was once tasked to capture my mother.

There had to be something I could do. I couldn't let myself cower in fear anymore. I had to act.

I didn't know what else to do, so I bit it, my newly transformed teeth sinking into its leathery claw. It wailed in pain as the venom from my mouth sunk into its skin. I spat the disgusting, metallic taste from my mouth and wiped my tongue with the back of my hand. When I looked back up, I saw its red eyes turning black.

It was hurt. But how? There were other marks—other bite marks scarred within its fur. Did it writhe like this every time?

I tried again, moving past the horrendous taste. As I bit it again, directly next to the last pair of my bite marks, it howled again.

When I looked at its face again, I figured it out.

I sunk my teeth in its claw again, and when the creature started to fall to the ground, its grip on me loosening, I jumped onto its back and gave it one more taste of my venom. It wailed as we spiraled downward and didn't stop until it exploded into a puff of ethereal smoke just before hitting the ground, sending me tumbling to the earth.

But I couldn't even feel the pain. I'd killed it.

I stood up against my demon and killed it.

My venom must have been the answer. Cassius turned me. Maybe only someone with his venom could destroy it.

I laughed on the ground, reveling in this victory and in my newfound power to take on a new life. I was in charge of what had power over me. I would never let myself be scared again.

"Wooow. How did you do that? I'm quite impressed."

That voice.

I looked up and saw Cassius grinning down at me, and my stomach dropped. "No . . ." I breathed.

Where was William?

His smile soured into a scowl as he bent down and ripped me up by my hair. I winced in pain, but I refused to give him the satisfaction of making me squeal or cry.

When his eyes met mine, I spat on his face, and he dropped me. I fell to the ground, my head throbbing from where he'd grabbed hold of my hair.

"You are much less dignified than your mother," he said, wiping his face in disgust.

"You wouldn't know anything about dignity, you monster," I said, getting to my feet.

He smirked, then grabbed me by the arms, his nails digging into my skin. "Perhaps you take after your father," he said, spitting out the word *father* like it was a curse.

"I'm sure it kills you that I'm not more like *you*."

He threw me to the ground, and the pain broke through me like a shock of lightning to my back. I looked up at him. "I'm sure it killed you that she didn't love you. That she was afraid of you."

He jumped on top of me and pinned my arms above my head. "She loved me," he said, moving closer so our faces nearly touched. "I loved your mother. She was the most beautiful thing I'd ever seen." He put his face against mine and breathed in the scent of my hair. I squirmed, but I couldn't get away, and his grip only tightened. "But that ungrateful little tramp didn't care about what I'd done for her. She just went off and slept with that blacksmith and got pregnant with you."

"How dare you," I growled, and kneed him in the gut. He recoiled enough for me to slip away from his grasp, but then he let out a yell and grabbed one of my arms again, this time using his teeth to split my skin from the bottom of my wrist-bone to the tip of my elbow. I cried out in pain as the blood trailed down my arm, his hand still latched onto my wrist. I frowned as the dark red stream dripped from my elbow to the grass below.

I was bleeding.

How was I bleeding?

He grabbed my other wrist and then pinned me against the mansion. The smoke was thick, and the heat from the fire singed my skin. He moved close, his body pressing against mine. He smiled wickedly and looked into my eyes, hungry. "You do look just like her, you know," he said, and my stomach turned. "Maybe I should take you instead—make you mine."

"If she didn't even want you, why would I?"

"I wasn't asking."

"Get off of me!" I pushed my back against the wall, utilizing his grip on my upper body, and kicked him away with both of my feet.

The moment he hit the ground, I heard something clatter to the ground beside him. When I spotted it, I saw my chance.

A lot of dangerous guests will be coming, William had said.

As Cassius got to his feet and jumped toward me, I sunk to the ground, grabbed the blade, and plunged it into his side. Black blood oozed from the wound as he screamed. The sound echoed into the sky, nearly drowning out the thundering of the dilapidating house behind us.

I kicked him to the ground and took out the blade—the silver blade Mr. Clarke had given me when I left the inn. The blade I'd tied in the seam of my skirt earlier that evening.

Now I was above him, and he was bleeding at my feet. It wasn't until then that I saw just how badly William had beaten him. Cassius' face was covered in black bruises, a stark contrast to his pale skin. "What did you do with him?" I asked, but he didn't reply. He just held his side, coiled on the ground like the bleeding snake that he was.

When I lifted the knife to plunge into him again, he said, "I did love Claire, you know. More than anything." My hand froze, and I watched as he looked up at me with those haunting crystal-like eyes. "I did." He winced in pain but kept his eyes on me. "You can understand that, right? You understand what love can do to someone, don't you?"

I scowled down at him, my hand gripping the blade tighter. "I understand love. What I don't understand is obsession."

He smirked. "There is a fine line between the two."

"Only to a monster."

He chuckled, then lunged at me, knocking the blade from my hand. He pulled himself on top of me and grabbed the knife, growling through the pain of his wounded torso. "Let me introduce you to your mother," he hissed, readying the blade. He smiled as he pierced it into my arm. When I wailed in pain, he leaned in to whisper, "Oh, but I'm going to make it hurt before I do."

The pain was white-hot, and I wondered how long it would take to heal. It didn't appear I had fully turned yet, so what was I capable of?

But Cassius didn't know. He thought he was toying with a human woman wounded in the grass.

He threw the blade behind him and pushed his hands against my shoulders, his right hand pressing into my freshly cut skin. As I thrashed to get away, he leaned in and bit me.

The moment after he sunk his fangs into me, he stopped. He sat up and looked down at me. "Why didn't that sting you?" he spat, as if I were a broken toy he wanted fixed.

I was the one laughing now, clutching my wounds. "You have no power over me," I said, lunging forward and biting him back, my fangs sinking into his neck. The shock paralyzed him—I doubted it was very painful for him, if at all. He was just in complete and utter shock.

I jumped over him and grabbed hold of the blade. I pointed it at him. "What did you do with William?" I asked. He held onto the spot I had bitten, as if he still couldn't believe it had happened.

Then he chuckled. "He's gone. You don't have to worry about him anymore." Anger ripped through me. I had never wanted to kill a person until this very moment.

"What did you do?" I asked.

He shrugged and let out a long, carefree sigh. "I didn't do anything. We just fought, and then I won." He smiled gleefully like he'd just won a game of tag, not killed a person.

"Where is he?" I asked again, moving closer, still pointing the dagger at him with both hands. He walked to me at a leisurely pace, an ugly smile still painted on his face.

"Just forget about him, Caroline, and tell me your secret."

"What secret?" I asked as he walked closer.

"Are you *special*?" He slapped my hands with one fierce swipe, sending the dagger somewhere in the grass. I fell down after it, but the smoke was too thick to see through anymore. I felt around for it, but Cassius picked me up by the back of my dress, pulling my whole body off the ground.

I kicked in the air, but he just looked up at me like I was a stray cat he found wandering around. "Tell me," he whispered, still wearing that unsettling grin. "Your secret."

Smoke blasted through a nearby window, and I violently coughed as it poured into my lungs. "TELL ME!" he screamed, throwing me to the ground. When my vision blurred, I tried to get my bearings. I wondered if he'd caught on yet, even just a little. I was much stronger than a human, and he couldn't infect me. I was bleeding red, but everything else led to me being one of his kind.

But he couldn't see it, even though it was staring him in the face.

When I opened my eyes, I turned my head and saw it—

the shining silver of the blade. When he reached down to grab me again—to toss me around like the ragdoll he treated me as—I rolled over and grabbed it, swiping it across his face.

He recoiled but didn't loosen his grip on me, even when a droplet of blood escaped from the fresh cut beneath his right eye. "You little—" He reached down to hit me—to take the knife and torture me further. But he was knocked down by William, who was covered in soot and holding his arm tight against his side.

"William!" I cried and launched myself at him, but before I could make it to him, Cassius struck me on the back of the head. My ears rang, and I couldn't hear a thing until after I saw William strike Cassius to the ground with his good arm.

While Cassius was still down, I fell to the ground and plunged the blade into his leg. He cried out in pain as I twisted it, but his voice got lost in the destruction around us.

"What do we do with him now?" I asked.

"We need to take him to the mirror. Quickly. Before the house burns down."

Chapter *Thirty*

"I'll be back," Cassius spat through grunts of pain. William took the knife from my hand and pointed it at the beast of a man lying in the soiled grass.

"Then maybe I should kill you right now. Save myself the headache later."

The two men glared at each other, then Cassius laughed, his head falling back as the laughter grew more and more chaotic. "If you did that, you'd never get my mind out of your head, and you'd have the Council to answer to."

William pushed the blade against Cassius' throat and leaned in close. "I'm sure they would make an exception. Just this once."

Cassius' amused look vanished as black blood trickled down his throat.

"William, stop! Let's just get him to the mirror. You

would never forgive yourself if you did this, and you could get yourself in trouble. As much as he deserves it, you shouldn't do it. Don't doom yourself to misery because of a serpent like him."

His eyes stayed on Cassius, the knife still pressed against the vampire's throat. But after glaring at the vampire beneath him a moment longer, William's shoulder dropped, and he threw the blade back into the grass. Cassius smiled, but before he could do anything, William knocked him out cold.

When the man's body went limp, William hoisted him over his shoulder. "The mirror can only be open at night," he said. "It will lock as soon as day breaks. We have to hurry."

He took my hand, and we ran into the building. As we rushed through the halls, we dodged falling beams and sparks of ember. "It's important we lock him away now. If we don't get him in there in time, we'll have to take him to another portal, and that could give him time to escape."

"There are more mirrors?" I asked as he pulled the latch and opened the door.

"Yes, every clan has one. They are the gates to the Shadow Realm. Our reflections are stored there. It's what separates us from mortals. It's what makes us not quite human."

"It's all right not to be human," I said as he tossed Cassius onto the floor to catch his breath. He stared at him a moment and raked his hand through his hair. When he turned to me, I saw the sorrow heavy in his eyes. He smiled softly and walked closer to stroke the side of my face.

"I wish it was all right not to be human," he said, moving a lock of hair behind my ear, as he often did. Although he was smiling, his eyes were still heavy. "But not being human might keep me from you, and I can't bear the thought."

As he caught my chin in his fingers, a smile broke across my face. "William . . . Charles didn't tell you? You don't know?"

He frowned. "What are you talking about?"

My eyes fell to Cassius. "We should put him in first." I said, then looked back up at him, "Before I tell you." My smile broadened.

William studied my face before finally nodding. "All right. We have to hurry," he said, picking up Cassius' limp body. "Turn the key." I turned the pendant that was sticking out of one of the symbols on the mirror. As William pushed him inside, I finally remembered where I'd seen them.

"This symbol was on my aunt's papers." Thoughts of Maggie flooded my mind—her teaching me not to go into the shadows. To be afraid of them. To learn of the evils in the dark and avoid them at all costs. "She knew," I whispered to myself, feeling the grooves and folds around the key. "I still can't believe she knew."

"What?" William asked weakly, pain showing on his face.

My hand stayed wrapped around the key, and I watched my fingers turn white with the pressure as I recalled all those moments in my life. All the times she told me to beware of the monsters in the closet. To be afraid of demons, vampires, and the creatures of the night.

But she never told me that I was one, too.

I looked at William. He had slumped onto the floor and was leaning against the wall, wincing in pain and holding onto his wounded torso. The roaring flames were getting louder on the other side of the door. I could hear the faint snaps and cracks as it threatened to pull us down with the rest of the house. We needed to go, but first, I had to tell him.

I let go of the key and walked over to him, kneeling in front of him so I could look straight in his eyes. Seeing him in so much pain splintered a part of my heart. "William," I said softly. "My aunt knew that I was one of you."

His stare was steady as he processed my words, and I smiled at the way he looked at me because I'd never adored anyone as much as I adored him. And even in this terrible circumstance, where the world was quite literally falling down around us, all I could see was him. Him and his tousled hair and soot-stained face, and those dark eyes I could never resist.

I pulled his fingers to my wrist so he could feel my slow, uneven pulse. "When Cassius bit my mother, he infected me," I said, curling my hand around his. "I've been turning into a vampire my whole life. I think coming here quickened my transformation, and when Cassius came out, it completed." I wasn't sure if that was enough information, but I knew we didn't have much time.

I searched his face for any hint of a reaction—confusion, surprise, joy—but that same steady gaze remained, unmoved.

"Your pulse," he said finally. "That's why it was so slow when we danced. And that's why you could see the bat in the basement. You're . . ." A smile brightened his weary face. "We're even more alike than we thought." He chuckled softly and brought his hands to my face. I let my cheek rest in the curve of his palm.

"We can be together," I said, tears welling in my eyes. "We don't have to worry."

His smile deepened, and he was about to say something when he started to cough—a cough that shook his whole upper body, his black blood escaping his mouth and splattering onto the floor. That's when he noticed.

He looked at my arm. At my face. And his smile disappeared. "Caroline. You're still human. Your blood—" as he said the word, he shivered hungrily, and he had to take a breath before he continued. "Your blood is red. I don't think you've completely turned yet. Are you thirsty? Ravenous for blood?"

I thought back on the people in the woods and how drinking their blood never once crossed my mind.

My stomach lurched. I had a feeling that the distinct lack of thirst wasn't a common trait amongst newly turned vampires.

"The mirror. Look into the mirror." He pointed to the open portal. Other than the key secured in the keyhole in its rim, it looked like any ordinary mirror, yet it was so much more. "If you have a reflection you're still human. Go look."

My legs buckled. I didn't want to look, but the walls in the house were shaking, and I needed to know what I was. I got up slowly and walked over to face it. When I peered inside, whatever warm blood I had left in my veins turned cold.

I could see myself. I still had a reflection. It was faint, but it was there.

"I don't understand," I said, turning to William. "I-I am a vampire. That's why I was in so much pain earlier—I was transforming. And that's why Cassius couldn't turn me tonight. That's why he couldn't really hurt me." I looked back into the mirror, the air shallow in my lungs. "No." I shook my head. "No."

This couldn't be it. It couldn't be real. I *had* to be a vampire. That's why everything happened the way it had tonight, just like my grandmother had said. It's why I could be with William. It's why I never belonged anywhere else.

"You haven't turned yet," he said, coughing as smoke

seeped into the room. "There's still time."

"What are you talking about?" I said, but my stomach just twisted more. I already knew I wouldn't like whatever it was he had to say.

He nodded to the high window near the top of the room. "It's not daylight yet. Once the portal has been opened, we have until daybreak to use it." His mouth stretched into a half-smile, but his eyes were sad. "You can still save your mortality."

I shook my head, my knotted stomach sinking. "I don't know what you mean." But I didn't want to know. I wished we didn't have to know.

His eyes motioned to the mirror. "When a person is turned into a vampire, their soul is taken from them and hidden in a world just beyond this one. We can reach it through there." I continued watching him, but with every word he spoke, my chest tightened. I didn't like where this was going.

His gaze returned to mine. "Vampires can't freely leave once they've gone inside. They have to be taken out with the key by a trusted human inviting them out into this world, or by a member of the Council. When Cassius was cast into the mirror, he was doomed from living as an immortal being in this human world, but he also couldn't retrieve his chance at mortality, either. Because he was a vampire."

The burning house could swallow us up at any moment, but still, I couldn't move. I couldn't speak. All I could do was look at him and ignore the stinging in my eyes.

"I love you Caroline," he said, and there was a shudder in his voice as he said it. "I love you so much that I'm willing to lose you if it means you'll be free."

"No, William, I—"

"You are a rare exception, Caroline," he said. "You are

both vampire and human right now. The mirror is open. You can freely go between the worlds. Go. Retrieve the human half of your soul, and let yourself be free. Give yourself the chance any other vampire would kill for."

The flames devouring the mansion drummed angrily against the door, threatening to come inside. "We have to leave."

"It can't come in here," he said, wincing as he repositioned himself against the wall. "This room is enchanted to protect the mirror."

The roar of the burning house boomed below us. "That won't matter when the whole mansion collapses on top of us," I said.

"That's true," he said with a small, sad laugh, then grimaced and placed a hand on his abdomen. I walked over and knelt beside him, bending over his drooping frame. A tear broke its way down my face when I saw the black blood soaking his tattered white shirt. I thought about how vampires had always been so much more human than I'd ever known.

And when I looked into his eyes, I saw the man that I loved. The one who made me feel safe and accepted. The man who made me feel more myself than I ever knew possible. And the more I studied his soot-smeared face and the warmth of his eyes, the more I realized that my decision was my own and that I knew what I was going to do.

He watched me, waiting for my rush to the mirror, but I didn't budge. The only movement I made was to make a point of shifting from my kneeling position in front of him to a sitting one. I needed him to see me. To see just how much he meant to me.

"I don't care what any other vampire would choose in this situation," I said. "This is my life, and I choose to be with you. Vampire or human, it doesn't matter to me. I don't care about being normal." I ran my fingers down the side of his face. "I care about *you.* I care about the life I want to have with you. You accept me for who I am—who I *truly* am. I love you. Why would I give up my own happiness simply because any other vampire wouldn't have done the same?" I shook my head. "I don't want that. I want *you.*"

I slid my hand in his and laced our fingers together. "I want a life with you," I said. "That's all I want. Not a human life. *Our* life."

His chin quivered as he held back tears. "Are you sure?" he whispered, one of the tears escaping. And as the emotion welled in his eyes, I couldn't fight back the tears in mine any longer.

"Yes," I whispered shakily. "I have never been more sure of anything in my life."

He lifted his hand from his torso and ran his fingers gently through my hair. Then he smiled and placed my face in his hands. He gently stroked my damp face with his fingers, banishing the tears from my cheeks. "Then be mine forever," he said, "and I'll never let you go."

The tears were spilling freely now, so all I could do was nod. Nod deliriously and cry. He pulled me close and kissed me, and I melted into him, kissing him like the world around us wasn't falling apart. And he kissed me like it wouldn't matter even if it did. Like we could create our own pocket in the universe through this kiss. A place only our own.

When our lips parted and the foundation below us quaked, we knew it was time to go. "What about the mirror?" I said, glancing at the portal beside us. "Could Cassius escape again?"

"No, but we should lock it before the mansion goes down," he said, but before he could get to his feet, I stopped him.

"I'll do it. You're in pain, and I want to see my reflection one last time." I made my way to the key and cranked it to seal the gate shut. As I did it, I saw my faint reflection in the mirror. I was almost gone. The last mortal part of me would soon disappear from this world forever. It would be hidden away in the realm of shadows where Cassius now lay almost lifeless.

I watched as it continued to dim. "Are you sure Cassius will never escape?" I asked.

"I suppose we can never be sure, but this seemed to have been his one shot. He gave your mother his key—the clan leader's key—and set up the possibility of someone using it one day. He'd relied on the hope that he could trick a human into letting him out, and his followers were still free. But after tonight, he will be out of chances. I can't imagine he will ever have an opportunity like tonight again."

I couldn't believe his plan had worked to begin with. That Cassius was such an expert on manipulation that he could pull something like tonight off. Something so shockingly disturbing.

As I watched the remnants of my reflection disappear, I swore I saw something. I wasn't sure if my mind was playing tricks on me or if what I saw was really there, but I swore I saw it. I swore I saw Cassius—his face behind the glass with that wicked, vindictive grin.

Before I could talk myself out of it, I did what needed to be done. I grabbed hold of the mirror, pulled it across the room, and pushed it down the stairs. I watched as the frame broke through the door, not fully satisfied until I heard it crash into a million pieces and saw its splintered remains get devoured by the blaze.

Chapter *Thirty-One*

After the blood-veined smoke dissipated from over the mansion and everything was still, Evelyn decided to take the villagers in the forest to the bottom of the hill. She was surprised at their willingness to follow her after everything they'd just witnessed, but they did. They followed her until they got to the foot of the hill, where the chaos between vampires and humans had ceased.

What she saw there was astonishing, but not in the way she would have expected. Amid the broken booths and undeniable wreckage of the festival everyone worked so hard to put on, Cassius' followers had been apprehended, each by one of the many vampires she and Charles had enlisted for this very possibility. And there was not a dead body to be seen.

It had worked. The preparations she and Charles had made proved to be successful in the end. They had requested the help of vampires from various clans, even the help of a member of the Council of Shadows—someone who was dear to the family, having worked with Charles when Evelyn brought Cassius before them all those years ago. An important witness to what had happened tonight.

As soon as she spotted her husband, she rushed to his side. "What happened?" she asked, inspecting the scratches and fang marks on his skin.

"There are many wounded humans we will need to care for immediately," he said, "but no one was killed. And we have the witness we need to put these horrible monsters away, just as we did Cassius."

"However, this time," called the nearby councilman, Cecil Harrison, holding one of the soon-to-be prisoners, "more precautions must be taken to ensure none of this ever happens again."

Evelyn nodded. "Of course. I cannot believe it happened at all." Her eyes fell to the ground. William had been right, and she had risked everyone's lives simply to better her own. The guilt stung her, but she pressed on. "Well, I suppose we need to call for the doctors. *Our* doctors. Ones who know how to deal with this. And you," she said to her husband. "You know what to do. I'll go find William and Caroline."

She turned around and started up the hill, where some of the others were already working to put out the fire. Panic flooded her gut. If anything happened to either of them, she'd never forgive herself. And she had a long life to suffer through it, reliving the pain every time she thought of her vampiric brother and the woman he loved. A woman who turned out to be one of them, too.

Her hair cascaded behind her as the wind picked up. Smoke rushed against her face. When she bent over to cough it out of her lungs, she saw one of the families from the forest. A stout woman, her hair damp with sweat, but she, her lanky husband, and their two boys all looked up at her. "Mr. Day, and . . . I'm assuming *Mrs.* Day?" she said, "Is everything all right? How is—"

"We wanted to thank you," his wife said quickly, and Evelyn's mouth clamped shut. "You saved us. All of us." One of her boys, about seven years old, jumped forward and hugged the head of the Ashdown clan, his little arms squeezing around her waist. The mother chuckled softly. "None of us will forget this. None of us will forget your courage—that you kept us safe."

"I assure you that this will be written about in the *Brakerton Heights Herald.* Everyone will know what happened here today, save a few details." The gaunt man smiled—something Evelyn hadn't witnessed before this very moment. "You have no need to fear. None of us will forget your bravery. Everyone in Brakerton Heights will know the truth." He paused, pursing his lips, then said, "And we'll stand behind you."

Evelyn didn't know what to say, but even if she did, she doubted she'd be able to speak. The knot in her stomach loosened just a bit, knowing that if all went well, perhaps she and her family could live normal lives after all—that this festival and everything that occurred wouldn't have been for nothing. The transition might not happen as smoothly as she would have hoped, considering what happened here tonight, but she finally had what she'd longed to have these last three decades. Hope.

Chapter *Thirty-Two*

One Week Later

"We'll be moving into a new office next month," Agnes said, grinning as she stacked the next batch of freshly inked papers. "Our latest issue is outselling the other papers by a landslide."

"Though they're also selling well," Mary added as she looked up from her desk. Agnes shot her a look, and she put her hands up. "I'm not saying that to diminish our success. Sheesh, I'm sorry."

Agnes turned back to me. "It's all thanks to you, Caroline. Thank you for everything." She reached over and grabbed my hands. I smiled, genuinely happy, but the new pain of being around humans was too much for me. I needed to go.

"I'm so glad I could help. I wish you both the best at

your new office," I said, "and I wish you luck in finding the additional employees you're searching for."

"We already have fifteen applications," Mary said, beaming. "I think we've inspired some of the other women in town. Especially you, Caroline. Everyone looks up to you. Are you sure you have to leave?" The two of them looked at me expectantly.

"I'm sorry, but I think I need to take some time off." My eyes trailed to the window, and I caught a glimpse of William waiting for me outside. A smile crept across my lips, and my heart skipped. I would never get tired of the effect he had on me.

"Where will you go?" she asked.

"I'm not sure yet," I said, but I thought back on the conversation William and I'd had the day before. '*We need to get you hunting as quickly as possible*,' he'd said. '*That should be the first thing we do.*' "But I think William has some ideas," I said, my smile widening as I said his name.

"You're a lucky woman. Do you know that?" Mary said with a sigh. "You came out of that festival with the success story of the century and a man who adores you."

I laughed. "Mary, just tell Thomas how you feel and you'll be in the same boat as I am."

Her cheeks flushed. "Perhaps."

"Besides, you'll get to revel in the success of the paper much more than I will, since you'll be staying here while *The Woman Speaks* continues on in its rise to popularity."

Her eyes darted to the window. "Still," she sighed.

The wind rushed in through the broken window before I could respond, and the smell of blood assaulted my senses. How I was able to smell it so clearly was beyond my comprehension, but it plagued me just the same.

I *really* had to go.

"Well, I must be off. Thank you both for everything," I

said. They stopped what they were doing and rushed over to hug me. I braced myself, preparing to resist my dangerous new urge.

"We wish you all the best," Mary said as she squeezed me, and Agnes nodded. I breathed a sigh of relief as they stepped away.

"We do," she agreed. "Please write to us. We still haven't heard nearly enough from you about what happened up there."

I thought of my time at Ashdown Manor—of discovering my mother's letters and learning about myself in more ways than I could count. And I thought of William. The way he unlocked a part of me I didn't know existed. A part of me I loved.

There was a lot I could tell them, but I wanted to keep that part to myself.

"I'll be sure to write," I said, wrapping myself in my new coat. After the fire at the mansion, William and I had to make a quick shopping trip for new clothes. This dark burgundy coat with velvet cuffs was my favorite purchase from the excursion, and judging by the rapidly declining temperature, the most necessary. "Good luck, you two, and thank you for everything." After giving them one final smile, I opened the rickety door of the soon-to-be-former office of *The Woman Speaks*. Before I left, I stopped. "Oh, and be sure to have Evelyn Bower over to your houses for tea sometime," I said. "She is lovely company, and I'm sure she and her husband would like it very much."

They nodded and said their goodbyes as I headed into the frigid late October afternoon. The air had a nasty bite, but it was nothing compared to the intensity of the blaring sun. I tipped my hat to further block the light from my eyes.

"How did it go?" William asked, pushing himself off the

building and walking over to thread his hand in mine.

"It was lovely."

"Good," he said, kissing me softly on the lips. "Are you ready to go?"

I nodded, and he smiled, his eyes crinkling at the sides. "Then let's go."

As William led me out of the city, I couldn't help but glance up at where the manor once stood. The fire had been caught and extinguished before it could cause further disaster or claim any lives, but everything inside had been burned from existence—turned to dust and ashes. My mother's diary, Maggie's trunk, William's old books and letters. Everything.

Perhaps we should have been sad about it, but we weren't. We couldn't be. There was a certain peace that came with losing the things of the past—of escaping everything we'd known before. We could no longer be tied down by it. Now, we only had the future. We could only look ahead.

We left Brakerton Heights without looking back. And we enjoyed the scenery of those first few steps.

As William led me through a sea of gold and ruby leaves, I couldn't stop smiling. I couldn't stop marveling at how pure and beautiful happiness could be. And though we didn't know where life would take us from here, it didn't matter. We had each other, and to us, that was enough.

Together, we were free.

ACKNOWLEDGMENTS

I want to give an extra special thanks to my husband, Alex, and my aunt, Kim, who were my amazing beta readers during my writing process. Their insight was very helpful and much appreciated.

I'd like to also thank my husband for his continuous support while I work on all my writing endeavors. Thank you, Alex, for everything you do for our family and for me.

I would also like to thank my parents for the support and encouragement they've always given me, both in my life and in my writing career. If it wasn't for you, I don't know if I'd be here today. So, thank you, Mom and Dad, for believing in me and always encouraging me to follow my dreams.

Lastly, I want to thank all of you readers for picking up my book and enjoying this journey with me. I hope to get to know you all more throughout my writing career and look forward to the adventures that await.

ABOUT THE AUTHOR

ELISE NELSON is an author of romance, poetry, comics, and more. She has a Bachelor of Arts degree from Boise State University, where she studied English literature, creative writing, and multimedia storytelling. When she isn't busy writing, she loves reading, laughing, and making memories with her family.

You can visit her website at
www.elisenelsonauthor.com

www.ingramcontent.com/pod-product-compliance
Lightning Source LLC
LaVergne TN
LVHW041058080826
845145LV00007B/1628

* 9 7 8 1 7 7 7 6 3 2 9 3 9 *